A LITTLE CLOSER . . .

Braden found himself watching how Damask's lips moved when she talked. Her lower lip was fuller than her upper one. Both were pink and soft looking.

He realized she was waiting for his reply. What had she said?

Braden took a step closer to Damask. Her robe buttoned high up to her neck and came down to her ankles. But still, it was a robe, and somehow in the quiet of the house at night, the atmosphere suddenly seemed intimate.

He took another step forward, bringing him very close to her. She didn't move backward as he'd expected but stood her ground. This close to her, he saw how smooth and soft the skin of her face was. Almost like velvet. No, smoother than velvet . . .

Slowly, he lowered his head until they were so close he could feel her warm breath, smell the intoxicating scent surrounding her. . . .

Back off! Back off while you still can! he told himself urgently.

Instead, he gently brushed his lips across hers. . . .

PROMISE ME LOVE

Elizabeth Graham

Zebra Books
Kensington Publishing Corp.
http://www.zebrabooks.com

For my husband, Lewis, with much love.
Thanks for all your help and support.
I couldn't have done it without you.

ZEBRA BOOKS are published by

Kensington Publishing Corp.
850 Third Avenue
New York, NY 10022

First Printing: May, 2000
10 9 8 7 6 5 4 3 2 1

Printed in the United States of America

Chapter One

Goose Creek, Pennsylvania—1880

Damask raised her head to stare at the big fieldstone building topping the hill.

Goose Creek Inn! How she'd loved the place that long-ago summer. Now she was here to stay. All three of them were.

Relief banished her fatigue from the long, miserable coach and train ride from Tennessee. Thank God Aunt Ada had urged them to come. Soon she would enfold them in her welcoming arms. They'd have a home again.

"Why are we standing here? Let's go up to the inn."

Cory's worn shoes tapped impatiently on the cobblestone walk of Goose Creek's Main Street. His one good suit of clothes was somewhat the worse for wear, and his brown hair needed smoothing, but for a boy of ten, he would do.

"Yes!" Emmy added her pleas. Nine-year-old Emmy's green dress and jacket were holding up better than her brother's outfit, and her auburn braids were still neat.

Damask smiled at her younger brother and sister. "In just a moment."

She smoothed the skirt of her gray traveling dress and tucked wisps of her auburn hair under her hat.

Main Street looked much the same as she remembered. The bank. A barbershop, a bakery, a haberdashery, other business places. At the end of the block a big, obviously new brick building stood. She wondered what it was.

Something clattered past on the street behind them. A farm wagon. Damask knew that sound well. She'd ridden in her family's wagon many a time.

An approaching woman gave the group a curious glance as she passed, probably thinking they were prospective inn guests, and Damask realized no one would recognize her—it had been nine years since the summer she'd spent here as a child of eleven.

From the corner of her eye Damask saw an older man approaching. He stopped beside her.

Reluctantly, she drew her gaze away from the inn beckoning from its hilltop and smiled at him. He must be in his late sixties, she thought, and his lined face and work-roughened hands, his worn clothes, bespoke a hard life.

But his smile erased ten years from his face. "You must be Ada's relations. Flora sent me down here to look for you the last two days."

"I'm sorry we're late. We ran into bad storms that delayed us. We were just getting ready to go up to the inn."

The man's smile faded, a sad look replacing it. He cleared his throat.

"I hate to be the one to have to tell you this, but Flora wanted you to know before you got up there."

Damask's heart lurched. "Tell me what?"

"Your aunt passed away night before last."

Pain ripped through Damask. She tried to swallow, but her throat felt dry as cotton. "Aunt Ada's dead?"

He gave a deep sigh and patted her shoulder, shaking his head as he glanced at Emmy and Cory. "I'm afraid so. Everyone will sure miss her. The funeral was this morning. I'm terribly sorry you had to miss it. We waited as long as we could for you to get here."

"Wh-what happened?"

"Doc said her heart just gave out on her. She'd had a weak heart for a long time, you know."

No, she didn't know. Aunt Ada hadn't mentioned anything like that in any of her letters.

The man suddenly stuck out his hand. "Forgot my manners. I'm Harold Kirk. Did odd jobs for Ada. She talked a lot about you and your family. Only relatives she had left. She was sure looking forward to you living with her."

Damask took his offered hand. "She was all we had left, too. I'm Damask and this is Emmy and Cory."

His concerned frown deepened.

Along with Damask's grief, fear swept through her. *What would they do now? Where would they go?*

After paying off the mortgage, she'd spent nearly all their money from the sale of their family's run-down farm on the trip here.

Harold gravely shook Emmy's and Cory's hands. "Glad to make your acquaintance but wish it didn't have to be under such bad circumstances."

Their faces solemn, both children returned his greetings, then gave Damask worried looks, as if they sensed her inner turmoil.

Her heart felt new pain. These two young ones had

gone through enough. "Everything will be all right," she told them, trying to put reassurance into her voice, hoping they believed her.

Although what she said wasn't true. How could it be true? All their hopes and plans were in ruins.

"I'll go with you up to the inn," Harold said. "Flora's still there, and that Braden Franklin."

Damask remembered Flora, a friendly widow with no family, who'd long been the inn's cook.

Disapproval had been in Harold's voice when he mentioned the last name. *Braden Franklin.* The name sounded vaguely familiar.

Harold leaned down and picked up her worn old traveling bag. She'd left their trunks at the railroad station. "I'll carry this for you."

"You don't have to bother," Damask said. "But . . . should we go up? I mean . . ." she floundered.

"It's no bother. Glad to do it, and of course you should," Harold said, his voice kind. He straightened up, holding the bag.

He turned left and walked away toward the turnoff to the inn. She stared at his back a moment.

What other choice did they have?

"Come along," she told Emmy and Cory, and the three turned and followed Harold.

Her peripheral vision caught several people on the street staring at them, but she didn't turn. She didn't want to talk to anyone else right then, nor hear their condolences.

The distance to the inn wasn't long. The summer she'd spent there, the road was kept in good repair, and many a carriage had made the journey to the busy hostelry. Now the road was overgrown and looked as if it hadn't been used much, except as a footpath.

"Are we going to stay here?" Emmy asked.

Damask found a smile for her little sister. "Yes,"

she answered, making her voice firm. But she didn't know for how long. She wouldn't tell Emmy that now, though.

Emmy sighed. "Good. I'm tired."

Cory had stopped to pick up a rock glittering with mica crystals. He turned it over in his hands, admiring it, then stuck it in his pocket, along with his other treasures.

Harold had slowed down to allow Cory to catch up with them. "Lots of those rocks around here," he said, his voice gruff.

Damask realized he was grieving for her aunt and hardly knew what to say to her. Any more than she felt like trying to make conversation with him.

The top of the hill widened out into a green meadow, covered with wildflowers on this warm, late April day. Their sweet smell filled Damask's nostrils. Oh, it was beautiful! Her memories of the summer she'd spent there had never left her, nor had her desire to return.

As they came closer, a new shock went through her. The inn's sturdy fieldstone walls still held firm, but the mortar was gone from between the blocks in many places, and white paint peeled from the shutters, the windows, and doorsills. The front porch roof sagged.

Aunt Ada must have fallen on hard times, Damask thought. Her heart ached for her aunt's troubles. Why hadn't she told her sister Myrtle, Damask's mother?

Because her parents had their own troubles, she answered herself. Aunt Ada knew they couldn't have helped with anything that took money.

Harold nodded at the inn. "Flora's out on the porch with her needlework," he said. "Never catch that woman idle."

His voice sounded admiring, Damask thought, glancing at the plump, gray-haired woman seated in a rocking chair, who lifted her head at their approach. The woman shaded her eyes with her hands, then stood, placing her sewing on the chair and smiling.

"Ach, it is good to see you," Flora said, "even on such a sad occasion." Tears filled her eyes, and she held out her arms toward Damask's little group.

"It's good to see you, too," Damask answered, not able to keep a tremble from her voice. She let Flora hug her to her ample bosom.

"And here are the little ones. Come, hug me," she commanded as Damask stepped back.

Cory looked alarmed, but Emmy did as Flora bade with no hesitation. Finally, Cory, his shoes scuffing along, sheepishly let the older woman embrace him.

"Such a fine family you have," Flora said. "It is no wonder Ada was so proud of you."

"Guess I'd better be gettin' on back," Harold said.

"Thanks for bringing the bag up," Damask told him.

"Glad to help. Good day, Flora." He smiled at her.

"And to you, Harold," she answered, her return smile lingering.

Harold turned and headed back across the meadow.

Flora sighed. "You must be tired. Such pity you did not get here for Ada's funeral. You should have seen the turnout. All Goose Creek loved Ada."

"Yes, I'm sorry, too," Damask said, struggling with her grief and worry. "But . . . maybe we shouldn't stay."

Flora looked at her in astonishment. "Not stay? And why should you not stay? You are her only flesh and blood!"

"I know, but . . ." Damask's voice trailed off. She was so tired, she fought to keep from staggering, but she held herself straight. She couldn't let Emmy and Cory see how dispirited she felt.

The inn's front door opened. A tall, broad-shouldered man of about thirty, with black hair and sea green eyes, stepped out onto the veranda. He wore dark, well-cut trousers, and the sleeves of his white shirt were rolled above his elbows, revealing strongly muscled arms.

He stared at Damask and her family, a muscle ticking in his jaw for a few moments before he gave them a polite smile.

A chill went over Damask. Despite his smile, this man wasn't glad to see them. Quite the opposite.

"There is no buts," Flora insisted. "The inn will be yours now. Come you inside and rest."

Astonishment filled Damask at the woman's words. *The inn would be theirs?*

The man had reached Flora's side. She turned and smiled at him but not with the warmth she'd given Damask and the children.

"This one is Braden Franklin," Flora said.

Oh, yes, the man Harold had mentioned. He must be a guest, Damask decided, although that didn't explain the unfriendliness he couldn't quite hide.

He extended his hand, and Damask put forth her own. His hand was warm and strong, and its touch sent an awareness through her that she didn't welcome. After what she'd just gone through with Warren Miller, she had no wish to feel an attraction toward any man.

"How do you do?" Braden Franklin said politely, but his voice, unlike his hand, was as cool as his expression.

Damask quickly withdrew her hand. "I'm Damask Aldon, and these are Cory and Emmy, my brother and sister."

He nodded. "I'm sorry for your loss. Ada was a wonderful woman."

Again his voice held no warmth, although it softened a bit at the end. Although he obviously didn't want to be friends with them, he'd cared for her aunt.

"Thank you," Damask said as formally as he had spoken to her.

Flora frowned at him, then turned again to Damask. "Come inside," she said once more, "and let us get you settled."

Damask picked up her bag.

"Let me take that," Braden Franklin said, reaching for its handle.

"No, that's fine. It isn't heavy."

He didn't protest further and, keeping her glance straight ahead, Damask walked by him and followed Flora into the spacious hallway, Emmy and Cory behind.

Damask drew in her breath as the ambience of the place took hold of her. Her aunt seemed very close, her presence filling the room. . . . Damask could almost hear her merry laughter, see her upright figure walking down the hallway to the big kitchen . . . .

You are right. I am still here.

The whisper seemed to come from inside Damask's head . . . or maybe it was all around her. . . .

What's the matter with you? Damask asked herself. Aunt Ada is *gone.* You have to accept that. You'll never see her again.

Damask swallowed hard and looked around. The floor of wide-planked pine boards was scuffed, in need of a coat of varnish, and the flowered wallpaper was faded and stained. The walnut table that had held the guest book, its wide pages invitingly open, still stood in the corner, but the tabletop was bare, the guest book gone.

A blue-gray cat with white markings sat in front of the table.

"Bluebell!" Damask exclaimed. "So you're still here?"

"Yah, but she is very old now," Flora said.

The cat meowed and moved forward, rubbing against Damask's ankle and purring.

Damask stooped to pet the animal, feeling a tiny bit better. "You remember me!"

"Sure she does," Flora said. "She much misses Ada."

Damask swallowed a lump in her throat, and she and the children followed Flora up the wide stairway in the middle of the hall. Bluebell stayed behind.

So did Braden Franklin. But Damask still felt his cool gaze on her back.

Partway up, Damask stumbled and glanced down to see a piece of sagging stair carpeting entangled in her shoe.

Flora turned, shaking her head. "Ach, watch the carpet. Bad shape it is in. I repair it, but it is too old."

So it was, faded and threadbare. Although scrupulously clean, as was everything else Damask had seen.

Flora stopped at a room halfway down the hall and swung the door wide. "Come, enter. You and the little Emmy will have this room and young Cory the next one."

From her confident manner, Flora must be in charge of the inn now, not merely its cook, Damask thought. "Do you have enough empty rooms to spare?" she asked.

Flora gave her a surprised look. "We have *all* the rooms empty. No one has stayed here for several years now."

New surprise hit Damask. "The inn's closed?"

"Did you not know?"

"No. Or I wouldn't have asked Aunt Ada if we could come here. I thought we could . . . help her. . . ."

Tears filled Damask's eyes. She tried to blink them back. "I'm sorry. None of this, none of us, is your concern."

Flora patted her shoulders. "Yah, it is. Ada loved all of you. She'd want you to stay."

Too tired to argue further, Damask set the traveling bag down. Despite her fatigue, something puzzled her. "But if the inn's closed, what is Braden Franklin doing here?"

"He was always a great friend of Ada's, and there is no boardinghouse here, no other place but the inn for people to stay."

"Then, he's been here awhile?"

Flora nodded. "Yah. For over a year now."

She gave Damask a sharp glance. "So tired you are, you will soon fall down. You take yourself a nap. You and Emmy." Flora smiled at the little girl drooping beside Damask, then turned to Cory.

"Young man, come with me and I will give you your room. Later we have a good supper."

"All right." Cory glanced at Damask.

She saw how hard he was trying not to show his own bewilderment. She smiled and nodded at him, and he straightened his shoulders and followed Flora out the door. Flora closed it behind her.

This was the room she'd stayed in that summer, Damask saw, memories sweeping over her again. There was the seat under the wide-silled window where she'd curled up with a book after she'd helped with dinner and the clearing up and looked down on the well-tended flower beds in the side yard. There was the white-painted rocker, the brass bedstead.

Even the same quilt, the double wedding ring pattern, was spread across the neatly made bed. Many a time she'd traced with her finger the looped rings, pieced with colorful blocks, finished with tiny, neat stitches.

The bed looked inviting. If she could just rest for an hour or two, they could sort all this out.

Damask sank down onto it, patting the space beside her. "Take your shoes off and lie down," she told Emmy. "And rest awhile."

Emmy did, sighing and curling up against her sister. "I like this place," she said. "I hope we can stay here."

Damask smoothed Emmy's auburn braids, so much like her own hair, now pulled into a knot at the back of her neck. "So do I, honey. So do I."

"What did that lady mean, that this was ours now?" Emmy asked.

"We'll talk about that later. Go to sleep now."

"All right," Emmy said obediently.

Too obediently. Ever since their parents had died of a fever two months before, the little girl had retreated inside herself. Cory was trying to be the man of the family now, but he, too, was suffering. Damask wished with all her heart for them to once more become the laughing, mischievous pair they'd been before the life they'd known had been destroyed.

And they would be again, she vowed. Somehow, she'd see to that.

Braden Franklin watched the young woman and her brother and sister follow Flora upstairs. Grief at his old friend Ada's sudden death still filled him, mixed with other less admirable emotions.

Ada had been half convinced to sell Goose Creek Inn to him before she'd gotten that letter from her niece, asking if she and her brother and sister could come to live there.

Overjoyed, Ada wrote back urging the three to come immediately. Then she'd told him things were different now. She couldn't think of selling. Her nieces and nephew needed a home there. The inn was their legacy.

Stunned, Braden hadn't tried to change her mind, recognizing Ada's determination to stick with her foolish, impractical decision.

Braden glanced around the wide hall. Hell, the place was too far gone to try to restore. And it couldn't be lived in for much longer without a lot of repairs.

Flora came back down the stairs, her round, pleasant face set in lines of worry. "You are still here? I thought you would be back at your department store."

Braden heard the emphasis she put on the last two words. She wasn't alone in her suspicion of the big store he'd built on Main Street. Some other Goose Creek residents felt the same way. But his innovative store was a big success with most of the town—especially the women.

"I'm just getting ready to go," he told Flora, forcing his turmoil of emotions back. He'd taken the morning off for Ada's funeral. Flora was a nice woman and he liked her. When he was growing up, she and Ada were among the few who'd treated him decently despite his dirty, ragged clothes.

Flora, with Ada's approval, had given him many a meal in the big inn kitchen. Flora wasn't to blame for any of this mess, and he couldn't fault her reasoning—either on the lack of need for a fancy store or on whom the inn should belong to now.

Since Ada had never married, her only remaining family.

Flora sighed and sat down on the old pine settle against one wall. "That girl is too young for to have the care of two children. She is little better than a child herself."

A sudden vision of Damask Aldon's breasts pushing out the bodice of her traveling suit came into his mind. Along with her clear gray eyes, the glimpses he'd had of her shiny auburn hair beneath her hat. No, she was no child. She was a full-grown woman.

To his surprise and consternation, these thoughts caused his body to stir. Damnation! That was all he needed—to feel a physical attraction to this female. He was engaged to a beautiful, desirable woman. Soon they would be married.

"Yes," he said, agreeing with Flora. "All the more reason she has no business being saddled with this crumbling hulk of a building."

Flora huffed. "Crumbling hulk! It is no such of a thing. It just needs some repairs."

"No, it needs to be razed and a new building, a fine house, built in its place."

As he said the words, another vision appeared in his mind. The mansion Verona wanted so badly. And he wanted, too, of course. A three-story wooden clapboard structure with a turreted tower on the side and elaborate carved embellishments.

Flora's mouth set. "Goose Creek Inn is more than a hundred years old. It does not deserve to be torn down."

"It's outlived its usefulness, Flora," Braden said gently.

Stubbornly, Flora shook her head. "You are wrong, Braden Franklin."

"I've got to go to the store," he said, rolling down his sleeves. He'd left his suit jacket in the room where

Ada had let him stay for more than a year while he was having his store built.

"You will be back for supper?" Flora asked. "Or will you sup with the Holmeses?"

Flora didn't like Verona's mother. Bernice Holmes was a bit full of herself, Braden had to admit, but who could blame her? Their large, productive farm was prosperous, their big new house impressive.

But they were still farmers. No doubt that was why Verona was so set on living in town, having the most expensive house in town. He couldn't blame her for that, either.

Wasn't he out to prove the same things to Goose Creek after its treatment of him and his family during his childhood?

Braden frowned at his thoughts. Brushing them aside, he summoned a smile. "Yes, I'll be eating here."

Flora nodded. "We will see you then."

Heading for his room, Braden frowned again at the thought of sitting down at Ada's laden supper table with these new people. It was bound to be an awkward meal.

Maybe he should drive out to the Holmes farm. He was certain of a welcome there.

He didn't want to, though.

And he didn't want to think of the reason why, because he knew it had something to do with the fresh-faced young woman he'd met for the first time just a few minutes earlier.

Chapter Two

"Here, have some *schnitz*. That will keep the hunger from eating you till supper is ready."

Flora held out a small plate to Emmy and Cory that held dried apple slices.

"Thank you," Emmy said in a small voice as she carefully lifted one slice.

"Oh, take more," Flora urged. "It won't spoil your supper."

Emmy glanced at Damask, who was putting cutlery on the long pine trestle table in the kitchen. Damask nodded, and Emmy took another slice.

Flora moved the plate toward Cory. "Here, a strong, big boy like you needs to eat to keep up his strength."

Cory didn't have to be told twice. He eagerly scooped up a handful of the dried delicacies. "Thanks," he remembered to say, Damask was glad to hear.

They were bound to be hungry. They'd eaten the

last of the food she'd brought from Tennessee at midmorning, and now it was late afternoon.

Flora's stewed chicken with dumplings and corn fritters sizzling in the iron skillet gave off appetizing aromas.

Damask realized seeing that everyone had plenty to eat was Flora's way of coping with the loss of her friend, Ada.

After her nap, Damask had washed her face, and changed into an old blue-checked gingham dress. Physically, she felt rested, but grief over her aunt's death, added to that for her parents, was very much with her.

Looking at the cut-glass spoon holder in the center of the table made a lump come to Damask's throat. If she closed her eyes, she could see her cheerful aunt arranging well-polished spoons in the container . . . lifting the lid of the tea caddy decorated with a fat red tomato.

Her presence seemed all around in this kitchen where she'd lived so much of her life. Damask suddenly remembered that moment when she'd first entered the house . . . and had imagined she heard her aunt's voice. . . .

A sound at the doorway made her glance in that direction. Braden Franklin stood there, wearing a dark brown suit coat, which he discarded while she watched. He hung it over a post of a ladder-back chair near the door, then rolled up his sleeves as they'd been when she first saw him. He didn't like being dressed up, she thought.

His sea green gaze found hers before she could turn her glance away.

Her breath suddenly became shallow. She forced her eyes back to the cutlery in her hands, annoyed and amazed at herself.

No man had ever caused her to have such a physical reaction before. Not even Warren—and they'd been courting for a year when, after her parents' death, he'd told her he couldn't take on the responsibility of raising Emmy and Cory.

Familiar pain and hurt pride swept over her at these thoughts. Warren hadn't loved her at all or he couldn't have walked away so easily. But she'd thought he had. Oh, yes, she'd been taken in.

"You're just in time for supper," Flora announced to Braden.

"I'm glad I didn't miss it."

His voice sounded neutral. His glance had been neutral, too, Damask thought, despite her reaction to it. For whatever reason he'd taken a dislike to her and Emmy and Cory, and he was trying hard not to show it now.

"You? Miss a meal? That will be the day."

Flora's voice sounded as if she were forcing her bantering comments. And again, as earlier, Damask felt Flora had mixed feelings about Braden. She liked him, but something was wrong between them.

In a few minutes they were all seated at the long table, Flora at one end, Damask and the children along one side, with Braden on the other, facing them.

Flora said the blessing, mentioning Ada in a simple, touching way that brought tears to Damask's eyes, then told them to help themselves.

Emmy and Cory needed no urging. Damask's heart hurt as she watched them eagerly dig into their food. Good food hadn't been plentiful around their homestead for the last two seasons of bad crops. And after their parents' death things had only gotten worse.

Damask had little appetite but made herself eat. She kept herself from glancing at Braden Franklin.

Flora kept a conversation going, talking of trivial, everyday things, but Damask and Braden contributed little.

After Damask and Emmy helped Flora clear the table of the main course, the older woman brought out several desserts that she said the neighbors had brought over the previous day.

Emmy and Cory stared in wide-eyed wonder at what Flora called shoofly pie, cherry custard pie, and vinegar pie. Such things were unknown in their home, although Damask remembered them from her summer at the inn.

When everyone was finished, Flora smiled at the children's sleepy eyes, their huge yawns. "I think it is time you young ones went off to bed."

"Yes." Damask rose to clear the dessert dishes.

"Leave them be. You see to the children and I finish here." Flora gave Damask a searching look. "Then come back downstairs. There are things we must discuss tonight."

Damask agreed, hoping the discussion would shed some light on the situations that puzzled her.

For once neither Emmy nor Cory argued about going to bed so early, and within a few minutes both were sound asleep. The April evening had turned chilly. Damask pulled the quilt over Emmy, a pang hitting her as she remembered Aunt Ada doing that for her, then looked in on Cory. He was also asleep, and she went in and tucked him in snugly.

Downstairs again, she paused at the kitchen door. The kitchen was once more tidy. Lamps were lit now, and Flora and Braden sat over steaming cups at the long table. A third cup sat at her place.

Flora glanced up, smiling as always. "Ah, you are here. I made chamomile tea."

"Thank you." Damask seated herself, relieved that

Braden seemed to be trying to avoid her glance as much as she was trying to avoid his. Although she had to admit she'd like to know more about him and why he was here.

She sipped the fragrant brew, then put her cup down, waiting for one of the two to start the discussion.

Flora gave a deep sigh, then turned to Damask. "The lawyer says Ada has left gifts for all three of us. We must be in his office tomorrow at ten o'clock for the reading of the will."

Startled, Damask darted a glance at Braden. He lifted his cup for another sip, still not looking at her.

He must be a very special friend if her aunt had included him in her will. But from the looks of things, Aunt Ada had little to leave anyone except this run-down inn. And Flora had said that would be left to her and Emmy and Cory.

Damask's thoughts upset her. She didn't want to think about such things with her aunt buried only that morning.

But she must. Not only was her future at stake, but her brother's and sister's, too. They were her responsibility now. She had to try to take care of them to the best of her ability.

Braden suddenly rose. "If that's everything, I'm going on to my room," he said, still in that forced neutral voice.

Flora looked at him for a moment, then sighed again and nodded. "That is all."

"Good night," he said, and left the room, grabbing his coat from the back of the chair as he went. Damask heard him mount the stairs.

She was relieved he'd gone. Annoyed with herself, she fought down another feeling. One of disappointment that he hadn't wanted to stay longer.

"I guess I should go to bed, too," she said, starting to rise.

Flora put a restraining hand on Damask's arm, and she sat back down. "Wait, dear. Some things I need explain to you. I believe to you and the little ones Ada left the inn and the property. But you see, Braden . . . he, too, wants the inn."

Damask stared at her, pieces falling into place. Now she understood why Braden didn't like her and Emmy and Cory. "Did he expect Aunt Ada to leave the inn to him?"

"I do not see how, but he tried to talk Ada into selling to him. Yah, she was the stubborn one. Not even listen, she would. Not after she got your letter."

Shock hit Damask at Flora's last words. No wonder Braden was unwelcoming. If she hadn't asked Aunt Ada for shelter, Braden might already be the inn's owner.

"So Braden wants to restore the inn and open it again?" Damask asked.

Flora sighed again, shaking her head. "No. To tear it down and build a mansion here on the hill for that girl he will marry, Verona Holmes."

Surprise, shock, and anger captured Damask in their grip. And something else she tried not to acknowledge.

Disappointment at learning Braden was engaged.

Flora patted her hand. "All this is much shock to you. Sometimes I think Braden is a dummkopf! But I know he is not like his bad father, who was much into the schnapps."

Damask drew in her breath. Braden *Franklin*. Now she remembered. Aunt Ada had told her about him. "He used to come to the back door and you brought him into the kitchen and fed him," she said.

"Yah. Before you were here. He went away and

made something of himself. Now, he comes back to prove good enough he finally is for this town."

She huffed. "And he does this by wanting to tear down the inn! And by building his fancy new store. And engaging himself to the Holmes girl."

Now all the puzzle pieces were in place. But that didn't solve anything or make Damask feel better. "So he hates me and Cory and Emmy because he thinks we're going to take what he wants."

Flora looked startled. "Ach, no, hate you he does not. He is mixed-up man. The pride rules him, not the common sense. Maybe he gets over this. I hope so, because in him there is good."

"So . . . if . . . Aunt Ada did leave us Goose Creek Inn . . . then he will try to persuade me to sell it to him."

It was more of a statement than a question, and Flora reluctantly nodded. "Yah, sure he will do that."

Damask smothered a yawn, her fatigue once more catching up with her.

Now it was Flora who rose, reaching for Damask's cup, placing it with hers and Braden's on a small tray. "Enough of this. To bed with you. Tomorrow all we will know."

But will we know how to deal with it? Damask wanted to ask but didn't. "Yes, you're right." She hugged the older woman. "Thanks for being so nice to us."

Flora hugged her back. "Not niceness," she protested. "You and the little Emmy and Cory are my family now. I am fond of you."

"We're fond of you, too. I . . . hope somehow this all works out for everyone."

"It would be *wunderschön*." Flora gave her a wry smile. "But that happens not often."

"No. Aunt Ada loved you like a sister, you know."

"Yah, I know. And I also loved her like sister. I miss her."

"So do I, although I hadn't seen her for years."

"That does not always matter."

"No," Damask agreed. "But I wish she were still here."

A shiver went over her as words echoed through her mind.

I am still here.

She had to stop being so fanciful, Damask told herself, bidding Flora good night.

She made her way up the stairs, light from the oil lamp on the stairway wall guiding her.

Emmy still slept soundly, as did Cory, Damask saw as she quietly opened his door and peeked inside.

She hoped she could do the same. But she very much doubted it.

Tomorrow would decide their future.

Damask, wearing her only good traveling gown, and Flora, in a black one, were seated in the lawyer's stuffy office by a quarter to ten. A neighbor had come up to stay with Emmy and Cory

Mr. Edwards sat behind his battered old desk, looking uncomfortable and ill at ease. The wall clock struck ten, and he cleared his throat. "Do you know what is keeping Mr. Franklin?"

Flora grimaced. "He is no doubt at that store of his."

"We can't proceed without him," Mr. Edwards said.

Damask clenched her hands into fists, her nerves tensing. Why wasn't Braden here? She wanted to get this over with.

The door opened and Braden came in, again wearing his dark brown suit. "I'm sorry if I'm late," he apologized.

"Only a minute or so." Mr. Edwards waved to the remaining empty chair beside Damask, and Braden seated himself.

Damn, but I don't want to be here! Braden thought. Why had he even come? To hear this man tell him that his friend Ada had left him a piece of furniture? Or maybe one of her treasured books?

At once he felt ashamed of himself. Ada didn't owe him anything. It was the other way around. He owed her a debt he could never repay now that she was gone. She'd been the one who encouraged him to stay in school despite the teasing he daily encountered from the other children because of his ragged clothes, his often-bruised body from his father's beatings when he was in a drunken rage. She'd told Braden over and over he was smart and strong. He could accomplish whatever he made up his mind to do.

"We are here to listen to the reading of the last will and testament of Ada Rose Harris," Mr. Edwards intoned. "Being of sound mind and body on the day she made out this will, the twenty-second of March, 1880."

Surprise went through Braden. Ada had made a new will less than a month earlier?

"To my longtime friend and companion, Mrs. Flora Schneider, I leave the contents of her room at Goose Creek Inn. I also leave her the right to remain at the inn as long as she wishes."

Braden heard Flora take in a quick breath.

"Goose Creek Inn, and the twenty acres around it, my home and place of business for forty years, I leave . . ."

Mr. Edwards paused and cleared his throat. Over the tops of his spectacles he looked at the three people seated before him. His mouth had tightened, Braden saw, as if he disapproved of what he must read next.

". . . jointly and equally to Mr. Braden Franklin and Damask, Cornelius, and Emmaline Aldon. Damask will act for her brother and sister. Neither Damask nor Braden may sell or otherwise dispose of Goose Creek Inn without the full approval and consent of the other party."

Beside him, Braden heard Damask's gasp of surprise. He stared at Mr. Edwards, feeling as if the man had punched him in the gut. In a moment he realized his mouth was hanging open and closed it.

Never in a million years had he expected this.

He turned toward Damask, seeing the same astonished look on her face that he'd no doubt worn a moment before. As if feeling his gaze, she turned her head.

Her eyes were the clearest gray he'd ever seen, and he felt as if he were falling into them.

He pulled himself together and jerked his head around toward the lawyer, who still had that disapproving expression on his face.

"Is this some kind of joke?" Braden demanded.

Mr. Edwards shook his gray head. "No, Mr. Franklin, it is no joke. I tried to persuade Mrs. Harris not to make out such a will, but she couldn't be swayed. She informed me it was her property, and she would do what she pleased with it."

Into the silence of the room, Flora's full-bodied laugh suddenly rang out. "I am not surprised," she said. "It is just like Ada to do something as this."

"Wh-what does this mean?" Damask asked, then grimaced at how stupid that sounded. She knew what it meant . . . she was just so stunned, she couldn't take it in yet.

Mr. Edwards's mouth pursed. "It means, Miss Aldon, that you and Mr. Franklin will have to work this out between yourselves. Legally, you have no recourse but to either accept Mrs. Harris's bequest as it stands or to refuse it."

Damask gasped at that suggestion. She couldn't look at Braden, but she burned to tell the lawyer that she and Cory and Emmy wanted to preserve the inn, not tear it down.

Why had her aunt done this? What was her motive?

"Refuse it? How . . . could I do that? My brother and sister and I have no home. And I . . . love the inn."

Damask's words caused an uncomfortable feeling to go through Braden. He tried to dismiss it. The foolish girl hadn't had a chance yet to see what bad condition the building was in. He'd make her a good offer for her family's half and she could buy a small house. Surely she'd see that was the only practical solution.

"I, too, have no intention of refusing the bequest," Braden said crisply.

Mr. Edwards nodded, no surprise on his face. He folded the papers he held and laid them on his desk. "Then I will see to having a new deed made up. This concludes our business. Good day to you all."

Flora rose, followed by Damask. Braden followed them out of the room and down the steep flight of stairs, back into the morning sunshine, none of them speaking.

On the sidewalk, Braden turned to Damask. "I'm prepared to offer you a more than fair price for your share of the inn," he said. "More than the entire building and the land and the outbuildings are worth."

"No," Damask said almost before he'd finished speaking. Her voice was as firm as his had been.

He stared at her, fighting down anger. "You're refusing without even thinking it over?"

"Yes," she said. "Flora told me you want to tear down the inn and build a house. I can't let you do that!"

Braden frowned at her. "It's the only sensible thing to do. The inn needs too many repairs."

"I don't care," Damask said. "I'll repair it. I want to live there. I want to open the inn again."

Braden gave a sharp bark of laughter. "You? How do you think you can do that? Do you have the money it would take?"

Damask's mouth was firm, too. "No. But I'll figure out a way. I'm not afraid of work. I can do a lot of it myself."

She was completely serious, Braden saw. His frown deepened. "You forget I have to agree to that arrangement, and I'll never do that," he said flatly.

Her generous breasts rose as she took a deep breath. "You're wrong," she countered. "The will didn't say anything about repairs or reopening the inn."

Braden stared at her, realizing she was right. Ada *hadn't* forbidden either of them doing anything to the inn. Only that they agree before selling . . . or otherwise disposing of it.

"You won't be able to do what you want," he said flatly.

"I'm going to try. And we're going to live there until you change your mind."

A flash of anger hit him, mixed with a contrary bit of admiration for her spirit. "All right," he said coolly. "And I will also continue to live there until *you* change your mind."

They stood facing each other like the combatants they were.

"*Gott in Himmel!*" Flora finally said. "Let us go

home. We cannot stand on the street arguing for all
the town to hear us.''

Braden knew she was right. Already, several people
had slowed down to stare at them, listen to their
raised voices. He was establishing himself as a solid
businessman in this town that had so disdained his
family. He couldn't afford this kind of scene.

"Yes," he agreed tightly, "let's go back to the inn
and discuss it further."

Damask lifted her rounded chin in that stubborn
way that reminded him of Ada. "What is there to
discuss? You've said you won't change your mind—
and I have no intention of changing mine."

Again, he swallowed his anger. "I'm going back to
my store. Maybe by tonight you'll be ready to listen
to reason."

She gave him an even, unsmiling look. "Maybe by
then *you* will be."

Don't lose your temper. You'll only hurt yourself. Braden
spun on his heel and walked rapidly away toward
the corner of Main and Walnut, where his new store
building stood.

Anger still simmered inside him.

Home, Flora had called the inn. He knew Damask
and her family already thought of it as such, too. It
couldn't be their home!

He would treat all of them fairly. More than fairly.
He'd see that Flora always had a place to live, plenty
to live on.

But he wouldn't let Damask thwart his dream.

He *would* have his mansion on the hill.

And he'd share it with Verona, the most beautiful
girl in Goose Creek.

He waited for the usual feeling of satisfaction to
hit him, but it was long in coming . . . and flawed in
some way when it did.

Chapter Three

When Flora and Damask got back to the inn, they found Emmy and Cory outside, exploring.

Mrs. Burton, the neighbor who'd looked after the children, was avid for news and was dumbfounded to find out the details of Ada's will.

No more so than I, Damask thought. She'd talked a big plan to Braden, but she didn't know how, with almost no money, she could implement it.

At Flora's urging, Mrs. Burton stayed for dinner, another feast compared to what Damask's family was used to.

"Braden I expected for dinner," Flora said, "but then . . ."

She glanced toward Damask, and Damask felt herself reddening, mentally finishing Flora's sentence. No doubt Braden didn't want to be in her presence at all. When he'd left, he'd been furious with her.

Well, she wasn't so pleased with him, either! Wanting to turn his friend's home and business to rubble so he could build a fancy new house on the site!

Emmy and Cory again ate as if they didn't know where their next meal was coming from and hurried off for more exploring. Mrs. Burton made short work of her meal and helping with the cleanup, and her keen black eyes gleamed when she hurried off.

Flora huffed out a sigh. "Now all over town it will be that you and Braden fight over the property."

Damask didn't like that idea, but in a small town such as Goose Creek, it was bound to happen, especially since several people had already heard their raised voices earlier.

Something else had been bothering Damask. "Why do you think Aunt Ada left such a will, when she knew Braden wanted to demolish the inn?"

Flora shook her head. "It wonders me, also. But Ada had reasons. She was not foolish woman."

"Oh, Flora, am I a fool to refuse Braden's offer?" Damask asked. "Am I completely selfish? Not thinking of my responsibility for Emmy and Cory?"

Flora studied her, then shook her head. "No. The inn falls not down, as Braden says. These thick fieldstone walls will outlive both you and me. A crime it would be to destroy it."

"But Braden's right—I don't have money for repairs. Or even for us to live on! I'd expected to earn our keep by helping Aunt Ada run the inn."

"How you think Ada and I have lived these last few years?"

"I don't know," Damask admitted. "I wondered about that."

"We have the cows—two Jerseys with thick cream for the butter. And eggs from the chickens. The ducks and geese make babies. The garden dirt grows good vegetables. The orchard has the fruit."

Damask nodded. "Yes, I can see you had enough food for yourselves."

Flora smiled. "Not only for us enough—but for the neighbors, too. I sell butter and cream all over town. And my jams and jellies and kuchen and such. Also the good brown eggs and the ducks and geese. That buys us the coffee and tea and the other things."

"Of course we'll help, but we can't let you do all that for us," Damask protested.

Flora gave her a sly smile. "Then I cannot stay here in my old room, since no longer I cook for the inn."

"That's not the same thing!"

"And why is it not? It seems to me the same."

Damask stared at her, at a loss for words.

Flora nodded. "It will work itself out. You see. You wait."

"I can't sit and wait. I have to keep busy."

Flora's eyes sparkled. "I said nothing about sitting. Work there is plenty of here."

The inn could wait for a bit. Making sure they had enough food for the coming year was the most important thing. Damask smiled. "Then I want to get busy. Where do I start?"

"Last week Harold plows up the garden patch. It is now time for the planting."

"I've done a lot of that. My parents had a small farm."

"Ada talked often about your mama. Her only sister. She was much grieved when she died of the fever."

Damask swallowed a lump in her throat. "Yes, so was I to lose her and my papa."

"Much you have lost for such a young woman," Ada said, her voice soft. "Maybe now no more losses."

"I hope so," Damask said. She forced a smile for Flora. "Can we start planting today?"

"We can," Flora said, satisfaction in her voice.

"Good. I love to plant seeds. It's so exciting when they start poking out of the ground."

"More so when you pick them and cook them in the kettle," answered the ever-practical Flora.

Braden rode his gelding, Jasper, down the long drive leading to the barns and stables of the big Holmes farm. When he dismounted, a stable hand led Jasper off.

Verona's father had done well, Braden thought, looking around the neat, bustling farmyard. When dairy farming started booming after the Civil War, he'd shrewdly invested in the best stock and now had the most prosperous farm in the county. Or several counties, for that matter.

Braden glanced down at himself. Not wanting to go back to the inn to change after he'd closed the store at five, he still wore his suit trousers. He'd left his coat and cravat at the store. The three-mile ride out from Goose Creek had left a coating of dust on his shoes, brought a film of perspiration to his face and arms, although the evening was cooling now.

But Verona wouldn't care, he assured himself. She'd be glad to see him. And he'd enjoy her sweetness after his tangle with tart-tongued Damask this morning.

Anger isn't the only emotion she arouses in you.

Where had that unwanted thought come from? He pushed it aside and headed for the front of the large white house. He stepped up on the wide porch, which sported huge columns like those of a southern plantation.

A dark-haired young woman wearing a black dress and a ruffled white apron opened the door.

"Good evening, Mr. Franklin," said the maid, who most places in Goose Creek would be called a hired girl and wouldn't be wearing a uniform.

"Good evening, Ruby," he answered, noticing as always her struggle to maintain her dignity when she greeted him.

From the gleam in her eye, he thought it pleased her that the son of no-account Lonnie Franklin was now a successful, well-to-do businessman. Worthy of Verona Holmes, her employer's daughter.

Or maybe it didn't.

He was used to both reactions now, after more than a year back here, and neither bothered him. Not very much, at least.

"Come into the parlor and I'll s—inquire if Miss Verona can receive you."

Suppressing a smile at her prim, stilted words, Braden followed her into the marble-floored foyer, then into the parlor.

The room was hideous, Braden thought as always. Every available surface was covered with antimacassars and doilies and trinkets, and crowded with dark, heavy furniture. The two windows might as well not have been there, since dark velvet drapes kept out the light. A few minutes in here and he was desperate for fresh air and sunshine.

Verona was as proud as her parents were of the pretentious new house.

And won't you love the way she decorates the house you'll share with her?

He frowned at that wayward thought. What was wrong with him today? He loved his sweet Verona and she loved him. She'd made that plain often enough.

"Darling! What are you doing here?"

Verona swept into the room, bringing a cloud of almost cloyingly sweet perfume in her wake. Before he could fully rise, she was leaning over him. She clasped his upper arms, giving him a display of her cleavage, and pressed her lips against his, her pointed little tongue darting between them.

She knew a surprising lot about kissing to be such a sheltered girl, Braden thought as he returned her kiss. He'd not have to worry about coaxing a frightened virgin into his arms on their wedding night.

And yet . . . sometimes he got the feeling that she didn't really *want* to do these things. . . .

He dismissed that thought. Obviously, if she didn't want to, she wouldn't. He'd never demanded anything of her.

"I came to see you," Braden answered when he could get his breath.

She stepped back, releasing his arms and wrinkling her pert little nose. "You smell of the road!"

No one would guess that only a few years ago she'd been helping her mother in the kitchen like any other farm girl.

He smiled at her. "Why wouldn't I? Since I've ridden Jasper out here?"

"You should have brought your buggy and we could have gone for a ride after supper."

She looked suggestively up at him from under long lashes, and he knew what she left unsaid: that they could have stopped the buggy on the darkened road.

"I needed the ride," he said, still keeping his smile.

"At least you should have told me you were coming tonight," she said, pouting prettily. "I thought you said tomorrow, and here I am looking my worst and wearing this old rag."

Her gown was of ice-blue satin and better suited to a ballroom than a farmhouse parlor, but it set off her pale blond prettiness and light blue eyes to advantage and no doubt that was her aim.

"You look beautiful as always, and I couldn't wait until tomorrow," he said.

Her pout left, and she gave him a gratified smile. "Why, what a sweet thing to say!"

"It's true," he answered. And it was, but maybe not in quite the way it sounded to her.

Verona seated herself beside him in an uncomfortable-looking gilded chair. "Did the old woman leave you one of her tables?" she asked coyly.

Braden frowned at her playfully slighting words. He didn't like to hear Ada spoken of in that way. But then, it was his own fault. Hadn't he told Verona that's all he expected?

He had to tell her. Might as well get it over with. "No, she left me half shares in the inn and the acreage."

Verona laughed, giving him a disbelieving look. "What a legacy that would be!"

"I'm not joking."

Her pretty face sobered. "What are you talking about?"

Braden drew in a deep breath and let it out. He didn't want to have to tell her this but knew he must.

"Ada left the property equally to me and to her nieces and nephew."

Verona shot out of her chair as if a bee had stung her. "You can't be serious!"

He nodded. "Yes, I am. I don't know why she did such a thing."

Verona frowned, then her face cleared and she smiled. "But you can buy these relatives' share, and we can build our grand house on the hill."

It wasn't a question. She had supreme confidence he could do that.

"Yes, I'm sure I can, eventually. At the moment, Damask, who's the only one of age and is in charge, is refusing to consider such a thing. They're all staying on in the inn—as is Flora."

Verona's eyes narrowed. "Staying on? Why?"

"I imagine because they have very little money to live anywhere else."

He knew that wasn't the only reason, but he didn't want to get into all that with Verona.

She smiled again. "Good. Then soon she'll be happy to sell to you."

"That's right," Braden answered. Somehow, this conversation was distasteful to him. It sounded as if the two of them, both with plenty of money, were plotting against a poor family with none in order to get their way.

And weren't they?

No. What he and Verona wanted was the only sensible thing to do. Trying to restore that moldering old inn was a foolish idea.

"And where are you going to live now that these people have arrived?" Verona asked. "You know we—"

She hesitated for a moment.

Then she smiled brightly, but it seemed a bit forced. "We have plenty of room. Mama and Papa would be more than happy to have you here. And so would I."

Braden didn't say anything for a few moments. Why wasn't he jumping at this chance to literally have Verona in his bed? Most men wouldn't hesitate a moment.

"I'm staying on at the inn, too," he finally said.

She looked jolted, but yet Braden thought he detected relief in her expression, too, puzzling him.

"You can't do that! Why, the whole town will be gossiping about you staying there with that young woman."

"Her brother and sister are also there, as well as Flora."

Verona frowned. She tapped one small black slipper against the Brussels carpet.

"That won't do at all," she said tightly. "You must move out."

A flash of anger went through him. He didn't like people telling him what to do. Especially the woman he intended to marry in the near future.

"No, I won't," he said evenly, his smile gone. "If I'm to persuade Damask to sell her share of the inn to me, I must be there as much as possible to try to wear her down."

He grimaced at his choice of words. They sounded cold and callous. "What I mean is, I have to keep telling her to use some common sense and do what's practical."

Verona's face smoothed out. She stopped her foot tapping and sat back down in her chair. "I'm sorry. I just don't want everyone gossiping," she said, her voice now soft, her smile back in place.

Mollified, Braden reached over and took her small white hand in his own and squeezed it. "You let me worry about that. All you need to do is keep yourself pretty for my visits."

For a moment he saw something flash in her eyes, as if he'd angered her with his remark, then it was gone.

She put her other hand on top of his and squeezed back. "I'll try to do that," she purred. "But next time give me some warning before you come. You will stay for supper?"

A picture of the old inn's big, cheerful kitchen came into his mind. Flora, Damask, and the two children sitting around the trestle table which was loaded with Flora's bountiful dishes.

"Of course I'll stay," he told his lovely fiancée.

"Good." She leaned forward, offering her puckered lips to him.

He leaned forward and kissed her with all the feeling he could muster, blotting out the oddly inviting picture of the old inn kitchen that still lingered in his mind.

"Where is Mr. Franklin?" Emmy asked Damask, smothering a yawn.

Damask, sitting on the edge of the bed she shared with the child, pulled the quilt up a little higher, under Emmy's chin. "I don't know. I suppose he has things to do. His life is none of our concern, you know."

Emmy gave her an earnest look. "But I like him."

Surprise went through Damask. What an odd thing for Emmy to say about a man who'd barely spoken to her.

Maybe she sees some of that good Flora insists he has inside. Children often see more clearly than adults.

No, she didn't believe that, she told herself firmly.

"Is he going to keep on staying here?" Emmy persisted.

"I don't know," Damask said again.

She'd been asking herself this same question all afternoon, trying not to admit that she wanted him to stay, even while she was horrified at herself for such feelings.

He was promised to another woman. And he'd declared himself her enemy, determined to destroy what she intended to preserve.

Damask kissed Emmy's cheek and rose. "Now go to sleep. You can't hold your eyes open."

"Yes, I can," Emmy insisted, but even as she spoke, her eyelids fluttered closed.

Damask watched her for a few moments. The child looked so young and vulnerable. Too thin. Emmy needed lots more good food to put some meat on her bones. So did Cory.

Braden's offer to buy their share of the property would solve all their problems. Allow them to buy a small house, big enough for Flora. Give them enough to live on without worry.

And here she was, stubbornly determined to keep this old building from being torn down, replaced with a mansion.

No, it was more than stubbornness. Something inside her told her she must do this. . . .

It was almost as if Aunt Ada's spirit *did* still inhabit these old rooms . . . telling her she was doing the right thing in fighting Braden. . . .

Don't be fanciful.

And why on earth should she want Braden to stay here? She'd met the man only yesterday. She didn't really know him, but what she did know, she didn't like.

That wasn't exactly true. She liked his looks . . . and his deep voice . . . that air of confidence. . . .

And she hated the kind of person he truly was. A man who could destroy the home of a woman he'd called his friend, who'd fed him . . . probably clothed him, during his childhood.

Damask quietly left the room, opened Cory's door to see him sprawled fast asleep across his bed. She covered him, then, out in the quiet hall again, hesitated.

Flora was already in bed. Their long afternoon of planting had left her exhausted.

Physically, Damask was tired, too, but not sleepy.

The events of the day were still too much with her, keeping her mind in turmoil.

She needed some of Flora's chamomile tea, she decided, and headed for the kitchen. The teakettle, gaily decorated with a painted peach, sat on the back of the stove, full of water for the morning coffee and porridge, thin wisps of steam coming from its spout.

Damask found the tea, wrapped in a cloth, in a metal can in the cupboard. She measured out a teaspoon of the fragrant flowers, put them in a cup, and poured the boiling water over them.

The kitchen door opened and closed.

Startled, Damask looked up.

Braden Franklin stood just inside the door, his suit coat draped over his arm, the first few buttons of his white shirt undone. Even from across the room, Damask could see the black curls on his chest.

She felt prickles on her arm. Gooseflesh. Just the sight of this man was causing that.

He looked just as surprised to see her.

"I thought everyone would be in bed," he said, coming farther into the room.

"The others are. I . . . wasn't sleepy." Damask turned back to her cup, reached for the honey jar.

She felt him behind her and her fingers fumbled on the jar. She grabbed it just before it overturned.

"That tea smells good," Braden said.

Panic rose in her. Too close behind. She had to get out of here. "I'm taking a cup up to bed with me," she said without turning.

"Good idea." He moved from behind to stand beside her, giving her a smile. "I think I'll do the same."

"I—Emmy thought you weren't coming back," she blurted out before she could stop herself.

He raised his heavy black brows. "*Emmy* thought that?"

Damask felt herself reddening and was furious. "She likes you," she mumbled, and was even angrier. She needed to stuff a gag in her mouth. She stirred her honey into her tea with such a fierce motion that some of it slopped out onto the worktable top.

Without looking at Braden, she reached for the dishcloth draped over the dishpan to dry, and her fingers closed over his. He'd had the same idea.

A tremor shivered through her at the contact. His fingers felt just as they looked—strong and warm. She had an insane urge to stroke her own fingers down their hair-roughened length, squeeze her hand around his. . . .

She jerked her hand away, and he moved his, and then she picked up the dishcloth and mopped up the spill.

"I like Emmy, too," Braden finally said.

What caused that odd note in his deep voice? Damask wondered. Was he also reacting to the accidental touch, or merely surprised at what she'd said about her sister?

Enough of this nonsense! Damask picked up her cup, moved back a step, and turned toward Braden, hoping her face didn't show her muddled feelings.

"There's plenty of hot water in the kettle," she said briskly. "And I'm sure you know where the tea's kept."

He wasn't smiling. His eyes seemed to be trying to see right through her. She had an absurd feeling that maybe they could.

"Yes, I know where the tea is kept."

Braden tried to keep his voice neutral but knew he hadn't succeeded. The touch of Damask's hand had unsettled him. He still felt it.

"I see the garden is planted," he said, forcing his mind onto what was bothering him. As he'd walked around to the back door, the full moon had revealed how industrious the two women had been that day.

Damask blinked at his abrupt change of subject and backed up another step. "We worked all afternoon."

"So you're planning to stay on here?" Again, he heard the tension in his voice but couldn't prevent it. Or deny it wasn't all caused by the sight of the neat rows laid out in the garden patch.

Damask's eyes flashed. "Yes! Of course I am. I told you that this morning."

Braden felt his jaw muscles tighten. "I thought maybe you'd reconsidered."

"I'm not wishy-washy," she said firmly.

"I'd never accuse you of that. But I hoped you might decide to have some common sense."

Damask stuck her chin up. "I have plenty of sense, common or uncommon," she said between clenched teeth.

She had a pretty chin . . . and he had to admire her spirit. "Good. I'm glad to hear that. I'm sure when you've had time to think my offer over, you'll see it's the only practical thing to do."

Her rounded chin came up a bit more. "And I'm certain that when *you've* had time to think, you'll realize what a selfish, ungrateful wretch *you* are. Aunt Ada loved you, and you'd repay her by destroying this inn she loved."

Despite the fact he knew how wrongheaded Damask was, he felt as if she'd hit him in the stomach.

He *wasn't* ungrateful. He would have done anything for Ada. But she'd refused to accept a cent from him except for his room and board.

"You're not looking at this in the right way," he finally said.

"Yes, I am. You just won't admit it because I'm opposing your plans," Damask said, trying to control the anger that made her tremble.

Her head high, she walked by him. He didn't move an inch, and the sleeve of her gown brushed against his bare arm as she passed. Even through the fabric she could feel his warmth, and contrarily, she shivered in reaction.

She felt his gaze on her back as she marched across the room to the hall door, but he didn't say anything else.

Good. She'd at least had the last word with the infuriating man.

So why didn't she feel more satisfied?

Chapter Four

Verona picked a white rose from the bed along the east side of the house and dropped it into her basket, a bit of dirt falling from its stem onto the bodice of her dress.

She frowned and flicked at the speck, her frown deepening as, instead of falling off, it made a streak on the pristine white muslin surface.

"Oh, hell and damnation!" she muttered, then stiffened when she heard voices coming from the big front veranda.

The louder, deeper one she recognized as her father's.

She hoped he hadn't heard her swear. Even more, she hoped whoever was with him hadn't. That simply wouldn't do.

A sudden wild longing for her carefree childhood days swept over her. She'd been such a tomboy, climbing trees with her older brother, Oliver, and Russell Gifford from the neighboring farm. She'd sworn right along with the boys, and it hadn't bothered them a bit. They'd had such fun. . . .

Appalled at her thoughts, Verona pushed them away. She was a lady now, engaged to Braden Franklin, the most up-and-coming businessman in town, she reminded herself.

She'd had other chances, of course, but no one had appealed to her . . . until Braden. He was so handsome and, as her mother said, had such a promising future.

Still, she hadn't been all that taken with the idea, but her mother kept on rubbing it in that she'd turned down all the other eligible young men who'd shown interest. Did she really want to be an old maid?

Verona had decided she didn't. Old maids, no matter how prosperous their families, were looked down on, whispered and laughed about.

So she'd managed to attract Braden with the feminine wiles Miss Pritchett had taught her. And some Miss Pritchett had told her about when her mother wasn't around. She'd flirted with Braden and lured him on to declare himself by promising him all the delights of the marriage bed. Even suggesting they wouldn't have to wait for the wedding . . .

And she had hooked him, much to her mother's delight.

She grimaced. *Hooked him.* Just as if he were a fish.

No, she amended hastily, she'd attracted him and then they'd fallen in love with each other. She was a proper young lady now, and she must act like one at all times. Even in her thoughts.

Verona sighed. Oh, but sometimes it was so hard! Especially when she was with Braden. When he irritated her, she sometimes forgot her ladylike ways and said what she thought instead of what he wanted to hear.

Just as she had last night when Braden had told her about that niece of Ada's staying at the inn along with him. That had made her so angry, she couldn't see straight.

Braden had gotten mad, too, bringing her to her senses.

It would never do to make him *really* angry. Why, he might break the engagement, and then where would she be?

Facing the town's gossip and pity because she was unmarried. Stuck in her family's house forever, when she'd belatedly realized how much she wanted her own house . . . that beautiful house Braden had promised to build for her.

She had to keep a closer watch on her temper. And how could she ask for more? Braden was rich and *so* good-looking.

Of course she wanted to marry him.

Didn't she?

Verona pushed away the momentary doubt. Yes! She did.

Braden certainly wasn't from one of the best families in the county. Far from it! His family was way down at the bottom of the Goose Creek social pile.

But it was easy enough to forget Braden's upbringing. Most of the town already had because he had plenty of money now and had built that wonderful new store.

As her mama had said, Verona was no longer a spring chicken. She couldn't hope to find anyone better than Braden.

Verona moved closer to the front of the house, stopping before the side flower bed, which contained a mixture of spring flowers, fading now, and early summer perennials.

She could hear the voices clearer, and again she

stiffened. Russell Gifford was the other person! What was *he* doing here?

Setting her basket beside her, Verona bent over the flower bed, dawdling over her selection, keeping her ears open.

"I've already leased the property. I'm going to start taking our produce in every Saturday," Russell said. "That empty space on the corner of Main and Elm will be just the spot for an open-air market."

Verona drew in her breath. What on earth was Russell talking about? Was he planning to make a spectacle of himself by hawking his farm vegetables to every passerby?

Trust Russell to think of something like this. When they were children, he always had the crackbrained schemes that got them in trouble.

Verona waited for her father's booming laugh, his ridicule for Russell's silly plan.

Instead, her father said, "That's one of the best ideas I've heard in a while."

Surprise went over Verona. Her father's tone was admiring, his words approving. And he meant every one of them, Verona knew. Her papa was no good at pretending things.

Unlike her and her mother.

"I'm glad you think so," Russell said. "We always have so much in our gardens by midsummer, we can't use it all, no matter how much Mama puts by. And there's a lot of people in the town now who don't have much of a garden."

"That's true. Bernice has jars in the cellar from so many years back, the stuff has to be thrown away."

"I wanted to give you first crack at going in as partners with me on this. If it works well this year with our extra vegetables, next spring we can plant more—set aside a few acres—and expand the business."

Russell's father had died the year before, leaving the farm to his mother and to Russell, so now he was free to run it as he pleased.

Verona sniffed. Run it in the ground, most likely.

And to come up with harebrained ideas! Surely her father wasn't going to get involved.

There was another silence, longer this time. Verona relaxed. Of course he wasn't. Her papa had good sense.

"I see no reason not to, Russell," Wallace said. "Thanks for asking me."

"No need to thank me. It'll be an honor to work with you. Maybe Oliver would want to try this, too."

"I bet he would. We can talk to him."

And now they were getting her brother involved!

Verona saw red. Before she thought, she marched around the corner of the house, her garden shears still in her hand.

"Papa! What is the matter with you?" she demanded.

Her father stared at her in amazement, his mouth hanging open.

Verona's glance swung to Russell. Her anger increased when he grinned at her, just as if he had when they were children together.

"Why, hello, Ronie," he said, using his old nickname for her. "Haven't seen you in a coon's age."

That wasn't true. She saw him every Sunday in church, and spoke to him, too. Although that was the extent of their conversation.

And she *hated* that nickname!

She stuck her chin up and sniffed. "What do you mean by trying to talk my father and my brother into this . . . this undignified idea? Just because you want to be the laughingstock of Goose Creek, you don't have to try to drag us into it, too!"

"Verona, that will be enough," her father said. His voice wasn't loud, but it carried authority.

Verona abruptly realized what she'd just done. Got involved with her father's business, which he didn't allow. Even from her mother.

She swallowed her anger. "I'm sorry, Papa," she said, feeling her face reddening.

Once more, her temper had gotten the best of her common sense. Damn! Oh, damn, damn, damn!

Her father gave her a disapproving look. "You should be. I let you and your mama run the house any way you see fit, but *I* run the farm."

And well she knew it. She'd heard her mother come out the loser in many an argument. Such as when, fifteen years ago, Papa had wanted to mortgage the farm he'd inherited from his parents and invest the money in dairy cattle.

Mama had had a fit, wailing and weeping, saying they'd all be in the poorhouse, but it hadn't helped. Papa had gone ahead and done it anyway.

And look where they were now. They had the biggest, most prosperous dairy farm in three counties.

Now, of course, Mama was proud as punch, acting like she'd gone along with the idea from the beginning. Papa let her talk, but Verona often saw a little knowing smile at the corner of his mouth.

Out of the corner of her eye, Verona saw Russell was trying not to grin.

She fought down her returning anger. She *wouldn't* give Russell something to grin about and then carry the tale home with him for his mother to spread all over the community.

Yep, Ronie got her comeuppance from her dad again. That girl just can't learn to keep her mouth shut.

Yes, she could. She *would*.

"Good day, Russell," Verona said coolly, and turned on her heel. She was standing very close to one of the big white pillars, and she'd forgotten she still held the garden shears.

Her arm swung around and the shears' tips stuck into the nearest column with a loud thunk, jarring Verona, almost making her fall. Her face burning, she finally got her balance back and jerked the shears out, leaving two jagged holes.

Her head up, Verona marched back to the side yard, listening for Russell's laughter.

To her great relief, it didn't come.

But her father's loud sigh did.

"I thought once Verona got herself engaged to be married, she'd learn to curb her temper and settle down and lose her flighty ways. Girl never stops to think before she says or does something. Of course, I've never been sure her marrying that Braden Franklin was a good idea."

Verona didn't wait for Russell's comment, whatever it might be. Her lips pressed tightly together, scowling fiercely, she reached the flower bed again. She stared unseeingly at it for a few moments, reliving the humiliating scene she'd just gone through.

She didn't feel like cutting any more flowers. Or engaging in any other ladylike pursuits.

Verona held the garden shears up. And, as she'd many times done with a pocket knife in a game of mumblety-peg, let them fly.

The shears skewered an innocent purple iris and brought it to the ground.

Verona glared at it with satisfaction. Leaving her basket and shears where they sat, she walked around the back of the house to the kitchen door.

Glancing through the glass pane, she saw Ruby

polishing silver at the worktable. Her mother wasn't in sight.

Good, Verona thought, going inside. She didn't want to have to talk to her mother just then.

Ruby glanced up from her task, smiling.

Verona forced a return smile and, leaving the kitchen, went down the long hall toward the stairs. Her hand on the banister, she stopped, then turned and walked the few feet to the ornate double front door and glanced out the small window to the side.

Russell and her father still sat talking earnestly together. As if sensing her look, Russell raised his head and glanced toward the door.

Verona hastily moved away. How on earth had she and Russell been such pals when she was a child?

She couldn't *stand* him now!

Flora and Damask stood in front of the inn, looking at the sagging middle of the front porch roof. Several of the posts had rotted and badly needed replacing. Maybe the entire roof needed replacing.

Yesterday, they'd finished planting the vegetable garden. By the day's end, Damask had an aching back and shoulders, but a feeling of great satisfaction in the neat rows.

Braden hadn't come back to the inn for dinner, but he was there at the supper table. Flora treated him the same as always, but he avoided catching Damask's eye, as she did his, and somehow they both managed not to say a word to each other during the meal.

If Cory and Emmy noticed the strained atmosphere, it didn't stop them from talking to Braden.

They were both hungry for male attention, Damask saw, stricken. And Braden talked easily with the children, treating them with respect. There was no hint in his voice or manner that he was engaged in a battle of wills with their sister.

Damask's heart, hardened to Braden, had softened a little as she'd watched the interplay among the three.

He wasn't all bad, or he couldn't be this kind to Emmy and Cory. He wouldn't have been Ada's friend, either.

But that didn't erase the fact that what he wanted to do was wrong. And would break Ada's heart if she were here to see him. Somehow, Damask knew that with certainty.

She frowned. Although Flora *had* said her aunt had considered selling the property to Braden at one time . . .

Before she'd gotten Damask's letter asking if they could come and live at the inn.

Was that it? Had Aunt Ada counted on Damask to help her restore the inn? This made little sense since Damask had no money, either. But she had a strong back.

Damask realized she was concentrating on these thoughts so she wouldn't have to think about last night . . . when Braden had come into the kitchen . . . when her hand had touched his and . . .

She took a deep breath and picked up her fork. She would not think about that. She would not, would not. . . .

During the rest of the meal she'd kept her eyes on her plate as much as possible and had tried to keep her mind a blank.

Which had been impossible.

Damask picked up a piece of broken slate from the ground. *Forget all that.*

A thunderstorm accompanied by heavy winds had

swept through the area late last night, blowing loose some of the roof slates.

"In the attic we will have new leaks," Flora said, glancing at the slate fragment. "With every bad storm, we get this."

Damask tried hard not to let her dismay show. After her stubborn stand with Braden, she wouldn't give up now. But already she could see the extent of the repairs needed was much beyond what she'd thought from her cursory look at the inn when she arrived.

"I was the oldest child, so I did a lot of farm work," Damask said firmly. "I can replace slates. Our farm-house had a slate roof and I helped Papa repair it many a time."

Flora gave her a surprised look. "Helped him?"

Damask shrugged. "I handed him the slates and nails," she admitted, "but I watched what he did and I remember. It isn't that hard."

"Not hard, maybe, but easy to fall and break your-self."

Damask smiled at Flora's colorful description of the injuries she might risk. "I'll be careful," she promised. "I don't want to break myself."

"For now we use another kettle under the leak. We talk about replacing slates some other time."

Damask tilted her head, her smile widening despite her worries. "Flora, you treat me as if I'm your child!"

Flora's return smile held a touch of sadness. "I wish that you were. I would be proud to claim a daughter such like you."

Damask remembered long-widowed Flora had lost several children in infancy. "I'm sorry you have no children."

Flora waved away her apology. "No need, no need. Now, let us see what else two women may be able to do."

"Those young scamps can quit their playing long enough for some chores."

Damask called Emmy and Cory, who were playing a game of tag in the wildflower-covered meadow.

Obediently, they hurried over. Too obediently, Damask thought. She'd like to see some of their normal impishness back.

"We need more wood for the kitchen range," she told them. "And, Cory, you can draw a couple of buckets of water from the well. Fill the stove reservoir with one."

"All right, Damask," Cory said. He headed purposefully for the woodpile behind the inn, Emmy trotting along beside him.

"They are good children," Flora said. "Your mama and papa raised them well."

"Yes," Damask agreed, blinking back tears. Why had her parents died? Why were they chosen to get that fatal fever?

"Are you ready to go inside?" Flora asked a moment later.

"Yes," Damask said again, pushing away her unhappy thoughts.

Her parents were gone and nothing would bring them back. All she could do was take care of Emmy and Cory as they would have done. Once the inn was repaired and open again, they would have an income. Their future would be brighter.

Two of the porch steps were badly rotted, and one corner of the porch had a hole in it big enough to require replacing several boards.

"I can fix the steps and the porch floor, too," Damask said, forcing a confidence she didn't feel into her voice.

Flora sighed. "These last years, I tell Ada let Harold do repairs before they get big, but she would not listen. She had not enough money for the material, she said.''

Damask drew in her breath in shock. The inn's guest list must have dwindled to nothing.

Why hadn't Aunt Ada let her family know how bad things were? *Because she knew your family was having its own hard struggle. What could they have done?*

The foyer wallpaper was stained with brown blotches, and up toward the ceiling, it was coming loose in several places.

"I can do that, too. Mama and I wallpapered our house several times." The confidence in Damask's voice wasn't feigned this time. Wallpapering wasn't hard. Tedious and time-consuming, but not difficult.

She fought to sustain that confidence in her abilities during the rest of their tour, with its myriad discoveries of peeling wallpaper in nearly every room, stained ceilings in most of them, too, some sagging from undetected leaks.

At last they came to Ada's small sitting room adjoining her bedroom. Damask paused in the doorway, memories sweeping over her as she looked at the full bookshelves on the right side of the fireplace.

It was in this room, when she was eleven, that she'd acquired her love of books. Aunt Ada was an avid reader, straining her eyes with the flickering oil lamps every evening here after her daily work was finished.

She'd sat there in her favorite chair, an old rocker. . . . Damask could almost see her there now. . . .

Damask stiffened, her breath catching in her throat.

Her aunt sat in the rocker before the fireplace, gray head bent intently over a book, her finger moving down the lines on the pages.

Damask blinked and the vision disappeared. She

shook her head. Her imagination was working over-
time today.

It is not your imagination . . . I told you I am still here . . .
a voice whispered in her head . . . or in the air around
her.

She had to stop this. Her aunt was gone. She took
a deep breath and turned to Flora. "I still have the
books Aunt Ada gave me. I've read them until they're
almost falling apart."

Flora chuckled. "Yah, I guess you take after her.
Ada was the reader for sure. You talk like her, too.
Not like the country girls do."

Damask grimaced. Flora was right. Due to her fascination with books and reading, she didn't talk like a
farm girl, a fact that had earned her much ridicule
during her growing-up years at the country school
she'd attended.

This room, like most of the others, needed work.
A dark brown stain marred the wallpaper in one corner of the ceiling and several strips of the faded paper
were loose.

Damask moved to a small round table covered with
a white cloth. Her aunt Ada's old Bible lay on the
table's top. Damask moved her hand down its black
leather cover, fighting the memories.

Several other books lay on the table. Damask picked
one up, noting it was a book of fairy tales she'd loved
the summer she was here. Ada had never outgrown
her love of make-believe. It was one of her most
endearing qualities.

"Emmy will like this," she said.

Flora moved to her side, peering at the book. She
clucked her tongue. "Ach, these others are the library
books she brought home weeks ago," she said, picking up the other books in the stack. "I must return
them."

Damask gave her a surprised, pleased look. "Goose Creek has a public library?"

Flora nodded. "A very little one. Ada always had the books from there."

"So will I," Damask said, smiling widely. "Here, why don't you give the books to me and I'll return them."

Looking relieved, Flora gave her the other books. "That would be good. My feet aren't so good for the walking these days."

"Mine are fine," Damask assured her, already looking forward to the bliss of being in a room full of books.

Flora was right, Damask thought, Goose Creek's library was little, in the front room of an equally small, brick house on Elm Street.

Their assessment of the needed repairs for the inn was complete. Dinner—from which again Braden was missing—cooked, eaten, and the dishes washed. Flora had gone to her room for a short nap, and Damask was returning the books.

At Damask's entry, a woman looked up from behind a desk cluttered with books sitting across one corner of the room.

"Good afternoon," the woman said, her dark brown eyes full of curiosity.

Just like the eyes of the other people Damask had encountered on the way here. Curiosity and speculation. No doubt Mrs. Burton's report of Aunt Ada's strange will was all over town by now.

Damask returned the other woman's greeting, realizing she was younger than appeared at first glance. It was her spectacles and her brown hair, severely pulled back into a tight bun, that made her seem older. But her wide smile made her face pretty.

Damask walked across the room and laid the books she carried on the desk. "These are books my aunt Ada had taken out."

The woman nodded, her smile fading. "I lost a dear friend when Ada died. She did so love books."

"Yes," Damask agreed. "She passed that love along to me."

Damask extended her hand. "I'm Damask Aldon."

The woman rose and took Damask's hand. "I'm Geneva Dale. Ada spoke of you often. I'm so glad you're here. Now the inn won't be torn down!"

Damask gave her a surprised but gratified look. Yes, the news had made the rounds, and here was one person solidly on her side. "If I can save it, it certainly won't."

Geneva frowned. "Oh, dear. Are you doubtful of that?"

Damask felt an instant empathy with this woman, and didn't at all mind her questions. "Yes," she admitted. "I am. Flora and I went around the place this morning seeing what needs to be done. It's almost overwhelming. And we don't have much money."

Much money? They had *no* money.

Geneva bit her lip. "I wish I could help, but my pay here is barely enough to keep me alive." She gave a wry smile. "Good thing I don't eat a lot."

"You don't have a family?" Damask asked, marveling at how it seemed so easy to talk of personal things with this woman she'd just met.

Geneva shrugged. "Oh, yes, I have a family. But I'm determined to prove I can earn my living—and don't have to either stay at home and be pitied, or marry some man I don't even like in order to keep from starving!"

Damask laughed in surprise, liking Geneva more every minute. "I wouldn't want to do that, either."

Geneva bit her lip again. "I'm sorry. My big mouth's run away with me again. I know you've just lost your parents and now your aunt. I love my family even though I don't always get along with them. You see, I have three older, happily married sisters, and my parents don't know what to make of me."

Impulsively, Damask reached out her hand and squeezed Geneva's hand, lying on the desktop. "Don't worry about it. I understand how you feel."

Geneva looked amazed. "Do you, really? You're so pretty, you must have a dozen men after you."

"I'm not pretty! I have red hair and freckles, and I'm too tall. And I've had only one man interested in me in my whole life."

That last remark brought the familiar pain and scalded pride to the surface again.

Geneva tilted her head and regarded Damask closely. "Your hair is a wonderful shade of deep auburn and you have about six freckles on your nose. And I've never seen anyone with eyes that shade of gray before. You're not too tall, either. What happened to the man?"

Damask sucked in her breath, not wanting to talk about this. But Geneva stood there, her big brown eyes warm and compassionate. She wasn't asking out of just a desire for gossip.

"He jilted me when my parents died. He couldn't face raising my younger sister and brother."

This was the first time she'd told anyone about Warren's defection. It didn't hurt as much as she'd expected to talk of it.

"Oh, what a beast! You see, that's what I mean. Men are too selfish. There's not a one I'd marry."

Geneva's pale cheeks flushed a deep pink. She looked away from Damask.

Why, there was *one* man Geneva looked on with favor, Damask thought. Was the interest not returned? Was that why she was embarrassed at what she'd just said?

But her words had hit home. "Many of them are selfish," Damask said.

Warren certainly was. And she'd met another one two days ago. She frowned at that thought. Yes, Braden Franklin's self-centeredness was just as bad as Warren's, although a different kind.

And despite the fact he was promised to another and Damask didn't even like him, she was strongly attracted to him, no matter how much she tried to deny it. Or fight it.

Geneva turned to face her again, her blush fading. "My, here we are, chattering away like we've known each other all our lives. Isn't that strange?"

Damask forced her disturbing thoughts away and smiled at her. "I guess so. But you're very easy to talk to—and nice."

Geneva smiled back. "So are you. Maybe we can be friends."

"I'd like that," Damask said.

"So would I."

"I'd better get back to the inn. I want to get started on some repairs this afternoon."

"Will Braden let you?" Geneva asked. "I mean, if he owns half the inn, don't you have to agree on everything?"

Damask laughed at that absurd idea. "We don't agree on *anything* so far. But he can't stop me—short of using physical force—and I don't think even he would do that."

Geneva's dark brows lifted. "You don't like him, do you?"

"Of course I don't like him. He wants to destroy the inn!"

"Yes, he's wrong about that, but I think deep down he's a good man. He had a terrible childhood."

Damask nodded. "Flora says that, too, but that doesn't mean—"

The door opened and Harold came in, carrying two books.

"Afternoon, Miss Damask," he said, smiling at her. "Gettin' settled in?"

That wasn't the term she would have used, but she nodded. "I'm going to start repairing the front porch steps this afternoon."

His mouth fell open. "Why, Miss Damask, a young lady like you can't do that kind of work by yourself."

"Of course I can," Damask said firmly. She turned back to Geneva. "What do I owe you for the book fines?"

Geneva waved her hand. "Oh, forget it. Under the circumstances, you don't owe anything."

"All right. Thank you." Damask looked hungrily around at the book-lined walls but turned resolutely away. She had a lot of work to do these next weeks. And Aunt Ada's sitting room had more than enough books for her spare moments.

Harold put his books down on the desk and turned to her again. His face was set in resolute lines. "Miss Damask, I don't have any work lined up for the next few days. I'll be up in a little while to help you."

Startled, Damask shook her head. "No, Harold. I don't have any money to pay you."

He snorted. "Who said anything about money? Ada gave me jobs to do for years and paid me more than enough. I guess I can help her niece out a little now.

Especially since it's for such a worthy cause. I don't want to see that whippersnapper start tearing down Goose Creek Inn any more than you do.''

Damask swallowed. His help would make such a difference. And he truly wanted to do this. "All right, Harold. You keep account of the work you do, and when the inn's running again, I'll pay you.''

Oh, and wasn't she the sure one? Already talking about reopening the inn. As if that would happen soon.

Harold gave her a look full of respect. "All right, if that's the way you want it.''

"It is.'' Damask turned back to Geneva. "Good-bye.''

"Good-bye,'' Geneva echoed, her face alight with interest.

There was no backing down now, Damask thought, preceding Harold out the door. She wasn't a quitter, and she'd see this through whatever happened.

Whatever Braden Franklin did to try to stop her.

Chapter Five

"Mr. Franklin, could I have a few words with you?"

Braden, seated at his desk in his large, well-furnished office, going over the last week's records, glanced up at Jacob Gilroy, his store manager.

Jacob looked harried, which was nothing new. He almost always looked harried, especially near the end of the day.

"Of course. Come in and sit down." Braden placed a ruler to mark his place on the line he was examining and gave the man his full attention.

Jacob raked his fingers through his thinning brown hair and seated himself in front of his employer's desk.

"It's that new girl we hired as a clerk in the . . . uh . . . women's section," Jacob said, his face reddening.

Braden suppressed a smile. Jacob couldn't bring himself to say lingerie department. "Yes," Braden prompted, "go on."

Jacob raked his hair again. "She just doesn't know how to handle the type of ladies who frequent that department."

"What's she doing wrong?" Braden asked patiently.

"She's insulting the customers!" Jacob burst out.

Braden sighed, knowing he'd have to drag every word out of Jacob. "In what way?"

The man's flush deepened. "Mrs. Holmes came in just a little while ago, looking for . . . some . . . private items, and the wretched girl told her she'd never fit into the size she was trying on."

A vivid picture of Verona's mother trying to squeeze her ample figure into a too-small item of underwear popped into Braden's mind. He clamped his lips together so Jacob couldn't see he was doing his best not to laugh out loud.

"The girl has been here only a few days," Braden said when he got his mirth under control. "Give her time."

Jacob's agitation increased. He got up from his chair and leaned over the desk. "But that won't help! She's a Lathrop, and she'll always be a Lathrop. You know that family."

Braden's amusement disappeared. His body grew rigid. He stared at the man standing before him.

He's a Franklin, and he'll always be a Franklin. That whole family's just no-account.

How many times had he heard statements like that? How many times had he blindly struck out with his fists, then retreated to the old cabin in the woods to nurse his misery?

"What did you just say?" Braden asked, his voice deadly soft. He rose to his full six-foot-one-inch height.

Jacob stared at him, then retreated a step. "Wh-

why, I just said that Lorene is a Lathrop and she'll always—"

His voice broke off, his eyes filled with fear. He retreated another step. "I didn't mean anything," he gabbled.

"Jacob, you're a good store manager," Braden said, still in that deadly soft voice that was worse than a shout.

"I'm not going to fire you right now. But if I ever again hear you make a remark such as that, or if any of the employees tell me you have, you will be out of my store that instant. Do I make myself clear?"

Jacob retreated again. He nodded frantically. "Oh, yes, sir, Mr. Franklin, perfectly clear."

"First thing in the morning, send Lorene Lathrop in to see me," Braden said. "I'll have a talk with her."

Jacob bobbed his head again. "Yes, sir. Will there be anything else?"

Braden looked at him coldly. "No, Jacob. You may go."

The man scuttled from the office, closing the door very quietly. Braden sat back down, staring unseeingly at the open ledger before him.

Finally, a muscle ticking in his jaw, he got up from his chair, grabbed his suit coat from its peg on the wall, and left the office.

Jacob was gone, and the store was closed for the day. Quiet reigned in the aisles, the counters filled with merchandise.

The store still had a new smell, which exhilarated Braden when he unlocked the door every morning and came in an hour before anyone else. He liked to roam the aisles, pick up an item here and there, glance at the entire big room, go up the stairs to the upper floor equally full of a myriad of items for sale.

His, all his. Pride would fill him that he'd accomplished so much. Goose Creek had to acknowledge that he was a man of substance now. One of the town's leaders. His store employed more people than any other business in town, paid them better wages, too.

Braden slammed his fist into the wall outside his office door. Plaster cracked. When he drew back his throbbing hand, it was bleeding, the knuckles raw and cut.

How many people, his own employees included, sneered behind his back as he passed by?

He's one of those trifling Franklins. The whole family's nothing but trash and always will be.

Why in God's name had he returned to this town that had given him so much grief? Why hadn't he built his store in some other place, where no one knew anything about his family? Where he would be respected for what he'd accomplished, not for his family background or lack of it.

Why had he let his damned pride drive him to come back here and show them all?

He dug a handkerchief from his pocket, wrapped it around his hand, then let himself out, locking the massive mahogany front door behind him. At the moment Main Street was deserted. Good. He couldn't be responsible for what he said to anyone right now.

He loosened his shirt at the neck, then rapidly strode down the street until he reached the road that climbed the hill to the inn. Although the incline was steep, he pushed himself forward, grimly making his strides as long as possible. When he reached the meadow at the top of the hill, he paused to take a deep breath, then another.

He glanced over at the inn. Two people were kneeling on the front steps—a man and a woman. The woman lifted her hand, and the evening sun shone on her auburn hair, striking gold glints from it, and on something metal she held. She brought her hand down, and a sound came across the meadow to him.

Hammering. Harold and Damask were out there, and she was hammering something.

Braden unwrapped his hand, saw the bleeding had stopped, and stuffed the handkerchief back into his pocket.

He started walking, almost running, again, and in a few more strides saw Damask driving nails into a section of new wood on the step. Harold hammered on the other step.

What did they think they were doing? This shabby old inn wasn't going to be repaired; it was going to be torn down!

They heard him coming and both turned toward him. "Evening, Braden," Harold said calmly.

Damask, clad in her faded blue-checked dress, looked at his taut face, then deliberately turned back to her work. She placed a nail, held it with her left hand, then again lifted her right, still holding the hammer. She struck the nail with the sideways blow that only someone experienced at this work could do, driving it evenly into the step.

Braden's anger and frustration grew as he recognized her skill. She wasn't bluffing when she said she could do a lot of the repair work herself.

Along with these feelings another grew, one that had been with him since the first moment he'd seen her. Attraction. Looking down at her bent head, with its auburn curls, her graceful, womanly figure, a rush of desire hit him.

He wanted to pull her to her feet, into his arms, and kiss her delectable mouth until she gasped for breath and begged for more.

And he was a complete, utter fool.

Braden forced his mind and body to quiet, as he'd

taught himself to do over the years, forced control back into himself. There was no use protesting what Damask and Harold were doing. Legally, he couldn't stop them.

And he didn't want to cause a scene, either, he admitted. He'd already lost his temper once today. That was enough.

"Good evening," he said blandly, glancing toward Harold to include him in the greeting. "Looks like I'd better use the back door."

"Oh, we can move," Damask said. "We've just about finished with the steps."

Her voice held a note of pride in a job well done.

Braden couldn't dispute it.

But he sure as hell wasn't going to compliment her on it, either.

"Don't bother. It won't hurt me to walk around back," he said, his voice still bland. He turned and headed toward the side yard, not looking back for another glance at Damask although everything inside clamored for him to do just that.

"Mr. Braden!" a voice called from behind the inn.

A child's voice. In a few moments Emmy appeared, Cory behind her, both coming to a halt in front of him.

Emmy's hair, so like her sister's, was coming loose from its neat braids. Her calico dress was torn at the hem and soiled. But her gray eyes shone, and a smile curved her mouth.

She somehow reminded him of his own sister, Peggy, who'd left Goose Creek years ago and never written a single letter home. Peggy was a few years older than Braden and, until she left, she'd mothered him as well as she could since their own mother had died when Braden was a baby. He didn't know where she was now. He suddenly wished he did.

Braden forced a smile for the little girl. None of this was her fault. "Hello, Emmy. What kind of day have you had?"

"Oh, it's been wonderful! Cory and I 'splored the woods and we found a little cabin way back inside there. It has a bed and a table and everything."

Braden's heart lurched. His face tightened again. He knew the cabin she meant. His childhood retreat when the world of Goose Creek got too much for him. His own private place of refuge. Where no one could find him or torment him.

The moments ticked by as Braden looked at the two children, who'd backed off a little, their own faces tightening. Then his face relaxed.

He no longer needed that refuge.

He smiled again at Cory and Emmy. They looked relieved.

"That used to be my cabin," he told them. "Or at least I called it mine. It belonged to your aunt Ada, of course."

"Did you stay in it?" Cory asked.

Braden nodded. "Yes, many a night I slept there, listening to the woods noises."

Emmy's eyes were wide. "By yourself?"

"Yes, by myself." And glad to be away from his raving father.

"Weren't you scared?" Emmy asked.

"No," he said truthfully. "I felt safer there than anywhere else."

The old pain hit him. He hoped these two children never had to feel anything like that.

Emmy gave him her wide smile that made something inside him soften. "You must have been very brave."

"No braver than you two."

"I'm going to sleep in the cabin some night," Cory

announced, puffing his chest out. "I'm not afraid, either."

Emmy gave him an astonished look. "Damask won't let you."

"I won't tell her, silly," Cory said scornfully.

Emmy considered. "Can I go with you?" she asked in a moment.

"Nope," Cory said, "you're a girl."

He gave Braden a smug look, obviously expecting his approval.

Consternation went through Braden. He'd gotten himself into a pickle. "Uh . . . I don't think it's a good idea for either one of you to plan on doing that. You're . . . uh . . . too young."

Cory frowned. "But you just said *you* did. How old were you?"

"Twelve. I was twelve," Braden said, hoping his face didn't betray him. In truth, he'd been only about seven the first time.

Why was he getting involved with these children? He didn't want to become close to Damask or her family. That wouldn't help his cause.

It wouldn't hurt it, either. There was that old saying, you can catch more flies with honey than with vinegar. He sure didn't help his cause the other night in the kitchen.

He'd regretted that ever since it happened. Or at least the way it ended. Although he knew he should, he couldn't bring himself to regret those moments with Damask.

Cory looked at him intently, as if trying to decide whether or not to believe him. Emmy had her hands folded over her chest, her small, rounded chin tilted up just like Damask had done that evening. . . .

Dammit! Why couldn't he get his mind off how the

girl looked and how she made him feel and onto the important thing.

Which was getting her to sell her family's share of the inn to him.

Forcefulness hadn't worked. Cocksureness hadn't worked. Maybe pleasantness would.

But how on earth could he be *pleasant* with Damask when every time he was in her presence he wanted to shake her.

Or kiss her.

You're promised to Verona. Why do you keep forgetting that?

"Emmy . . . Cory . . ." a voice called.

Damask's voice.

Braden turned and saw her heading purposefully toward him and the children, still holding the hammer she'd wielded so skillfully a few minutes before.

"There you are," she said. "It's time for your evening chores."

She took care to look only at the children and not him, Braden noticed.

"All right, Damask," Cory said obediently, all his bravado gone. "Come on, Emmy."

The little girl's face became serious, and she trotted along behind Cory as he headed for the woodpile.

Braden blinked in surprise. In an instant they'd transformed from naturally curious, lively children to overconscientious miniature adults.

And now he was alone with Damask and had a chance to put his new strategy into operation.

He smiled at her. Her abundant auburn hair had come loose from its coil on her neck. Bright tendrils escaped everywhere. Her fair skin was flushed, and there was a smudge of dirt on one cheek. Her dress was old and worn, and its bodice fit snugly over her rounded breasts.

And just as he had when he watched her hammer the nail, he wanted to pull her into his arms and kiss her until she begged for more.

Or, more likely, soundly slapped him.

"Looks as if you and Harold have been busy," he said, forcing his voice to sound careless and not reveal either of his contrary emotions—lust and irritated frustration.

She gave him a wary look, then nodded. "Yes."

She wasn't going to make this easy. He smiled. "I apologize for doubting your abilities with a hammer."

Her wary expression increased, with surprise added.

No wonder. This was the first time since they'd met that he'd so much as talked to her with more than ordinary politeness. Except for those few moments in the kitchen.

"I don't lie," she finally said.

Defensiveness was still in her voice, but its tones had softened just a bit, he thought.

But how could he answer that without admitting he'd believed she'd lied?

He decided on evasion.

"Most women don't know carpentry skills," he countered. "You can't blame me for doubting."

Damask gave him a straight look. "Maybe not. But I *can* blame you for wanting to destroy the inn."

Oh, hell! Their truce had lasted less than a minute. Now what? "I don't *want* to destroy the inn. I won't take any pleasure in it."

He paused, surprised at his words. In all his planning, he'd never once actually thought about the process of tearing down the old building. What it would involve.

His mind pictured huge sledgehammers pounding

at the weathered gray fieldstone walls, breaking the ancient windowpanes. . . .

Inwardly, he recoiled from the vision. He felt his jaw muscles tightening.

"I'm only being practical," he said, forcing his tones to remain even. "I can sit down with you, show you how much money it will take—*would* take," he hastily corrected himself, irritated at the momentary slip when he'd sounded as if reclaiming the inn was a possibility.

When it wasn't. She couldn't do it on her own, and he certainly wasn't going to help her. No, no. Who helped her wasn't the point. It was a hopeless project. Why did he keep forgetting that, too?

"Is money all you ever think about?" Damask demanded, her gray eyes turning smoky.

That sight transfixed him for a moment. "Of course not, but *you* might consider thinking about it once in a while."

Her mouth tightened. "I do, but I also think about everything I can do that doesn't cost anything but my labor."

"No matter how handy you are with a hammer and saw," he said, forcing his voice to stay calm and reasonable, "some things you can't do. For instance, the whole porch roof has to come off."

Her chin raised. "Harold is going to continue to help."

She was getting upset; her breasts were rising and falling with her breaths. Braden's eyes couldn't seem to stop following that rise and fall. . . .

Desperately, he pulled himself together. Things were going downhill fast.

He'd make one more appeal to her reason.

"Damask, one old man and one young woman can't possibly do everything that must be done here." He frowned. That hadn't come out right. *None* of the repairs must be done. *Wouldn't* be done.

He started again. "What I mean is it's foolish and pointless for you to embark on this project when I'm never going to agree to reopening the inn."

Oh, hell and damnation! Neither had that changed her mind. All he'd done was get her back up.

"We already went through this. Remember, nothing in the will specified we *have* to agree on that point."

She was right, and she'd made him feel like a fool for forgetting that important fact. What could he do if somehow she got the inn in shape to reopen?

Not a damned thing. But that wouldn't happen. The odds were strongly against her.

His hand was throbbing again. He glanced down, saw it was bleeding once more, reached for his handkerchief, and rewrapped it.

He glanced up to see Damask's concerned gaze fixed on his injury.

"You've hurt yourself! What happened?"

Her voice sounded concerned, too, as if she truly cared. Without warning, warmth filled him. How long had it been since he'd felt that kind of concern from another human being?

Not since Mr. Johnson died.

No, no. What was wrong with him? Verona cared for him. She showed it every time he saw her.

She shows she wants you—that's not the same thing.

He shrugged, finishing tucking in the ends of the cloth. "It's nothing."

He'd be damned if he'd admit how it happened.

She walked across to him, picked up his hand, and started unwrapping the handkerchief.

Her hand brushing across his wrists was pain and ecstasy combined. He jerked his hand back. "It's all right," he said roughly, to keep her from seeing how her touch affected him.

She stepped back, the expression in her eyes making him wonder if that small touch had bothered her, too. "You need salve on it. I'm sure Flora has something."

"No doubt. I'll tend to it later."

The back door opened and, as if summoned, Flora came out into the yard. Her sharp glance at once took everything in.

"Ach, what you do?" she exclaimed, hurrying over to Braden.

With a deep sigh, Braden gave up. "I hurt my hand."

Flora clucked her tongue. "Come along inside."

Damask followed them into the kitchen.

Flora already had Braden's hand soaking in a basin of warm water. From a few feet away, Damask could see the raw, bleeding knuckles.

"Have you been in a fight?" Flora asked, her voice astounded as she rubbed soap on a clean rag and started scrubbing.

Braden winced. "No," he said shortly, not looking in Damask's direction.

"Then, your fist you must have stuck through a wall."

Braden's quick, startled glance told Damask Flora had guessed more or less correctly.

"Not quite through," he said in a moment, his voice wry.

Flora clucked her tongue again. "Such a doing for a grown man!" she scolded. "The anger gets people in much trouble."

"I know that," Braden said quietly. His glance found Damask still standing halfway across the big room.

She sucked in her breath at the expression on his
face. A blend of emotions came and went on his
strong features. Anger . . . and hurt . . . deep hurt.
His face suddenly looked vulnerable . . . like a boy's.

She didn't know what had happened . . . knew Braden didn't intend to tell them, either. At least not
now. Maybe never.

But that didn't matter. Somehow she felt closer to
him, as if she could see behind the façade of strength
and control he presented to the world, to the real
man beneath.

A man who wasn't cold and callous, money hungry,
and grasping. But sensitive and kind. Warm and
caring.

Damask turned away, shook her head to clear it of
these notions. When she glanced up again, Braden's
iron control had once more taken over.

"Stop fussing over me," he told Flora, pulling his
hand out of the basin. "It's just a few scratches."

"It is more than that. Your hand will be much sore
for several days."

Doggedly, Flora patted his hand dry, applied an
ointment so strong, its fumes made him cough, then
bound it up in a clean white cloth.

"Thank you, Flora," Braden said, giving her a grin
that looked forced. "I hate to think what you'd do
if I broke my leg."

Flora waggled her finger at him. "I would go fetch
the doctor," she said.

"Good."

Damask suddenly became aware that she was standing in the middle of the floor, still holding a hammer,
and had left Harold working away out front.

And she'd had another argument with Braden that
neither had won.

But maybe she could at least have the last word.

"I must go back and help Harold finish repairing the steps," she said briskly. "We're almost finished with the second one."

Damask turned and walked toward the hall door, jauntily swinging the hammer as she went.

She could feel Braden's gaze scorching her back.

And just as on that first day she'd come to the inn, it made her shiver.

Chapter Six

"Oh, Braden, do sit there beside Verona," Bernice Holmes simpered from her seat beside her husband on the horsehair sofa.

"Of course," Braden said. He smiled and seated himself on the love seat beside his pretty fiancée—who was giving him a surprised look.

No wonder. For some reason, he'd been about to sit down in an overstuffed chair instead of with Verona.

The love seat wasn't very big. The sleeve of his suit coat brushed against the sleeve of Verona's pink silk gown, and she moved a bit closer so that he felt the warmth of her body against his own.

Braden was uncomfortable. He wanted to move away, but there was no room. What was wrong with him? He should be enjoying the proximity of Verona's lush body so close to his own. After all, her physical charms were a big part of her attraction.

"I was shopping at your store a few days ago, Braden," Bernice said. Bernice's faded blond looks were much like her daughter's. "My, I must say it's certainly a big place. I've never in my life seen so many things for sale at one store!"

Wallace Holmes hid a yawn between his fingers. He still got up before dawn to do farm chores and after supper was ready for bed.

"That's what I had in mind when I built it, Mrs. Holmes," Braden answered politely. "I trust you found everything you were looking for."

She frowned. "Actually, I didn't. One of your salesgirls was most unpleasant, and I left. You really need to be more careful in the people you hire, Braden," she said primly. "Some of the girls aren't from the best families."

Braden tensed, anger rising. First his store manager, and now his fiancée's mother, complaining about a salesclerk's family background. He'd discovered Lorene hadn't been disrespectful to Mrs. Holmes. She'd merely suggested the woman try on a larger size undergarment.

Had everyone in town forgotten that *he* certainly hadn't come from one of the best families?

Didn't you want them to forget? Isn't that why you came back here? To prove to Goose Creek that you're as good or better than any of them?

Yes, he wanted the town to be impressed with what he'd accomplished . . . but that didn't mean forgetting his origins. . . .

Braden wrestled with his muddled feelings. "No, I'm sure they aren't, Mrs. Holmes," he finally said, not able to keep his voice from sounding a little clipped. "The *best families* would have no need to send their daughters out to clerk in a store, would they?"

Verona turned to him with a little tinkling laugh. "I should hope not! Can't you just see *me* behind one of those counters?"

Bernice gave a little gasp as if the very idea of such a thing would give her the vapors. "No, my dear," she said, preening. "You will never have to worry your pretty head about such a thing."

Braden saw his sarcasm had gone right over both their heads. Verona and her mother *were* determined to forget his humble origins. Verona's father was nodding, almost asleep, and, as always when the conversation got away from farming, was totally uninterested in either listening or joining in.

As for the other indisputable fact—that not too long ago the Holmeses had been a struggling, hard-working farm family—that, too, was in the past, purposefully forgotten. At least by Verona and her mother.

You knew all this from the beginning. Verona was the best Goose Creek had to offer. And she wanted you—after turning down the old doctor's son and a couple of others higher in Goose Creek's social order than you'll ever be. You can't deny that flattered you.

Bernice glanced at her husband, who'd just let out a snore.

"My goodness, I think I must take Mr. Holmes up to bed!" She rose with considerable effort and shook Wallace's shoulder.

He opened his eyes with a start, staring around with confusion. Then he shook his head and also got to his feet.

"Come along," Bernice said. "Let's leave these two lovebirds alone for a little while."

She gave Verona and Braden an arch glance, which he saw didn't bother Verona at all. No, the expression on her face told him she couldn't wait for her parents to go upstairs.

But yet . . . something about her expression didn't quite ring true.

What's wrong with you tonight? he asked himself crossly. Stop picking at everything. And he wanted to be alone with her, too, didn't he? Verona wasn't skimpy with her affections. He wouldn't have to coax kisses and caresses out of her.

Verona's parents left the room.

The cluttered, crowded parlor suddenly seemed very hot. Braden felt perspiration break out on his forehead. He tried to edge away from Verona, but there was no room.

Fresh air—yes, that's what he needed. He got up from the love seat so suddenly, Verona gave him a startled glance.

"What's the matter?" she asked, tilting her blond head so that the carefully arranged ringlets around her face bobbed.

For God's sake—did she have to try to pose every *second?*

"Nothing," he said. "It seems warm in here. I thought we might go out on the veranda."

Too late he realized how she'd take that invitation—as a chance for more serious kisses and caresses than could be managed in the parlor.

Too late? What did he mean? Hadn't he gone home from here more than once with his body throbbing painfully from unreleased desire?

But to his relief, instead Verona twisted her pretty mouth into a grimace. "Oh, the bugs will be out by now." She held out her arm, her full sleeve falling back to reveal her rounded white flesh. "For some reason, all the bugs just seem to love to make a meal of me."

She tilted her head again, her grimace turning into a pout, obviously waiting for a compliment.

The words stuck in his throat. "I guess I'd better get going. I have to get up at five."

Verona's feigned pout turned into a real one. "I don't see why you have to go to your store so early. Isn't that why you have a manager?"

Braden shook his head. "No. Even the best manager couldn't feel about the store as I do. I need to be there as much as I can this first year."

Verona turned her pout into a coaxing smile. She patted the seat beside her. "But it's still early. Come and sit back down."

She lowered her head and glanced up at him from under her long lashes.

Good Lord, did she have to act like a flirt all the time? Braden realized he was objecting to things that had never bothered him before, but he couldn't seem to help it.

"I'm tired tonight. I think I'd better go along home."

Verona lifted her head, her coaxing smile widening. "Oh, all right, we'll go outside," she said.

Alarm went through Braden. He backed up a little. "No, that wasn't a good idea," he said hastily. "You're right, the bugs will bite your delicate skin."

Verona's smile faded, a frown replacing it.

"What on earth is wrong with you lately?" she demanded. "You hardly ever come out here—it's been nearly a week—and when you do, you act like you can't wait to get away."

Braden forced a smile. "There's just a lot going on now with the store."

Verona's ice-blue eyes gleamed. She got up from the love seat and moved close to him.

"We need to get married," she said, her voice low and seductive. "But first we must get our beautiful house built. When can we start on it?"

Frustration went through him at this reminder of his stymied plans. "I don't know. I'm having no luck persuading Damask to sell her share of the property to me. Instead, she's doing repairs."

Verona's frown was back. "*Damask,* is it?" she asked coolly. "I thought you said she didn't have any money for repairs."

Braden tensed. "She and Harold, the handyman Ada used, found some boards and nails somewhere and they're doing the work themselves."

Verona's frown was rapidly turning into a scowl. "I can't believe this! You mean you're just sitting around and letting her do all this?"

"No, I'm not just sitting around," Braden said, his mouth tightening. "I have a business to run and I spend long hours doing it. You just told me I spend too much time at the store."

Maybe you do. You have a good manager. Maybe you need some time off.

No, he didn't. He couldn't afford to take any time off now. He had to keep on top of things.

Verona ignored his last words. "By now I expected that shabby old building would be torn down."

Braden stiffened. "Ada hasn't been dead two weeks yet. It's indecent to talk about tearing down the inn this soon."

Verona shrugged impatiently. "Why are you letting this woman take over? Why don't you stop her?"

"How?" Braden demanded, his irritation increasing. "Nothing in Ada's will gives me that right. And I can't bodily force her to stop."

Verona's pretty mouth curled until it wasn't pretty at all. "I bet I'd think of something. I wouldn't just let her do as she pleases."

"I'm not!" Braden said, his irritation and frustration overflowing. "Legally, my hands are tied. You should be able to see that."

For a moment, Verona didn't say anything. Then,

again, her face smoothed out and her charming smile reappeared. She put her slender arms around Braden's neck and gazed up at him adoringly.

"Darling, I'm sorry for getting cross. I know how hard this is for you since that foolish old woman left such a stupid will."

Braden stiffened. "Ada wasn't a foolish old woman. She was my friend. I don't understand her purpose in making that will, but she didn't have to leave me anything. I'm no blood kin. Damask's family is."

Verona pressed herself against him. "Yes, I know all that's true," she cooed.

She lifted her face, her small, pointed tongue coming out and licking her lips slowly.

"I just get so impatient for us to be married. So that we can be together all the time. Surely, you can think of something to do that will make that Damask person change her mind."

Her body was plastered against him. But for the first time, his lower regions weren't stirring themselves to heated arousal.

Verona puckered her full lips in the way he'd thought deliciously erotic not long before, and let her lashes flutter closed.

Go on, you have to at least kiss her good-bye.

Reluctantly, Braden put his arms around his intended and pressed his lips to hers. At his first touch, Verona's lips relaxed and opened. She pushed her tongue against his lips coaxingly.

Braden kissed her as warmly as he could manage, but he kept his mouth closed, and as soon as decently possible, he ended the kiss and moved back.

He threw a hasty glance toward the door. "We'd better say good night. Wouldn't want your parents to come back down and find us like this."

Verona tossed her blond curls. "You know my

mother wouldn't be at all shocked to find us kissing. After all, we are engaged to be married!''

Both statements were true, Braden acknowledged. And Verona had every right to be annoyed with his behavior. He was annoyed with himself.

But just the same, he didn't want to kiss her any more tonight, and he wasn't going to.

"I'm sorry," he said apologetically. "I'm tired. I shouldn't have come out here tonight but gone on to bed."

She looked at him for a minute, her face set in unhappy lines. "You're certainly not very good company."

"I know, and I'm going home right now, before I get in any more trouble with you," he said, trying to end on a joking note.

But Verona wasn't having any of that. She nodded coolly. "Good night, Braden. I hope the next time you deign to grace us with your presence, you're in a better mood."

"I will be," Braden said, feeling a rush of relief that he could leave.

He hurried out to the stables where he'd left Jasper. The stable hand was dozing, and Braden told him to go to bed, he'd manage with the horse. His hand was healed now. He'd taken the bandage off yesterday.

Jasper nickered a greeting and Braden rubbed his head. "At least I'm not in any trouble with you, am I, boy?" he muttered.

Riding back to the town through the soft spring night, he pondered over the evening just past. Ever since Damask and her family had come into his life, nothing had gone right. He always seemed to be in an emotional turmoil now.

And tonight he'd come very close to having a serious misunderstanding with Verona. Over nothing. Or everything.

Hell, he didn't know what was wrong. It was as if he were seeing her with different eyes now. And not much liking what he saw.

"Stop being an idiot," he advised himself, his words echoing in the stillness of the deserted road. "Nothing's changed. She's a beautiful woman and you love her. She'll make a good wife, and marriage to her will cement your position in Goose Creek. Her family is one of the most highly respected in the county. And that's what you want. It's why you came back here in the first place."

Of course it was. And he mustn't forget it.

Although he didn't like hearing his ambitions and dreams described like that, even if only to the night breezes.

He'd worked hard for all he had.

But you had a bit of good luck along the way, too. You can't deny that.

No, he couldn't, and he never tried to.

He wondered if Damask was in bed or still doing inn repairs. She and Harold had finished replacing the rotten boards on the front steps and porch floor. They'd done a damn good job of it, too, he had to admit.

Yesterday morning at breakfast, Damask had poured him a cup of coffee and he'd noticed a large blister on her palm. Maybe she'd helped her father on their farm, but she wasn't used to spending days hammering nails into boards.

And she shouldn't be doing it now.

He drew himself up short. No reason for him to be concerned about her overworking. She had only to say the word, and he'd buy her family's share of the inn. She could move them to a little house.

And what about Flora? Ada's will gave her a home in the inn for as long as she wanted to stay. How can she do that if you tear it down?

Frustration went through him again. He couldn't help what Ada had put in her will! She hadn't said the inn couldn't be sold or destroyed—just that both he and Damask had to agree.

And from the looks of things, that would happen about the same time pigs flew.

Braden was tired and ready to call it a night by the time he got back to Goose Creek. The inn was dark except for one light upstairs in Ada's study. Damask was probably in there, reading.

Braden rode around back and put Jasper in his stall, took the bridle and saddle off, and rubbed the horse down while he ate his ration of oats.

What was Damask reading? he wondered. And had she gotten ready for bed and was in the study in her nightgown and robe, as she'd been one night when he'd passed by on the way to his own room?

He tried to turn off his wandering thoughts. It was none of his affair what she was reading or wearing. All he wanted to do was get her out of his life so he could continue with his plans.

But if she was alone, he could try again to persuade her into accepting his offer. He'd raise it. Surely that would make her see reason.

As always, the back door was unlocked. He let himself into the silent house and walked quietly upstairs.

Light still spilled out into the hall from the sitting room. And Damask was indeed in there. But she wasn't reading.

She was singing.

Her voice was low, so as not to wake the others, he guessed, but its sweetness still came through.

Braden walked down the hall, pausing when he came to the sitting room doorway.

His breath caught in his throat.

Damask sat in the small rocking chair before the now-cold fireplace, Emmy in her robe-covered lap, softly singing an old lullaby to the child. Emmy leaned against her sister, her pose suggesting utter love and security, her eyes almost closed.

An open book lay facedown on a table behind Damask. A lamp lent highlights to her russet hair, a warm peach glow to her cheeks. Her arm held Emmy protectively close.

The scene clutched at his heart in a way that hadn't happened in a long time. He remembered his sister, Peggy, rocking and singing to him when he was very young. Ada and Flora had fed him, given him some measure of comfort on his worst days growing up.

But no one else had ever sung to him.

He didn't know how long he stood, watching, listening, but he must have made some sound, because Damask glanced toward the door. Her eyes widened when she saw him, her arm instinctively drawing Emmy, who'd fallen asleep, closer.

Damn. He didn't want her to think he was spying. He walked into the room to stand in front of them, pasting a smile on his face to reassure her.

Frowning, Damask put a finger to her mouth to warn him to be quiet. "What do you want?" she whispered.

Her voice didn't sound very friendly, he noted. Had he expected it to? They ate some meals together but exchanged very little conversation—both were always wary and aloof.

"I'd like to talk to you," he whispered back.

Damask started to struggle to her feet, lifting Emmy. "I have to put her to bed."

Braden stepped forward. "Here, let me take her. She's too heavy for you to carry."

For a moment he thought Damask would refuse, but then she nodded and he slipped his arms under the sleeping child. She was a lightweight, even asleep, too much so. She needed some meat on her bones.

Damask followed him out of the room to the adjacent bedroom she shared with Emmy. The door stood ajar and he pushed it open with his foot. Another lamp, turned low, burned in here, too. The room was tidy, the bedding thrown back.

Gently, Braden slid Emmy into the closest side of the bed and pulled up the covers. Emmy, still solidly asleep, didn't so much as flutter an eyelash. Her small cheeks were rosy with sleep. Impulsively, Braden touched one of them. It was warm and soft beneath his hand, and something inside him stirred.

He needed children of his own. That thought was surprising to him, and he wondered why. After all, he was engaged. And soon he'd have a wife to give him children.

For some reason, he couldn't picture how children of his and Verona's would look. Their coloring was so different. . . .

They were so different.

He pushed that errant thought aside.

Damask had followed him in and stood at the bedside.

Close enough for him to touch if he had a mind to. She smelled faintly, tantalizingly, of flowers. He saw her hair was slightly damp, as if she'd recently washed it, tumbling over her shoulders in burnished curls.

She reached over and smoothed the covers. Braden straightened and smiled at her. After a moment's hesitation, she smiled back.

The smile lit her face, turned it from merely pretty to beautiful. He wanted to touch her, wanted it so strongly he moved back a step to stop himself from implementing the urge.

He gestured toward the sitting room and Damask nodded. He left the room, Damask behind him, leaving the door ajar, as it had been before.

Once back in the sitting room, Damask didn't reseat herself. She stood, her back to the fireplace, looking at him. "What did you want to talk about?"

Nothing, I don't want to talk at all. I want to pull you into my arms and kiss you like you've never been kissed before.

His thoughts appalled him. Desperately, he reminded himself that he was promised to Verona. That he loved Verona and fully intended to marry her.

Then why did he persist in having these kinds of thoughts, these kinds of feelings for this girl-woman he'd met such a short time before?

"As if I didn't know," Damask continued when he remained silent.

Her speaking voice was musical, too, he noted as if for the first time. No wonder she could sing so well.

Braden pulled himself together, determined to banish his unwanted thoughts. "You're right," he conceded.

Damask sighed and covered a yawn with her slender hand. Her gray eyes had dark smudges under them. She looked drawn and pale, a bit thinner, too. Damn, she was working too hard!

And she wouldn't have to be, he reminded himself.

What would she feel like in his arms? Soft and cuddly?

He tightened his jaw as if that would block out these disturbing thoughts and desires.

"I'm increasing my offer. I'm willing to pay you

the full amount the property is worth—not just your share.''

Damask frowned. She swayed on her feet a little. She was exhausted.

He wanted to pick her up and cradle her on his lap as she'd cradled Emmy.

His jaw tightened more. He had to finish this and get away from her. ''I'm not here to harangue you,'' he said quickly.

Finally, Damask shook her head. ''I can't do it. Maybe I'm a fool, but the inn is all I have left of Aunt Ada . . . I didn't even get to see her before she died. It's all I have left of my family. I had to sell our farm in Tennessee.''

Her unexpected words pierced him to the heart. Made him ashamed of himself. But there was no reason for him to feel that way. Damask's mission was doomed to failure. He was only trying to save her more futile effort.

Oh, and wasn't he the noble one!

''Ada wasn't thinking clearly when she made out that will,'' he finally said. ''It doesn't make sense.''

Damask's eyes widened, making her look younger and at the same time older. A woman, not a girl. A lovely woman who'd melt into his arms.

He took a couple of deep breaths.

''So you think she should have left it entirely to you?'' she asked.

''No, of course not.''

''Oh, then, you think she should have left it completely to my family.''

Braden stared at her, not able to help admiring her quick mind. ''Neither one.''

''All right, maybe she should have left it all to Flora,'' Damask went on doggedly. ''You can bet Flora wouldn't give up on saving it.''

Braden found himself watching how Damask's lips moved when she talked. Her lower lip was fuller than her upper one. Both were pink and soft looking.

He realized she was waiting for his reply. What had she said? Oh, yes, that maybe Ada should have left the inn to Flora.

Braden took a step closer to Damask. Her robe buttoned high up to her neck and came down to her ankles. But still, it was a robe, and somehow in the quiet of the house at night, the atmosphere suddenly seemed intimate.

Damask's delectable mouth was open a little. Her eyes were fixed on him.

He took another step forward, bringing him very close to her. She didn't move backward as he'd expected but stood her ground. This close to her, he saw how smooth and soft the skin of her face was. Almost like velvet. No, smoother than velvet . . .

He had to touch it, to see if it felt as it looked. His fingers barely grazed her skin, moving down her face in a feather-light touch that somehow seemed to be connected to all the nerve ends in his body. A flood of sensation went through him.

Still, she didn't move back.

His hand moved farther down her face to cup her chin, feel its soft roundness. . . .

Beneath his hand he felt her slight tremble. *His* touch bothered *her*, too. Exultation rose in him.

Slowly, he lowered his head until they were so close he could feel her warm breath, smell the intoxicating scent surrounding her. . . .

Back off! Back off while you still can! he told himself urgently.

Instead, he gently brushed his lips across hers.

Chapter Seven

Damask drew in her breath at the whisper-soft touch of Braden's lips against her own. Alarm bells clanged inside her.

She should move back, go to her room, and firmly close the door.

But she didn't do any of those things. She felt her lips part under that gossamer touch, heard Braden's own intake of breath at her action.

His lips were on hers again, pressing this time, imparting an urgency that trembled through her body, made her respond in kind.

Her lips parted a little more and Braden's touch became harder, more urgent. He reached out, and she moved forward into his embrace. His arms felt so good . . . so right somehow wrapped around her; she slid her own arms around him.

Braden deepened the kiss. Damask responded. The kiss went on and on. Damask closed her eyes to savor every nuance. . . .

A sudden cry came from the room next door.

Damask stiffened in Braden's arms and pushed herself away from him. Shock traveled through her.

What had they done?

What had *she* done?

She whirled and left the room at a near run, hastening next door to the bed she shared with Emmy.

The girl was sitting up in bed, wild-eyed, tears running down her face.

"Where were you, Damask? I was scared."

Damask sat down on the bed, gathering Emmy to her. Ever since their parents' death, bad dreams had frequently bothered her sister.

"I'm here now. It's all right."

Damask's peripheral vision caught Braden moving past the door, toward his own room at the end of the hall, she assumed.

Again, shock washed over her.

She'd let Braden kiss her. Kissed him back with an eagerness to match his own—the man who was trying to destroy this inn she loved, which meant so much more to her than a mere building.

Hadn't her experience with Warren taught her anything?

And that wasn't the worst of it. She'd kissed a man who was engaged to be married. Promised to another woman.

Disbelieving shame flooded over her. How could she have done that? What on earth had come over her? One moment they were arguing and the next they were in each other's arms.

Shame isn't the only thing you feel. She forced the thought away.

Emmy's cries turned to sniffles. Finally, the little girl sagged against her sister.

Damask eased Emmy back down on her pillow, then went to the door and closed it firmly.

A lot of good that would do now. She should have come in here when Braden first touched her. Before that, even.

She hadn't, though, and she couldn't undo the kiss.

But she *could* give Braden a wide berth and make sure she was never alone with him again.

So you admit you're afraid to be alone with him? That you can't trust yourself not to fall into his arms if you are?

The loud crack of an ax blade against wood brought Damask out of the uneasy sleep she'd finally found not long before.

She glanced at the window. It was barely dawn. Emmy still slept peacefully. She'd had no more bad dreams last night.

Damask sat up in bed, shaking her head to clear it, and listened.

Someone was splitting wood. Who? And why so early?

It wouldn't be Harold. And it certainly wouldn't be Flora. Or Cory. That left only one person—Braden.

A roiling mix of emotions hit her. She didn't want to think about Braden.

Damask swung her legs out of bed. She washed at the basin, grimacing at her pale face, her dark-circled eyes, in the small mirror above the washstand, wondering why her bottom lip felt so tender.

Because you were kissed soundly last night. By a man with burgeoning whiskers.

Damask ignored that unwelcome reminder and quickly put on her one other everyday dress—this one of printed calico.

Easing open the door, she listened for noises from downstairs. All was quiet. Flora rose very early and had an ample breakfast cooked every morning before Damask got downstairs, much to Damask's chagrin.

She was surprised the noise hadn't woken Flora, but since it apparently hadn't, this morning *she'd* cook breakfast, Damask thought, forcing her mind to stay on that mundane chore and not wander to the man outside, chopping wood.

The kitchen was clean and tidy as always. Bluebell meowed at the back door for her morning saucer of milk.

Damask poured the milk from the big bowl on the worktable. Taking a deep breath, she opened the door, steeling herself for the sight of Braden.

To her relief, she didn't see him. He must be at the farthest woodpile behind the barn, she realized.

"Here you are." Damask set the saucer on the porch, then headed purposefully for the stove to get the fire started.

When Flora came downstairs half an hour later, Emmy and Cory behind her, Damask's biscuits were already in the oven and she was stirring flour for gravy into pan drippings from the bacon cooked and in the warming oven.

Flora sniffed the air and smiled. "You have beat me up! Something smells good."

"I hope it's breakfast," Damask said, smiling back, Flora's friendly face lifting her spirits a little.

"Yah," Flora agreed, her smile turning into a grin. "Since the meal you have already cooked, we will eat before Cory and I milk the cows."

She tilted her head. "Is that Braden chopping the wood so early?"

"It must be," Damask answered, quickly turning back to her gravy making. She didn't want to take a chance that Flora could see in her eyes what had happened between her and Braden last night.

How was she going to face him across the breakfast table?

Emmy began setting the table, her usual job. Cory lifted a stove lid and added another stick of wood.

"Let me cook the eggs," Flora said, going to the stove.

Damask shook her head. "No, that's all I have left to do. Pour yourself some coffee and sit down for once."

After protesting, Flora finally did just that but got up and insisted on helping put the food on the table a few minutes later.

Cory had been sent to fetch Braden for the meal, and both came back just as Damask put the last biscuit into a basket and covered it with a cloth.

"My, but you have been busy this morning," Flora said. "Out cutting the wood before you break your fast."

"I enjoyed it," Braden answered, sounding a little out of breath from his exertions.

The old shirt he wore was damp with sweat, and his hair needed brushing.

She remembered all too well how his arms had felt around her last night.

He went to the washstand in the corner and washed his face and hands.

"Just the same, it was good of you to do it," Flora said. "Thank you."

"No need to thank me. Why shouldn't I? I live here, too."

I live here, too.

Damask's hands froze on the bread basket. What an odd thing for him to say, when his goal was to demolish the inn.

She heard Braden pull out his accustomed chair and sit down, but she didn't look up. Everyone else seated themselves, and Damask still stood at the stove.

"What you do, fussing around over there?" Flora asked. "Come, sit and eat what you have cooked."

She couldn't put it off any longer. Damask brought the biscuits to the table, pulled out her own chair, and sat, wishing she weren't directly across the table from Braden.

Damask passed the biscuits to Flora. The older woman gave her a look, then frowned. "You do not sleep good. You have the circles under the eyes."

Damask forced a smile she hoped was bright enough to satisfy sharp-eyed Flora. "Why, I slept very well," she said, also forcing brightness into her voice.

Maybe Braden would believe last night had meant nothing to her.

"You do not look fine, you look like you work too hard," Flora declared, taking two biscuits, then passing the basket on to Braden.

Flora frowned at him, too. "You also have the circles. You, too, rest not well."

Damask stole a glance at Braden. Flora was right. He looked as if he hadn't slept all night. She held her breath, hoping Flora wouldn't make the connection.

Flora sighed. "You young people believe you can burn the candle at all ends and get away with it." She waggled her finger at both of them. "Not so. When old as me you get, you will pay for it."

Flora didn't suspect what had gone on last night. Damask let out her breath in relief. And why did she want Braden to think their kisses meant nothing?

If *she* were engaged and her fiancé kissed another woman, it would be important to her. But his fiancée would probably never learn of the incident. Damask didn't think Braden would tell her.

And what could *she* do about it? Damask asked herself. Lean across the breakfast table and apologize? Of course not. Neither could she seek Braden out later and do so. Her heart quailed at the prospect.

No, as she'd decided last night, all either of them could do was forget it happened. And vow it never would again. Braden must have come to the same conclusion. Guilt was eating at him or he wouldn't have stayed awake most of the night the same as she.

Maybe there's more than guilt involved.

No. She wasn't that foolish, and neither was Braden.

"You bake very good the biscuits, Damask," Flora said. "And the gravy and rest of meal. You will make some lucky man a good wife one of the days."

"Thank you," Damask managed to say with a forced smile. The last thing in the world she wanted to think about now was becoming a wife to any man.

"Isn't that so, Braden?" Flora asked, her eyes twinkling. "If you were not already spoken for, you would be setting your hat for her, is not that right?"

Emmy giggled. Cory hid a grin behind his hand.

Damask wished the floor would rise up and swallow her.

Her side vision told her Braden had glanced up at Flora's bantering words. Damask turned her head a little toward him. His smile was as forced-looking as her own.

"Yes, Damask knows how to cook," he said politely, not rising to Flora's bait.

Flora snorted. "Is that the best you can do?" she demanded, her voice still teasing.

Damask got up abruptly and went to the stove. "More coffee, anyone?" she asked, again too brightly.

"Why, sure," Flora said, picking up her cup and holding it out as Damask brought over the blue enamel coffeepot.

Damask filled it, hoping she'd distracted Flora enough so the other woman wouldn't continue the train of conversation she'd begun.

But now, of course, Damask realized, she had to offer Braden coffee, too.

She turned toward him. "Ready for more?" she asked in that sprightly voice that wasn't hers at all.

Braden lifted his head, and their glances met. For a split second Damask saw all that had happened between them last night in his sea green eyes.

The coffeepot wobbled. She quickly looked away from Braden, steadied it with her other hand, and filled his cup.

Back in her chair, Damask tried to steady her uneven breathing as well.

Braden was in just as much of a turmoil as she was. And well he should be. He felt guilt because he was betrothed. He *should* feel guilt . . . they *both* should.

And that was *all* she saw in his troubled glance, she assured herself.

She'd never been so glad for a meal to end.

"I'll clean up in here since you the meal cooked," Flora insisted. "Emmy helps me, won't you?"

Emmy agreed.

"Thanks for breakfast," Braden said, his glance somewhere between her and Flora.

"You're welcome," Damask answered automatically, thinking what a strange phrase that was. Braden wasn't welcome here, not to her. They were adversaries, and that wouldn't change.

She'd also like him gone so she wouldn't have to fight her attraction to him, she admitted.

Damask caught herself looking after Braden as he left the room to go upstairs, then quickly turned aside.

"What do you today?" Flora asked. "Is Harold coming to help?"

Damask didn't miss the hopeful note in Flora's voice as she asked the last question. Flora and Harold liked each other, she knew. More than liked each other, she thought. Why had they never married? Flora had been widowed for a long time, and Harold for quite a while. His son, Edmond, was grown, in his twenties, and, like his father, he was a fine carpenter.

"No, Harold isn't coming today. He has a job to do for Millie Thornton."

Flora sniffed. "He will be sorry he took that. Millie will have him do everything three times over. Nothing suits that woman."

Damask heard an odd note in Flora's voice. Why, she was jealous of Millie, Damask realized.

"About what you do today you did not answer me," Flora said, rattling dishes in the pan as Emmy cleared the table.

The porch floor and steps were finished. But, of course, the porch roof wasn't. And that was a job she and Harold couldn't do by themselves. She didn't know how it would get done. Maybe it wouldn't.

Damask frowned, trying to dismiss that worry. There was another repair she *could* do by herself, though. "Oh, I'll think of something," she told Flora.

Maybe the hard, miserable job would work off some of her disturbed feelings about what had happened last night.

Before Flora could question her further, Damask hurried outside to the barn.

Braden came downstairs half an hour later wearing a gray suit and a crisp white shirt and cravat, his hair slicked back. He let himself out the front door and walked across the neatly repaired front porch and down the now-sound steps.

He felt full of restless energy even after the wood chopping and despite the fact he'd slept hardly at all the night before. Maybe the walk to the store would dissipate some of it.

At the bottom of the steps he turned right. He stopped short when he saw the long ladder propped against the side of the building. He glanced up and saw Damask sitting on the ridgepole.

He drew in his breath. *Straddling* it, to be more accurate. She held a nail between her teeth, a hammer in one hand, and while he watched, she leaned over, perilously close to upsetting her balance, and placed a slate she held in the other hand against the side of the roof.

She lowered the hand holding the hammer to steady the slate, while with the other she reached for one of the nails between her lips and placed it against the slate.

Braden opened his mouth to shout at her, then thought better of it. A sudden noise such as that might be enough to make her fall.

And the ground was a long way down from the third story.

Braden swallowed, fear sweeping over him as he thought about just how far.

Damask lifted her hammer and took aim at the nail. When her arm was halfway down, Braden heard a crunching sound and realized her weight had broken a slate under her. She swayed, catching herself but letting go of her hammer and nail.

The broken slate fell like a chunk of lead. Braden jumped backward, but it landed on one of his well-polished brown shoes, thankfully flat instead of sideways, breaking into two pieces. The hammer and nail had come down just a few feet away.

"Dammit!" Braden swore. Anger mixed with his

fear for Damask's safety. He looked up at the ridge-pole again.

She looked down at him, her mouth open, her eyes wide.

"Get the hell down from there," Braden ordered. "Are you crazy? You'll break your fool neck."

Even from that distance he saw her stiffen. He groaned inwardly. Oh, that was just the right thing to say to a stubborn woman like Damask.

She turned away and, to his immense relief, he saw she was heading for the ladder.

He hurried over and steadied it while she climbed down. She'd pinned her dress between her legs to keep from getting tangled up in it.

When her feet touched the ground, Braden saw she was trembling. "Just what did you think you were doing?" he demanded.

She slowly turned to face him.

Her face was set in firm lines despite the trembling of her slender body.

"That seems obvious," she said coolly. "I was repairing the roof."

He snorted. "Oh, is that what you call it?"

The front door banged and Flora came hurrying out, drying her hands on her snowy-white apron.

"Oh, thank God you are all right! I heard sounds and thought you fall."

"It's a miracle she didn't," Braden said grimly.

Damask drew up her slim shoulders. "I wasn't about to fall."

"Oh, yes, you were." Braden stalked across to the ladder and lifted it.

"You leave that ladder where it is!" Damask demanded. She hurried over, the hammer clutched in her hand.

"So you can get back up there and this time kill yourself? I don't think so."

Damask grabbed the other side of the ladder and tugged. "Put it down!"

"No."

From either side of the ladder they glared at each other, neither giving an inch.

"Stop it, you two," Flora said. "You are both being the children."

Flora's correct assessment of the situation rankled even more with Braden.

His glare darkened. "I'm not letting go of this ladder until you promise me you won't attempt this foolishness again."

Damask's glare matched his own. "Then take your coat off. You'll be here awhile."

"Will you stop acting like an idiot?"

"I'm not doing anything of the sort. I'm just trying to do a repair job. And *you're* trying to stop me."

Braden saw Cory and Emmy were now an interested audience, along with Flora.

Dammit, he wasn't going to give in to this hard-headed woman. She knew this job was beyond her abilities, but her pride would keep her from admitting it. Her pride would quite possibly get her injured or killed if she insisted on doing this by herself.

He had two choices. He could go hire someone to come up here and make these roof repairs—in which case he'd be giving in and admitting that she'd won this skirmish in their battle about the inn.

Or he could help her himself. That wouldn't be a hell of a lot better choice. But it was the only one he had.

He hoped he could get through this without Damask discovering his secret. He looked up at the top of the inn and repressed a shudder. It was a long way up there.

And a long way down.

He half turned toward Cory. "Will you go to my store and tell my manager I won't be in today?" he asked the boy.

Cory nodded and took off at a lope toward the meadow.

Damask stared after him, then jerked back around to again glare at Braden. "You had no right to send Cory to your store without asking me."

"Would you have given your consent?" he asked.

"Probably not," she shot back.

"He'll be all right. It's not far."

"I know that. But it wasn't your place to send him." She shifted her grip on the ladder. "Do you intend to spend the morning standing there, holding one side of this ladder?"

"No, I intend to spend it repairing this damnable roof," he said coolly.

She stared at him. "What do you mean?"

"I feel an obligation to keep you from maiming or killing yourself."

She kept on staring at him. Finally, she huffed out a breath. "You really will stand here all day if I don't agree, won't you?"

"Yes," he said unhesitatingly.

Damask let go of her side of the ladder. "All right. Neither of us is accomplishing anything like this. You can help me repair the roof," she said ungraciously.

Behind him, Braden heard Flora release a sigh of relief.

"Thank God you two are finally agreeing."

That wasn't exactly what had happened, but Braden didn't argue further.

"I'm going upstairs to change my clothes. I want

you to promise me you won't set one foot on that ladder until I come back."

Damask nodded stiffly.

Braden eyed her pinned-up dress with disapproval. "And if you insist on doing this, you'd better put on some trousers."

"I don't have any."

"You can borrow a pair of mine," he said crisply. "They'll be too long, of course, but a hell of a lot safer than what you're wearing."

After a moment, she nodded again. "All right."

Braden leaned the ladder against the building and headed toward the house, Damask following, Emmy and Flora bringing up the rear.

Half an hour later, Braden straddled the ridgepole.

His palms were sweating, and perspiration rolled down the side of his face. He didn't dare look down at the ground so far beneath him.

Cory had returned from his errand, and he and Emmy had gone off somewhere.

Damask stood on the highest rung of the ladder, a wooden box holding slates and nails balanced on the roof in front of her.

She wore a pair of Braden's old trousers, rolled up several times, and one of his old shirts with the sleeves equally rolled. She should have looked ridiculous and unattractive, but strangely, she didn't, Braden concluded.

The masculine garb only accentuated her essential womanliness. Made him remember those stolen moments when he'd held her in his arms, tasted her sweet lips.

Wanted more.

He quickly turned those thoughts off. He had to concentrate on the job at hand or he could very well fall himself.

Take it one step at a time. Just hold the slate, take the nail from Damask—

"Braden Franklin," a high-pitched female voice said from below. "What in the world are you doing up on that roof?"

Braden tensed. *Oh, God, no. Why now?* He closed his eyes.

That was a mistake. His head swam; he felt himself swaying.

Desperately, he clung to the ridgepole. After a moment, his head cleared a little and he cautiously glanced down.

On the ground below the ladder stood an elegantly dressed woman holding a tiny silken parasol over her bobbing blond ringlets.

Her voice was lilting and sweet and she smiled brightly, but something about her posture told Braden she didn't feel pleased or happy.

He took a deep breath, then another one.

"Good morning, Verona," Braden said. "What are you doing here?"

Chapter Eight

Damask nearly dropped her box of supplies.

Verona!

Braden's intended was the owner of that sugar-sweet voice?

Cautiously, Damask twisted on the ladder and glanced downward.

The woman standing there wore a sweet smile. She was petite and pretty, dressed in the height of fashion. But her pale blue silk gown was hardly suitable for walking up a hill on a warm late spring day. Even if she did have a parasol.

"Why, I came to see you, of course," Verona said, tilting her head to the side and glancing up at Braden from under long lashes.

"Papa dropped me off at your store, but your manager told me you wouldn't be in this morning. I couldn't *imagine* what was so important you'd neglect the Emporium. So I just *had* to walk all the way up here to find out!"

The woman's voice seemed to have lost a bit of its sweetness, Damask thought.

"I'm not neglecting the store," Braden said, a slight edge to his tones. "Jacob Gilroy is a very capable manager."

Verona twirled her parasol, which exactly matched her dress, Damask noticed.

"Oh, I'm sure he is. But only last night you were telling me you had to be there all the time these first few months."

A lump settled in Damask's stomach. So Braden had been with his fiancée last night . . . he'd come straight from Verona to her . . . from kissing Verona to kissing her.

Stop it! Damask told herself. That was as much your fault as his. This woman has the *right* to kiss him . . . to be kissed by him. And why aren't you feeling guilty now, when you're faced with her?

"This won't take long," Braden said.

"But why are you up on that roof? It looks very dangerous."

Damask's tension grew. Would Braden tell his fiancée the truth? That he was doing this job because he feared Damask would fall?

"I can take care of myself, Verona." His voice sounded tight.

But he said nothing else, and Damask relaxed a little.

"Of course you can, darling," Verona purred. "But why are you up there?"

"I'm replacing broken slates."

Verona's mouth pursed. "Whatever for?"

Damask heard Braden's impatient sigh. "Because the roof is leaking."

The woman's pale blue eyes widened. "Why should

you care if the roof of this awful old building leaks? You're going to tear it down soon.''

Damask pressed her lips together and turned back around to face the inn, fighting to keep from disputing Verona's hurtful words.

"In the meantime, I'd like to sleep in comfort, not have to worry about rainwater dripping on my face at night.''

Braden's voice was cool. Verona had to know he was getting annoyed. Why didn't she stop questioning him?

Instead, she gave her tinkling laugh again. It sounded like icicles shattering on stones, Damask thought.

"Wouldn't it be simpler if you just moved out of the inn? Mama has a lovely guest room all cleaned and aired. You know how welcome you'd be.''

Verona's words evoked a vivid picture in Damask's mind: A night-quiet house . . . Braden sleeping in the guest room . . . probably not too far from Verona's room . . .

It's none of your business, she told herself sternly. It has nothing to do with you.

"We've gone over that before," Braden said tightly.

"Yes, and I still don't understand your reasons. Surely, you can force this Damask person to sell her part of the inn to you without staying here and trying to wear her down, as you said.''

Damask gasped, a jolt of anger going through her. Her head went up and she stared hotly at Braden. He'd been looking down at Verona, and his glance met hers.

He frowned and looked guilty. Damask's anger grew. Yes, he'd told Verona that. She could imagine how they'd laughed about it.

And why was Verona talking about her as if she

weren't even present? Was the other woman just so rude, she didn't care?

Her back stiff, Damask climbed backward down the ladder until she reached the bottom.

She turned and faced Verona, folding her arms over her chest, covered with Braden's too-big shirt.

"Braden can stay here until the cows come home, and I won't change my mind about selling him my family's share of the inn. No matter how much wearing down he does."

Verona backed up, her eyes going wide, her mouth hanging open. "Oh! You . . . you're this Damask person? Why didn't you say something?"

"What was I supposed to say?" Damask demanded. "And when?"

"But I thought . . . you were a boy. Braden's helper."

Jolted, Damask glanced down at her man's shirt with its rolled-up sleeves and her pants legs. Her hair was pinned back with one of Cory's caps on it to keep the sun off her face.

If she hadn't been so angry, it would be funny, Damask thought.

And, now, contrarily, she *wanted* Verona to know exactly what this situation was. "*I* was working on the roof," she said evenly, "and Braden offered to help *me* with the repairs."

Verona stared at Damask for another moment. Her expression gradually changed from dumbfounded amazement to something else. A calculating look. She was sizing Damask up. As a woman sized up a rival.

A mix of emotions went through Damask. Incredulity, anger mixed with amusement . . . finally one she didn't want to acknowledge.

She was sizing up Verona, too.

For the same reasons.

No, she wasn't, she instantly denied. She couldn't be. Braden belonged to Verona. And she didn't want him anyway.

Hard on that thought came a new one that took her breath away.

Was Braden's kiss last night coldly calculated? One of the ways he planned to "wear her down"?

The more she considered the idea, the more she admitted it was probably true. A new wave of anger and humiliation went over her.

Verona drew herself up. Her expression became one of dignified affront. As if *she* were the one who'd been wronged.

Turning, she lifted her head again to look up at Braden. "I thought maybe we could spend the day together, but, of course, I can see this is *much* more important."

"Yes, I'd say so," Braden said tightly.

Damask couldn't keep a grimly satisfied smile from turning up her mouth. Let him squirm. And let Verona smolder. They both deserved it.

Verona's glance returned to Damask, then her eyes narrowed with anger.

For a moment she stared at Damask, then her face relaxed and became once more the face of a pretty, guileless young woman.

Slowly, Verona turned again toward Braden. "I'm sorry, darling," she said sweetly. "I know how cross men get when they're working and someone interrupts them. Papa is the same. I'll leave now—but remember, tomorrow night you're coming for dinner. Good-bye now."

She lifted her parasol over her head, and again her glance met Damask's. Her pretty lips still smiled, but the look in her ice-blue eyes held a definite challenge.

You'd better leave my man alone, it said.

"Goodbye, Miss . . . what did you say your last name was?"

"Aldon," Damask said, holding herself very still. "Good-bye, Miss Holmes."

Verona gave Braden one last coquettish glance over her shoulder. "Don't forget now! We're going to have a very special meal."

"I won't. Good-bye, Verona," Braden said, relief plain in his voice.

Damask watched Verona sashay across the meadow, daintily holding her skirts up. She had exquisitely slender ankles and didn't seem to mind exposing them.

"Are you ready to get this job finished?" Braden called down to her.

"Yes," Damask answered shortly. She picked up her supply box and again climbed the ladder.

"I thought you might be so mad, you wouldn't work with me," he said in a moment.

New anger went over Damask. She raised her head, glared at him. "I want to get the job finished, too. And I thought *you* were working with *me*."

Braden's face was expressionless except for that odd tension he'd had ever since he climbed the ladder.

"So you did." He paused, then went on. "I'm sorry for what Verona said. And for what I told her."

His apology surprised and mollified Damask, but was it genuine? How could she tell? She couldn't. "I already knew you were trying to wear me down, as your fiancée said."

"She was rude. So was I."

"That's true," Damask acknowledged.

Your fiancée's more than just rude, she told him silently. *She's also selfish and calculating. Can't you see that?*

No, he was too busy looking at her lush figure, her beautiful face.

Damask's gaze roamed Braden's features, trying to read his true feelings. "Kissing me won't change my mind, either," she blurted out. Dismayed, she clamped her hand over her mouth.

The movement made the ladder sway. Damask grabbed at it with her other hand, and her box of supplies fell to the ground, hammer, nails, and all spilling on the way down.

Braden stared at her in disbelief. "My God, this is a nightmare."

Damask knew her face was redder than the chimney brick. "I'll get the things."

Braden waited while she gathered up the scattered items and climbed the ladder again.

"Are we finally ready to do this job?" he said evenly, his face expressionless.

"Yes," Damask said in the same tone.

She'd made a fool of herself, but maybe it was worth it. Braden hadn't denied her accusation. That must mean she was right. He'd kissed her only to change her mind about selling her share of the inn to him.

Embarrassment and anger went over her again, as well as disappointment. She'd thought he was a better person than that.

Why? If he was willing to take half of this inn, which should by rights belong to her and Emmy and Cory, why was she surprised at this?

He carefully fitted a slate in place. "Nail, please," he said.

Damask plucked one from the box and stretched her arm out to him.

Braden leaned forward very cautiously and took it. He placed it in the prebored hole in the slate, then, without looking toward her, reached out his hand again.

"Hammer," he requested tersely, his face tense.

Damask gave it to him, wishing she were anywhere but here. As Braden had just said, doing this job, working with each other, was going to be a nightmare.

Braden lifted the hammer, his motions still slow and careful, and brought it down on the slate. His aim was true. The nail went through the hole and into the roof.

Braden let out a deep breath.

Damask glanced at him. It wasn't all that hot, but perspiration dripped down his face. His jaw was still tense, a muscle working in it.

Her own jaw tightened. How she wished Verona hadn't come! This job was hard enough without both of them being wound as tight as springs. And they'd only just begun. Her heart sank.

It was going to be a very long morning.

They worked together in silence for the next two hours, moving their positions several times. Braden stayed tense, his every move deliberate and slow.

Damask's anger and embarrassment gradually faded. She was quick to anger and equally quick to get over it. She couldn't hold a grudge.

Unlike Braden. He must be one of those people who stayed angry, brooded over things.

She couldn't stand that kind of person.

Braden won't be in your life forever, she told herself. He'll marry Verona and run his store and you'll never have to deal with him again.

Yes, but when would that happen? This stalemate could go on for months. After the repairs that she and Harold could do were finished, then what? Braden wouldn't do anything else. She didn't have money to hire other people.

A sudden idea came to her. Maybe she could get a bank loan. Goose Creek had only a very small bank, but maybe they'd take her half of the inn as collateral. . . .

"Well, that's it," Braden said, relief in his voice, jolting her out of her troubled thoughts.

Of course she couldn't get a bank loan. Not with Braden owning half the property.

Damask glanced at him. The tension was gone from his face. He actually gave her a smile.

Damask couldn't help smiling back. "Are we finished?" she asked in surprise.

"At least for now. Until the next bad storm. Slate's brittle. Doesn't take too much to damage it, especially when it's old, like this is."

"The summer I stayed here, there were lots of storms—and they were worse up here on the hill. The lightning scared me to death."

Why had she told him that? She didn't want to get on truly friendly terms with him. She might reveal a weakness he could exploit to his own benefit.

Which he was obviously capable of doing. Despite what Flora said, he must have turned into a cold, ruthless man, or he wouldn't be so callous about the inn. He wouldn't be engaged to a woman like Verona.

He had an odd expression on his face. As if he understood and sympathized with her fears. "I don't blame you. Storms . . . and . . . other things can be frightening."

Damask was surprised at his unexpected remarks. His hesitating voice.

His foot was braced against one of the chimneys. He moved it and his shoe slipped away from its foothold. Braden's body twisted. His face paling, he grasped the chimney and clung to it, his eyes wide as he looked down at the ground far below.

She stared at him. What was wrong? He wasn't in any real danger of falling, but his stance, his pale sweating face, suggested imminent disaster.

Suddenly, understanding went through Damask. Why, he was afraid of heights! Her father had been that way. He'd been unable even to climb a ladder without enervating fear.

Anger at her wasn't the reason Braden had acted as he had while they were working. Why his movements had been so careful and deliberate, his manner so remote.

But he hadn't let on, and he'd finished the job despite his fear. Just as her father always had.

Reluctant admiration filled her.

"It's all right," she told him, her voice low and controlled as she'd heard her mother speak to her father in such situations. "Take it slow and easy. Gradually, let go of the chimney and turn around. . . ."

She talked him through it, and when they were both on the ground again, she let out a trembling sigh of relief and sat down abruptly on the grass.

"I'm glad that's over."

Braden sat down, too. Beside her. "You're not the only one."

Damask didn't answer. She took a few deep breaths and released them, letting the tension drain from her body.

"You did that very well," Braden said finally.

She didn't have to ask him what he meant. She plucked a blade of grass and pulled it between her fingers until it squeaked.

"Look, I'm not proud of being such a coward!" he said roughly.

Damask jerked her head up, surprise on her face. "You're not a coward. You're very brave."

He stared at her. "How can you say that? You saw

me up there, clinging to that chimney, shaking. . . ." He made a disgusted noise in his throat.

"A coward wouldn't have stayed up there working for two hours."

He scowled. "I won't let this rule my life."

She nodded. "My father was like that."

Surprise came to his face. "Your father had this . . . fear?"

Damask nodded again. "Yes, all his life. But he didn't let it stop him from doing anything he had to do. Neither do you."

She saw his Adam's apple bob as he swallowed.

He was silent as the moments ticked away. His face gradually relaxed.

"I couldn't have stood for Verona to see me as you just did," he finally said, his voice soft.

Shock washed over Damask at his unexpected words.

He was engaged to Verona, planning to live with her the rest of his life, yet he couldn't share this with her?

But Verona and Braden were two of a kind, weren't they? Wasn't that what she'd decided only this morning?

Her jumbled thoughts swirled. She didn't know how she felt about Braden. Her feelings changed daily. Hourly.

"Are you finished with the work?" Flora asked from the porch. "The dinner is ready for to eat."

"Yes," Braden said. He got to his feet and looked down at Damask.

"I didn't kiss you to try to change your mind about anything."

Despite their being in the front yard of the inn and Flora only a short distance away, his low tones were somehow intimate.

Damask looked back at him, still caught in that confusing snarl of feeling.

"Then, why *did* you kiss me?" she finally asked.

His face was unsmiling, his eyes gazed steadily into hers.

"For the same reason you kissed me, I think. Because I wanted to. Because I couldn't help myself."

Chapter Nine

"My, but it's nice out here!" Verona's mother said, smiling at her daughter. "I think May is the prettiest month of the year. Not too hot yet, but no more cold north winds either."

Verona nodded, not interested in Mama's idle chatter, her attention centered on her humiliation at the inn that morning. Dinner was over. She and her mother sat on the big front veranda, as was their custom after the noon meal.

When she'd come home, she'd said only that Braden had been too busy to visit with her. Mama accepted that explanation with no questions. Men spent most of their time working to make money. That was as it should be.

Verona needed to talk to someone. Some things were bothering her. She had no close girlfriends since she'd finished school. That left Mama.

Verona sighed. She might as well just plunge in and get it over with. Seeing Braden with that Damask person had jolted her. Even in man's garb, her hair stuck up any old way under a cap, Damask was pretty.

Verona realized she hadn't expected her to be pretty. Was that why Braden was still living in the inn? Did he have an eye for that girl?

She and Damask had sized each other up out there in the inn yard, and Verona had been furious. She'd left in a huff. She was halfway home in the carriage she'd hired from the livery stable before she admitted she wasn't mad at Braden because she was *jealous* at the thought of Braden being attracted to Damask.

What bothered Verona was the possibility of losing him . . . and therefore losing everything she burned for.

Verona's mouth tightened. She wanted to get married so the town wouldn't think of her as an old maid. She wanted to get away from her parents and live her own life.

She wanted to be mistress of a beautiful house on the hill above the town. Braden would give her all that. There was no reason for her to worry about that Damask person—she couldn't be a serious rival.

Verona shivered. But in return, Braden would expect certain things from her.

Oh, she was tired of all this playacting. At first she'd enjoyed dressing up in pretty clothes and flirting with Braden. After all, he was very good-looking. But by now she'd expected to be able to relax a little. Not have to talk in that affected way and bat her lashes and the rest of it.

She'd thought she and Braden could be at ease with each other and her fear of intimacy would lessen. She wouldn't have to pretend . . .

But that hadn't happened. They didn't seem to have anything much to talk about. So in desperation she had to keep on with the flirting. And by now, with her mother's silent approval, she'd gone way beyond that.

Verona took a deep breath and plunged ahead. "How did you feel about Papa before you were married?"

Mama gave her a surprised look. "What do you mean?"

Verona bit her lip. "When Braden kisses me . . . and I start to thinking about after we're married . . ."

Before they were married if Braden had decided to move into her parents' house. Thank God he hadn't! She'd *hated* having to act so eager, when in reality she was terrified at the idea.

Her voice trailed off. She hoped she didn't have to go into any more detail.

Braden thought she was as eager as he was for the marriage bed. But lately, he hadn't seemed very eager for her kisses . . . her promises of things to come. Had he realized she was just pretending?

Or *was* he interested in that Damask woman?

"Don't worry, dear," Mama said, patting her shoulder. "All girls feel like that. Everything will be fine. It's a woman's duty to submit to her husband. After a while, it won't bother you so much."

Giving her mother a horrified look, Verona sprang out of her chair. "You mean things won't change? I *still* won't like Braden kissing me, and . . . the rest of it?"

Mama frowned. "Now, Verona dear, don't get yourself all worked up. You know how Miss Pritchett told us ladies must never lose control of their emotions."

"Oh, damn Miss Pritchett!" Verona burst out. "She's not the one who'll have to go to bed with Braden!"

Mama's mouth dropped open in shock. "Why,

Verona Holmes! I can't believe I heard you correctly. What on earth would your father think?"

Verona scowled. "I don't care. It's his fault just like yours. You made me set my cap for Braden."

That wasn't exactly true—realizing Braden was the best catch she'd ever get a chance at now, she'd been willing enough. But she hadn't known how she'd feel later.

Her mother drew herself up straight, her mouth set in a thin line. "I'm going to pretend you didn't say those things. Or use that kind of language."

The front door opened and Verona's father came out just as her mother finished speaking.

He gave Verona a questioning look. "Something wrong?"

Verona forced herself to calm down. She couldn't possibly talk about this with Papa. "No," she said, seating herself again.

"Good." Papa sat down on the other side of Mama. "Nice day."

Verona saw the strain in Mama's smile. "Just what I was saying."

"After I sit a moment, I've got to ride over to Russell's and talk with him about the open market. I still can't believe it did so well the first week. Oliver wants to go into it with us."

Verona closed her eyes, trying to fight down her irritation. Her entire family was willing to turn themselves into peddlers!

"By next year we'll probably have to rent more space," her father said to her mother, beaming.

It wasn't working. Verona felt as if steam were coming out of her ears.

"Papa, I don't see how you think we can keep up our position in the community if you do something as vulgar as hawk vegetables from the street!"

Her father sighed. "Verona, don't start that hoity-toity business with me again. Why, you acted like a hotheaded little girl with Russell last week."

Verona looked at Mama for support. "Tell him," she pleaded.

Her mother gave Verona a frown, plainly telling her she was still upset. "You know I always leave business matters up to your father. He's done very well for us."

Verona jumped up from her chair again. "But, Mama! Don't you see—"

"That will be quite enough from you, dear," her mother said reprovingly. "You'd better go up to your room. I declare, you must be coming down with something!"

Fuming, Verona stalked into the house, where she almost collided with Ruby. "Why don't you watch where you're going?" Verona snapped.

"Sorry, Miss Verona," Ruby said, backing up, giving her a wide-eyed look.

Verona went upstairs, her head high. When she got to her room, she barely kept herself from slamming the door as hard as she could.

Standing in the middle of her big, fussily furnished room, she glared at the mahogany four-poster, with its white ruffles, and at the dressing table that was a girl's dream. Pots of face creams, bottles of perfumes, and a silver-backed brush and comb sat on its top.

She walked to the dressing table, picked up the brush, and flung it at the opposite wall. It hit with a satisfying thud, leaving a dent in the cabbage-rose wallpaper.

"I *hate* this room! I hate my life!" she said out loud, then flung herself across the big bed and burst into tears.

*   *   *

"Hello there," a vibrant masculine voice said into the quiet of Goose Creek's library.

Geneva Dale had been so engrossed in the book she read, a gothic romance full of love and adventure, that she'd incorporated the opening and closing of the library door into the story action.

The unexpected voice startled her so much, she dropped the book. Her heart jumped. She knew that voice.

The book landed on the floor, still open. Geneva gasped. The book was new, just coming in today's mail. And it had landed facedown, probably crumpling pages as it went.

"Now look what you've done!" she wailed, horrified. She picked up the book and turned it over, letting out a sigh of relief to find it still pristine.

"Sorry," the voice went on, amusement and something else in its tones now. "I didn't mean to get you all flustered."

Geneva raised her head and looked into the dark brown eyes of Edmond Kirk, Harold's son.

And the town's most eligible bachelor.

He smiled easily at her, the smile of a man who knew he was good-looking and thoroughly enjoyed it.

All the unmarried girls in Goose Creek had heart palpitations when Edmond deigned to smile at them.

No, not all, Geneva corrected herself. *She* didn't.

Geneva gave him a cool smile in return. "You didn't *fluster* me, Edmond. You *startled* me."

Edmond's smile widened, revealing his even, white teeth. "Startle, fluster, what's the difference. I made you drop your book."

"Well, yes," Geneva admitted, smoothing the page

and then closing the book. "But *startle* means that the fact I wasn't aware of your presence caused my reaction, and *fluster* would mean that your presence somehow bothered me. Which isn't the case at all," she finished primly.

Edmond looked bemused at her spate of words. He raised his hand. "I'm sure you'd know better than me, Geneva, since you're the town librarian."

He grinned. "And I sure wouldn't want to think that my presence somehow *bothered* you."

His voice held a suggestive note, and Geneva's face suddenly felt too warm. Edmond loved to tease. When they were younger, he'd sat behind her in school and teased the life out of her, threatening to dip her long braids into his inkwell. He never had, but the threat was enough to keep her uneasy all the time.

"Rest assured that isn't the case," Geneva said, her voice going from prim to cool.

"Good." Edmond placed two books on the desk. He had big hands, she noticed. Big but well-shaped, with the nails clean and trimmed. Odd that hands like that could do such painstaking work with wood.

"Pop's under the weather. He wanted me to bring these back and get him a couple more."

Geneva frowned. As did everyone else in town, she liked Harold. "I hope it's nothing serious."

"Nope. Just a touch of grippe. He'll be up and about in a few days."

"I'm glad to hear that."

"He's having a good time helping that new woman work on the old inn."

"Damask? I met her a few days ago and liked her a lot."

Edmond shrugged. "I haven't met her myself. Town's all in a stir over Ada's will. Some people are on Braden's side, and think the old building needs to be torn down, but more are on her side.''

Geneva couldn't tell how Edmond felt. He sounded pretty noncommittal. Geneva made her voice firm. "I'm one of those that is on her side. Goose Creek Inn is a beautiful old building. It would be a sin to destroy it.''

"Pop's kind of on a crusade. He's getting people interested in helping Ada's niece. Me, for one. When I have a free day or two, I'll go up and do some work."

Geneva gave him a surprised look. "You?"

He shrugged. "Why not? I kind of like to see the underdog win.''

"So do I,'' she said. "And there's no doubt Damask is the underdog in this situation.''

He nodded. "And that's funny, too. Because Braden's family was about at the bottom of the heap when he was growing up.''

"And some people don't intend to ever let him forget that,'' she said crisply.

Edmond looked surprised. "I don't feel like that, and I don't think most others do, either. He's a nice fella and the women in town are gaga over that new store of his.''

"I like Braden, but I don't want him to win this time,'' Geneva said.

"You're not alone in that. Pop doesn't, either. And some others, I guess.''

Edmond was standing too close to the desk. Somehow, it made the room feel smaller and made her feel strangely breathless.

She stood, signaling she didn't want to talk about this anymore. "What books does Harold want?"

Edmond shrugged again, making Geneva aware how broad his shoulders were. "You know the kind of stuff he likes, don't you? I'm not a reader.''

No, Edmond certainly wasn't—or a scholar of any kind. He'd barely scraped by in school, leaving as soon as he could.

"History ... biographies, that kind of thing," Geneva said. Standing, she saw how much taller he was than herself, making her have to look up at him. She didn't like to do that.

Edmond glanced around the room with its shelves of books on every wall. He grinned again. "I wouldn't know where to start. Pick me out a couple, will you?"

He gave her a winning smile, guaranteed to make any female recipient delighted to do his bidding.

She wasn't delighted. But it was part of her job to help patrons with their book selections.

"Of course." She walked by him, so close that the sleeve of her white blouse brushed against his arm, encased in a blue chambray shirt. Geneva shivered.

Quickly, Geneva drew her arm away, but not before Edmond had noticed her reaction.

His grin widened. "Maybe this roomful of books is giving you a chill. Want me to get your jacket?"

Oh, he was certainly full of himself! Geneva raised her chin a bit, not looking at him. "The room is not chilly at all."

She knew where every book in the entire room was located. She walked to the east wall and let her glance go over its shelves for a few moments, then plucked out a book. Moving to another section, she soon found the second one she wanted.

Geneva brought them to her desk and put them down. "These should keep Harold going for a few days."

She didn't look at Edmond as she slipped behind her desk again. After removing a small card from inside one of the book covers, she neatly printed

Harold's name and the date on it, then put the card in a wooden box on the desktop.

Finally, she glanced up.

Edmond was flipping through one of the books. "Pop's really something. Can't believe he actually likes to read all this dry stuff."

Geneva looked at his head bent over the book. What a pity that such a well-shaped head had nothing in it.

At once she felt ashamed of herself. Edmond wasn't brainless or dumb. He'd followed his father's trade and was a master carpenter. Several houses in Goose Creek had a piece of his custom-built furniture.

It was just that his likes and dislikes were so different from hers. She couldn't live without books. He couldn't care less if he ever read one.

And why should that concern her? She wasn't interested in him as more than a childhood friend. They were hardly even that anymore, since they'd both grown up.

Edmond lifted his head suddenly and caught her looking at him. She felt herself blushing again. Edmond certainly didn't need another female admiring his good looks. He was cocky enough already, she thought, waiting for his knowing grin.

But it didn't come. Instead, his dark brown glance met her equally dark one and held.

Our coloring is just the same, she thought inanely. *If we had children, they'd all look as alike as peas in a pod.*

She jerked her gaze away, picked up the other book, and removed its card.

"You'd be pretty if you quit pulling your hair back in that knot like you're punishing it for being curly," Edmond said.

A small, painful jab hit her somewhere inside. Geneva closed the book and placed it on top of the first one. "It's none of your business how I wear my hair."

Edmond laughed, and Geneva couldn't suppress another shiver. He had such a contagious laugh, everyone around him usually laughed right back, even if they didn't know why they were doing it.

"You're right, and you're shivering again. Sure you don't want me to get your jacket from the wall?"

He didn't miss a thing, did he?

"Edmond, I'm really busy today," Geneva said, her head still bent over her desk. "A new shipment of books came in this morning, and I have to sort and shelve them."

She indicated the carton beside her desk.

Edmond laughed again. "But first you have to read them all, I guess."

Too late she remembered she'd been immersed in a book when he came in. For the third time since he'd arrived, she felt herself reddening and was furious at herself. She *never* blushed like her silly sisters.

"That pink in your cheeks is very becoming," Edmond said, so close to her ear, she jumped and looked up.

He was leaning over her desk, grinning.

"Edmond Kirk, will you get out of here so I can get some work done?" she asked crossly.

He gave her a mock salute, the grin still in place. "Yessum, I'll do that. Right away, ma'am."

"You're the biggest fool in Goose Creek," she said, trying to make her voice severe.

"That's what all the girls tell me, ma'am," he said solemnly.

He picked up the two books and headed for the door.

Geneva watched him walk . . . no, *saunter* was the correct term for the way he moved. As if he had all the time in the world and intended to enjoy life to the fullest.

He reached the door, opened it, then turned to give her one more cocky grin.

"Tell Harold I hope he enjoys the books and gets over his ailment soon," Geneva said.

"I will, Geneva," Edmond answered. His voice seemed to linger on her name.

When the door closed behind him, the room suddenly seemed dark and drab, all its life leaving with him.

"Don't be such an idiot, Geneva Dale," she said into the silence of the room.

She looked at the box of books. As she'd told Edmond, she needed to catalog and shelve the new shipment. But it was Friday afternoon and nearly closing time. She could do it tomorrow.

Geneva picked up her novel again and found her place. She settled back in her chair, using the box of books as a footrest.

After a few minutes, she sat up and put the book back down. For some reason, she couldn't seem to get interested in it again.

No wonder. You just got a taste of real life, and that's better than any book can ever be.

Real life? Putting up with Edmond's teasing and acting so full of himself?

Edmond likes you. You could get him interested in you as a woman if you wanted. If you bothered to fix yourself up a little.

"Why?" she asked the empty room. "So Edmond can have a little fling, then discard me like he's done half the young women in town? No, thank you."

Aren't you being a little hard on him? The women fling themselves at him.

"I don't need any man to make me happy. I have

everything I want right now. A wonderful job where I can spend most of my time doing what I love best: reading. Enough income to let me be independent. I don't have to answer to anyone but myself. Half the wives in town would give anything to be where I am.''

I think you protest too much. No book can warm your bed at night, put its arms around you, give you children.

Geneva pushed her disturbing thoughts far back in her mind and got up. She might as well get the books cataloged.

She touched the back of her hair where it was pulled back so tight it made her temples ache.

Punishing her hair for being curly! What a ridiculous idea.

Edmond has acute sensibilities for a man who never cracks a book.

Of course that wasn't why she wore her hair like that. It was easy to do, stayed neat all day.

And maybe you fear appearing attractive to men. That might mean you'd have to get serious about one.

Geneva shook her neat head, trying to rid it of these unwelcome thoughts, buzzing around like bees inside.

Was Edmond attracted to her?

Or might he be if she loosened her hair, wore more becoming clothes?

Did she *want* him to be?

Damask, pail of hot water, rags, and brushes in hand, entered the sitting room. She was going to put new wallpaper in here, but first she must remove the old paper.

Looking at the stained, faded paper hanging down in strips in several places, she sighed. This would not be an easy task.

Why was she doing it? she wondered, her mood, which had been getting lower and lower each day, sinking even further. Why was she doing *any* of this?

Braden showed no signs of changing his mind. Why had she ever thought he would? After meeting Verona a few days ago, any hopes of that had died. Verona wanted her mansion on the hill even more than Braden did. And Verona had no nostalgic fondness for the inn as Braden seemed to have. Sometimes, anyway.

Since the day the week before when they'd worked on the roof, she hadn't been alone with him. The ending to that episode, when Braden had told her he'd kissed her because he wanted to, had so stunned Damask, she'd stared at him.

Braden had stared back.

Flora's second call from the porch that dinner was ready finally broke the mood. They went inside, sat across the table from each other, exchanged a little conversation.

But as little as possible on her part. She could hardly digest her food because she was still trying to digest what Braden had said.

What on earth did he mean, he'd kissed her because he wanted to? How could he want to kiss her, when he was engaged to the beautiful Verona?

No, that wasn't the important question. Braden *shouldn't* have wanted to kiss her because he was promised to another woman.

And she shouldn't want to kiss *him,* because of that indisputable fact. And also because he was intent on destroying everything she loved.

But she *had* wanted to.

She'd like to kiss him again.

He also said he had to kiss her . . . he couldn't help

himself . . . and that she felt the same. She didn't deny it, either.

Had to. As if fate or something beyond themselves decreed it.

That was ridiculous. She didn't believe any such nonsense.

Then, why hadn't she denied it?

Downstairs, she could hear Flora in the kitchen, singing a lively German song as she cleaned up from breakfast. Flora had wanted to help with the wallpaper, but Damask wouldn't let her. The older woman cooked most of the meals, she—with Cory's help now—milked the two cows morning and night, and tended to the butter making and many other household tasks. That was enough.

Children's laughter drifted up from the yard below the open window.

Damask smiled, the noise of Emmy and Cory playing momentarily brightening her mood. It was good to hear them. With each day that passed, they seemed to be settling in more, liking everything more. Acting like the young children they were.

Was it fair of her to let them come to love the inn, when soon they might be out of it, living in a tiny house somewhere in the town?

Was she a fool not to tell Braden she was ready to talk business with him? Ready to sell him their half of the inn? Especially since he'd given her a better offer?

Her mouth twisted. Probably. But something inside wouldn't let her do that. Not now. Not until she absolutely had to.

That time hadn't yet arrived. But she feared it might.

Standing here wasn't going to get this job done.

Damask set her bucket, rags, and brushes on the

floor. Before she began, she needed to put everything from the tabletops away so the items wouldn't get damaged.

The round table beside the old rocker where the lamp sat, where Damask sat reading for a few minutes each evening, held several books. Among them the book of fairy tales she was reading to Emmy in the evenings and Aunt Ada's old Bible.

Damask smoothed the leather cover, remembering the times she'd come in here to find her aunt in her rocker, reading this.

Just touching it made her feel as if Aunt Ada were close by . . . not really gone. . . .

Out of the corner of her eye, Damask saw a flash of movement and turned toward the rocker.

Her aunt sat there, rocking, reading, just as she'd pictured her.

While Damask watched, her breath frozen in her chest, the woman lifted her head . . . looked at Damask. Her lips moved, she pointed toward the table. . . .

Damask gasped. "Aunt Ada!" she cried.

The vision disappeared.

Damask stood there, her heart pounding. What had just happened? Had she seen a ghost? The first time, her second day here, when she'd thought she'd seen her aunt, she'd been able to dismiss as her overactive imagination.

But not today. Not *twice.* She hadn't imagined what had just happened a few moments ago.

Slowly, her heartbeat and breathing returned to normal. Damask realized she'd picked up the Bible and held it tightly clutched in her hand.

Could Aunt Ada have been trying to tell her something?

Damask rejected that. No! Why, she didn't even believe in ghosts, let alone believe they could make themselves visible in order to give a message to the living!

What had her aunt been pointing at? The table or the Bible? The Bible felt warm under her hands. Quickly, Damask placed it back on the tabletop. She swallowed. Backed off a little.

But the Bible drew her toward it again. Damask retraced her steps. She picked up the tome and sat down in an armchair. Drew a deep breath.

"All right, Aunt Ada," she said aloud. "If you want to tell me something, what is it?"

The Bible felt warmer. A whisper came into Damask's mind . . . or from somewhere close by. . . .

Turn the pages . . . keep turning them.

Curiously, Damask had lost her trepidation . . . and her disbelief. She did as the voice in her mind ordered, starting at the beginning and flipping through the delicate, thin pages. She waited, expecting another whisper in her mind to tell her when to stop.

But nothing happened. She kept on turning pages, disappointment filling her. Disappointment and a feeling she was behaving in an irrational manner. She stopped the page turning, started to close the Bible.

No! The voice commanded. *Look for it. You can find it.* The voice faded.

"But I don't know what to look for," Damask protested. "Tell me!"

There was no answer. Somehow, Damask knew the voice was gone . . . at least for now.

She drew a deep breath and opened the Bible again, this time in the middle of the volume. She let her hand rest on the paper. There was nothing on the page except the printed words. No message, no underlining. Nothing.

But her fingers felt a bumpy outline . . . something was under the page.

Her heart beating with excitement, Damask turned the page. An envelope lay there. With her name on it in Aunt Ada's handwriting.

Her hand trembling, Damask picked up the envelope and held it in her hands. It, too, was warm, but this time that didn't alarm her. She felt suddenly closer to her aunt than she ever had. As if the older woman weren't gone but was nearby. . . .

As those whispers she'd heard that first day had told her.

At last Damask broke the seal and drew out the single sheet of paper inside.

My dear Damask,

By the time you find this letter, you will consider yourself to be in dire straits. Don't despair! You're strong and capable. You can do what you've set out to do.

And everything you need is here. But you must find it for yourself.

My love,
Aunt Ada

Damask held the letter in her hand, drawing strength from it even while the wording puzzled her.

Everything she needed was here, but she must find it for herself? Find *what?*

Finally, she folded the letter and returned it to its envelope, then put it back into the Bible.

After carrying the Bible across the room, she carefully laid it on one of the bookshelves alongside the fireplace. Although she had no idea what her aunt meant by that cryptic message, she felt heartened, stronger. As if her aunt's presence *were* here, watching over her, approving of her attempts to keep Goose Creek Inn from being destroyed.

That wasn't all ... Aunt Ada wanted something else, too. . . .

Damask straightened. Enough of this. She'd best be about the job she had laid out for today. It wouldn't get done by itself.

Chapter Ten

Braden sat at his desk, looking unseeingly at the open ledger in front of him. Any minute now, a knock would sound on his office door, he'd say come in, and Jacob Gilroy would enter wearing a nervous, apologetic expression and with some problem he needed to discuss.

"Damn!" Braden slammed the point of the pencil he held down so hard on the desktop, it broke off, leaving a small hole in the polished surface.

He was sick of this daily routine. He was sick of having to attend to every tiny detail of his business.

Surprise hit him at these thoughts. When had this happened? When the store first opened, he'd been so eager to take care of every little thing, he couldn't wait to get to the store in the morning, didn't want to leave in the evening. Now that had changed.

Maybe it had started that night at the Holmeses, when he'd told Verona he had to put in these long hours at the store, and had felt a flicker of irritation at that thought.

Now he felt more than mere annoyance. The last few days he'd started feeling hemmed in, smothered.

He sat there, thinking. A large part of it was his own fault for starting things off this way. And he'd let his feelings override his common sense the day he'd been so angry at Jacob. . . .

Yes, he'd reacted like a young boy with a huge chip on his shoulder.

He must make some changes in the way things were done here before he reached the point where he couldn't handle his business effectively.

The expected hesitant knock came.

"Come in," Braden said, forcing his voice to sound cordial and not show the impatience he felt.

Jacob entered, his smile as tentative as his knock had been. "I'm sorry to disturb you, Mr. Franklin, but there's a matter I think needs your attention."

Braden forced a smile he didn't feel. "Sit down."

Jacob looked surprised but did as his employer said. Usually, he remained standing during these exchanges.

"You've worked for me since the day the Emporium opened—six months ago."

Alarm sprang into Jacob's pale brown eyes.

Braden sighed and raised his hand. "Don't worry, I'm not going to fire you. Just relax."

Jacob nodded but still looked wary. "Have I—have I done something that—"

"No," Braden interrupted. "That's what I want to talk to you about. I hired you to manage this store, and lately you haven't been doing that."

Jacob swallowed, his prominent Adam's apple bobbing up and down. "I'm sorry, sir, if—"

"Just hear me out," Braden said. "You haven't been

doing your job because you're afraid I might disapprove of some decision you make. Isn't that right?"

After a moment's hesitation, Jacob nodded.

"And that's because of the incident with Lorene Lathrop."

Jacob stared at him, the alarm back in his eyes.

"I hired you for this job because I thought you were an intelligent man, good at leadership. And it's my fault you haven't been exercising that quality."

Jacob kept on staring, not moving an inch.

"As of this moment I want you to feel you are fully in charge of this store. You need to consult me only on truly important issues. I think you understand what those might be. I'm going to put complete faith in your judgment."

Jacob's mouth fell open. After a moment, he got up and leaned over the desk, holding out his hand. "Thank you, Mr. Franklin," he said fervently.

Braden shook his manager's damp hand. "No thanks necessary, Jacob."

There. He'd taken care of this problem, he hoped. At least for the time being. He'd have to be on guard against his tendency to oversee every detail. That wasn't good leadership. His years with Mr. Johnson had taught him that.

He glanced down at the open ledger before him and closed it with a decisive snap.

He picked up the ledger and handed it to Jacob. "Give this to Edgar, please. Tell him I trust his figures to be accurate. That's why I hired him."

Jacob now looked stunned. "Yes, sir, Mr. Franklin. I will do that." He turned to go.

Braden looked down at his now-cleared desk. The restlessness that had plagued him for weeks intensified.

Damn, but he'd like a day off.

So take a day off. After all, you're the boss.

So he was. So he was.

Braden rose. "Jacob, I have some matters to attend to. I'm leaving now and I won't be back until tomorrow."

If Jacob had looked surprised a moment ago, now he looked astounded. And well he might, Braden reflected. Only two times he hadn't been at the store from an hour before it opened, with a brief dinner break, until after its closing—the day of Ada's funeral, and the morning he'd worked on the inn roof with Damask a few days ago.

He didn't want to think about Damask.

"Of course, Mr. Franklin," Jacob finally said. He left the door open for his employer to follow him out.

Braden did, glancing around the building that was his pride and joy. As always, it had several customers. And as always, it appeared they were being taken care of appropriately.

The counters were neat; the floor was clean; the sun struck gleams of light from the shining front windows.

Braden smiled at his manager. "Good-bye, Jacob. I'll see you tomorrow."

His stride light, he headed for the front door, pausing to smile and speak to the customers and his employees on the way. On the sidewalk, he paused.

He'd said he had matters to attend to, but truth to tell, no business had to be done today. From the dogwood tree in front of the store, a robin sang.

He was as free as that happy bird.

So what was he going to do with his newfound freedom?

He could pay a visit to Verona. He hadn't seen her since having supper at her parents' place a few days before. But it was only ten o'clock in the morning. She wouldn't be expecting him now. She probably wouldn't even be welcoming.

The supper had been strained, and he'd left soon afterward without talking in private with her.

He knew a lot of that was his fault. Every time he looked at Verona, he saw Damask's face, remembered their kiss. He should feel more guilty about that kiss than he did. He certainly wouldn't expect Verona to be kissing another man.

And he *did* feel guilty. Nothing like that would happen again.

But visiting Verona now wouldn't be a good idea.

He frowned momentarily at the relief that went through him at that decision. He should be eager to see his lovely fiancée, disappointed when he couldn't.

But he'd taken a day off and he intended to enjoy it. That is, when he thought of something to do besides work.

Mrs. Burton passed by, nodding, giving him a curious look, and he decided he'd have to make his decision while he walked . . . somewhere.

Automatically, he headed toward the hill that led up to the inn. Almost to the turnoff, he decided he'd go fishing. He hadn't done that since his return here.

Lord, he hadn't fished in *years*.

Taking the road up the hill in rapid strides, he filled his nostrils with the freshness of the May morning. On days like this he'd gone fishing as a child, at the branch of Goose Creek near the cabin in the woods.

That's where he'd go today. His old poles and hooks should still be in the cabin.

Approaching the inn, he glanced toward it. Flora was weeding the vegetable garden out back. The last few days Harold had been under the weather with the grippe and Damask had worked on the interior of the inn.

He hadn't talked to her alone since the morning they'd repaired the roof together. Which had ended with that moment of unexpected closeness between them . . .

No, he wouldn't think about that . . . about Damask. Every time he did, that familiar mixture of annoyance and attraction filled him.

Why had he kissed her? Why did he want to do it again?

Because he enjoyed it. Because she was sweet and warm and soft in his arms and her lips tasted like heaven.

Because he couldn't help it.

He pushed those thoughts aside, concentrating on the other, opposite effect she had on him.

Irritation. Like an oyster must feel when a grain of sand got in its shell and couldn't be dislodged.

She stubbornly refused to give up her foolish idea to restore and reopen the inn. He'd come up with no plan to stop her.

Ada's will made that impossible. For the hundredth time he wondered why Ada had left the inn to both of them. What had she wanted to accomplish?

The garden was flourishing under Flora's expert care. She continued to sell her butter, eggs, and baked products to the townspeople. And, of course, he paid her for the meals he ate at the inn, and for his lodging.

Damask and her brother and sister and Flora were getting along fine.

This stalemate could continue indefinitely.

Maybe Ada had planned for it to.

The thought surprised him, making him stop in his tracks. Why would she do that?

To keep the inn from being destroyed. No, that

didn't make sense. She could have left the entire property to Damask's family. The result would be the same. He'd still be trying to persuade Damask to sell to him.

There was another reason. A good, sensible one, too. Ada was no fool.

Maybe she wanted things to happen just as they had.

He stopped in his tracks. No, that couldn't be. . . .

Could his old friend Ada have been that devious? Maybe so. She changed her will only after inviting Damask and her brother and sister to come live with her. Did she know then she was failing . . . would live only a little while longer?

Knew he wouldn't let them become destitute.

Knew he'd do just what he'd done. Offered Damask twice what the run-down inn was worth so he could have his way, fulfill his dream of a mansion on this choice spot overlooking the town.

He frowned. That also didn't seem plausible, and he was going to forget his problems for one day and just enjoy himself.

Braden let himself in the front door. He heard a clatter of pans from the kitchen and guessed Damask was working in there. Good, he wouldn't have to encounter her.

Quietly, he headed upstairs to his room to change from his business clothes. A few minutes later, he came back down just as quietly. The sounds from the kitchen continued, and appetizing aromas wafted out. His stomach growled in response, but he ignored it. He'd eat later, after Damask had left the kitchen. There were always leftovers.

He let himself out the front door again to avoid going by the kitchen and walked around back. Flora looked up from her weeding, then, holding her hand on her back, groaned and straightened.

"Why are you here this time of day?" she asked, surprise in her voice. "It is too early for dinner."

Braden gave her an affectionate smile. Although he knew she disapproved of his plans, they'd always been friends. "I'm taking the day off. Going to do a little fishing in the creek."

Flora looked even more surprised. "That, I cannot believe. All you do is the work, work, work."

Braden shrugged. "All the more reason to take a day off."

Flora nodded slowly, an odd expression on her face. "Yah, that is so. You go to your old fishing place, you say?"

"Yes. I haven't been there since I came back. I wonder if there are still any fish there?"

Flora smiled at him again—almost a grin. "Oh, yah, plenty of fish."

"Good. Maybe I'll catch enough for a meal."

Flora nodded again. "Maybe you do that. I will have the skillet hot."

Braden lifted his hand in farewell, wondering again at her almost playful manner. She hadn't been like that with him since he'd come back and had begun trying to buy the inn from Ada. It was like old times, and it was pleasant. He wished she'd be like that all the time.

Oh, of course she should. Since your goal is to tear down the building she's lived in for forty years and loves as much as Ada did.

As much as Damask does.

Unexpected and unwelcome guilt hit him. He forced it aside. Damask and Flora were unrealistic, and once they were settled in a little house somewhere, they'd realize that. They'd be happy and content.

The path to the cabin was worn down. No doubt from Emmy's and Cory's footsteps. He hoped his cautions that day he'd talked to them about the cabin had kept them from trying any nighttime adventures, but he was sure they frequented it during the day.

The cabin door hung by one hinge. Braden entered and looked around, memories sweeping over him. The old metal cot frame was still there, rusted now. Worn sheets covered the corn-shuck mattress. The children must have brought the sheets from the inn. He'd had no such luxuries when this place had been his refuge.

The small fireplace hearth was swept clean, with no evidence of recent fires. Good. Playing in here was one thing, making fires was another.

A couple of battered wooden chairs sat against the wall, and the old table was still in one piece, scrubbed clean and covered with an ancient tablecloth.

There was even a canning jar filled with wildflowers in the middle of the table.

Emmy's touch, he thought, not able to keep from smiling. When he'd stayed here, flowers or tablecloths had been the things furthest from his mind.

No, he'd used his time here to restore his soul—and fear his father would discover his retreat.

Not that he ever had. His father had been too busy staying drunk to worry about anything. As long as Braden had kept out of his way, he'd been safe, and Braden had finally figured that out.

He glanced at the corner where he'd kept his fishing gear. One cane pole leaned there, a line dangling from it, a hook on the end.

Braden examined it and saw it would do. He should have stopped and gotten a can of worms from the vegetable garden. He was surprised Flora hadn't suggested that.

Never mind. He'd take his chances on finding something at the creek bank.

For a minute he couldn't remember where the path to the creek started. Then he saw a worn-down place in the undergrowth and headed that way. Yes, this was the path, and it, too, showed evidence of recent use.

He frowned. Emmy and Cory shouldn't be there unsupervised. What if they fell in?

You fished in that creek from the time you were six years old.

Yes, but he was never really a child. From the earliest times he could remember, he'd been older than his years from necessity and fear.

Emmy and Cory hadn't had that kind of childhood. They showed every evidence of attentive care and love. And with Damask's continued care, they'd get over losing their parents at such young ages.

Why did his thoughts return to Damask no matter where they started out?

He came to the end of the path and pushed the bushes apart, anticipating the sight of the clear flowing stream that had given him so many pleasant moments.

He stopped short. Quiet and intent, Emmy and Cory sat on the bank, holding fishing poles in the water.

They heard him rustling the bushes and both turned. Surprised smiles lit up their young faces.

"Mr. Braden!" Cory said. "Don't you have to work today?"

Braden walked to the bank and stood behind them. "I'm playing hooky."

Emmy laughed. "You can't play hooky. You don't

have to go to school, and school's out for the summer, anyway.''

Braden's eyes widened in mock surprise. "Is that right?"

Emmy laughed again, a delightful sound. "Of course it is."

"You've got a bite!" Cory yelled.

"Oh!" Emmy turned back around, and while Braden watched, soon landed a good-sized perch. She put it in the old bucket with a makeshift lid under a big willow tree near the bank.

"We almost have enough for supper," she said.

Braden gave her an impressed look. "If I catch a few more, will that be too many?"

She smiled up at him. "You're funny. Of course it won't be too many. Flora will be glad!"

"All right, then." Braden carefully seated himself beside Cory.

The boy handed over a dented can. "Here's some worms."

"Thanks." Braden baited his hook and threw it into the water.

Emmy sat down on the other side of him and expertly rebaited her own hook. She gave a contented little sigh. "I wish we could stay out here forever."

Something clutched at Braden's heart. He glanced down at her bent head of auburn curls fighting to get out of their confining braids. Her hair was so like Damask's. That same springiness, that same wonderful color . . .

Forget Damask, Braden ordered himself. He concentrated on his fishing. The sun was shining, but a refreshing breeze blew. The willow tree shaded them.

A sudden tug came at his line. Excitement filled him as he felt the fish trying to take the bait. In moments, he had landed a decent-sized sunfish.

He put the fish in the bucket and gave a contented sigh himself as he rebaited his own hook and swung his line in the water again.

He intended to enjoy this day to the hilt.

Damask made her way along the path to the creek, avoiding blackberry briers and other hazards as she balanced the woven basket she carried.

My, but it was a nice day! Too nice to be cooped up in the house. Maybe she'd stay for a little while after she ate dinner with the children on the creek bank.

Flora was taking her afternoon nap, which she wouldn't miss for the world. She'd spent the morning making butter and weeding the garden. Damask had stopped stripping wallpaper early to surprise her with dinner.

Duly surprised, Flora approved heartily of Damask's plan to take a picnic dinner to Cory and Emmy at the creek. She'd helped Damask pack the basket, insisting on including enough food for five people instead of only three.

Flora's attitude had radically changed. At first she'd worried about the children out on the creek bank by themselves.

"Ach, what if one of them falls in?" she'd asked the first day they'd wanted to go fishing.

"They both swim well," Damask had said. "Papa taught all of us when we were very young."

Flora had looked relieved and nodded. "That was smart of him to do."

The familiar pain of loss went over her. Papa had taught his children all kinds of things so they'd never fear anything they shouldn't. Or be in danger, either.

Coming out of her reverie, Damask frowned. She

knew she was nearly at the place where the children always fished, but she didn't hear a sound.

Worry hit her. *Was* she too careless with them? What if they'd fallen in and couldn't get out even if they were good swimmers? They could have hit their heads. . . .

Damask hurriedly pushed aside the last bit of underbrush and stopped short, her heart skipping a beat.

Three people were lined up on the creek bank.

Cory, Emmy . . . and Braden.

She'd seen him only at the supper table a few times since the day they'd fixed the roof. Their conversation was carefully polite during those meals. By unspoken agreement, they seemed to be avoiding each other.

Avoiding their senseless arguments over the inn.

Avoiding the chance of their glances meeting . . . which might remind them of the kiss they'd shared.

Remind *her*, maybe. What made her think Braden still remembered? He was engaged to a beautiful woman. As if she could ever, for a moment, forget that.

Emmy and Cory turned when they heard her.

"Damask! Why are you here?" Emmy asked. "Did we stay too long and miss dinner?" she asked worriedly.

Damask smiled and set the basket down. "No. I've brought dinner to you."

Cory's brown eyes lit up. "Oh, boy! What did you bring?"

Braden at last turned his head around, too. He smiled at her.

Damask's heart skipped another beat. He had such a wonderful smile, even when it was forced, as she was sure it was now. He was dressed in old trousers and shirt, but that didn't detract one bit from his good looks. Maybe it added to them. She always thought he looked too stiff and formal in his suit and collar and cravat.

Damask smiled back just as casually. "Well, fried chicken for one thing. And corn fritters. And a chunk of Flora's kuchen."

"Yay!" Cory yelled. He scrambled to his feet, carefully bringing his pole and line with him. Just as carefully, he leaned it against the far side of the willow tree.

Emmy did the same.

Braden got to his feet, holding his dripping line with its dangling worm and hook to his pole. "I hope you brought extras. I haven't had dinner yet."

Damask nodded. "There's plenty."

"Good." Braden put his pole alongside the two leaning against the tree trunk.

"But . . . what are you doing here? I thought you'd be at your store."

"He's playing hooky," Emmy said, and giggled. "Even if there isn't any school and he's all grown-up."

Braden's smile turned into a natural-looking grin as he gazed down at Emmy. "That's right."

Damask couldn't think of anything else to say.

The tension that always seemed to be between them was curiously absent. Maybe it was the presence of the children. Maybe it was because they were away from the inn. Maybe it was the beautiful day.

But another kind of tension still tightened her stomach. That acute awareness of Braden every time they were in the same room together . . . or now, like this.

She set the basket on the ground and began unpacking it, taking out an old tablecloth first and spreading the food and utensils on it.

Braden helped her. Damask took the utmost care that their hands didn't touch. Finally, all was ready, and they sat on the ground around the makeshift table.

Damask was relieved that Braden sat across from her and not beside her. The tablecloth was small, and it would have been easy for their hands and arms to touch if he'd sat to her left or right.

As always, the children ate as if they were starving. Damask filled her plate, then asked, "Have the fish been biting?"

Emmy looked up, her eyes bright. "Yes! We caught enough for supper."

Damask smiled at her, thinking how much better the children looked now. They'd both filled out and seemed happier, their once-pale cheeks now blooming with color.

And how long would that last if they had to move away from this place they loved so much?

Maybe they wouldn't have to move.

She told herself not to be foolish. Braden had plenty of money. He could wait them out as long as it took.

Yes, but from what she'd seen of Verona, that woman wouldn't be willing to wait very long for her mansion.

But she'll try to figure some way to get you out of the inn soon. Don't underestimate her.

Damask pushed her disturbing thoughts aside. She was going to enjoy this outing, too. And try to keep things pleasant between her and Braden . . . for the children's sake.

Emmy and Cory soon finished their meal and were ready to play.

"Don't wander far," Damask cautioned.

"We won't," Cory promised.

The two ran off down the path that led away from the creek, leaving Damask and Braden alone.

Damask quickly put the remains of the food back

in the basket. There wasn't much left. Good thing she'd let Flora put in extra. Her hands paused.

Had Flora known Braden would be here, and that's why she'd done that? She must have. Braden would have had to go right by her where she worked in the garden.

Why hadn't Flora told her?

Because she was probably afraid you wouldn't come if she did, she answered herself.

"I'll wash these dishes in the creek," Braden said, scooping them up.

"All right," Damask agreed, surprised. She watched him as he walked to the water's edge. His shoulders were so broad. Muscles rippled in his arms, making her remember how strong they'd felt that night in the sitting room. . . .

He's engaged. He's trying to ruin the life you want to live here. Why do you keep forgetting those things?

After he'd finished with the dishes and brought them back, she'd leave. When she'd considered staying, she'd thought the children would be here.

She could have stopped them from leaving. Maybe she wanted to be alone with him. . . .

No, she didn't. She had more sense than that.

Braden soon returned with the clean dishes. "That's better than taking them back dirty."

"Yes, thank you," Damask agreed, quickly packing them in the basket and standing. "I'd better be getting back."

He gave her an easy grin and sat down on the ground under the tree, putting his hands behind his back, leaning against the tree.

"What's your hurry? Maybe you need a day off as much as I do."

She looked at him . . . so relaxed-looking . . . so *good*-looking, and her resolve weakened. It would be wonderful just to sit down and relax for an hour or two.

Here, in this pastoral setting, she could forget all her troubles. . . .

But with the person causing most of the troubles sitting only a few feet away?

"You look deep in thought," Braden said. "Is it such a tough decision to make?"

She gave him a straight look. "Do you think we can be together for more than five minutes without getting into an argument?"

That wasn't what she feared. The real question was, could they stay out of each other's arms?

His smile still in place, Braden nodded. "Yes. If we make up our minds to forget our differences for a little while."

"All right," Damask said, snapping the lid down on the basket and reseating herself. She gave him a smile. "I think you're right. I need a little time off, too."

He nodded approvingly. "That's the girl. You've been working very hard."

She stared at him. Had he forgotten just *what* she was working on? Trying to repair the inn he wanted to tear down?

She didn't want to talk about that. It would get them arguing again. She just wanted to sit here. As Braden said, not think about anything disturbing or unpleasant for a little while.

Braden patted the space beside him. "Come and sit here, so you can lean against the tree."

Alarm went through her. Sit beside him? So close they were nearly touching? "I don't think that's a good idea."

His face changed, as if he read her thoughts. He

moved over a little so more space was left between them. "There. Plenty of room."

Damask walked over and sat down beside him, knowing at once it was a mistake. They were still too close together.

She could smell the clean scent of him, feel his warmth, remember the kiss they'd exchanged that night in the sitting room.

Remember the day they'd repaired the roof and he'd said he kissed her only because he wanted to.

Because he *had* to. Because he couldn't help himself.

She inched away from him until she could go no farther and still be leaning her back against the tree.

He noticed. His smile was wry. "I'm not going to pounce on you."

"I didn't think you would," she answered.

No, what worried her was her own reactions. He hadn't pounced that other time. He hadn't needed to. She practically fell into his arms.

"Good. Now that that's out of the way, what can we talk about?"

The idea of sitting here, relaxed, under this tree, and just talking to each other—like friends—was so novel, she gave him a startled look.

He smiled at her. "Strange thought, isn't it? But I bet we could do it if we tried."

Her mind was a blank. She couldn't think of a single subject to discuss.

Silence drew out between them.

"Would you like to hear about my future plans?"

She jerked her head around. Had this been just a ploy to start in on her again about the inn?

He waved his hand. "No. I'm not talking about the inn. Do you think I'm that devious?"

After a moment, she said, realizing it was true, "No, I don't guess so."

He huffed out a sigh. "I'm glad to hear that. I meant my *business* plans. The Emporium is only the beginning. I'm going to build other stores in other towns. Or cities."

He'd piqued her interest. "So one store isn't enough for you?"

"Not nearly. Frank Woolworth opened a five-and-dime store last year in Lancaster. It's thriving. I hear he plans to open a chain of them eventually, all across the country. No reason why I can't do the same thing with department stores."

He paused, then continued. "I believe prosperous times are ahead. It looks like the Democrats will nominate Winfield Hancock for the presidency this year. He's a Pennsylvania native and a good man. But James Garfield, who'll no doubt be the Republican nominee, has a better grasp on finance and the good of the country."

She stared at him in surprise. "I don't keep up with politics, but I had no idea your ambitions were so far-reaching."

"Yes," he said simply. "When I left here, I went to Philadelphia and got a job as a stock boy in a large men's clothing store. Lemuel Johnson, the owner, had no family. He took a liking to me, taught me all he knew about retailing. Eventually, I worked my way up to become his partner. When he retired, I bought out his share. I sold the store at a good profit a couple of years ago."

Damask's surprise grew. "So that's how you got your start."

"That's how. I worked hard, but I was lucky, too."

"Yes," she agreed.

He gave her a wry grin. "Oh, so you don't think my hard work had much to do with it?"

She couldn't help smiling back. "I didn't say that. Mr. Johnson must have been very impressed with you."

Braden's grin faded. "He was a lonely man. He'd always wanted sons. I filled that need for him."

Something in his voice made her see this wasn't easy for him to talk about.

"I think he filled a need in you, too," she said softly. "And I don't mean a drive to be successful."

Braden looked down at the ground, picked a blade of grass, and ran it between his fingers. Then he raised his head. Their glances met and held.

Damask felt a current go through her . . . a closeness she'd never expected to feel between them. An emotional closeness . . . a sharing . . .

"Yes, he did," Braden said quietly. "He never had sons, and I never truly had a father."

His words touched her heart. "I was blessed. I lost my parents, but while they were alive, we always had plenty of love, even if we were poor."

"Yes, you were blessed."

His gaze remained on her, and that feeling of closeness between them grew inside Damask. Would it be possible for them to become friends?

That wasn't likely. Not unless Braden gave up his plans for his house on this hill and decided not to fight her any longer.

She wouldn't think about that now. She wouldn't destroy this fleeting intimacy. But neither did she want it to increase . . . become something else, something more dangerous . . .

She'd better change the subject, get their conversation away from such deeply personal matters.

Damask turned away from him, tilted her head, and looked at the sky.

The blue dome was clear except for a few puffy white clouds drifting around. "The sky seems so near today. Almost near enough to reach up and touch."

Her voice was deliberately casual. She hoped he'd follow her lead.

Suddenly, without warning, a face loomed over hers.

Braden's.

"Did anyone ever tell you what amazing eyes you have?" he asked softly.

She swallowed. He was so near . . . his clean, masculine scent was overpowering. She started to get up, to move away, but he brought his strong hands down on her shoulders.

"Don't run away from me," he said, his voice still very soft.

"I'm not," she said. "But I want to get up."

"Why?" he asked.

He let go of her shoulders and lay down beside her. Their shoulders touched. She felt a shudder all through her body. He looked up at the sky, just as she'd been doing.

"Look at all that blue sky . . . those clouds. Makes all our petty problems and worries seem pretty unimportant, doesn't it?"

She forced herself not to look at him. His pose was entirely too intimate, too suggestive. She couldn't think of philosophical things while he was so close.

Suddenly, she couldn't think of anything but the kiss they'd shared.

Desperately, she tried to marshal her defenses. Tried to summon anger against him for what he wanted to do to the inn, to her life and Emmy's and Cory's.

But she couldn't. Stretched out beside her, his sea green eyes fixed on the sky, he was a different man from that hard, cold one who cared nothing for their feelings, their lives. . . .

She was silent so long, he turned his head toward her, catching her gaze on him.

She felt herself reddening. She felt herself being drawn toward him, knew she should resist with every fiber of her being.

He was spoken for. He was still her enemy!

But the longing inside her was stronger than her guilt or her common sense. Stronger than anything.

When she finally let her gaze meet his, he was looking at her.

The hunger in his eyes made her draw in her breath.

Made her admit her own hunger was just as deep.

Chapter Eleven

The springy grass underneath their heads had a wild, fresh smell. An intermittent breeze cooled the air. The creek made pleasant sounds as its current ran over the rocks in the streambed. Overhead, birdsong filled the air.

Braden felt alive in a way he hadn't felt since childhood. Every sense was attuned to his surroundings . . . to Damask.

Her eyes were the color of storm clouds lit from within—glowing . . . luminous. He'd never seen eyes that color or with that depth. He could easily get lost in them.

He drew in his breath as her expression changed. Her face held the same hunger she must see in his own. He reached out a hand to stroke the well-remembered softness of her cheek. Its velvety feel under his fingertips made a tremor go down his hand into his arm.

She lay very still, looking at him. As if she couldn't

get enough of the sight of him—just as he felt about her.

Braden's hand moved downward. Damask tilted her head, arching her neck so that the line of her throat was accessible. He spread his fingers out, seeing his darker skin against the whiteness of her own, feeling her throbbing pulse, her warmth, wondering how his touch felt to her. . . .

When she closed her eyes, he felt suddenly bereft without that gray glow gazing into his own eyes.

Damask wore a faded lilac day dress with a high neckline and tiny jet buttons to the waist. After undoing the first few, he spread the material back on either side. The top of her breasts was visible now. Braden bent his head and placed feather-light kisses on the delicate skin.

Her eyes opened, widened . . . her pink lips fell open, too. With a groan, Braden covered her mouth with his. Her lips were so smooth, so soft, so responsive under his own.

He couldn't stop kissing her. He felt intoxicated with the feel and scent of her. He rolled onto his side, taking her with him so that their bodies were tightly pressed against each other. He could feel her every soft hollow and curve, just as she must be able to feel his hardness. . . .

Shrieks of children's laughter split the late spring air.

Against him, Braden felt Damask stiffen, just as she had that first time they'd kissed when Emmy cried out in her sleep.

Emmy and Cory mustn't find them like this.

Although every cell in his throbbing body told him that he couldn't stop, he rolled to a sitting posture, then got to his feet. His side vision saw Damask frantically buttoning her dress, smoothing her hair.

His heated body still throbbed. He'd like nothing better than to plunge into the creek and cool himself down. If he'd been alone, he'd strip and do just that.

He wouldn't need to cool down if he were alone . . . if Damask weren't here. This must stop. He was promised to Verona. How could he keep forgetting that?

Emmy and Cory burst out of the woods, Cory holding a frog in his hand and chasing Emmy, Emmy shrieking with feigned terror. At the creek bank, Cory let the frog go.

Damask got to her feet and picked up the picnic basket. She smiled at the children as they stopped by the willow tree.

She didn't smile at Braden or even glance his way.

"Ready to go home?" she asked the children.

Her voice sounded strangely husky.

Emmy's face fell. "Can't we stay awhile longer? It's not late, and maybe we can catch some more fish."

"Please, Damask, let us stay," Cory begged.

"I'll stay with them," Braden said. His own voice didn't sound normal, either. "I'd like to fish a bit more, too."

Fishing wasn't what he yearned for. He clenched his hands at his sides. He wanted to walk down the shaded woods path with Damask . . . he wanted to . . .

It didn't matter what he wanted. Since his body seemed to pay no attention to his mind or his good sense, he had to avoid being alone with her.

Finally, Damask turned to him, their glances meeting. The expression in her eyes, on her face, made him draw in his breath. Guilt was there . . . and anguish . . . and confusion.

And something else . . . that he couldn't put a name to. Maybe he was afraid to . . . or to admit he felt an emotion coursing through his veins as unfamiliar as her look.

"All right," Damask said, still in that husky tone, still avoiding looking at him.

"But don't go back into the woods anymore. Stay right here," she told the children.

"We will, Damask," both children chorused.

She walked away, her posture straight, and disappeared into the underbrush.

Braden listened until he could hear her no longer.

This can't go on, Braden told himself again.

And what was he going to do about it? Tell Verona? Break his engagement?

What about leaving here, going back to Philadelphia? He could buy another store there. Or maybe now was the time to move on to another small town not too far from here, to build a second department store.

He should never have returned to Goose Creek. But things were going fine until Ada died and left that crazy will. Until Damask appeared and changed his life.

Was that the truth? Did he feel real love for Verona? Or had he fooled himself into believing so because marrying her would complete his carefully laid-out plans?

Damask went in the inn's back door, into the hallway. At once the aroma of something cooking hit her nostrils.

"Flora's chicken corn soup," Damask said aloud. Few foods smelled or tasted better.

She'd keep her mind on that. Forget what just happened between her and Braden.

But how could she, when her body still felt the

touch of his . . . her lips still tingled where his lips had pressed against them.

When she still longed to be in his arms. Lost in the world they created when they were together.

You can because you must. He's not yours and never will be.

Desolation swept over her in a frightening surge. She fought against it, finally went on into the kitchen.

Flora stood at the huge black range, stirring the contents of a big soup pot with a wooden spoon.

She turned and gave Damask a surprised look. "Ach, you are back early. I thought you might take a few hours off for to rest."

"I did," Damask said, feeling her face warm. Could Flora tell by looking at her what had happened by the creek? Was her hair mussed, grass stains on her skirts?

Flora shook her head. "Not long enough. You are too pale, and you are losing the weight."

Damask set the picnic basket on the worktable and started unpacking it. "I don't see how I could be, eating your wonderful food. And why didn't you tell me Braden was there with the children?"

Flora turned back to her soup, shrugging her plump shoulders. "I suppose I did not remember."

Damask snorted. "I suppose you aren't telling me the truth. Were you afraid I wouldn't go if I knew he was there?"

Flora shrugged again. "Maybe so."

A sudden strong urge came over her to tell Flora what had happened today . . . what had happened that night in the sitting room. . . .

Maybe Flora could give her some good advice.

You don't need advice. You know what you've done is wrong. And so does Braden.

The urge to confess faded. Damask finished with the picnic basket and put it in the pantry.

"That's a big pot of soup," she said.

"Yah," Flora answered. "I take some of it to Harold. Edmond tells me he is not getting over the grippe. He's still in the bed."

Flora's voice sounded worried. More worried than it should for someone who was just a friend.

"I didn't know that. Yes, taking him soup is a good idea. Does he live alone?"

"Edmond lives with him. But I think, like two men alone, they not much cooking do."

"You're probably right." Damask came to stand beside her. "Can I pack something else to take?"

"Yah. Some of my kuchen. I made two pans with the wild strawberries. And will you go with me?"

"Of course," Damask agreed, getting one of the fruit and custard cakes out of the pantry and putting a clean cloth over it.

It would probably do her good to get away from here for a little while. The children were safe with Braden.

Safe? How could she feel that he was a safe guardian for Emmy and Cory, when he was such a threat to all three of their lives?

She didn't understand it, but she did. Even more so after the talk they'd had today. She'd felt closer to him, felt she knew him better.

Oh, she was getting to know him all right!

How could she have kissed him again? How far would that embrace have gone if the children hadn't come back?

Worrying about it would get her nowhere. She'd managed to forget Warren. To recover from his shoddy treatment of her. She'd manage this tangle, too.

A few minutes later, Damask and Flora were on their way down the hill with the food, Damask insisting on carrying the jar of soup, Flora the lighter wrapped kuchen.

Harold lived in a small frame house on Walnut Street, a side street off Main. The house was well-kept, the yard neat, Damask noted as they made their way up the walk.

Flora was panting with exertion.

Damask looked at her with concern. "That walk was too much for you. We need a buggy."

Flora laughed. "What we need and what we have are two different things, yah?"

Damask's conscience smote her. "If I accepted Braden's offer, we could afford a little house like this one. A buggy, too."

Flora patted Damask's shoulder. "But the inn with all its happy memories that we love would be gone."

"Yes, but maybe—"

"No maybes," Flora said firmly. "You do right. Stop the worry about it. Everything will come out fine."

Damask didn't see how that was possible, but she said no more. They walked up on the porch, where a small dog was yapping and whining for their attention.

Damask leaned down to pet him.

"That is Edmond's Towser," Flora said, smiling.

She knocked, and a handsome young man opened the door leading into a tiny entryway.

"Flora! It's good to see you." He turned to Damask with a grin. "And you're Ada's niece. The one who's doing battle with Braden. Come on in."

"Yes, I'm Damask," she told him, smiling back, feeling heartened. He must be Edmond, Damask thought. And he seemed to like the idea of her "doing battle" with Braden.

He stood back, and Damask followed Flora inside.

"We have come to see your papa," Flora said. "We bring him some good soup to make him well again."

Edmond looked at the food they carried with interest, making Damask remember Flora's comment about the two men probably not doing any more cooking than they had to.

"Pop'll like that," Edmond said.

"He sleeps?" Flora asked. "We do not wish to disturb."

Edmond laughed. "You won't. He's reading. Says he gets enough sleep at night. He's getting pretty grumpy. Wants to be up and about."

He led them to a small bedroom to the left off the narrow hallway. The door was open.

"You got company!" Edmond announced.

Harold was propped up with pillows behind his head, a book in his hand. He gave them a surprised look and put the book down on his lap.

Edmond pulled over two straight-backed chairs.

Flora handed the kuchen to him and motioned for Damask to do the same with the soup. "Here, take this to kitchen and put into bowl for your papa. It still will be hot from the stove."

Watching Edmond leave, Damask thought he was a good-natured young man as well as being very handsome.

Flora sat down in one of the chairs, and Damask took the other one.

Flora frowned at Harold. "The doctor have you seen?"

He frowned back. "Yep," he said grumpily. "Twice. Told me I'm gettin' old and I got to expect it will take longer to get over the grippe now. And everything else, too."

Flora's frown turned into a smile. "You are not so

old," she said. "I think you have lots more life in you."

After a moment, Harold gave her a grudging smile. "That's what I tried to tell him, but he's a young know-it-all."

The old doctor had retired, Damask remembered Flora saying, and his son had taken over. Some of the townspeople, especially the older ones, were having a hard time accepting him.

And Harold's glance seemed to be lingering on Flora, she noticed.

Edmond came back carrying a tray with a steaming bowl of Flora's soup. He arranged it in front of his father. "Had a hard time keeping from eating this myself."

"Eat, eat!" Flora said, waving her hand. "I make more when this is gone."

"I was hoping you'd say that," Edmond said. He disappeared again.

Harold dipped his spoon in the soup and raised it to his mouth. He gave Flora a smile. "You're still the best cook in town."

To Damask's surprise, color came to Flora's round cheeks. "Thank you," she said.

Harold's glance lingered on Flora for a moment. Turning to Damask, he asked, "How are you getting along? Bet you're trying to do too much by yourself."

"No, I'm not. I've finished one guest room and I'm working on the second. I have it about half wallpapered."

"Damask, she is the fastest worker I ever saw," Flora said. "You are right, Harold, too much she does."

"Doc tells me I'm going to be laid up for another week or so," Harold said. "But I don't think I'm going to pay him any mind."

"Yes, you are," Edmond said, coming back with

another bowl of soup and a third chair. He turned to Damask. "Sounds like you could use some help, but it can't be Pop for a while."

He sat down at the foot of his father's bed. "Hope you ladies don't mind me eating in front of you. Don't think I can wait."

Flora waved her hand. "Go ahead, eat," she urged.

"You're danged right she could use some help," Harold said. "A whole lot of it."

"Keep your suspenders on, Pop," Edmond said. He took a sip of soup and then sighed. "Flora, you ought to open up a restaurant."

Harold's glare was back, directed at his son. "If you think I'm going to stay in this bed till I grow to it, you've got another think coming!"

"You'll do what Doc says. I've got a strong back."

He turned to Damask. "I've got some free time coming up. I could put in a couple of days' work on the inn. I've always loved that old place."

Damask stared at him in surprise. "That would be wonderful, but I can't afford to pay you now."

Edmond waved that concern aside. "I don't want pay. I'd like to do this for the inn. I'd hate to see it torn down."

Finally, she nodded. "I'd be glad to accept your help, but I want you to keep track of how much time you put in. When the inn's making money again, I'll pay you."

She'd told Harold the same thing. And that was an optimistic statement. It might never happen.

He grinned. "It's hard for you to accept help from others, isn't it?"

Damask smiled back. "No, but I don't expect people to help me with this. It was my own idea to try to get the inn repaired and opened again, I imagine plenty of people think it's foolish."

"I don't," Edmond said firmly.

"Edmond, he does the fine carpenter work," Flora said, beaming with approval at the young man.

He beamed back. "Then that's all settled." He turned to Damask again. "I could start in a few days, if that's all right."

A picture of Braden coming back to the inn to find Edmond hard at work there filled her mind.

Braden wouldn't like it.

He didn't have to like it.

"That would be fine," she said. "Thank you so much."

"You're welcome. I might be able to round up a few more men who have some free time."

Damask swallowed. "Oh, I couldn't accept—"

"Yes, you can. Stop worrying about it. You'd be surprised how many people in this town don't want to see that inn torn down," he told her.

"Yah, that is right," Flora put in. "I talk to my customers when I bring the butter and eggs."

"There's no reason why it has to be," Edmond said. He finished his soup and stood up.

Damask swallowed. "I can't afford to buy materials, either."

Edmond gave her his good-humored smile again. "Pop and I have some leftover boards and such in the shed. I bet there's some stuff in the barn up there, too."

"Maybe so . . . I'm not sure. But—"

Waving his hand, Edmond got up. "You ladies go ahead and visit with Pop. I think I'll go on downtown and talk to some people."

Damask nodded, too stunned to speak.

In the space of a few minutes, she'd gone from feeling she had little chance of success, that she was probably foolish to keep on struggling, to bright hope.

If you think it's going to be that easy, you're a fool. Braden Franklin is a smart, hard man. He's as determined as you are to have his way.

She knew that, but her hopes refused to be dashed.

She'd seen another side of him a few hours ago. A side that wasn't hard and ruthless. Ambitious, yes, but there wasn't anything wrong in having dreams. Nothing would be accomplished without that.

And maybe it would be possible to change his mind about this particular dream. Maybe if he saw several of the townspeople working on the inn, he'd have a change of heart.

Even if that was possible, which was highly unlikely, what about his fiancée? Could she imagine Verona having a change of heart, too?

No. But stranger things have happened, Damask told herself.

Chapter Twelve

Verona settled herself on the veranda, carefully pulling the folds of her pale yellow muslin dress out from under her in order not to wrinkle them. The dress was new. This was the first time she'd worn it, and its color flattered her fair complexion, made her blond curls look even brighter.

But the pretty new gown didn't give her the pleasure it should have. As it would have before she and Braden got involved with each other. Before she'd managed to get him to propose marriage to her.

She half expected Braden to come for supper tonight, but she wasn't sure. He hadn't been definite about it the last time she'd seen him.

Verona waited for her mood to brighten at the thought of seeing her handsome fiancé in a few hours, but it didn't. All she could think about was having to put on her act for him and pretend she was dying of impatience for their wedding night.

When the truth was, she dreaded it like poison.

Verona hastily put those thoughts out of her mind. She'd worry about that when she had to.

It didn't look as if that night would come anytime soon.

Braden wasn't doing a thing to get Ada's family out of the inn. Neither had he persuaded that Damask woman to sell their half of the property to him.

Verona acknowledged she was no closer to getting her beautiful mansion on the hill overlooking Goose Creek than she'd been weeks ago.

Was that the only reason she wanted to marry Braden?

The sudden thought appalled her. No, she loved him, of course. As Mama had said, she was just nervous, like all brides were. She needed to try to hurry things along so she could get that first night over with.

And what if it doesn't get any better, ever, as Mama said? Would she just get used to it?

Those unwelcome thoughts she pushed far back in her mind. She had enough to worry about. Things weren't going right around here, either. Papa was still letting Russell take his produce to that silly open market in town. Russell came over at least twice a week, and he and her father, and now her brother, Oliver, sat around grinning like jackasses and talking about expanding by next year.

She heard footsteps and glanced up.

As if her thoughts had conjured him, Russell walked toward her, that same stupid grin on his face.

Did he think *she* was going to talk to him about the market? Praise him for his brilliant idea?

Verona drew herself up, giving Russell a haughty glance. Annoyed, she felt her heart beating a little faster. She took a couple of deep breaths to calm down.

She *wouldn't* let him get her upset!

"Good afternoon, Ronie," he said, sitting down beside her. "You're looking pretty today. Is that a new dress?"

She darted him a glance, surprised that he'd noticed. Braden paid attention to things like that. But she'd never expected Russell to. He'd even said she was pretty.

Then she remembered she was mad at Russell. "What if it is?"

"What's got your bun in a snit?" he asked, a hint of laughter barely held in check in his voice.

Verona huffed, jerking her glance away. "I truly appreciate your gentlemanly way of expressing things."

Russell laughed, a rich, full-bodied sound. Unexpectedly, a shiver went down her arms.

"Ronie, you tickle me when you try to act like such a lady."

She whipped her head around, glaring at him. "I *am* a lady!"

He laughed again and shook his head. "I bet if I tried hard enough, I could get you to shimmy up that maple tree in the backyard with me like you used to."

For a moment, she had a wild urge to do just that. She could picture them high in the branches. . . .

Horrified, she sat up straighter and made her glare stronger. "Why don't you go home, Russell Gifford? I'm waiting for someone."

Instead, Russell crossed his legs and made himself more comfortable. "I bet I know who. That rich fellow you managed to snag. Hard to believe his pappy was the most no-account man in Goose Creek."

"I don't have to stay here and listen to your insults!" Verona got to her feet.

Russell put one of his big hands on her arm. "Now, don't go off mad, Ronie. I swear you haven't changed a bit. You should have been born with red hair. You sure have the temper for it. I wasn't trying to insult Braden. I admire him for what he's accomplished. But what's this I hear about him wanting to tear down the old inn?"

"That's none of your business! Besides, that old place needs to come down."

She shook his hand off her arm, horrified at how again that tingle went up it.

Russell tilted his head and gave her a knowing grin. "So you can build your fancy new house there? What do you want with something like that, Ronie? Why, you're a country girl. Always will be no matter how many fancy dresses you wear or how much you try to act the lady."

His words went straight inside her to a place she was trying to forget.

"I *hate* you!" she told him.

Before she thought, Verona drew her hand back and gave him a resounding slap.

He put his hand to his reddening cheek. "There! See? Would a lady have done that?"

He gave her another insolent grin.

"Yes! And if you don't stop grinning like that, I'll give you another one."

She barely stopped herself from stamping her foot. Or *his* foot.

He laughed out loud. "Go ahead," he dared her.

She'd never been able to resist a dare. She drew her hand back again, then heard the front door opening.

Papa or Mama. She lowered her hand.

"Good to see you, Russell," her father's genial voice said from behind. "Need to talk some more business?"

"Yep," Russell replied.

Again, Verona could hear the barely held back laughter in his voice.

Oh, how she'd like to kick him where it would do the most good!

She couldn't stay out here another second. She'd wait for Braden inside.

With as much dignity as she could muster, her head high, Verona went inside and upstairs to the privacy of her room.

"Good morning, Mr. Franklin," Sanford Wright, the town barber, said respectfully. Perhaps a shade *too* respectfully. His tone was almost distant, which for a garrulous man like Sanford was strange.

"Morning, Sanford," Braden replied, giving the man a smile.

Sanford's return smile was very reserved—which was also not as usual.

"I'm in luck—first customer of the day," Braden said affably, seating himself in the barber chair.

The barber didn't comment on this obvious fact. He stepped up behind Braden.

"What will it be, Mr. Franklin?"

Why did Sanford keep calling him Mr. Franklin in that stiff way instead of Braden, as he always did?

"Oh, the usual cut—you know how I like it," Braden answered. No, he wasn't imagining things. There was a distinct chill in Sanford's voice.

Sanford enveloped Braden in the big, white cover-up. Braden heard him behind, rattling around in his barber tools.

The door to the small Main Street shop opened, and Tildon Yates entered.

"Morning, Tildon!" Sanford said jovially. "How's the world treating you?"

"Oh, can't complain, I guess."

Tildon, leaning on his cane, came in and lowered himself heavily to one of the chairs along the side wall.

The old man spent most of his days in the barbershop, talking to customers. Over eighty, he wasn't much good for anything else, he told everyone. He was an interesting old man and told good yarns.

"Good morning, Tildon," Braden said, again smiling.

Unsmiling, Tildon stared at him for a moment. Finally, he nodded. "Mornin', Mr. Franklin," he said in a clipped tone.

Braden's bafflement deepened. What was going on? Tildon was friendly with everyone.

He glanced at Tildon again. The old man was staring at him intently, his mouth set.

The bell jangled again, and Durward Vail came in. Owner of the livery stable, the portly, middle-aged man was one of the town's more prosperous citizens.

"Morning, Durward!" Sanford's voice was full of good cheer. "Ain't seen you in a while."

Durward's eyes swept coolly over Braden and dismissed him. Ignoring Braden, he greeted Sanford and Tildon, then seated himself next to the old man.

What in *hell* was going on? Braden asked himself. Why was he suddenly the town pariah?

"Is it true what I hear about you, Mr. Franklin?" Tildon's quavery old voice said into the unusual silence.

Braden gave him a startled glance. Tildon was pointing his cane at him, giving him an accusing look, as if he were a criminal.

"Since I have no idea what you're talking about,

Tildon, I can't answer that,'' Braden answered, keeping his voice genial.

"Why, I'm a-hearing that you're trying to put that sweet young niece of Ada's and her brother and sister right out on the street! Going to tear that old inn down right around their heads."

Braden closed his eyes for a moment. "Ada's nieces and nephew own half of the inn property," Braden said as pleasantly as he could manage. "So it would be a bit hard for me to do that."

Tildon glared at him and shook his cane. "No, it wouldn't. The poor girl ain't got any money, and she's out there a-workin' her fingers to the bone trying to fix the place up."

Braden opened his mouth to refute the man's words, then closed it again.

What Tildon had said was the truth.

And put like that, it did, indeed, make Braden sound like a heartless scoundrel.

He realized Sanford's scissors had stilled. They were no longer trimming his hair.

Durward stared at him with almost as unfriendly a look as Tildon's.

Braden took in a deep breath, then huffed it out. "I'm doing no such thing," he finally said. "What Damask does is entirely her own affair. I've offered her a more than fair price for her family's share of the property. She refuses to accept it."

Durward's glance sharpened.

Too late, Braden realized how overly familiar it had sounded for him to call Damask by her given name under these circumstances.

Tildon's cane still pointed at Braden. "I don't blame her a bit. Goose Creek Inn's a heap older than I am. It's a town landmark!"

Durward nodded in agreement. "That's so. I've

heard some of the bigwigs stayed there during the War Between the States."

"They did," Sanford put in. "Why, that inn has been there since before the War for Independence!"

With a small shock, Braden realized he hadn't known either of those facts. If they *were* facts.

"Well, if it's *that* old, it sure needs to be torn down!" he said lightly, trying to cool the atmosphere a little.

Durward and Tildon looked at him as though they couldn't believe what he'd just said. Sanford's scissors had stilled again. No doubt he was also giving the back of Braden's head the same kind of look.

Braden was suddenly glad he wasn't getting a shave.

He'd just said a very stupid thing. The question was how to retract it.

Pretend he hadn't meant it, that he was only joking? But if he did, he'd be agreeing with these men.

Acknowledging that the inn shouldn't be leveled.

Dammit! He'd backed himself into a corner. He forced a pleasant expression onto his face. "Many buildings a lot more historic than you think this one is are torn down every day."

Tildon stubbornly shook his head. "Not in Goose Creek they ain't."

"Nope," Durward put in. "Can't say as I remember any others that old here at all."

"Goose Creek Inn is the oldest building we have," Sanford said. "By far."

Braden tried to think of something else to say but couldn't.

An uncomfortable insight went through him. If these men were so firmly against his plans, then that must mean others also were.

Why had he thought he'd have the support of the whole town? Just because he was a wealthy man?

Because he'd built the newest, most successful business the town had?

Had he actually thought everyone would enjoy the sight of his and Verona's big white mansion up on that hill?

For the first time, he realized how simple-minded he'd been to believe that.

True, he'd known there would be some envy, that was only natural and couldn't be avoided. People always envied the ones that fortune favored. That hadn't bothered him. It had even been an enjoyable thought.

Oh, stop being so pompous, he told himself. *People with money, you mean.*

But he'd never given a thought to the possibility that he'd have true opposition to his plans. That some townspeople would object for the reasons just presented here a few minutes ago.

How many people felt the way these three did?

If a lot did, it could hurt his business. Maybe even ruin it. Ruin all his future plans.

Maybe he should just give up this idea . . . there were plenty of other attractive places to build a house. . . .

No! He couldn't. It had been part of his dream for too long. Ever since he'd become partners with Mr. Johnson, he'd burned to come back here, build a house on that hill, the most choice spot in town.

All during his growing-up years, he'd been looked down on. It had been a pleasant thought that the town would at last have to look up at him. Not only figuratively, but in reality.

But he'd also wanted to have the townspeople's respect. What a foolish, naive idea.

"You're all finished," Sanford said into the silence

that had fallen. He whipped off the covering cloth and brushed Braden's shoulders free of hair.

Sanford's voice was still cool. Both men facing Braden were giving him unfriendly looks.

Braden stood. He fished in his pockets. "Here you are," he said to Sanford in hearty tones, giving him more than his customary large tip.

"Thank you, Mr. Franklin," Sanford said, not even looking at the money.

His expression was the same as the other two in the room.

Damn it all to hell! What was he going to do about this? Braden asked himself.

"Good day, Tildon, Durward," he said, forcing his expression to remain cordial and not reveal his inner turmoil.

Tildon still glared at him. "Braden, you was raised in this town just like I was. I know you wasn't treated so good when you was growin' up. But you've made somethin' of yourself now, and most people wish you well in your business dealings. But that could change. It's plain shameful that young girl and Harold slaved away on that building and you're planning to destroy it."

"I certainly didn't encourage them to," Braden said evenly.

Durward let out a sound of disdain. "I guess not! Why, I hear poor old Harold worked out in the rain and got himself a bad case of the grippe."

"What?" Braden stared. "Harold didn't work out in—"

His words broke off. He didn't know when Harold had worked, or under what conditions. Why in hell should he? The old man was doing it of his own free will.

Tildon nodded, pounding his cane on the floor. "Yep, that's what I heared too. Might die, they say."

Braden took a deep breath. "I believe that things are getting out of hand," he said. "I haven't heard anything about Harold being on his deathbed."

But would he have? He hadn't even been at the inn much lately.

Guilt and worry hit him.

"Don't 'pear like you wanted to hear anything," Tildon said darkly.

Braden pressed his lips together. He turned and left the small shop.

What kind of a mess was brewing here?

His plans had been general knowledge around town for quite a while. No one had ever spoken a word of disapproval to him before.

Who had gotten people so riled up? And why?

The obvious answer occurred to him.

The person who had the most to gain in this dispute.

Damask.

Right now he had to stop by and see Harold. Find out for himself if the old man was truly seriously ill.

And then he was going to have it out with her.

Today.

Chapter Thirteen

Braden made short work of the few blocks between the barbershop and Harold's house.

He strode up the walk and knocked on the door. No one came to answer. Braden frowned. That must mean either that Harold was still bedfast or no one was at home. The first thought seemed more likely.

Hardly anyone in Goose Creek locked their doors. Braden turned the knob, and the door opened easily under his hand, letting him into a small hall.

"Anyone home?" Braden said into the silence.

"Hell, yes," said Harold's grumpy voice from a room to the left. "Come on in. I could use some company."

Maybe you won't want mine, Braden thought as he closed the door behind him and entered the room.

Harold was propped up in bed, a book lying open on his lap. His eyes widened at the sight of Braden.

"Well, sit down. I didn't expect to see you."

"I guess not."

Feeling uncomfortable, Braden took a chair. It had never occurred to him to visit Harold. But he liked the old man and was relieved to see that, contrary to the barbershop trio's dark forebodings, he didn't look very ill.

"How are you getting along?"

Harold shrugged, frowning. "Doc says as well as can be expected. Gettin' old, he tells me. But I'm sure sick of this dang bed!"

"I bet you are," Braden said sympathetically. "Is there anything you need I could get you?"

Harold looked surprised again at Braden's offer. He shook his head, then grinned. "I'd like a miracle pill to get rid of the fever and these aches and pains."

Braden grinned back. "Wish I could give you that."

Harold's grin faded. He gave Braden a straight look. "Not that I don't appreciate your visit, but you don't strike me as a man who goes around visiting sick-beds."

Braden's discomfort returned. "I was in the barber-shop and some of the men said you were bad off."

Harold snorted. "Bet one of 'em was old Tildon. He always thinks everybody's dying."

"Yes, it was." Braden took a deep breath. He had something to say and he might as well get it over with.

"Harold, I don't think you should work on the inn. At your age, it's too hard on you. Maybe it did contribute to your getting the grippe."

Harold's frown returned. He jerked himself more upright in the bed. "Sitting around doing nothing would have me in my grave for sure. I'm not about to do that."

"I didn't mean you should."

Harold's frown darkened. "Then, what did you

mean? Miss Damask hasn't got anyone else to help her. Of course, I'm sure that doesn't bother *you* any.''

Braden had thought Harold resented him. Now he knew for sure. "I'm beginning to think pretty soon I'm going to be ridden out of town on a rail," he said wryly, a touch of annoyance in his voice.

"Lots of people don't like what you want to do," Harold said, his voice stiff. "And I sure don't like you coming here and trying to get me to stop helping that little girl.''

"Harold, I didn't come here for anything like that," Braden protested, startled at the other man's interpretation of his visit. "I just wanted to make sure—"

He broke off as the front door opened again.

"Is anybody here?" Flora's cheerful voice asked.

Harold's eyes lit up. "Come on back, Flora," he called.

She did, carrying a basket, a smile on her face. She stopped short when she saw Braden, then her smile widened.

Braden rose, feeling more uncomfortable by the second.

"So you, too, have come to visit. That is good." She nodded approvingly.

"Hello, Flora," Braden said. "I was just going. I'll leave you two to visit."

As Braden let himself out the door, he reflected that neither Harold nor Flora had protested his departure.

No, they seemed eager to have him gone.

And he was relieved to go, but he wished he'd been able to convince Harold he'd had no ulterior motives for his visit.

Had he?

No. His conscience was clear.

He straightened his shoulders and headed back up the street.

He hoped Damask was at the inn. It was ten o'clock and he hadn't even been to the store yet this morning. Not that Jacob couldn't handle things. Since Braden had delegated some of his authority, the store seemed to be doing fine without his constant presence.

Of course Damask would be at the inn. Where else would she be?

She might be down in the town, trying to stir up more resentment against him.

Braden's mouth set grimly at that reminder of why he was hunting her up. He hurried his steps. He was damnably tired of all this!

The wildflowers on the hillside meadow were fading now, almost gone. But it was still a lovely place. He looked across to the inn as he rapidly approached it.

His house would have a fine setting.

His beautiful white house, right where the inn now sat.

In his mind's eye, the inn stubbornly refused to disappear and let his vision replace it. That unsettled him a little. No wonder, after what he'd just been through at the barbershop and Harold's.

He let himself into the wide hall. No sounds came from the kitchen. It was still too early to cook dinner.

No sounds from any of the other downstairs rooms, either.

Damask must be upstairs, then. She'd better be. If she wasn't in the inn, he'd go back to town and find her.

Braden tried to take the stairs two at a time, but the graceful old stairway steps were too deep. The stairway had a nice curve to it. He'd have to try to incorporate something like that into his house.

The woodwork and the moldings were beautiful, too. Maybe he could keep some of them, use them in the new house . . . no, Verona wouldn't like that. She wanted everything new and of the latest design.

He frowned. It would be a shame to destroy some of the things here.

Maybe it would be a crime to destroy any of it.

He pushed that disturbing thought aside and went looking for Damask, finding her in the sitting room.

She stood on the top rung of a ladder, reaching toward the ceiling with a trowel heaped with plaster.

The movement made her old blue work dress stretch tight against her breasts, revealing their roundness, their enticing curves. . . .

Hearing him at the door, she twisted her body on the ladder, turned toward him, and the ladder swayed drunkenly.

Fear leapt into Braden's chest. He sprinted across the room.

A big glob of plaster fell and splattered on the floor, barely missing him. Damask plunged the trowel back into the container, frowning at him. "Why are you here?"

Braden grabbed the ladder, trying to steady it. "What in hell are you trying to do?" he asked, ignoring her question.

Her face set, she looked down at him. "You can plainly see what I'm *doing*. Not *trying* to do."

His fear was slowly fading. But he wouldn't want to be up on that ladder.

"All I see is that you're likely to fall and break your neck any minute. Why aren't you using the ladder we had for the roof?"

"It's too heavy for me to carry up the stairs."

Braden's jaw tightened. Now he was supposed to tell her he'd go fetch the sturdier ladder for her. Like hell. He wouldn't get roped into another job.

"Get down from there."

"This hardens very fast. I have to get it on the ceiling."

She turned around again, making the ladder sway, and dipped her trowel into the plaster mix once more.

Swearing silently, he looked up at her.

"At least come down long enough for me to tighten the screws in this damned thing."

She spread the plaster across a hole where the lathing showed through and smoothed it out. "I already tried that. It didn't work."

Braden steadied the ladder and ground his teeth. "What do you expect me to do? Buy you a new ladder? Help you with your muleheaded plans?"

She dipped another trowel full and applied it. The ladder swayed.

Braden cursed again.

He had to admit she was doing a good job.

"I don't expect you to do anything," she finally said. "Why won't you let me work in peace?"

"Because I don't want to find you lying on the floor badly injured or dead."

Instead of replying, she smoothed more plaster. Then she awkwardly descended the ladder, holding the pan and trowel in one hand.

Relief surged through Braden. She'd decided to have some sense! Her bottom swayed enticingly as she came backward down the ladder. He couldn't seem to take his eyes off it.

On the floor once more, she turned to him. "I ran out of plaster. I have to mix up a new batch."

He stared at her. "You mean you're going back up there?"

"Yes." She started for the bag of plaster and pail of water sitting on the brick hearth.

"Wait." Braden grabbed her bare forearm. Her

skin was warm and smooth, just as it had been that day by the creek.

She tried to jerk away from him, then gave him an exasperated look. "Why?"

Her lips would be just as smooth, too. He knew. He'd tasted their delights.

Get your mind on your business, he told himself.

"Because I'm not letting you climb that ladder again."

She'd stopped trying to get loose from his grasp. A look he couldn't define came over her face.

"Oh? Did you change your mind? *Are* you planning to help me with this job, too?" she asked sweetly.

If he held on to her much longer, he would forget why he came here, and she'd be in his arms again. Her lips would be beneath his own, sweet and hot. . . .

He let go of her arm and moved back a step. "No, I'm not going to help you patch this damned ceiling," he said evenly.

She nodded. "I thought you'd say that." She turned again and walked toward her supplies.

He wouldn't touch her again.

But he had to stop her.

Braden moved to the ladder and pulled it down from the wall.

Outraged, Damask rushed toward him. "What are you doing?"

Braden laid the ladder on the floor, sat down on it, and folded his arms across his chest. "As you said to me a minute ago, I believe you can figure that out."

She folded her arms across her breasts, pushing them in a little. "Are you planning to sit there all day?"

Braden imagined his hands where hers were, kneading that yielding flesh. His lower body began to ache and harden. He hoped she didn't notice the effect she had on him.

She'd accused him of kissing her to try to change her mind. That had never occurred to him.

But that didn't mean it couldn't occur to her . . . again.

He hoped that possibility would cool his heated body. It didn't.

"If necessary," he said between his teeth. "I don't have much planned. I can take the day off."

The mention of a day off again made him think of the afternoon at the creek. His body hardened more.

Damask's gray eyes flashed. "I don't believe you have nothing better to do than prevent me from replastering this ceiling."

Braden abruptly remembered why he was here. "You're right."

She looked a little relieved. "I'm right? Then you're going to let me get on with my work?"

"I didn't say that." He shifted so that he was a little more comfortable and so she couldn't see the effect she was having on his lower parts.

Wariness came back into her face. "Then, what do you want?"

I want to pull you down on top of me and kiss you senseless. Roll you over on your back and lay myself against you. And more than that . . .

Get back to business, he told himself sternly.

"I came here to talk to you."

She sighed wearily and sat down on the edge of the old rocker. "I haven't changed my mind. There's no use trying to persuade me to sell to you."

He gave her an even look. "That's not what I want to talk about."

She raised her brows. "Oh? What else could you possibly have to say to me?"

Her words took him back once more to the creek.
When he *had* talked to her about things other than
their dispute.

When he'd shared his dreams with her and she'd
listened with every evidence of understanding and
sympathy . . .

Dammit! Why couldn't he keep his mind where it
belonged? And that wasn't on Damask's body. Or her
understanding heart.

He swallowed and sat up straighter. "I want you to
stop spreading lies and rumors around town," he
said evenly.

She shot out of the chair and put her hands on
her shapely hips.

"What are you talking about? I've never spread any
lies or rumors!"

"Oh? Then, why did the men in the barbershop
this morning tell me what a villain I am? What a
historic landmark the inn is? How poor Harold is
heading for the grave because he's the only one who's
been helping you?"

She stared at him, her mouth open. "I have no
idea. But *I* certainly didn't tell anyone such things.
Is Harold worse?" she asked worriedly.

"No, no. I went to see him just a little while ago.
He's fretting about having to stay in bed, but he's
not worse."

"Oh, good." She stared at him again. "*You* went
to visit him?"

Her tone was disbelieving. No wonder.

"Yes, I did."

"Why?"

"Because I wanted to see for myself if the gossipers
were telling the truth about how sick he was!"

"Oh." She nodded as if she accepted that reason.
Annoyance swept through Braden. "If I'd told you

I went to see him just because I wanted to, just because I like him, you'd never have believed me, would you?''

"No," she said.

"So you think I'm selfish and grasping with no thought for anyone but myself."

He saw her swallow. "No," she said slowly. "I . . . I don't think that, either. I know you have . . . a softer side. You're very good with Emmy and Cory. I trust you with them."

Braden's irritation faded. He felt as if she'd paid him a high compliment. "Thank you," he said.

He believed her when she said she wasn't the one getting people stirred up around town. If he'd thought about it more deeply, he'd have realized he couldn't see her doing that. He wouldn't have rushed over here to accuse her.

"I believe you aren't the guilty party on the rumor-mongering. But I can't stop you from doing anything you want. Either trying to get people on your side or working here. Even if you promise not to climb this wreck of a ladder again, there are plenty of other things you can do."

She shrugged, then smiled. "You're right. So, are you going to let me get on with my work?"

"Will you promise not to climb this ladder again today?"

She looked at him for a moment. "All right, I promise I won't climb this ladder . . . today."

He sighed and rose. "I suppose that's the best I can hope for."

"I'm afraid so."

They were standing only a few feet apart. If he stepped forward, she'd be in his arms. He'd be holding her close, breathing in her sweet scent, feeling her soft body pressed against his hardness. . . .

Leave . . . now, he commanded himself.

He had to admire her spunk and determination.

But he also had to think of his own life and what he wanted.

And he was no longer certain he knew. Something inside him seemed to be changing.

But he was sure of one thing. If he stayed much longer, he'd have Damask in his arms.

In broad daylight. In the middle of the sitting room. He could picture that all too clearly.

"I've got to go," he said.

He turned and left the room, thinking he heard her soft sigh—of disappointment?

No, he was dreaming . . . and he was engaged . . . and the next thing he must do is talk to Verona about his changing feelings.

He wasn't looking forward to that at all.

Chapter Fourteen

Astride Jasper, riding out to the Holmes farm, Braden felt increasingly out of sorts. What a hell of a day this was turning out to be.

After leaving the inn, he'd stopped at the store to tell Jacob he might not be in today.

He hadn't wanted to leave Damask.

With an effort he pushed thoughts of Damask out of his mind.

He was going to see Verona, his intended wife. And he'd better stop forgetting that fact.

It was dinnertime when he arrived, and of course Mrs. Holmes urged him to eat.

He couldn't refuse, but he wasn't hungry. Too much had gone on today. And he wanted to get this last confrontation over with.

What was he going to say to his beloved? Or was she truly his beloved? Maybe she was just part of his plan to make Goose Creek sit up and take notice of him at last.

No, he couldn't fool himself that much. Could he? Hell, he didn't know for sure.

Verona didn't act overjoyed to see him, either, which he'd expected. But then, she never did lately, and after today's talk, there was no telling how she'd act.

When they were seated around the table in the ornately furnished dining room, Bernice gave him a bright smile.

Too bright, maybe, Braden thought, tensing. He'd never felt at ease with Verona's mother.

"How are the plans for your and Verona's new house progressing?" she asked.

This was no casual question. Braden inwardly groaned, wondering how to answer her.

"The plans are all finished, ma'am," he said politely.

Bernice raised her brows. "Oh, is that right? So we can expect construction to begin soon?"

She was putting him on the spot—and didn't care. She was doing it for a purpose.

Seated at the other end of the table, Verona's father gave him an intent look.

Verona's face held an expression he couldn't read. But he knew whatever it meant, she wasn't happy.

"No, I didn't mean that," Braden said to Bernice Holmes. "Miss Aldon hasn't agreed to sell me her family's share of the inn property yet."

From the flicker in Mrs. Holmes's eyes, he knew Verona had already told her this. Of course she had. Even if she hadn't, the whole town knew how Damask had stymied him.

Hell, maybe the county!

Mrs. Holmes raised her brows even higher. "My goodness! Surely, you can think of some way to persuade her. And . . . well . . . it's hardly the thing for both of you to be living there."

What was she getting at? This wasn't something she'd just found out, either.

"Miss Aldon and her family have as much right as I do to stay there," he said.

Verona's mother gave him another overly bright smile. "Oh, I'm sure she does. I was thinking more in terms of you moving out." She sighed. "Goose Creek could use a boardinghouse."

Or an inn. It used to have that. And it could again if he were willing.

No, it would take more than that, and wouldn't be that easy, no matter what Damask thought.

"But *we* have plenty of space, you know. Two spare bedrooms."

The idea of living in this fussy, overfurnished house made sweat break out on Braden's forehead. God, he couldn't stand that!

Did he think a house for which Verona chose the furniture would be much different?

Braden cleared his throat, giving Verona another quick glance. She looked as surprised as he felt.

So, despite her own suggestions along these lines earlier, she hadn't put her mother up to this.

"I don't believe that's a good idea," Wallace said, his voice heavy with disapproval.

Clearly, Wallace also hadn't known his wife planned to bring this matter up now.

Bernice's smile faded. She looked at her husband. "Why ever not, dear? Braden is almost family now."

"Almost isn't the same as being family. Too many gossips in Goose Creek."

He turned to Braden, his face serious. "As I understand it, you're no nearer setting a wedding date than you were a couple of months ago?"

Why, he doesn't want me to marry Verona, Braden realized, surprise running through him. *He'd just as soon we never set a wedding date. And he doesn't want me living under his roof now.*

Was Wallace Holmes concerned for his daughter's virtue? If so, this was a recent development. He'd left Verona and Braden alone in the parlor and out on the veranda many a night with no apparent qualms.

"Yes, that's so, sir," Braden said, keeping his voice even and casual.

"I don't like this way of doing things," Wallace said, his voice even more disapproving. "When two people decide they want to marry, they should go ahead and do it."

"Wallace!" Bernice said, her voice scandalized at her husband's bluntness. "Verona and Braden haven't been engaged long."

Wallace's heavy, dark brows drew together. "Long enough. Long enough."

Verona suddenly stood up and threw her napkin down on the table. "Excuse me," she said in clipped tones. "I'm not very hungry."

She turned and left the room. In a few moments, Braden heard the front door open, then close.

Damn and blast! How could Verona leave him alone with her parents when her father was in this kind of mood?

"What in thunder has got into that girl?" Wallace growled. He picked up his fork and began eating.

Bernice Holmes sighed. Taking her husband's cue, she, too, picked up her fork and daintily speared a piece of meat.

"It's just bridal nerves, dear," she said soothingly. "I remember feeling like I was going to jump out of my skin before we were married."

Wallace lifted his head and scowled at her. "I don't

see how she could have bridal nerves when the wedding hasn't even been planned. Or the date set.''

He turned, his scowl encompassing Braden.

This had gone far enough, Braden decided.

He, too, rose and laid his napkin on the tablecloth. "Will you excuse me?" he asked politely.

Bernice gave him a relieved smile. "Oh, yes, Braden, go on and find Verona. I'm sure you two lovebirds have a lot to talk about.''

As Braden left the room, he distinctly heard Wallace Holmes's disgusted snort.

Verona was on the veranda, sitting stiffly in one of the big wicker chairs, her foot tapping the floor, her mouth set.

Braden sat down beside her. An hour earlier he'd dreaded this talk, known it was going to be difficult. Now, after what had just happened in the dining room, he dreaded it even more.

Verona kept facing straight ahead.

The silence drew out.

He had to break it. Braden reached for Verona's slender hand, enfolded it in his own. It was cold and limp in his grasp, but at least she didn't jerk it away.

"You're looking very pretty today," he told her.

In fact, he hadn't noticed her appearance until just now.

But she did look pretty, as always. Her pale yellow gown flattered her fair skin, and every one of her blond curls was in place.

"Thank you," she said remotely, keeping her head turned away.

Braden sighed in exasperation. "Verona, we need to talk. We *have* to talk," he emphasized.

She darted a quick, angry look at him. "We're *always* talking. Talking, talking, talking! I'm sick of it. I want to *do* something!"

"Do you think I don't?"

"I'm beginning to wonder. You don't seem to mind this Damask woman stopping our plans in their tracks."

She gave him another irate look. "Of course, that might have something to do with her being young and pretty . . . and living under the same roof as you."

Guilt and anger surged over Braden, with guilt the strongest. "That's a hell of a thing to say to your fiancé!"

Did he really feel that outraged? There was truth in what Verona said.

But not the way Verona meant it. As if he'd bedded Damask and planned to keep on doing it.

He'd had those desires.

But he hadn't acted on them. And didn't intend to.

Verona gave him a cool look. "I believe any woman would think the same thing under the circumstances."

"Don't you trust me?"

The instant the words were out of his mouth, he wished them back. He'd kissed Damask . . . more than once.

Verona tossed her blond curls. "I thought I could, but this has been going on too long now."

A muscle jerked in Braden's jaw. "Only a few weeks. I see no way of hurrying things along. I found out today a lot of the townspeople are against me on this."

"What? Who?" she demanded.

Braden told her what had happened in the barbershop. And of his visit to Harold later.

She sat tapping her foot again, her face closed and angry. And again, there was that elusive something in her expression he couldn't define.

It was like a blend of confusion and doubt . . . and a touch of fear and regret. Why did he find that hard to understand? With what had been going on, no wonder she felt those things.

Braden took a deep breath and said what had been pressing on his mind most of the day.

"Maybe we should just forget our plans for the house. Let the inn stay."

She gasped, jumped to her feet, and stood facing him, her hands on her hips. "You promised me that house where the inn stands, and that's what I want!"

He'd had about all he could take for one day.

"Is that the only reason you want to marry me? To get your mansion on that hill?" he asked her just as hotly.

She stared at him, the anger draining from her face, replaced by pallor. Now she, too, looked guilty, as if he'd just discovered the truth about their relationship.

"Of course not!" she said angrily. "Why would you think such a thing of me?"

"Because that seems to be all you can talk about every time we're together," he rebutted.

"Every woman wants a house of her own! And up until now you wanted to build there as much as I did. *You're* the one who thought of it in the first place."

Braden swallowed as her telling point hit home.

"I know, but I'm beginning to think it isn't worth all the hassle. There are lots of pretty places to build. What about that nice little rise on the west side, where we've looked at the sunset many a time?"

She glared at him. "I don't *want* any other house. Any other place. That's the best spot in town, and you know it."

"Yes, it is, but that isn't the only consideration."

"Do you really think half the town is going to fight you on this?" she asked incredulously.

"How do I know? As a businessman, I can't afford to risk the bad will of the community."

"So you're actually afraid of a bunch of gossipy townspeople?"

"No! That's not it." Braden paused.

"Then, what is it?" Verona prodded.

"I don't *want* the townspeople to think badly of me," he said, tight-lipped, hating to admit it but knowing it was true.

Verona gave him another incredulous look. "But didn't you come back here to show all the people who treated you badly as a child that you were a big success now?"

Braden drew a deep breath and let it out. "Yes. I did. But . . . things have changed."

"*What* things?" she demanded. "Don't tell me. I already know. That Damask woman coming here."

Braden couldn't deny it. They looked at each other for a moment.

She pursed her lips. "I'm sure there's also gossip about you and that woman staying in the inn together."

Braden frowned. "I can't figure you out today. A few minutes ago, you acted like you had no idea your mother was going to suggest me moving in here. Now you're all for it."

For a moment, that blend of confusion and other emotions came across her face. Then it disappeared. She drew herself up.

"I realized my mother was right. My parents aren't going to let the town make a laughingstock out of me."

"Don't be ridiculous," he snapped. "No one's spreading that kind of gossip."

"How can you be sure?" she countered. "Until today, you didn't know they were talking about you and that woman fighting over the inn."

Braden suddenly remembered the moment in the barbershop when he'd called Damask by her first name and Durward's glance had sharpened.

Verona could be right about this.

Hell, Verona's parents were right, too. He should move out of the inn, set a date for their wedding in the near future, and marry Verona.

And then what? Move in here with her? Or build a house somewhere else, no matter how much she protested?

Neither of those solutions appealed to him.

Like Verona, he, too wanted to live on that hill overlooking the town.

No other place would do.

But he was no longer sure he wanted to build a mansion there.

With nothing settled, Braden left Verona standing on the veranda and went to the stables. Confusion and anger filling him, he urged Jasper into a gallop heading home.

Home! He had to stop thinking about the inn as home. It wasn't his home; it never had been.

It was the closest thing to a home you had, growing up. After your sister left, Ada and Flora gave you your only taste of love and family life.

Yes, that was true. And he was grateful. But it had nothing to do with his present predicament. The inn was old. It had outlived its usefulness. The old always had to go, to make room for the new. That was the way of life everywhere.

So why was he having these doubts now? He hadn't

before Ada's death, when he'd almost had her talked into selling to him.

But then the town hadn't been against his plans. The town hadn't *known* about his plans. He wanted not only the townspeople's respect but also their liking. His present path didn't seem to be making that happen.

What you want to do isn't right, a voice that sounded like Ada's whispered in his mind's ear. *The inn belongs on that hill.*

He swallowed, felt gooseflesh rising.

He'd worked too hard to give it all up now. If he didn't build that mansion where Verona wanted it, he'd lose her. The most beautiful girl in town, her father the most prosperous farmer in three counties.

Marrying her, building the house, would make all his dreams come true.

The whisper came again

Maybe it's time to change your dreams. . . .

Carefully holding a jar of soup, Verona let herself into Harold's yard. She'd driven the buggy to town and left it at the livery stable, just a block away.

The midafternoon sun was still warm on her back. Braden had left about two hours before.

She tried not to think about their argument. She'd angrily accused him and he'd accused her right back. It had left her feeling confused and angry and even more unsettled.

And had also made her realize she'd have to do something herself or she'd never have her house on the hill overlooking the town.

Never have Braden for a husband, she'd hastily amended.

Of course she wanted that, too. No matter what

her mother said, surely after the first few times, what women and men did together in bed wouldn't be so unpleasant.

At least, then, she wouldn't have to pretend a passion she didn't feel. Would she? No, of course not.

Yes, and maybe you want to look down on the town just a little bit yourself. Prove once and for all that your family is as good as any around.

Verona shrugged. Maybe she did. She guessed she hadn't forgotten those early days when her family was struggling just to get by.

That Damask woman might be gathering sympathy from the townspeople, but she wasn't getting help from them. Harold was the only one who'd helped her and Harold was laid up with the grippe. But soon he'd be back at the inn, working with Damask.

Verona decided she needed to pay Harold a visit.

She told Mama it was time she started doing a few things for the community, since she'd soon be one of the town's leading matrons. She asked her mother to show her how to make the delicious chicken noodle soup for which she was famous.

Mama wouldn't allow Ruby to attempt that recipe. In fact, Mama still did much of the cooking because she enjoyed it and because Papa insisted.

Mama had been delighted. Verona had stood over the hot stove for an hour and a half, measuring and stirring. To her gratified relief, the finished product had smelled and tasted almost as good as her mother's.

She hoped it softened Harold up enough so that her plan would work.

Her first knock on Harold's door went unanswered. The second time she knocked louder, and from somewhere inside she heard a dog start yapping.

A voice bellowed, "Come in!"

The voice sounded grumpy, but she recognized it as Harold's.

Verona turned the knob and the door opened. At once a small black and white dog jumped up on her, still yapping, its tail wagging frantically.

"Get down!" she told it in low tones.

It obeyed but stayed right beside her, whining.

She walked into the small entry. To the left was an open doorway.

"Mr. Kirk?" she called.

"Come on in," the same voice said, its tones still annoyed.

She hesitated. If he was in a bad mood, it might not be a good time to set her proposition before him. But she couldn't sit around any longer, waiting for Braden to do something.

Verona smoothed her skirt and felt her curls, then, the dog following, she went to the open doorway.

Since she'd lived in Goose Creek all her life, she knew Harold Kirk. She'd seen him around town and at church.

He sported several days' growth of gray beard, and his hair was rumpled as if he'd recently been sleeping.

His sour look changed to a startled one. No wonder. He certainly hadn't expected to see *her*.

Verona smiled widely and held out the jar. "I heard you were sick and I brought you some chicken noodle soup. I made it myself."

His startled look intensified. "That's neighborly of you, Miss Holmes. I didn't expect to see you and Braden both on the same day."

He motioned to a chair close by his bed. "Sit down."

Verona did, carefully arranging her skirts so they wouldn't get wrinkled. Since Harold hadn't told her what to do with it, she still held her soup jar.

The dog settled down beside her with a satisfied sigh, putting its head on her slipper.

Harold laughed. "Towser's taken a shine to you, looks like."

She smiled and reached down to pat the dog. "He's a cute little thing," she said. He was, she realized. Her family had never owned anything but big farm dogs.

"Would you like some soup now?" she asked hopefully.

He shook his head. "Thanks just the same, but I'm not hungry. Flora brought me some earlier."

"Oh," Verona said, chagrined that someone else had gotten here first.

Without the soup to put Harold in a mellow mood, her plan wouldn't be so easy to implement. She'd just have to lead up to it gradually.

"You're looking good," she said brightly. "You'll soon be up and about."

He shook his head, his mouth turning down at the corners. "Doc says I got to stay here another week."

"Oh, that's too bad," Verona sympathized. She took a deep breath. "You've probably been doing too much. All that work up at the inn is too hard for a man your age."

Harold frowned at her. "I wasn't doing anything too hard. And I'm not that old, either, young lady."

Verona bit her lip, realizing she'd made a mistake. "Oh, no, you're not really *old,*" she said quickly. "I just meant that kind of work takes several men to do it."

Harold nodded. "Lot of it does. And Edmond is rounding some men up to help."

His eyes glinted, and he gave her a sideways look that held a touch of triumph.

Verona's eyes narrowed. Her lips pressed together.

Maybe Edmond would find others willing to work for nothing and maybe he wouldn't. The townspeople were probably gossiping about Braden and Damask living under the same roof. But she doubted if many people would openly criticize Braden about the inn, since he was now the most well-to-do businessman in Goose Creek.

She needed to stop pussyfooting around and get down to business.

Verona summoned another smile. "Mr. Kirk, I want to offer you a business proposal."

"A business proposal? Your papa need some work done?"

"No," she hastened on. "I want to give you the opportunity to do the fine carpentry work on the new house Braden plans to build."

He gave her another surprised look. "He's decided to build his house somewhere else?"

Verona's smile faded. "No, of course not."

Harold grinned. "Young lady, you shouldn't be in a hurry to make such offers. 'Pears to me that house may never get built up there on the hill. Did Braden send you? I can't believe he'd do that after—"

The front door opened. "Pop!" a young male voice called. "You got some company."

Footsteps sounded in the hall. Verona turned her head toward the door. Into the room came Edmond and Damask.

The little dog jumped up and ran over to Edmond, whining a welcome.

"Why, hello, Verona," Edmond said, surprise evident in his face. He bent to pet the dog.

Verona managed a smile, while inside she raged. Why did they have to come now? "I . . . just brought your father some soup." She held up the jar.

"How are you, Damask?" Harold asked. Affection

and respect were in his voice as he greeted the other woman.

Damask's smile and voice were warm. "I'm fine. I've got some of Flora's fresh-baked yeast rolls to go with the soup she brought earlier."

She smiled at Verona as if they'd never exchanged those nasty comments in the inn's front yard. "Seems Harold will have enough soup for a while."

"Yes," Verona croaked. She *had* to get out of here! She stood, holding out the jar to Edmond. He took it.

Damask wore a faded old calico dress and a worn bonnet. Her hands were red and rough from hard work.

Verona asked herself how she could be worried about this woman and Braden living in the same residence.

She was a lady from a prosperous family. Damask was . . . nothing.

Verona felt a flash of shame at that spiteful thought, but held her head up high. "I was just leaving. Goodbye, Mr. Kirk," she said, trying for dignity. "I hope you're soon back to health."

His eyes gleamed at her. "Oh, I will be, missy, never fear. I'll be up there working on that old inn again before you know it."

Verona pressed her lips together to keep from showing her anger.

"It . . . was nice seeing you," she said in the general direction of Edmond and Damask.

"I have to get back to work," Edmond said. "I just came by to see if you were all right, Pop."

"Verona, since it's so close, would you mind taking these books back to the library and getting me a couple more?" Harold asked. "Geneva knows what I like."

Oh, hell and damn! Verona fumed, then caught herself. She had to watch her temper.

"I can do that, Pop," Edmond said.

"No, you need to get back to work. I'm sure Verona doesn't mind."

Forcing a pleasant expression on her face, she turned back, took the two books.

The gleam in Harold's eyes was stronger.

Why, he'd done this on purpose just to annoy her!

She opened the door and Towser bounded over, yapping eagerly.

"Towser, come back here, you can't go," Edmond said.

He gave Verona a surprised look. "He usually doesn't much like women."

Verona managed another smile. "I guess I should feel flattered."

Edmond grinned at her. "Yep, you should."

Walking toward the library, still fuming, Verona had a strange thought. She wished Harold had looked at her as he had Damask. As if she were a *real* lady, one he liked and respected.

Don't be ridiculous, she told herself. You are a real lady. Damask is just a poor relation of that old woman who died. You've got more than she'll ever have.

She wished she could truly believe that.

Geneva looked up when Verona entered the library, giving Verona the third surprised look she'd had that day.

She explained her errand, and Geneva hurried off to find Harold's new books.

Verona didn't know Geneva very well. They'd gone to school together but weren't friends. She envied Geneva, Verona thought, then was amazed.

How could she envy her? Geneva worked all day at a boring job that didn't pay much.

But she was independent. She had her own house in back of the library and didn't answer to anyone. For a minute that seemed like heaven.

Verona reminded herself she wanted a lot more than those things. A lovely house, nice clothes, a fine carriage. And to realize that dream, she'd either have to stay at home forever or marry Braden.

Or someone else who could give her all those things.

But she'd already turned down the other men who could.

Russell Gifford's face floated into her mind, grinning hatefully at her just as he had the other day. She gritted her teeth. Was she crazy? Russell had been her childhood pal, but now she couldn't stand him. Besides, he was far from rich.

"Here, these should do Harold for a few days. He reads more than anyone I know—except me." Geneva laughed. "Do you like to read?"

Her question took Verona aback. She hadn't opened a book except the Bible and her mother's cookbook since she left school. "Not really," she said.

Geneva smiled warmly at her, and Verona realized the other woman was quite pretty when she smiled. "You're missing a lot."

Verona shrugged and picked up the books. "I'd better get these back."

"Tell Edmond he can return them when he has time," Geneva said.

"All right," Verona answered. Geneva's voice had changed when she said Edmond's name. Softened.

Was the town's old maid librarian sweet on Goose Creek's most handsome bachelor? Besides Braden, of course. And he couldn't be considered a bachelor, since he was engaged.

You'll be an old maid, too, if you don't marry Braden, she reminded herself. Pitied, like Geneva, no matter how independent she is.

She *would* marry Braden. And she would get all the things she wanted. Including her house where the inn now sat.

Are you sure that's what you really, truly want? Or just what you think you should want? Now that your father's made so much money.

What was wrong with her lately? Why did she keep having all these stupid doubts? Yes, she *did* truly want all these things. She'd be a fool not to. Any woman would be.

And to that end, she had to help things along.

She frowned as she remembered how Damask and Edmond's arrival had prevented her from presenting her proposal to Harold. Damask was probably still there, too, so she couldn't do it when she dropped off these books.

Anyway, Harold wasn't acting very receptive. That last question, about whether Braden had put her up to this, had rattled her. He might not have gone along with her offer that he not work on the inn any more in return for all the carpentry work on the new house.

Maybe she'd been saved from making a fool of herself. Yes, she probably needed to forget that idea and come up with another.

She set her mouth. Things had dragged on long enough.

It was time for drastic measures.

But what could get Damask and her family out of the inn for good? And the wonderful mansion built there?

Verona stopped her brisk walk as an idea came to her, one so startling it took her breath away. It scared her a little, too.

But the more she thought it over, the better it seemed. Yes, it would work . . . it would work perfectly.

A slow smile widened her mouth.

And no matter how he protested, she would make Braden agree to do it.

Chapter Fifteen

A loud thud from outside the inn, followed closely by another, brought Braden out of a deep sleep.

He sat bolt upright in bed.

Now what was Damask up to? He knew Harold wasn't working on the inn today. Only yesterday Harold had told him he'd be in bed for at least another week.

Glancing toward his window, he saw it was barely daylight. What could Damask be doing by herself so early in the morning to make that racket?

Probably something that might injure or kill her.

Braden jumped out of bed, quickly washed and dressed, and headed downstairs, mentally geared to forcibly stop Damask again if it was necessary.

He grimaced. Or at least *try* to stop her.

He jerked open the front door, then stopped in surprise.

Edmond and several other men, Durward Vail among them, were tearing down the old porch roof and throwing the rotten lumber and shingles on the lawn.

Durward glanced up, then quickly down again, but not before Braden saw the unfriendly expression in his eyes.

Braden's surprise turned to annoyance.

What in hell did they think they were doing?

That was obvious, wasn't it, he answered himself. They'd gotten a group together and were repairing the roof. No, they were *replacing* most of it.

"Excuse me," Braden heard Damask say from behind him. He turned.

She carried a tray holding several steaming cups of coffee, obviously meant for the workers.

She wasn't smiling. Neither was she frowning. She looked as if she were trying very hard to have no expression on her face.

Unsmiling himself, Braden moved aside to let her through.

"Here you are," Damask said brightly to the men. She set the tray on a small table against the wall. She wore one of her old work dresses and her hair was pulled back and tied in a scarf. But she was still beautiful.

"I can sure use that," Edmond said. He gave Damask a slow, appreciative smile as he walked over and picked up one of the cups.

Damask returned it, the smile lighting up her face.

Braden clenched his hands at his sides. For a moment, he wanted to punch Edmond.

Are you crazy? he asked himself, amazed at his sudden violent urge.

Edmond gave every young, attractive woman that kind of look. Besides, it was none of his business.

But he didn't have to like it.

He almost headed for work without breakfast, but

common sense stopped him. If he didn't eat, he'd have a throbbing headache by midmorning. And maybe food would calm him down.

Give him some idea of what he should do about this latest development.

You can't do a damn thing about it. Ada fixed that when she left such a ridiculous will.

Braden turned and headed for the kitchen. Emmy and Cory were eating breakfast. The milk pails sat on the worktable. Cory and Flora had already finished milking the cows. Flora was at the stove, her back turned. He took a couple of deep breaths, trying to get a hold on himself.

"Good morning, Mr. Braden," Emmy said, smiling. Cory also greeted him with a smile.

"Morning." He gave a general greeting to the three of them. Despite his roiling emotions, a small, warm feeling went through him. He liked these children. They weren't to blame for what their sister was allowing to be done.

He sat down and helped himself to eggs, bacon, and biscuits.

Flora placed a steaming cup beside his plate. She touched his arm, and he glanced up at her.

"Goose Creek Inn is not yet ready for to be torn down," she told him quietly.

He opened his mouth to refute her statement, then, with a glance at the children, closed it again. He wouldn't argue with them present. Besides, he couldn't wholly disagree with Flora. Not anymore. What angered him wasn't the repairs but the circumstances.

He didn't like Edmond and the others putting him in a bad light, he had to admit.

Flora took the coffeepot back to the stove, then seated herself.

Braden looked at his plate. He wasn't hungry, but he'd better eat. He picked up his fork, and Damask came into the kitchen.

"The men like the coffee, yah?" Flora asked.

"They certainly did," Damask said. She sat down, not looking at Braden.

If you can give Edmond a sweet smile, you ought to be able to spare one for me, he told her silently.

Then he told himself how irrational that was. He hadn't smiled at her, either.

The children made short work of their meal and hurried toward the door. "Don't you go bothering the men," Damask warned.

"We won't," they chorused, and disappeared. In a few moments, Braden heard the front door open and close again.

Naturally, the children would be fascinated with watching the work. It was nothing to them who did it.

Flora finished her meal and started on the cleanup.

"I'll do the dishes since you want to weed the garden," Damask offered.

Flora agreed and left.

Now he and Damask were alone in the big room. The silence lengthened. Braden looked with distaste at his plate of congealing eggs. He gulped down his coffee, pushed his chair back, and rose.

"Aren't you going to raise a ruckus?" Damask asked, still without lifting her eyes to his.

He stood there, looking at her bent head. Already, tendrils of springy auburn hair had worked themselves loose from their coil. He ached to reach down, let one of them curl around his finger. . . .

He pushed his chair in and stepped back.

"Why? It wouldn't change anything," he said, forcing his voice to stay low-pitched, reasonable.

Finally, she turned, looked at him.

The full force of her eyes with their dark fringe of lashes hit him, making him draw in his breath. He felt his pulse rate speed up.

"Anger would be a natural reaction to having your plans ruined."

"My plans aren't ruined," he said, hearing the lack of conviction in his voice. "Only delayed."

Her eyes flickered. "That may be," she conceded. "But if I saw you with a sledgehammer, advancing on the inn, I'd probably pick up a stick and stop you."

He winced at that, saw she'd noticed his reaction. Surprise danced over her features. Her mouth opened a little.

Her lips were so pink, so soft. So completely kissable.

"You don't like to picture the inn being torn down, do you?" she asked bluntly.

He felt his facial muscles tightening as he stared back at her.

"I have to go to the store," he finally said. He turned and left without a backward glance, but he felt her gaze on him as he walked across the room.

Opening the front door again, he saw the men were making rapid progress. A third of the old roof was down now.

Edmond smiled at him, but no one else did. Braden kept his gaze straight ahead as he walked down the steps, avoiding flying debris, and headed across the meadow.

This was an awkward situation. He didn't want to make enemies of any of the townspeople, but neither could he stand by and approve while they destroyed his dream.

That's funny, his mind told him. *You're the one who's the destroyer . . . or wants to be.*

No! That wasn't what he wanted.

What is it, then? You can't have your new house here without getting rid of the old building first.

Pushing the disquieting thoughts to the back of his mind, he was relieved when he got far enough away, he could no longer hear the men's crowbars and hammers.

At the store, he forced himself to greet his employees, then hurried into his office and closed the door.

Seated at his desk, he opened the big folder that held the building plans for his next store and tried to become engrossed in them.

His head soon began throbbing because he hadn't eaten breakfast, but he was still too disturbed to want anything to eat. Doggedly, he stared at his blueprints, his detailed drawings, until the pages blurred.

Finally, hunger pains struck, too. He glanced at the clock on the wall. Only ten o'clock. He lowered his head again. At twelve, he straightened the pages in the folder and put it away.

He dreaded returning to the inn, but he'd be damned if he'd stay away. He wouldn't let those men think they could run him off, make him feel in the wrong. The inn belonged to him as much as it did to Damask!

It doesn't belong to either of you, Ada's voice whispered in his head. *The inn belongs to the town . . . you and Damask are only its caretakers . . . it will outlast you . . . your grandchildren should play in it.*

Braden dropped the folder. Papers fanned out across the floor. Cursing, he bent to pick them up.

A knock sounded on his door. Not a timid one now. "Come in," Braden muttered.

Jacob entered, then stopped right inside the door. "Is anything wrong?" he asked.

Braden picked up the last of the papers and stood, placing them on the desktop. "No. Did you need to see me about something?"

Jacob hesitated, then nodded. "Sales fell off this last week," he said. "For the first time since the store opened."

Alarm went through Braden. Were townspeople boycotting the store because of what they perceived as his wrongful actions?

Would they go that far? Were their feelings about the inn that strong?

"Thank you, Jacob." Braden forced a smile. "Let's not worry about it yet. I'm sure it's only temporary."

Jacob's furrowed brow smoothed. "All right, Mr. Franklin."

He left, Braden right behind him.

Topping the hill, Braden saw with relief no one was outside working. Either they'd stopped for the day or gone home to eat.

Reaching the inn, he saw they'd made a lot of progress. That afternoon and another day, and the new porch roof would be finished.

Somebody had to pay for the new posts and shingles. He knew it wasn't Damask. Had the men taken up a collection and bought the materials? Worse yet, maybe others in the town had contributed.

Embarrassment flooded over Braden.

He was being put in an impossible position.

No one's putting you there. You're doing it yourself.

Glowering, he headed for the back, since the front porch was strewn with debris. He heard talk and laughter from the kitchen as soon as he opened the back door.

Oh, hell! He should have realized Flora would cook dinner for the men.

His stomach rumbled loudly, reminding him he hadn't eaten since the previous night. But he'd be damned if he'd eat with the men obviously enjoying themselves in the kitchen. He'd wait until they finished.

But they'd seen him, and now they turned and looked at him. Not very friendly glances, either, except for good-natured Edmond.

"Come, eat," Flora urged. "There is plenty of room."

Damask stood at the stove, dishing up food. She didn't turn.

Feeling very much the outsider, and not liking it a bit, Braden shook his head. "Thanks, but I'm not very hungry. I just came home to get something I forgot this morning."

His stomach again rumbled loudly and, irritated, he saw grins on more than one of the men's faces as he headed for the stairs.

Home. He'd called the inn home again.

What kind of man wants to lay waste to his own home?

Scowling, he hurried upstairs, then to his room. Leaving the door open, he jerked out his top bureau drawer, where he kept a few business papers, grabbing the first thing he saw.

Hearing a sound from the door, he glanced over.

Damask stood there. Her hair had come loose at the sides, her blue dress was smudged with dirt, and one pocket of her apron had a torn corner, where she must have snagged it. Her face was flushed.

All that made no difference. Standing there, twisting a corner of her apron around her finger, she was beautiful. She bit her lower lip, and Braden could feel the sensation in his own mouth, his teeth.

They stared at each other. Braden took a step toward her. "Damask . . ."

She whirled and left the room.

Braden followed.

She was walking quickly down the hall to the stairs, and he hurried to catch up with her. Finally, he did, reaching out to grasp her upper arm to stop her flight.

"What do you want?" he asked her.

The words were too evocative, making him think of all the things he wanted from her . . . all the things he could never have. . . .

She jerked her arm, trying to free it. "I want you to let me go!"

He did, and she started to walk away again. Once more he grabbed for her.

Her eyes flashed at him. "Will you stop that?"

"You must have had something to say to me or you wouldn't have come to my room."

Her gaze dropped. "It wasn't important," she muttered.

"I don't believe you." This time he wasn't releasing her until she told him.

Slowly, she raised her head, her glance meeting his. He felt jolted by her eyes. Those glowing gray orbs. They gazed into his own with such honesty, it took his breath away.

"I . . ." she paused and moistened her lips with her tongue.

Braden felt his body's automatic reaction.

"I only wanted to tell you," she continued in a rush, as if she had to get it all out before she lost her nerve, "that I don't want us to be . . . enemies."

Braden stared at her, the feel of her warm, pliant flesh delightful beneath his fingers, then regretfully released her. "How could we not be? If you get what you want, I'm going to be unhappy, and if I do, you will be.''

He realized he'd conceded she might get her way. Just a slip of the tongue, he told himself.

"I don't for the life of me understand why Ada set things up so that we had to be enemies.''

She bit her lip again, and once more he felt it all the way down his body. "I don't think that was Aunt Ada's purpose. She was too good a person to be that malicious. She loved both of us.''

"You're right," Braden admitted, "but if that's so, why did she do it? She must have had a reason.''

Damask's eyes darkened to a storm-cloud color. "Yes," she whispered, "I'm sure she did.''

He wanted her in his arms . . . he *had* to have her in his arms. His whole body throbbed with need.

"Damask . . .'' His voice was a whisper, too. He reached for her, and she moved willingly into his embrace. His arms closed around her, and a shudder went through him. She felt so right, so perfect. As if this were the way it was meant to be.

But it isn't. You know that.

He ignored that warning voice.

She belonged in his arms.

For long moments they stood like that, her head resting against his chest, her soft body pressed against his hardness.

Tenderness welled up inside him. He wanted not only to make love with her but to keep her from all harm, protect her always. . . .

He looked down at her head, covered with the scarf. He plucked the scarf away, ran his hand over the shining, yielding waves.

She moved against him, pushing herself closer.

"Raise your head," he whispered. "I want to look at you.''

She stiffened against him, and he thought she was going to pull away. Instinctively, his arms tightened around her.

Then she lifted her head, her soft lips slightly open, gazing at him.

This is wrong and you know it. She didn't care, she couldn't help it. A force stronger than morality was driving her.

How could she ever have thought she loved Warren? Those puny feelings were nothing like the way she felt now, held close to Braden's warm, hard body.

She could feel his arousal pressing into her stomach. It inflamed her own desire. Her heart was pounding in her chest, her breath coming faster.

When Braden lowered his head, she raised her own to meet him halfway. He smelled clean and good, like soap and the outdoors. The first brush of his lips against hers was as light as a butterfly's touch, but it sang through all her nerve endings with its promise of more to come.

She opened her lips to him before he could urge her to do so, hearing his sharp intake of breath. He clutched her closer, pressed his lips harder on hers, pushed his tongue inside her mouth. Explored the soft warmth opened to him, retreated, then pushed again.

Damask gasped. Heat flooded her body, pooled in her lower parts. Eagerly, she returned his kisses, wanted more. He finally released her mouth, his lips moving down her throat to the pulsing hollow there. . . .

The sound of men's voices and laughter came up the stairwell. Then the slam of the front door.

Damask tried to cling to the dream she was lost in, trying desperately to stay locked in Braden's arms.

But she couldn't.

She dropped her arms from around him, tried to pull away.

For a moment, he resisted her tug. She could see he was still lost in the dream, his eyes unfocused.

She tugged harder, and clarity came back to his eyes, his face tightened. He let go of her too suddenly, and she swayed a little. He reached for her to steady her, but she moved back out of his reach.

They stood, looking at each other.

Damask pressed her lips together. She wouldn't go running off, not this time. She had to say something to him, make some acknowledgment of what had just happened between them.

"I'm . . . sorry," she began, then stopped.

No, she wasn't sorry at all. She should be; of course she should be. But she wasn't.

"I . . . we . . . can't keep on letting this happen. It isn't right. You're engaged."

"Don't you think I know that all too well?" he asked.

Of course he did. She'd sounded like an idiot.

"I have to get back to the store," Braden said, his voice strained, his face tight.

Her face flamed. Maybe *she* had no regrets they'd kissed, but he did.

"I must go help Flora in the kitchen." She almost fled down the stairs. Halfway down, she stopped and turned toward where he still stood.

"I saved you a plate of food in the warming oven," she said, then hurried on down.

Braden watched her go, so full of conflicting emotions, he couldn't separate them out.

Damask had said she was sorry for what had happened between them. She'd looked as if she felt that way, too.

He wasn't sorry. No matter how wrong it had been, he wasn't sorry.

His body was still hard and needy. Still desperately wanting her. And that wasn't all. She roused more than a physical hunger in him. She touched him emotionally, too. Tender feelings toward her were still very much with him.

I saved you a plate of food.

Why did that sound so intimate? Like something a wife would say to her husband?

He shook his head, trying to brush away that unexpected, crazy thought.

Instead, another thought came.

Maybe it wasn't so crazy. Maybe it wasn't crazy at all.

Chapter Sixteen

Wishing her stomach weren't tied up in knots, wishing she could enjoy the soft spring evening, Damask walked slowly through the woods toward the creek. She had plenty of time for what she wanted to do.

No, not *wanted* to do. What she *had* to do.

She'd spent the afternoon keeping the men replacing the roof supplied with cold, fresh well water and Flora's fresh-baked kuchen and coffee.

By the time the men stopped for the day, it was evident they'd be finished tomorrow, unless it rained.

This morning, when the men had shown up, she'd been delighted, but she was also dismayed because she couldn't pay them. They'd told her to consider this a community service. They didn't want the old inn torn down and assured her most of the town residents felt the same way.

Damask had finally, reluctantly, agreed. She should be overjoyed. And she was, of course. Their help was heaven sent. But she couldn't consider the work a gift.

And all afternoon, she'd silently chastised herself for letting Braden kiss her again. For kissing him back. For wanting more than a kiss.

How can we be anything but enemies? he'd asked her.

He was right. Even if he weren't engaged to Verona, they could never be . . . lovers. They couldn't even be friends. The inn stood between them like a mountain.

She swallowed. And after she told him what she planned to do. . . .

Before the men went home, they'd offered her a proposition that stunned her. But she'd accepted it. She would have been a fool not to.

Braden had come back to the inn and eaten supper and then headed out this way, without exchanging more than a dozen words with anyone. She hadn't even tried to talk to him there. She wanted more privacy.

But contrarily, Damask was also nervous about being alone with him, especially out in the woods.

She'd explain why she came at once, because if they were alone together for more than five minutes, they'd probably be in each other's arms just as they'd been earlier.

Unless they were fighting. Which was a definite possibility after she told him her plans.

Pushing back the last bit of underbrush, Damask came out into the small clearing by the creek and drew in her breath.

As she'd hoped, Braden sat on the creek bank, gazing out over the water.

He must have heard her, for his head jerked around. A look of surprise came over his face, then he turned away again.

You certainly got a big welcome, she told herself wryly.

But what did she expect? Naturally, after what had happened earlier today, he'd be trying to avoid her.

Just as she should be trying to avoid him.

And she would. But she had to do this. She owed him that much.

Damask stood there for a few moments, looking at him. She'd have to join him, since he apparently had no intention of rising.

She walked over and sat down beside him, being careful not to sit close. But Braden moved away from her another few inches just the same. Like her, he was taking no chances.

She'd intended to tell him what she must and then leave. But now she reconsidered.

Maybe she'd better lead up to it gradually. There was no point in making this any more unpleasant than it had to be.

And maybe she was fooling herself. It would be impossible to make this conversation pleasant. She just wanted to be with him a little longer.

And that was a dangerous longing she couldn't indulge.

"It's a beautiful evening," Damask said.

For a moment she thought he wasn't going to talk to her at all, but then he said, "Yes, it is."

Evening sounds filled the air around them. Birds sleepily settled themselves for the night with soft chirps. The bushes rustled as small animals found their way back to their shelters, and the creek made melodious noises as it flowed over the rocks in its bed.

She ought to move even farther away but couldn't be that obvious. What should she say next?

"My sister Peggy used to fish with me here," Braden said into the silence. "She could catch more fish than anyone I ever knew."

She was surprised at his words, his tone. Suddenly, she could picture him as a boy, like Cory, sitting here with his big sister as Cory sometimes sat with her.

"Do you ever see her now?" she asked.

"No. We lost touch years ago." His voice sounded wistful.

"Maybe you could find her," Damask suggested.

After a few moments of silence, Braden said, his voice strained, "Yes, maybe I could. But she's never come back to Goose Creek. She might not want to see me now."

"You'll never know until you try," Damask said, hearing the echo of her mother's voice in her words. How many times had she been told that growing up?

Damask felt a softness growing inside her and fought against it. Right now, she didn't want to feel sympathy for him or his miserable childhood. It would only make what she had to say harder.

But her hand went out and touched him on the shoulder, a small, comforting gesture. His warmth came through his shirt into her fingers, and at once she drew back her hand, moved farther away, exasperated at herself for not sticking to her resolve.

He gave her a quick glance, then looked away.

In a moment, she breathed easier again. He was wary, too. Nothing would happen between them this evening.

At least nothing of a romantic nature.

"I've always loved this place," she told him. "Everything about it. I didn't fish much that summer I visited, but I sat on this bank many a day with a book."

Braden glanced at her again. Her words, her tone, had been as wistful as his own about his sister.

He'd come here to be alone, to try to think things through to some kind of clarity. To try to figure out what to do. About both the mess with the inn and with his personal life.

He hadn't been worth a damn at the store this afternoon. He couldn't concentrate on anything because his troubled thoughts kept intruding.

But he couldn't be sorry Damask was here, although he wondered why she'd come. To talk about this physical attraction that drew them together like steel to a magnet whenever they were alone together?

Just as it had today in the upstairs hall.

Even now, when they were sitting a distance apart, he felt the pull between them and fought against it.

Did she believe talking would change anything? If so, she was wrong.

And maybe he was wrong. She could have come for an entirely different reason. He wouldn't think about it. He'd give her time, let her bring up whatever it was.

But he found he was curious about her relationship with Ada.

"How did you happen to come and visit here alone?"

Damask kept facing straight ahead. "I don't know exactly. Aunt Ada wrote and asked if I could come, and my parents let me."

That nostalgic sadness was still in her voice.

She loved this place. In just a short time it had become home to her.

She had no other home now.

Just as he had no home . . . except the inn.

The inn was the only real home he'd ever had.

That thought hit him with the force of a blow. He felt as if someone had punched him in the stomach.

You love this place, too. You want your fancy house on this hill, but you can't stand the thought of the inn being demolished to get that house.

No, he couldn't, he admitted. If he got his way, and Damask sold her family's share of the property to him, he wouldn't be able to do that. Or to see it done.

So what will you do? Concede defeat?

He clenched his jaw muscles so hard, a sharp pain hit him. Hell, he didn't know! He'd gotten where he was by making fast, sound decisions.

Now he was waffling around like a green boy.

Beside him, Damask cleared her throat. She moved a bit farther away.

He turned his head toward her. She was pleating a fold of her skirt between her fingers, her head bent.

She looked up and their glances met . . . and held. Her eyes were troubled. Once more he felt that peculiar spell stealing over him. His rational brain receded, allowing his emotions to take over. . . .

"Braden, I have something to tell you," Damask said, her voice resolute, each word clearly enunciated.

Relieved . . . yet disappointed, he said, "All right."

Her breasts rose and fell as she took a deep breath and then released it.

Braden realized he was watching those movements with fascination and jerked his head away.

"The men who worked at the inn today made a . . . business proposal."

Surprised, he turned toward her again. "What do you mean?"

She took another deep breath and released it. This time he kept his gaze slightly to the side of her face, but his awareness of her flowed through his veins just the same.

"They offered to lend me money for the materials to finish the inn repairs and to work to get it open again."

His surprise grew but no negative feelings. He

hadn't been expecting this, but it didn't bother him now. As it would have only that morning. "Is that right?"

She looked taken aback at his mild reaction. No wonder. This sudden change on his part was a bit unsettling to him, too.

"Yes. A majority of the townspeople don't want to see the inn go. They're willing to finance the rest of the repairs and to do the work to insure that doesn't happen."

"Why are you telling me this? You could have just gone ahead and arranged everything. You know I can't stop you."

What would she say if he told her he no longer even wanted to stop her? That, in fact, he wanted to share her dream. But he couldn't do that yet.

Not until he'd talked to Verona. Sometime in these last few minutes another realization had come to him.

He couldn't marry Verona. He didn't love her.

Her gaze wasn't focused directly on his now, either. "I know. But I couldn't do that. It wouldn't be fair to you."

He was still battling with his turmoil of emotions, and her words made shame go over him. Was she worried about being fair to him? When he'd never had those concerns for her?

"That's very decent of you," he finally said.

Surprise and relief evident in her voice, she asked, "Aren't you going to fight me on this?"

"How?" He was relieved his voice sounded so calm and reasonable when inside he felt just the opposite.

She shrugged. "I don't know, but I never imagined you'd have this reaction. Don't you even care?"

He burned to tell her of the awakening he'd just had. Tell her he no longer intended to fight for his former goals. That his goals had changed . . . and she could be included in them if she wanted . . .

But first he had to face Verona.

"I . . . can't talk about it right now," he told her honestly. "But you go ahead with your plans."

Damask let out her breath and got to her feet. A small smile curved her mouth. "I'm glad that's over. You don't know how I dreaded it."

She was going to leave. He had to think of some way to stop her.

Was he out of his mind? Let her leave! That was best for them both.

He got up, too, and smiled at Damask. "We've done enough fighting."

"That's true. I hate fighting."

They stood only a few feet apart. No farther than they had earlier that day at the inn. No farther than they had before, when they'd ended up in each other's arms.

All he had to do was move toward her, hold out his arms. . . .

You're pretty sure of yourself. What if this time she slaps your face?

He didn't think she would, but he didn't move those few feet toward her, although every muscle in his legs and feet strained forward.

He glanced up, where the sunset painted the sky with glowing color. "Looks like tomorrow will be a fair day. The men should be able to get the roof finished."

Damask's eyes were still filled with surprise. And maybe something else. Disappointment?

"Yes. I hope so. Good night, Braden."

"Good night." He watched as she turned away, found the path through the woods, and disappeared from view.

Braden let out his breath, still fighting himself to keep from following her, holding her close against his heart again.

He should have walked back to the inn with her. It would soon be dark. But he'd wait a few minutes, give her a head start.

Sitting down on the bank of the creek again, he stared unseeingly across its width.

He expected Verona would have a holy fit when he told her he wanted to break their engagement. He couldn't avoid that . . . he'd proposed to Verona of his own free will. Promised her his future . . . promised her a lifetime of love.

But that promise couldn't be fulfilled if the love had died.

Or had never been there in the first place.

Maybe Verona would accept this . . . admit her own feelings for Braden didn't run deep. He didn't know.

But one thing he *did* know. Damask deserved to live in the inn she loved. Run it again if she wanted to.

And there might be a future for them down the road.

If he was very, very lucky.

Relief still coursed through Damask as she made her way back to the inn. It was hard to believe Braden had calmly accepted the idea that she was going to open the inn again. She'd expected anger and arguments.

She frowned. He didn't seem to care what she did anymore. He'd seemed remote, or as if he was holding his feelings in check.

Which was exactly what she was doing. And if he'd

made one move toward her, she wouldn't have been able to resist him. But Braden hadn't taken that step.

And she wished he had, no use denying it.

But that was her foolish, emotional side. Her sensible side was glad. Whatever was between them could never grow because Braden was already spoken for. And now it seemed he was at last realizing that.

Pain washed over her.

She fought it. She would put her feelings out of her mind and concentrate on the important things. It looked as if she and the children could have a life in Goose Creek after all.

Her problems had been solved with the town's offer of help.

No, that wasn't true. Not *all* her problems . . . not the most important one . . . not the one that couldn't be solved. . . .

As much as she loved the inn, she loved Braden more.

Damask stopped short on the path, the words spinning through her mind.

She loved Braden.

No! Just because her physical desire for him was so strong it overwhelmed her good sense when they were together didn't mean she loved him. It *couldn't* mean that. She wouldn't let it!

Braden loved Verona. He felt only desire for her, and that didn't mean anything. Warren had desired her, too, but had dropped her like a hot potato when he realized marrying her would mean taking on the responsibility of Cory and Emmy.

How could she have these feelings for Braden so soon after her experience with Warren? Hadn't she learned anything about protecting her heart?

Men often felt desire for more than one woman.

And they assuaged that desire outside of marriage. Then went on to marry the women they loved.

Sickness went through her as those thoughts made what she and Braden had together seem ugly.

Braden had said no words of love to her ever. He felt nothing for her except unrequited lust. She'd been a fool to let him kiss her, to kiss him back. More than once. More than twice!

Yesterday, she'd brazenly kissed him when the men were downstairs, just feet away. . . .

Verona was Braden's intended wife. Verona was the one in the right.

All *she* had was her self-respect . . . and other people's respect for her. And she could have lost that in the blink of an eye if anyone had seen her and Braden embracing.

This foolish emotion she thought she felt for Braden had to be buried deep and never revealed to anyone.

Least of all to herself. Because she couldn't survive if she admitted she loved him and he was never going to return that love.

Chapter Seventeen

The next evening, after his talk with Damask at the creek, Braden sat in the Holmeses' stuffy parlor. He loosened his cravat for the second time in a few minutes and recrossed his legs.

He hated this room, but he had no other choice. He didn't want to suggest going out on the veranda for fear Verona would get the wrong idea.

Although lately she hadn't taken any opportunity that presented itself as an excuse for kissing and cuddling. Of course, neither had he.

As if to emphasize this point, Verona hadn't seated herself beside him but was perched on the uncomfortable little gilt chair she often sat on.

He'd deliberately waited until after the supper hour. Verona's parents had been in the parlor, and both had given him surprised looks at his late arrival but had soon excused themselves and gone upstairs.

Leaving him alone with his intended wife. He winced inwardly at the thought.

After tonight that would no longer be true.

Looking at Verona's perfect blond curls, her rose silk gown, her carefully tended hands, her pretty, pouting mouth, a vision of Damask's tumbled autumn fire of hair, her wide, wonderful smile, came into Braden's mind's eye.

How could he ever have believed he and Verona would be happy together? He should have realized that was impossible after the day he'd repaired the inn roof and been overcome with his fear of high places. Damask had gotten him through that, and he'd confessed to her he'd never be able to tell Verona about this problem he had.

If he couldn't share that with her, how could he share his life?

He'd blinded himself to his true feelings, his true motives. He'd seen only how decorative Verona was, how suitable a hostess she'd be for a man in his position.

Yes, what a fool he'd been.

Verona stopped fiddling with her dress, glanced his way. She took a deep breath, then gave him a brilliant smile, which didn't look natural. She seemed as unsettled as he was tonight.

She rose, came over, and stood before him, then leaned over and put a small hand on either of his shoulders and gazed into his eyes.

Her gown's neckline dipped low. He could see part of her lush breasts, as he was sure she intended. But, as always when she behaved in this manner, her actions didn't quite ring true. She seemed to be forcing herself.

Before he could move, she'd pressed her mouth against his, her small tongue teasing at his lips.

Oh, Lord, why was she doing this now? He wanted desperately to push her away but didn't. He wouldn't humiliate her by making it obvious she no longer held any sexual attraction for him.

But he couldn't passionately return her kiss, then the next minute announce he wanted to break their engagement.

How was he going to do that, anyway, without revealing another woman now held his interest? She already suspected as much.

He doubted if she'd accept the other, equally important reason—that they weren't right for each other. Never had been.

Relief swept over him when, after a few moments, Verona drew back and straightened up.

She tilted her head and pursed her lips into a little pout. "What's wrong, darling?" she asked, her voice falsely sweet. "Are you tired tonight?"

"A little." He paused. "And I need to talk to you about something important."

"I need to talk to you, too," she said. "About something *very* important."

Surprised, he stared at her. Did she suspect what he was going to say? No, of course not, or she wouldn't be acting like she wanted him to carry her off to bed.

Or, rather, *trying* to act that way and not succeeding very well.

Giving him another slow smile, Verona sat down beside him and slipped her hand into his.

Again, he had the distinct feeling that even more so than usual, she was having to make herself do these things.

Braden was beginning to sweat. No way could he gradually lead up to what he must say. He'd have to come out with it and take what came.

And he should have done it as soon as her parents left the room.

Verona reached up and loosened his cravat. "I

don't know why you're all dressed up,'' she said in sugar-sweet tones. ''Won't you be more comfortable if you take off that awful thing?''

Following words with action, she slipped the cravat off, tossing it aside, then unbuttoned his shirt, her fingers lingering on his neck.

She gave him another too sweet smile. ''There, isn't that better? Of course, it would be even nicer if you had no shirt on at all.''

This had gone far enough. Braden grasped her hand and moved it back to her side. ''Please don't do that.''

He heard the stiffness and strain in his voice.

Her smile dimmed. ''I don't know what's wrong with you lately, Braden. I was only trying to be nice.''

''Verona,'' he said, his voice strangled, ''I have to tell you something!''

She tilted her head. ''Later. Ladies first.'' She gave him an arch smile that rang as false as her previous actions and words.

Again, he saw her intake of breath, then its release, as if she were gathering her nerve.

Her voice very even and precise, as if the words had been memorized so she wouldn't forget them, she said, ''I have thought of a perfect solution to our problems with that Damask person.''

''Verona!'' Braden started to rise, get away from her smothering closeness, tell her what he must.

''No, wait! You must listen to my plan.''

He heard the edge of panic in her voice, and the next words tumbled out in a rush.

''All you have to do is burn down the inn the next dark night.''

Disbelief swept over him. Surely, he hadn't heard her correctly. He jerked himself up, stared at her. ''What did you say?''

Verona tilted her head again. Her chest rapidly rose and fell.

"You must burn down the inn."

Braden's incredulity turned to stunned horror. "Have you lost your mind?"

"No," she said, again in that precise manner that sounded so unnatural, as if she'd learned it by rote. "It can't fail. With the inn gone, the land won't be worth much. She will have to sell her family's share to you. And then we can build our lovely house."

He was caught in a nightmare. "I can't believe you're saying these things."

Verona narrowed her eyes. "It's the only practical solution."

"Burning people in their beds is a practical solution to you?"

Frowning, she tossed her head. "Of course I didn't mean for you to do that! You'll have to think of some way to get them out of the building."

Braden's mouth set into a hard line. "I don't have to think of anything. I'm going to forget you ever mentioned such a horrible plan."

Her frown deepened. She jumped up and put her hands on her hips. "You're a coward!" she accused. "You're afraid to do it!"

He kept on staring at her, feeling as if he'd never seen her before.

"Verona, I once thought we were two of a kind—both selfish and ready to grasp what we wanted. An ornate mansion, all of Goose Creek looking up to us in every way. But I was wrong. How could you think I'd even consider what you're suggesting?"

She drew herself up as tall as possible and folded her hands across her chest. "If you won't take this chance to solve our problems, I will not marry you."

Relief swept over him in a tidal wave.

My God, *she* had done it for him! He didn't have to.

"Then it's over," he said, not able to keep the relief from his voice. "I came here tonight to tell you I wanted to break our engagement. I don't love you. And it's obvious you don't love me."

Verona's mouth fell open. Her eyes widened in surprise. She blinked and moved back a step.

"I was right—you and that Damask woman *are* involved with each other!"

Braden's relief fled. He should have stopped her earlier. He should have told her he'd realized they weren't right for each other. Dread filled him. Now it was too late.

No, it had always been too late. She wouldn't have believed him then, either. She still would have pounced on Damask as the reason.

Of course Damask was a big part of it. But not the whole. He could never marry Verona now even if he'd never seen Damask.

"Verona, calm down. Let's talk this over like sensible people."

Fierce anger burned in her eyes. "There's nothing to talk over. You promised to marry me, to build me a beautiful house on that hill. And you're going to! Mama and Papa will make you!"

His dread grew. "Verona, *you* broke the engagement first."

"I didn't mean it. You know that."

He stared at her, realization going through him. She'd thought threatening to break their engagement would make him do what she wanted.

"You were trying to force me to commit a terrible crime, and it didn't work," he cut her off, his voice grim.

He wished to God she hadn't been bluffing. That she'd truly wanted out as much as he did.

"I don't care!" she shrilled. "You promised me! Papa will take you to court if you don't marry me!"

"I doubt that," Braden said, desperately trying to keep this from getting out of hand. "I don't think he even wants me to marry you."

"Mama does! *I* do!"

"You don't want *me*. I don't think you ever did. You want only what I can give you."

Verona clenched her jaw. "Marriage is a bargain between two people. I . . . I'll give you what you want in bed and you'll give me a lovely house, nice clothes, a carriage."

The layers were being peeled off Verona one by one. The more he saw, the less he liked her.

"You'll 'give me what I want in bed'? I thought you wanted me, too."

She shrugged. "Oh, I just pretended all that. Mama says I'll get used to it after a while, and it won't be so bad."

"Get used to it? Won't be so bad?" he asked, wondering why he bothered. They were finished. "I expect a little more than that from the woman I marry."

Anger flared in her eyes again. "Yes, I bet you do! No doubt you've already had it from that Damask woman."

Remembering the passionate kisses he and Damask had shared, he couldn't stop a flicker of guilt across his face.

Verona drew her breath in sharply. "I knew I was right! You *have* bedded her!"

"No! I have not."

Her lip curled. "I don't believe you. *She'd* let you do anything you wanted. *She's* not a lady like me."

Anger flared inside him. He took a step nearer. "Damask is more of a lady than you could ever be. I won't have you talking about her like that."

Verona's face hardened. "I'll talk about her any way I want to. To anyone I feel like. You can't stop me!"

"Listen to me. Stop this right now." He took another step toward her.

She backed up. "Stay away from me!" she screamed as if she feared for her life.

Braden stopped. "Oh, for God's sake, quit acting like an idiot."

Her movements swift, Verona reached over to a nearby table, picked up a china figurine, and hurled it at his head.

Braden sidestepped, and the knickknack crashed against the wall beside him and shattered.

"Get out of here! I hate you!" Verona screamed.

Verona picked up another figurine and lifted it. "Go!"

She was beyond reason now. He'd leave, give her a chance to calm down. Expecting to see her parents come flying down the stairs, demanding to know what the ruckus was about, Braden hurried out.

He rode off on Jasper, his mind in turmoil. The night breeze was cool on his chest, and he realized his shirt was still unbuttoned partway, his cravat still on the Holmeses' sofa.

His plans to talk calmly with Verona, convince her it would be to their mutual advantage to break off their engagement, had turned into a disaster.

He still found it almost impossible to believe Verona had demanded he burn down the inn. How could she conceive such a terrible idea?

Only a short time ago, he'd planned to marry her, live with her the rest of their lives.

"A fool like you doesn't deserve to be saved from such a horrible fate," he said aloud, relief coursing through him again.

And again, it didn't last long. The night air made him start thinking more clearly.

Did he truly believe tonight's argument had ended things between Verona and him cleanly and forever?

No. He doubted Mrs. Holmes would take the broken engagement well. She'd been as excited about the prospect of Verona becoming his wife as Verona had.

And although Verona had screamed at him to go, said she hated him, he couldn't trust her to leave things as they were.

Verona was furious, feeling like a woman scorned. She'd threatened to blacken Damask's good name. He didn't doubt she meant it.

As hard as it was for him to believe, she'd been serious about burning the inn. If she could dream up a scheme like that, she wouldn't hesitate to spread filthy gossip about Damask around town. She might even be able to convince her mother to do the same.

Her family was highly respected in the area. Damask was well-liked, but morally, as far as the townspeople were concerned, Verona was the wronged person. Many people would no doubt agree that Damask had stolen Braden from her.

And everywhere Damask went, she'd be the target of scornful glances, vicious talk. She couldn't stand that. She might not even want to live here anymore. She could lose all she'd fought for. A place of business and a home for her family.

Verona had even threatened to have her family take it to court. Bring a breach of promise suit. And if that happened, Damask would be dragged into the mire.

Damn! He couldn't let that happen. But what could he do to prevent it?

There was only one solution. He must marry Verona after all.

Sickness coursed through him. No, he wouldn't do that. *Couldn't.*

What a hellish marriage it would be for both of them.

He could do one other thing. Marry Damask now. Before Verona and Mrs. Holmes had time to do anything to hurt her.

The thought was so sudden, so unexpected, it made him draw up on the reins. Jasper obediently slowed down and stopped in the middle of the deserted country road.

Since yesterday evening at the creek, he'd known that he wanted Damask in his life. But he'd gone no further than that. He'd thought to break off with Verona, then court Damask properly. . . .

The physical pull between them was very strong. He'd never felt anything like it with another woman. And he knew Damask felt it, too.

And desire wasn't all he felt. Although they'd fought each other since their first meeting, he liked and admired her. She had character and spirit. Kindness and love. She was raising Cory and Emmy as well as any mother.

She'd be a good mother to his children.

A picture filled his mind: a house full of babies with Damask's glorious hair and eyes. Maybe some of them with his own coloring. Or a combination of the two.

Jasper nickered questioningly at the stop, twitched restlessly.

Braden flicked the reins, and the horse eagerly

moved forward again, going smoothly from walk to trot into an easy canter.

It was too late tonight to talk to Damask. She would no doubt be in bed by the time he got back to the inn.

But tomorrow . . . yes, tomorrow morning . . .

He'd go down to the store and tell Jacob he'd be gone for a while.

He smiled. Maybe all day. He'd persuade Damask to come for a walk in the woods with him. They could go to the creek. . . .

Memories of the morning before flooded over him. God, how wonderful Damask had felt in his arms. The passion she'd shown was genuine . . . he wanted that again . . . he wanted it every night for the rest of his life. . . .

Did he think it would be that simple? All he had to do was ask her, and she'd fall into his arms?

He frowned. Maybe not that easy. But he had to persuade her . . . now. He couldn't take a chance on waiting.

If they were married, Verona or her mother couldn't hurt Damask. If they did spread gossip, it would soon die down.

Doubt suddenly hit him. Was he thinking clearly? How could marrying her stop gossip? It might very well make it worse, confirm Verona's lies.

That was possible, but he had no other choice. Except marrying Verona.

He shuddered.

Somehow, he'd persuade her they must marry now. If they were married, at least he'd be able to protect her from the threat of court action. The Holmeses wouldn't go to court for just a monetary settlement.

Tomorrow, under the willow's shade, by the bank

of the sparkling stream, he would ask Damask to become his wife.

As Braden galloped off, Verona heard her parents thumping down the stairway.

Oh, damnation! She fought her anger. Now she'd have to explain . . . tell them Braden had broken off the engagement. And why . . .

Quickly, she began picking up the figurine pieces. It had been one of Mama's favorites—a shepherdess holding a long crook.

Mama would be angry with her for that as well as the rest of it.

And it wasn't her fault! Braden hadn't even listened to her brilliant plan. He'd just made her feel like an awful person for even considering such a thing, she'd blurted out her ultimatum without thinking.

She'd never dreamed he'd take her seriously.

Or that *he'd* come here tonight to break off with *her.*

Her anger surged again.

Because of that Damask woman! Verona was sure that was the true reason, despite his denials. But as much as she'd like to, she wouldn't go around telling people that Braden had bedded Damask. Her mother would probably kill her if she did. Her parents wouldn't consider any kind of legal action against Braden, either. . . .

No, she'd lost him, lost her only chance to marry a man with plenty of money who could give her a lovely home and all the other things she wanted.

When Mama heard the whole story, she'd say it was her own fault. Papa, too, would probably think that. Although, he might not care that much. She didn't think he'd ever really liked the idea of her marrying Braden.

He'd just gone along with what he thought would make her happy.

And marrying Braden would do that. She pushed down the voice inside her head that was telling her maybe this was for the best.

No, it wasn't. Oh, why had she made him leave? Why had she let her temper get the best of her again?

Her plan would have worked! Both of them would get what they wanted. Braden wanted that mansion as much as she did. He was the one who made the plans to build it.

You're right. So, why don't you burn down the inn yourself?

The thought took her breath away. She dropped the pieces of the figurine back on the floor. No, she couldn't do that. She was a woman. This plan required a man.

Her parents had reached the bottom of the steps, and she could hear them hurrying down the hall.

Oh, *what* was she going to tell them?

If the job was done, if the inn was gone, Braden would soon forget Damask, since he wouldn't be seeing her every day.

After all, *she* was much prettier than Damask. She could go to Braden, tell him she was sorry she'd lost her temper, and that she didn't mean all the things she'd said.

Verona swallowed. She could even let him . . . bed her . . . if she had to.

Yes, they could still have a fine marriage, be the envy of all Goose Creek. If she was strong enough to do this.

Braden would accept her apology. He'd realize she'd been strong and brave and had solved their problems. The way would be clear for them to marry, to build the mansion on the hill. . . .

"Verona," her mother said from the doorway, her voice outraged. "What on earth is going on down here?"

Verona stepped back from the scattered porcelain on the carpet. Braden's cravat was still on the couch. Verona snatched it up and stuck it down behind a cushion. She took a deep breath and turned to face her parents with a rueful smile.

"Oh, it's nothing much, Mama, Papa. Braden and I just had a little spat, and I'm afraid I lost my temper. I'm so sorry I broke your shepherdess."

Mama frowned. "That was my favorite piece. How *could* you be so careless? And you scared us to death when we heard you screaming like that. Thank goodness, it wasn't anything serious."

Mama's face gradually relaxed. As Verona had hoped, her mother didn't want to know the details. She only wanted things to go along smoothly.

"You're a grown woman, Verona," her father said, his voice heavy with disapproval. "It's about time you learned to control that temper of yours. Not many men are willing to put up with their wives throwing things at them."

Verona hung her head. "I know, Papa, and I'm so ashamed of myself. I'll go apologize to Braden in a day or so."

She peeked at him from under her lashes. His frown didn't clear. He was still giving her a searching look, as if he didn't believe what she was saying. Almost, as if he'd been hoping for the worst . . . that Braden wasn't going to be her husband after all.

"Yes, you do that," her mother said approvingly. "You're right. Give it a day or two, then you go tell him how sorry you are."

Her mother didn't wish that, though.

And neither did she, Verona told herself firmly, forcing back the doubt that kept trying to creep in.

She wasn't a coward! She'd always been as daredevil as her brothers . . . and Russell . . . when they were growing up.

Tomorrow night the moon would be only a thin sliver. She'd tell her parents she was going to visit her brother and his family overnight and ride Lady to Goose Creek.

She could do this, and she would.

Chapter Eighteen

Damask came into the sitting room, carrying a pail and trowel. The decrepit ladder still leaned against the wall. She'd promised Braden only that she wouldn't use it for the one day, and it had to do. She intended to finish repairing the plaster on the ceiling today no matter what.

Yesterday, the men had finished the porch roof. It was amazing how much better the entire front of the inn looked now, with the new roof and freshly painted new posts.

Harold had sent word with Edmond that he'd be back to work in just a few more days. Edmond had laughed and said his father meant what he said—he was sick of resting.

Three of the upstairs guest rooms were almost ready for occupancy. She needed Harold's help for a few things yet.

But soon the inn would be ready to house guests again. She'd have to see about putting advertising in some of the big city papers, especially the Philadelphia ones. And she'd have to make some flyers for the train station.

Flora was bustling around, chattering about their future plans.

Damask knew she should be excited. But the truth was, she was scared.

Braden hadn't given her the fight she'd expected when she'd told him, two evenings ago, she planned to reopen the inn. He hadn't even argued about it.

Her realization that same evening that she loved Braden, no matter how she tried to deny it, had overshadowed his unexpected capitulation.

She was still fighting against that hopeless love. But now she realized something else.

Braden hadn't conceded anything to her.

Ownership of the inn property was still divided between them. He could stand by and let her reopen the inn, but he hadn't offered to give up his share. Or to abandon his plans for a mansion on this hillside.

Of course he hadn't, because he probably thought she would fail in her attempts to make Goose Creek Inn once more a thriving concern.

What did she know about running an inn? Nothing at all.

Flora was a wonderful cook, but Aunt Ada had done the rest of it. And with all her experience, her aunt hadn't been able to turn a profit the last few years she'd kept the inn open. Apparently there had never been a very good profit from the time she'd opened it more than forty years ago.

Damask fought off a wave of depression. It was pretty nervy of her to think she could turn things around.

But what else could she do, except give up? Sell

her share to Braden, move the children and Flora into a small house somewhere in town.

And watch Braden tear down the inn, build his house in its place, live there with Verona. No! She couldn't do that.

At the creek, she'd believed Braden not only didn't intend to oppose her plan but actually approved of it. Just because he'd been pleasant. That meant nothing, except as he said, he couldn't stop her. He'd probably been secretly amused, knowing she was getting herself into deep water.

She was taking a big chance with Emmy's and Cory's future. If the inn failed again, she'd be honor bound to repay the money the townspeople had advanced, no matter what they said. She couldn't live with herself otherwise.

And how could she ever repay the money?

A sudden burst of song came from Flora in the kitchen, as well as tantalizing smells drifting up the stairwell.

Flora was making shoofly pies. One of the delectable molasses confections was for the family—and one she intended to take to Harold.

Damask smiled, feeling a little better. She'd asked Flora if she wanted her to come along on the visit, and Flora had looked a bit flustered, and said no, she'd be fine, and didn't want to take Damask from her work.

As if summoned by her thoughts, Flora appeared in the doorway.

"I go now to Harold. The children are down with the Millers' young ones. They ask if they can stay for dinner and I say yes. That is all right?"

"Yes, that's fine," Damask said, glad they'd found friends near their own ages. They needed that.

"Good-bye now. Don't work so hard." Flora spotted

the ladder leaning against the wall and frowned. "You do not climb on that rickety thing! I won't go if you say you do."

"It's not that bad," Damask said. "See, it has all its rungs."

"You still should not do it with no one in the house. What if you fall?"

Damask sighed. "I won't fall, and I'm almost finished patching the ceiling."

"All right," Flora finally said. "But be very careful."

"I will," Damask assured her, relieved when the older woman turned and left.

Now to get to work. She set the ladder against the wall in front of the fireplace, then mixed a small pail of plaster.

Cautiously, holding the pail and trowel in one hand, holding to the ladder's side with the other, she climbed the ladder, wincing at its old-age groans but hoping it would hold her weight again today.

Halfway up, the groans increased, and then the rung she stood on broke. Her feet fell to the next rung, which also gave way. The third rung wobbled but held.

Her heart thudding, Damask dropped the pail and trowel, grasped the ladder's sides, and hung on, fighting for balance.

Her desperate movements made the ladder shift, slip, and fall forward against the brick of the fireplace, where it steadied.

Damask carefully tested the next rung. It held, and so did the others as she gingerly descended. On the floor again, she heaved a sigh of relief, her knees shaking.

She was safe, and the ladder hadn't fallen against the new wallpaper, damaging it, she saw, relieved. The solid fireplace brick couldn't be hurt.

And she wouldn't be using this ladder again. She grasped its sides and moved it away, laying it on the floor against the far wall.

Coming back to clean up the pile of spilled plaster, which had luckily missed the carpet, she frowned.

One of the fireplace bricks stood at an angle. The old ladder, hard as that was to believe, must have damaged it after all.

Damask reached up to try to press the brick back into place and saw that it wasn't damaged. It just jutted out in a peculiar way, almost as if it was supposed to. But it hadn't been that way before. She'd surely have noticed.

She pressed harder against the brick. A creaking sound came from the oak paneling of the wall next to the fireplace, and then a section of the wall moved aside. A musty odor came out into the sitting room.

Stunned, Damask stared.

Behind the paneling was a small open space containing a cot, a tiny table, and a straight-backed chair. A few books and a stack of papers sat on the table, as well as a pewter candlestick.

It was a secret room!

Why was it there? Why had Flora never mentioned it? Or Aunt Ada, for that matter, the summer she stayed at the inn?

The spilled plaster forgotten, Damask walked to the opening. Did she dare go inside? How could she resist?

Damask glanced at the angled brick again. It was safe. It couldn't move back by itself and lock her in there.

Her heart thumping with excitement, she slipped inside the room and looked around.

The walls and low ceiling were of rough plaster, once white but now dingy. Damask pushed on the cot's mattress, and dust flew out, making her sneeze. Whatever this room's purpose, it apparently hadn't been used for a long time.

She went to the table. A half-used candle sat in the holder, a box of matches alongside.

The top book, unlike the mattress, wasn't very dusty and didn't look that old. Damask picked it up and walked closer to the doorway in order to see better.

The Underground Rail Road. A record of Facts, Authentic Narratives, Letters, &c . . . By William Still, For many years connected with the Anti-Slavery Office in Philadelphia, and chairman of the Acting Vigilance Committee of the Philadelphia Branch of the Underground Rail Road.

She drew in her breath. Why was this book here? She'd known, of course, that her aunt was strongly against slavery.

Could fugitive slaves have been hidden in this room?

Damask replaced the book on the table and picked up the one underneath, which looked like a ledger.

It was. Damask turned the pages, her surprise growing. Records were here from the time her aunt bought the inn until just a few months before.

Why was the ledger here instead of down with her aunt's other inn records in the sitting room desk? Damask opened it again at the first page, the first entry.

Made in 1840, it was the record of a loan made from a Mr. Maynard Lowell to Miss Ada Harris. Neat entries followed, where Ada had repaid the loan, never missing a payment.

Damask turned the pages, finding them the records

of more loans from private individuals, all meticulously repaid.

The last loan had been paid in full only a few months before her aunt had died.

The third book was another ledgerlike book. After paging through it, Damask understood the significance of the book about the Underground Rail Road.

This one was a record of fugitive slaves whom Ada had helped. By hiding them in this room. By giving them money to speed them on their way.

Damask closed the third book and placed it on the bottom of the stack again, then put the other two on top.

Sitting there, she tried to take it all in.

Now she understood why Ada had always been short of money, even in the many years the inn had made a good profit. Why she'd let the inn repairs go until she finally had to close it down.

She had almost bankrupted herself by helping others and never revealed it to a soul. Even Flora must not know, or she would have told her.

Damask got up from the chair and walked to the cot. Dazed, she sat on the mattress, her hand resting on the knob topping one of the metal bedposts. It moved beneath her hand, and idly she turned the knob, her mind whirling with the discoveries she'd just made.

They put an entirely new light on everything. Maybe she *would* be able to make a profit running the inn, after all. Aunt Ada had. She'd just given it all away.

A small sliding noise came from a few feet away.

Damask frowned. The room seemed to be getting darker. . . .

She leapt to her feet just as the sliding door clicked shut, leaving her in darkness.

Her heart stopped beating, then began pounding.

She ran toward where she thought the opening was and frantically searched for a latch, the edge of the paneling, anything to get her out of here!

She found nothing. Her heart finally slowed its frantic beating as she took deep breaths and slowly let them out.

Why had the door closed? How could she get it open again?

Think, she commanded herself. The door couldn't have closed from the outside unless someone pushed it. No one was here except her, and anyway, no one could have moved the brick without her seeing.

Then the door had closed from the inside. Somehow, she must have done it herself.

The bedpost. She'd turned the knob on the bedpost!

It was so dark in here. Thin streaks of light came through from slits in the inner walls, but that didn't dispel the inky blackness.

Carefully, she walked to where she thought the cot stood, swept her outstretched hands around, and finally made contact with the metal frame.

She sat down on the cot again, searching for the post she'd touched before. Her hand shaking, she tried to turn the knob in the opposite direction from the way she had a few minutes ago.

It wouldn't turn.

Maybe she was wrong in the direction. She tried it the other way, but it still wouldn't move.

Maybe another bed knob *opened* the door! Lunging across the cot, she tried the other knob at the bed's foot, then both knobs at the head.

None of them would turn, not even a tiny bit.

The mechanism must work only one way from this side. The person in here could close the door, but it could be opened only from the outside.

That made sense. The hidden people couldn't

know when it was safe to leave this hideaway. They would have had to depend upon the person helping them to know that.

To release them from their prison.

Damask shuddered, goose bumps rising on her arms.

What was she going to do? Flora would be back soon but might not come up here. She'd probably work in her garden until time to cook dinner. And when she did come up to see why Damask wasn't responding to her call, what would she find?

A trowel and a pile of hardened plaster on the floor. No doubt the fireplace brick was neatly closed, leaving no sign of what had happened.

Just as she'd never noticed anything different about that one brick. Whoever built this room had done an excellent job. They had to, or the room couldn't have served its purpose.

And the room had been built long before Ada's time. Her records made that clear. Probably no one but Ada knew about it.

Flora would be worried. She'd search elsewhere in the inn, then the outdoors. Finally, she'd decide Damask had gone down to Goose Creek . . . she'd wait for her to return. . . .

Damask swallowed. She had to get herself out of this predicament.

When she heard Flora in the sitting room, she'd pound on the wall. How thick were these walls? Could she hear Flora?

Could Flora hear *her?*

Panic welled up again, and she fought it down. She must stay calm and came up with a plan.

She could die in here. There was no food, no water. Instantly, at that thought, thirst hit Damask. She fought down the feeling.

A small rustle came from a corner.

Her heart pounding, she jerked her feet up on the cot. A mouse . . . or maybe a rat!

Stop this! Stop it right this second.

Cautiously, Damask lowered her feet to the floor and felt her way to the table. Fumbling on its top, she knocked the box of matches off.

The rustle from the corner came again. Frantically, she felt around the floor, found the matches, and managed to strike one.

The brief flare of light showed her the candle and, fingers shaking, she got it lit.

She darted a glance to the corner and let out her breath in relief when she saw nothing. Trembling, she sat down in the chair and watched the feeble light, so grateful for its comfort, tears welled in her eyes.

So must the people closed up in this room for maybe weeks at a time have felt. Although they were no doubt supplied with candles, they were still closed up in here. Almost like being in a coffin, she thought morbidly.

Damask checked the matches, relieved more than half a box was left. Regretfully, she pinched the candle out and gasped as the room was again plunged into blackness with only those tiny slits of light.

Holding the candlestick, she fumbled her way to the sliding door. Huddling close, she turned her head so her ear was against the panel. She'd sit here until Flora came up and then she'd pound on the door with the heavy pewter candlestick.

Surely, oh, surely she'd be able to hear Flora if she called out.

Wouldn't she?

Fear still pounding through her, Damask settled down to wait.

*   *   *

Braden hurried up the hill, eager to reach the inn.
Jacob hadn't even looked surprised when Braden told
him he'd probably be gone much of today. In fact,
he'd seemed gratified to be left in charge of the store.

From halfway across the meadow, and not for the
first time, Braden appreciated how much better the
inn looked with the porch roof replaced, new posts
gleaming with a coat of fresh paint.

The repair gave the inn back its solid look. As if it
could stand for another hundred years or so.

As far as he was concerned, it could.

Braden stopped in his tracks, surprised at his
thoughts. The burning desire for a mansion on this
hill had left him. Had it gone with his broken engagement to Verona?

He wasn't sure, but he felt lighter, happier, just
looking at the inn and accepting its right to be exactly
where it was.

*Ah, yes, you have changed your bad dream into a good
one* . . . . a voice whispered in his head. A hauntingly
familiar voice.

Ada's.

The voice no longer bothered him. This was Ada's
beloved home. Why shouldn't some part of her still
be around?

He increased his pace and almost ran onto the
porch, opened the door.

Standing in the wide front hall, he listened. No
sounds came from anywhere in the house. A delicious
smell wafted out from the kitchen. Someone had
recently been baking.

Braden walked back to the kitchen just to make
sure Damask wasn't there. The big room was neat

and empty. A shoofly pie sat on the scrubbed work-table. That was what smelled so good.

Maybe by dinnertime things would be settled between him and Damask and they could share a piece of this.

What if Damask threw him out on his ear? This sudden proposal of marriage might not sit well with her.

All he could do was try. And if she agreed to marry him, the tricky part would be to get her to also agree to marry very soon, within the next few days.

After glancing quickly in all the downstairs rooms, he found them empty, then climbed the stairs.

At the top, he stopped and listened again. Not a sound came to his ears. She surely couldn't be work-ing that quietly.

She'd been patching the sitting room ceiling the other day, the day he'd sat on the ladder to prevent her using it. Maybe she was in there now, resting for a few minutes.

The sitting room door stood open. He glanced inside, disappointment hitting him not to see Damask in her favorite rocker—or anywhere in the room.

She could be in her bedroom . . . taking a nap? Although that idea didn't sound like Damask, he still went to her room and quietly opened the door.

It, too, was empty.

Then, she had to be outside. He walked across the room and glanced out the side window. No one was in the garden either. Only a few birds, and a rabbit helping itself to some lettuce.

Frowning, he walked back down the hall. Could she be in the woods? Fishing with the children . . . or just sitting on the creek bank?

His frown faded, replaced by a smile. If so, that was just where he wanted her to be!

He came to the sitting room again, passed by, then paused. He'd caught a glimpse of something, something that didn't look right.

Braden turned and went back, then walked across the room. A pile of plaster was splattered on the wood floor by the side of the fireplace, a trowel beside it.

Damask wouldn't leave a mess like this.

He glanced around. The ladder still leaned against the wall where he'd placed it a few days before.

But now several rungs were broken.

Had Damask climbed that miserable ladder although she'd promised him she wouldn't and the rungs had broken? Had she fallen and hurt herself?

She promised you only that she wouldn't use the ladder for that one day.

Fear hit him. "Dammit!" he said loudly and fervently. "Why in hell didn't she listen to me?"

And where was she?

Flora must have taken her to the doctor. How? They had no buggy. Flora couldn't carry her.

Nothing made sense, but urgency overtook him. Something was wrong. He could feel it.

Hurrying toward the door, he heard a muffled thud from somewhere behind him.

Braden stopped, turned around, but saw nothing. The sound came again. It seemed to be coming from the wall by the fireplace.

Rats?

No, it didn't sound like that. Again, the thud came, and this time he was sure it came from behind the paneled wall.

He ran across the room, put his ear against the panels, and heard Damask's voice faintly calling his name.

"I'm here!" he shouted back. "I'll get you."

A guest room was on the other side of that wall.

Had she gotten shut up in there? Injured and in pain from her fall?

Braden sprinted out of the room and flung open the door into the next one. This room was also empty. Wildly, he lifted the quilt and looked under the bed just to make sure she hadn't somehow gotten caught under it.

Straightening, Braden heard another thud, but fainter this time. He rushed back to the sitting room, again put his ear against the panel, and heard Damask calling.

"Don't worry, I'll find you!" he said as loudly as he could, hoping she could hear him.

She wasn't in the guest room and she wasn't in here.

That was impossible. Impossible but yet . . . .

Realization hit him. There was a space between those rooms!

Somehow, Damask was trapped in that space!

But how had she gotten in? Where was the door? Was there a sliding panel somewhere? A mechanism that locked and unlocked it?

Her voice was too muffled to tell him. He'd have to find it himself. Frantically, he pushed and prodded all over the smooth pine panels and the baseboards but found nothing.

The lock had to be somewhere else, which made sense. On the panels it would be too easily discovered.

Braden stepped back from the wall, looked at the pile of plaster, then raised his eyes to where Damask must have had the ladder leaning in front of the fireplace.

Yes! That's right, a voice whispered. *Look carefully at the fireplace. . . .*

This time Ada's voice didn't seem to be in his head

but somewhere nearby. His side vision caught a glimpse of something . . . someone in the old rocker.

Braden jerked his head around. The chair was empty.

But it rocked gently back and forth.

Feeling the hair on the back of his neck standing out, he hurried to the fireplace and examined the bricks. At first they all seemed to be the same, but then he saw one that looked a bit different. A piece of mortar was missing from one side.

Holding his breath, he pushed on that side of the brick.

Nothing happened.

Chapter Nineteen

Braden's heart plunged. Maybe he was wrong. He pushed again, harder this time, and heard a click. The brick moved outward, and the section of wall slid back.

Damask fell out of the opening, sprawling on her stomach.

Braden ran to her, his heart in his throat. He dropped to his knees, gathered her close to him for a fierce hug, then held her away to look at her.

"Are you all right?"

"Yes," she said, but she swallowed convulsively and he could see the tracks of tears on her cheeks. Otherwise she seemed unhurt.

He pulled her to him for another hug and felt her body trembling in his arms. Her hair smelled like the wildflowers in the meadow, and her body was soft and warm. He wanted to hold her close to him forever. Cared for and safe.

Finally, her trembling slowed down, stopped. She

pulled back a little, a wary expression on her face, as if she'd only just realized he was holding her close.

She pushed at her hair, which had come loose from its roll, and was tumbling about her shoulders. "I was so scared no one would hear me and I'd have to stay there all night . . . or longer."

She shuddered, and Braden realized just how frightened she'd been.

"But *I* heard you. I will *always* hear you." Tenderly, he ran a finger down her cheek.

Damask got to her feet, moving away from him.

Suddenly, he remembered the last time they'd been together . . . at the creek. She'd been wary of him then, too . . . moved away from him. As he had her.

Now that wariness was gone . . . on his part.

But not on hers, because she didn't know anything about what had happened last night.

Everything inside him screamed to tell her that moment how he felt. Tell her he was no longer promised to Verona. Tell her he wanted to marry her— *now.*

But he had to curb his urgency, go slow and easy. This was one of the most important times of his life. He had to do it right.

He couldn't say he wanted to marry her as soon as possible for fear Verona planned to try to ruin her reputation. If he could help it, she'd never know about Verona's threats.

But neither could he profess undying love. He'd thought he loved Verona, and look where that had gotten him. Was there even such a thing as real love between a man and woman? he wondered.

He could tell her he longed to have her in his bed. That he liked and respected her and wanted to take care of her. Those were all the truth.

"You'll never believe what I found in there!" Damask said.

He came out of his reverie. Damask's wariness seemed to be gone; her expression now held only eagerness to tell him what she'd discovered. His mood lightened. Maybe it wouldn't be so hard to persuade her.

Braden put his worried thoughts aside for the moment. He couldn't plunge into a proposal right now, anyway. And he was curious, too. "What?"

"Aunt Ada was hiding runaway slaves," she told him. "Come on, let me show you the records. But we'd better make sure the door stays open this time. I accidentally closed it by turning the bed knob."

"You're right. We don't want to take any chances. If *both* of us get locked up in there, who'd rescue us?"

She shuddered again. "I don't even want to think about that!"

He dragged the big armchair over and wedged it in the doorway.

Once inside, he examined the bed knob, told her a rod must run through it and the hollow post under it, then beneath the floor to the fireplace brick.

Damask showed him the books, told him what she'd surmised. He agreed with her suppositions, as astonished as she.

"So that's why Ada let the inn get so run-down."

"Yes," Damask said, feeling herself tense. Would he take the next step? Realize it was possible she could run the inn successfully.

And think that maybe the other evening at the creek he'd made a mistake when he'd agreed to not oppose her reopening the inn.

But he said nothing, just ran his long fingers over the books on the table, as if lost in thought.

Remembering how wonderful his hands had felt

caressing her a few minutes ago, Damask shivered, clasping her hands across her arms.

Braden looked up and put the book down. "Let's get out of here. I can almost feel the fear of the people who stayed here. It's in the walls and floors."

"Yes," Damask agreed, relieved he'd mistaken the reason for her shiver. "But I can also feel their hope of a better life. One that Aunt Ada spent a great deal of her own life to insure."

She went ahead of him, back out into the sitting room.

Braden removed the chair from the opening in the wall, then turned to her. "Do you want to close it up again?"

His gaze was so intent on hers. So searching. He looked as if he wanted to tell her something, something important. . . .

Why had he come here this morning? she suddenly wondered. Why had he come into the sitting room? He must have been looking for her.

"Yes. I'll tell Flora, but I don't want the children to know. They couldn't resist it."

"You're right. When I was their ages, I certainly couldn't have."

He walked to the fireplace, pressed the brick back in place, and the door slid shut. "Whoever built this did a superb job. No one would ever guess that room is there."

"No," Damask said. He had on one of the well-fitting suits he wore to the store, and it emphasized his broad shoulders and chest.

Hastily, she dropped that thought. So he must have just come from town. It was too early for dinner. What was he doing here?

"Of course, if you took measurements, you'd see

there was space unaccounted for," Braden went on, still looking at the paneled wall.

He turned to her. "Ada must have been very well respected in the community for no one to have suspected, to have searched the inn thoroughly."

" 'It is not easy to apprehend them because there are a great number of people who would rather facilitate the escape . . . than apprehend the runaway.' "

Braden stared at her.

Damask smiled. "It's a quote from a letter by George Washington to a friend. Aunt Ada copied it into her records."

Braden smiled back. "What he said was very true—and why the Underground Rail Road was so successful. Because of people like your aunt."

His glance met hers and held. Damask felt her breath coming faster. She felt the pull between them, that mysterious tug that drew them together no matter how much they fought it.

And she must fight it now. She couldn't let herself fall into his arms again . . . not ever again. He wasn't for her. He belonged to Verona.

He gave her a tender smile. "Do you know how scared I was? When I heard your voice in that wall and didn't know where you were or how to find you?"

Don't smile at me like that, she told him silently. *You mustn't!*

"How *did* you figure it out?" she asked him, desperately trying to keep her mind on something, anything, besides the way she felt about him . . . the way he made her feel.

His smile faded. But he still gazed at her.

"You're going to think I'm crazy, but I heard Ada telling me to look at the fireplace."

A shiver went over Damask. Involuntarily, she glanced at the old rocker. It sat there empty, still.

"Did you . . . see her in the rocking chair?" she asked.

Braden's eyes widened. "Have you seen her? Heard her?"

"Yes," Damask answered. "A few times."

She started to tell him about the letter she'd found in the Bible but didn't. That episode was still too strange for her to want to talk about it, and she'd never figured out what her aunt meant about everything she needed being here.

Besides, no matter how you feel about him, Braden still wants his mansion on this hill. That hasn't changed.

But it was hard to think of him as her adversary when he stood so close. When she remembered how good it felt to be enfolded in his strong arms. To have his mouth closing over hers . . .

"I didn't actually see her," Braden said. "But I looked over and the rocker was moving."

Goose bumps rose on Damask's arms again. And not only because she was listening to Braden's ghostly experience.

Get out of this room while you still can.

Her throat felt dry, and so did her lips. She licked them, then saw Braden's gaze locked on her mouth.

She felt herself reddening. "You might have saved my life," she told him lightly. "I don't know how to thank you."

He moved a step closer to her. "You don't have to thank me."

Damask knew she should move away, go downstairs, outside . . . anywhere to get away from him.

But she didn't. Her feet seemed glued to the floor.

Braden moved a step closer, then another. If he took one more step, he'd be close enough to pull her into his arms.

He took the step.

He reached for her, and suddenly her feet could move quite well. She went into his arms with a little sigh of pleasure and contentment and nestled her head against his chest.

Her sigh went through Braden like a knife. He wanted to protect her, he *needed* to protect her. That's why he was here now. To offer her a lifetime of that protection.

Don't be so noble. The pleasures of the flesh figure strongly in your willingness to marry her.

Yes. But he wasn't the only one who felt desire. Damask wanted him, too.

That was evident in the way she pressed against him. He could feel every lovely curve and hollow of her body. As she must feel his fast-increasing hardness.

He wasn't supposed to be doing this. He came here to propose to her.

But he had to lead up to it gradually. Asking a woman to marry you wasn't something you handled like a business deal. He had to get her in the proper frame of mind, so she'd see that marriage to him wouldn't be just a good bargain for them both. There was pleasure to be had also.

Lots of pleasure . . .

Damask lifted her head, her eyes gazing into his, her lips slightly parted. Braden's inner dialogue faded away.

He traced the curve of her lips with a gentle finger, and to his surprise, she opened her mouth a little more, lifted her head.

No man with blood in his veins could turn down that invitation. He pressed his lips on hers, pulled her closer, and after a moment let his tongue explore the velvety softness she offered so willingly.

He heard her intake of breath. Her tongue touched his, then withdrew.

The delicate touch inflamed him. He plunged his tongue into her mouth, withdrew it, then plunged again, imitating that other movement his lower parts were urging him to do.

Damask stiffened for a moment, and he thought she was going to pull away, but then her body softened again, and she began kissing him back with a passion that astounded him.

Braden scooped her up in his arms and moved to the sofa. He lay her down on her side, facing him, then came down beside her. His fingers fumbled with the buttons on her dress, those same tiny buttons that had thwarted him that day at the creek.

Finally, he had a few of them open, pushed aside, so that only the white cotton of Damask's shift was between them. Her nipples were taut, pushing against the cloth, as if eager to be free of their restraint.

With a groan, Braden lowered his head to one nipple, kissed it through the cloth, felt it tighten and pucker under his mouth. He fought a strong urge to tear the shift apart, leaving her bare to his avid gaze and touch.

He couldn't to that. Couldn't take a chance on scaring her. Although she was eager and pliant against him, somehow he was sure she was untouched.

Settling for pulling her nipple into his mouth, he sucked on it until he heard her own groan of pleasure.

Did I actually make that sound? Damask wondered as Braden continued doing those wonderful things to her.

It was so strange. When he sucked on her nipple, something deep inside her contracted, as if there were a silken cord running between those two places.

She squirmed against Braden, trying to get closer to him to ease that throbbing ache.

Braden lifted his head from her breast, and at once she felt bereft. "Don't stop," she told him. "Oh, please don't stop!"

His smile also held the heat his body was creating against hers. "I don't plan to."

He lowered his head to the other breast.

Damask thought she might die of sheer pleasure. She squirmed again, realizing her skirts had gotten hiked up and her bare thighs were pressed against that most male part of him. She had an intense urge to move her thighs apart for him.

She did.

Braden groaned deep in his throat again. His hand cupping her bottom, he pressed his hard maleness against her female core.

Pleasure such as she'd never known before surged over her in a great wave.

Moaning, she clutched at Braden. He took her lips again, his tongue making those movements that now his lower body was also doing.

Finally, she lay quiet in his arms. His head was against her breast and he was also still and quiet.

A door slammed downstairs. "Damask, do you still work up there?" Flora called.

Damask came back to herself with a start.

Here she was, lying on a couch with Braden, half undressed, his mouth on her breast. And he'd caused her to experience the most incredible feelings. . . .

Never mind that! Button your dress! Get up from there!

Panic filling her, Damask pushed Braden away. She'd forgotten the couch was so narrow. He fell on the floor with a loud thump.

Her eyes widened. "I'm sorry!"

"What is wrong up there?" Flora's worried voice called. "Do you fall?"

Braden got to his feet, giving her a startled look.

"No! I'm fine! I'll be down in just a minute," Damask called back, frantically working her bodice buttons. Oh, why did they have to be so small?

"Here, let me," Braden offered.

"No, I can do it." Damask pushed his hand away, her face flaming as she recalled what he'd just done to her. What *she* had just done.

Braden's voice had sounded strained, too, as if his feelings were the same as hers. Embarrassed shock.

Her buttons finally done, Damask got off the couch and smoothed down her wrinkled skirts. She threw a worried glance at the door, expecting to see Flora any second.

"Damask, I have to talk to you," Braden said. "That's why I came back here this morning. I have something very important to say to you."

Damask froze, staring at him. His face had lost all the passion it had held only moments before. He'd straightened his suit, and his hair looked as if he'd just brushed it.

He was no longer the lover who'd given her such bliss. He looked just like what he was—a successful businessman.

And she knew what he wanted to talk about. The only thing of importance between them.

He regretted giving her no opposition on her proposal to open the inn again. He planned to tell her he'd changed his mind and that he'd fight her every step of the way.

Especially now that he'd found out her aunt had done well. That her lack of money had been no fault of Goose Creek Inn's.

"There you are!" Flora said from the doorway. "I hear you not up here. I worry you fall."

"We can't talk now," Damask told him in low tones, holding her head high, embarrassment again sweeping over her.

Braden frowned. "When, then?" he urged.

"Tonight, up here, after everyone's in bed," she said, then stopped, appalled.

What would he think of her? After what had just happened between them?

He'll think that you want to continue this.

He nodded. "All right."

"My, you are home early, Braden," Flora said. "Dinner is not ready."

The smile he gave Flora looked forced. "That's all right. I felt the need of some exercise. I'm going to change and go chop some wood."

Flora looked from one to the other of them. Then she smiled widely. "Yah, that is good thing to do. Sitting at the desk all day not good for the blood."

She turned her knowing smile on Damask.

"You have done enough. Come down now and talk to me while I make the dinner."

Oh, Lord, now Flora had the wrong idea.

What wrong idea? What she's imagining happened sure enough.

Damask managed to smile back. "All right."

Without looking at Braden, she turned and walked toward the door.

Behind her, she heard Flora's gasp. "What is that mess on the floor?"

Damask remembered she hadn't cleaned up the spilled plaster. She stopped and turned. "It's a long story. I'll clean it up in a minute and tell you all about it."

She wasn't going to exchange another word with Braden.

Until tonight. Then she'd have to. She'd already promised.

Chapter Twenty

"Why, Miss Geneva, I believe your hair is coming down in the back."

At Edmond's teasing words, Geneva reached toward her neat bun. Her arm brushed against his shirtsleeve. The tiny contact made her pulse beat faster.

"Where?" she asked. Walking down the deserted street with him in the dusk was a daring thing to do. She felt a small thrill.

"Right here." Edmond tugged at her bun, and it came undone, spilling hair pins everywhere.

"Oh!" Geneva clutched at her tumbling hair. "Why did you do that?"

She could barely make out his grin in the dusky light.

"Just couldn't resist. I've been wanting to do that for a long time."

Another thrill surged through her. He'd been noticing her hair for a long time?

He'd shown up at the library that evening to return Harold's books and get more, and they'd talked. Edmond told her of his plans to open a small furniture factory in Goose Creek, doing the best pieces himself.

His enthusiasm had gotten her so interested, she'd been amazed to finally realize it was an hour past closing time. And even more amazed at her instant acceptance of his invitation to walk with him and his terrier. Towser was getting fat because Harold gave him leftovers of the food people brought him during his illness.

"I'll never find my hairpins. It's too dark."

She felt Edmond's hand on her hair, stroking down its waves. She knew she should make him stop, but it felt too good.

"I'm glad," he said, his voice satisfied . . . and somehow intimate in the dim evening light. "Hair like yours doesn't belong scrunched up in a knot."

She laughed, hearing its shaky sound. "Now, wouldn't I cause a scandal if I left my hair down all the time."

"Not all the time . . . but sometimes . . . like now."

She drew in her breath. Edmond's voice was even more intimate on those last words.

They turned the corner onto Main Street. Geneva thought she saw a figure dart into a doorway ahead of them but decided her eyes were playing tricks on her. Who would be doing something like that? When all the stores and businesses were closed?

They walked on down Main, Edmond teasing her as usual—but not as usual, either.

And both of them knew it.

Halfway down the block, Towser suddenly turned and ran back down the walk. He stopped at a doorway and began barking and whining.

Maybe she *had* seen someone a minute ago.

Edmond called the dog, and he came trotting back to them. Probably it was only a cat, or a boy out exploring when he was supposed to be safely home.

Her hair felt so loose and free falling around her shoulders. It made her feel young and carefree and pretty—even with her spectacles on. She glanced at Edmond, made out the gleam in his dark eye.

Perhaps she'd been too hard on him. He *was* the most handsome single man in town. No wonder all the girls threw themselves at him.

And *she*, plain Geneva Dale, was walking with him in the evening. And he thought her hair was beautiful.

Edmond was a little closer now. He reached over and slipped his hand around her waist.

Geneva let it stay.

Huffing out her breath in relief, her dark cloak flapping around her, Verona hurried up Main Street toward the turnoff to the inn.

When Edmond's little dog, Towser, who'd been all over her at Harold's house that day, came running to her yapping and whining, she almost died, sure Edmond and Geneva would walk over and recognize her. How would she ever explain her presence there?

She'd ridden her mare out before sunset, supposedly heading for her brother Oliver's house a couple of miles down the road. Instead, she'd left the animal tied in a grove of trees at the edge of town. Later, she'd ride back to Oliver's and stay the night.

It was a cloudy, moonless night, too, as she'd hoped.

At the top of the hill, she paused for breath, glancing across the meadow toward the inn.

A light still shone in an upstairs window on this side. Good. She didn't want them to be asleep—just not downstairs. She reached in the cloak's big pocket and found the jar of coal oil. That should make it easy.

Glad of her dark cloak, Verona hurried across the meadow and around to the back of the inn. To her disappointment, a light shone here, too—in the kitchen, she supposed.

She walked around the back porch to the window and cautiously leaned over far enough to see inside, then sucked in her breath.

It was the kitchen. Braden stood by the table, facing her, and that Damask woman faced him. Braden took a step closer to Damask, and she backed up. Braden had an odd look on his face, one Verona couldn't put a name to.

Her mouth twisted. What was Braden doing? Trying to steal a kiss now that he was no longer engaged? Well, he *thought* he wasn't engaged.

That would soon change.

Behind her, Verona heard a happy whine, then a series of yaps. She gasped and moved away from the window.

It was Edmond's dog—he'd followed her up here! "Go away!" Verona whispered fiercely. "Go home!"

Instead, Towser yapped even louder, dancing around her.

She heard the back door open. "What's going on? Bluebell, are you out there?"

Braden! Verona did the only thing she could think of. She dived under the bottom of the porch, where a section of lattice was hanging to the side, frantically pulling it back in place. She'd run right through a big spiderweb, and she shuddered, trying to get it off.

Towser followed, whining to get under the porch with her.

"Get out of here, dog, go on home," Braden said. "Bluebell, if you're under that porch, you'd better come out now. I'm not going to stand here all night."

Thank God, Braden had attributed the noise she'd made to the dog. Verona crawled farther under the porch, trying to be quiet. She feared Braden might come and look under here for what she assumed was a cat.

The spiderweb was sticky and clung to her cloak. She couldn't see a thing. What if a big spider were crawling on her, mad because she'd destroyed its web? There were probably lots more spiders with webs under here, too. She shuddered again.

Towser stayed where he was, whining and yapping.

"All right, Bluebell, I'm going inside," Braden said, his voice annoyed. "You've had your chance. That dog isn't big enough to hurt you, anyway."

The back door closed again.

Verona let out her breath in relief. Braden was gone and surely Towser would soon get tired of yapping and go home. And she could get on with her plan.

Close by, she heard rustling sounds. Her heart leapt in her chest. There could be coons in here, too . . . or skunks . . . even snakes.

Something jumped on her. Verona screamed, then clamped her hand on her mouth. Had Braden heard her?

A loud purr started, accompanied by ecstatic rubbing. A *cat*. It must be the one Braden called.

Towser's yaps increased in intensity. He scratched at the lattice, trying to paw it open.

Verona held on to it with all her strength, but a rotten piece gave way in her hand and she fell backward, her head hitting something hard before the cat jumped on her stomach.

"Go away!" Verona said, her head throbbing. She felt a warm trickle down the back of her neck. She was bleeding! She scrambled to her knees, the cat still clinging to the front of her gown. She frantically grabbed for the lattice before the dog could get in.

She wasn't quick enough. Towser poked his head in, still yapping. The cat hissed and dug its claws into Verona's stomach through her gown, where the cloak had come open.

Verona yelped with pain and pushed the cat off, then forced the lattice back far enough so that Towser had to remove his head.

Holding the lattice closed with one hand, Verona searched for her injury with the other, letting out a little cry when she found it. Her hand came away sticky with blood, but it didn't feel deep. Surely, it would stop bleeding soon.

The light from the kitchen window disappeared, leaving her in inky darkness.

Verona swallowed, trying not to think what might be under here with her.

Concentrate on your plan. Braden must be going upstairs. Good. He hadn't heard her scream. She could get started.

Just as soon as she got rid of this blasted dog. She felt something brush against her leg and jumped before she realized it was the cat. In a moment, she heard growls and hisses from in front of her, followed instantly by hysterical barks. The cat was teasing the dog.

Her heart sank. Now Braden would be back down to check.

Verona waited, letting out a sigh of relief when she heard nothing else from the house. But God only knew what Towser would do when she crawled out from under here. Or the cat, either.

She hadn't made really careful plans. Now, she'd better do that, except it was hard to think with the dog yapping and the cat hissing and growling.

Verona forced herself to concentrate and ignore the racket. Everyone was upstairs but not asleep yet. That meant they'd all be able to escape when they smelled smoke, but, she hoped not until the blaze was well enough advanced that it would destroy the inn.

Verona again felt for the jar of coal oil in her pocket. Her heart lurched.

It was gone!

It must have fallen out when she fell.

That meant she'd have to feel around under here, not knowing what she'd encounter. Why hadn't she thought to wear gloves?

Pushing on the lattice with one hand, Verona twisted herself around like a pretzel. Her flesh shrinking, she pushed the other hand along in the dirt as far as she could reach, finally touching something hard and cold. It was the jar, thank goodness. She picked it up and slipped it back into the cloak's pocket.

All right. When the dog left, she would creep out of here, pour the coal oil in several different places, then light them with the matches she'd brought. . . .

Where was she going to pour the coal oil? The inn was made of stone. Stone didn't burn.

Her mouth dropped open. Why on earth hadn't she thought of that?

But there were the windowsills and the doors. And the porch! Yes, if the porch burned, surely the blaze would be hot enough to catch the inside.

A sudden vision came into her mind—hot red

flames licking at the doors and windows, creeping inside, flaring against the curtains, then the wallpaper of the kitchen . . . spreading. . . .

She swallowed. A cold, hard knot formed in her stomach. She saw the flames roaring up the stairwell. . . .

What if there wasn't enough smoke to alert Braden and the others in time to get out? What if Braden had gone on to bed and was already asleep . . . and everyone else was, too?

And even if they *were* awake, how could they get down and outside if the stairs were burning? They'd have to jump from the upstairs windows. . . .

All the way to the ground . . .

Flora was an old woman . . . and there were the two children. And *Braden* . . . she wouldn't even want that Damask woman to *die*. . . .

She could be responsible for causing five deaths.

No! Verona recoiled from the thought, the awful pictures still unreeling in her mind.

The knot in her stomach hardened, twisted. She felt sick and fought the nausea down. Cold sweat broke out on her forehead. She shivered, feeling clammy all over.

She couldn't do this.

How had she ever thought it possible? To have demanded this of Braden? No wonder he'd reacted with such horror.

Verona had relaxed her hold on the lattice, and Towser pushed through with happy yips. Bluebell shot out through the opening with one last hiss and growl.

Towser pushed his head into Verona's lap, and she absently rubbed his ears, still feeling dazed and sick.

The scratches on her stomach stung, and her head still throbbed, but none of that mattered.

She had to get out of here, get back to her mare, and ride to her brother's. "Come on, let's go," she said in low tones to the dog, who followed her as she crawled out from under the porch.

She walked around the side of the building, noticing a light was still lit in an upstairs room. Possibly Braden's, but she didn't care. She didn't seem to care about much of anything right now.

She had fought her temper all her life, but it had been merely an annoyance.

This was different. Tonight, it had nearly led her to do a terrible, terrible thing.

No, she couldn't excuse herself that easily. It was more than just bad temper. She'd been completely selfish, thinking only of what she wanted and not caring about Braden or anyone else.

It started raining when she got to the meadow, a hard downpour, soaking her in seconds. Verona drew the cloak's hood up over her head and trudged on down the hill, feeling her way through the darkness, Towser still with her.

At the bottom, the rain stopped for the moment, and the clouds parted enough for the inky blackness to lift so that she could see her way through the town.

Once on Main Street again, Towser yipped at her, then trotted off, back to his home and master, Verona assumed.

She felt very alone when he'd disappeared, her spirits sinking further. All she wanted now to was to get to the grove of trees where she'd left her mare.

How could she go to Oliver's house looking like this? Soaking wet, her head cut. She couldn't, she decided. She'd go back home and put Lady away in the barn, then sneak up to her room.

And what would she say to her parents tomorrow

when they asked why she came home in the middle of the night?

She brushed that concern aside. She'd worry about it later, when she had to.

Finally, there was the grove of trees just ahead. She heaved a sigh of relief as she hurried over to where she'd tied her mount, listening for Lady's eager nicker at her approach.

Nothing but silence greeted her.

Verona stopped short, her heart sinking.

Lady was gone.

That couldn't be! She must have left her somewhere else. Trying to keep her panic at bay, Verona walked a little farther along the road.

No, that was the only grove that size anywhere in the area. Lady must have gotten frightened and managed to pull loose. She was probably home by now.

Verona hoped her mare somehow got to the barn without alerting the household, but she doubted it. She closed her eyes. Papa might be out looking for her, and how was she going to explain herself?

There was nothing to do but walk home and hope for the best. And no use bemoaning her fate.

She had brought all this on herself.

The jar of coal oil in her pocket bounced against her leg as she walked.

Verona took it out, looked at with loathing, tossed it on the road, and kept going.

The rain started again, a slow, steady drizzle that soon had her shivering and made the night pitch-black. She managed to stay on the road only because it was lighter than the surroundings.

Misery overwhelmed her. Her head bent, tears in her eyes, she trudged along, not paying enough attention to how or where she was putting her feet.

One foot came down in a hole, painfully wrenching

her ankle. Verona pressed her lips together and kept going, but within a few minutes her ankle was swollen and the pain was intense.

This stretch of road was bordered by fields, with no sheltering trees.

She had to stop for a while. Her ankle hurt too much to continue, and she was so tired. She'd been too upset to sleep much last night.

Verona moved off the road a few feet and lay down. She drew her sodden cloak around her, trying to arrange its hood for a makeshift pillow. Burying her head in her arm to block some of the drizzle from her face, she heaved a weary sigh and closed her eyes.

Chapter Twenty-One

As she climbed the steps, Damask heard Braden downstairs trying to settle the barking dog. She went into the sitting room and seated herself on the rocker, leaving the armchair opposite for Braden.

When she'd encountered him in the kitchen a few minutes before, he'd reminded her of her promise to talk to him tonight.

Whatever the talk was about, he could do it from the armchair. No more of the kind of thing that had happened that morning.

Her face flamed just thinking about it. Involuntarily, her hand went to her bodice, checking to see if all the buttons were fastened.

Braden had unfastened them . . . he'd kissed her hardened nipples right through her underclothes. . . .

How she'd wanted him to tear her chemise from her, put his heated lips on her bare skin. She had actually begged him not to stop!

Oh, that sounded like she was ready to be firm with him. How could she promise herself it wouldn't happen again tonight? Why hadn't she insisted they stay in the kitchen and talk?

When she'd suggested it, Braden had said no, he wanted them to be more comfortable, and like a fool she'd let him have his way.

Maybe it was her way, too, and she didn't want to admit it. Maybe she was glad of a chance to continue what they started that morning.

No! That wasn't true. Braden was engaged to Verona. He could never be hers. And that wasn't the only thing keeping them apart.

He wanted an elaborate new house on this hill.

She wanted this wonderful old inn.

They were worlds apart in how they wanted to live their lives.

No matter how much she loved him.

Her heart ached at that thought. Yes, she loved him, and she couldn't stop herself from doing so.

And Braden loved Verona, not her.

Her heart leapt as she heard the stairs creak. He was coming up!

Climbing the wide stairs, Braden slowed his steps, trying to think of how to accomplish what he wanted.

To get Damask to agree to become his wife.

His wife.

He liked the sound of that. It seemed right. As it never had with Verona.

One thing was certain, he had to improve over his performance that morning. All he'd achieved then was almost taking Damask's virginity. If Flora hadn't arrived when she did, that would surely have happened.

Of course, Damask hadn't been reluctant—far from it. But still, it was his ultimate responsibility to see full lovemaking between them didn't happen until the time was right.

Which was after they were married. And he had to make sure that event took place very soon.

The trouble was, he didn't seem able to think at all when Damask was in his arms. All he could do was feel.

But he couldn't walk in on her now and baldly say "I want you to marry me before Verona can spread gossip about you and me all over town."

Of course he could, but he doubted if it would work. Damask was no coward. She'd most likely tell him she'd take her chances with town gossip.

All right. He'd tell her he was no longer engaged. He'd somehow get her in his arms, hold her, and kiss her. And *stop* with kissing. Then he'd ask her to be his wife. He'd tell her . . . what?

Not that he loved her. Because he didn't. But he *did* want to protect her . . . take care of her. He liked and respected her. He was strongly physically attracted to her.

Those were reasons enough for marriage.

It sounded so easy. He knew it wouldn't be.

Braden went on upstairs and to the sitting room.

Damask sat in the old rocker, her back very straight. Although he thought she heard him at the door, she didn't turn.

He frowned. Not a good sign. That probably meant she wanted no repeat of the morning's events.

Of course she didn't. She still thought he was engaged. He had to get that out of the way first.

Braden walked across the room and seated himself in the armchair across from Damask.

Her face was composed, her slim hands folded in

her lap. The only sign she might not be as calm as she appeared was one foot tapping softly on the floor.

He gave her a warm smile.

After a moment, she smiled back, which made her gray eyes glow as if lit from within. She *was* lit with an inner light, he thought.

He took a deep breath and released it.

"I'm no longer engaged to Verona," he announced, his voice firmer, his tones more clipped than he'd intended. But he was wound up tight as a spring.

Her eyes widened with surprise . . . with something else? Gladness? Joy?

"You're . . . not?"

"No. I . . . we broke it off last night."

He wouldn't give her the details. He couldn't bring himself to discuss Verona's vicious idea. He could still hardly believe it himself. Or its aftermath, with Verona raging at him.

"Oh."

Damask couldn't seem to think of anything else to say. Braden's sudden announcement had stunned her. She hadn't expected this . . . not at all.

When they shared those passionate moments on the sofa that morning Braden was already free. Some of Damask's guilt dissolved. But had he told her only because he thought it was something she needed to know . . . or did it mean more than that?

Could it be *she* was the reason? That he cared for her as she did him?

Even if that were so, they still had other problems between them. But those other problems might be worked out. Now that the most important barrier between them was gone . . .

"Why didn't you tell me this morning?"

His smile faded, his expression became serious. "I planned to, I wanted to. But . . . ."

He didn't have to finish. Damask felt her face flame again. They'd done little talking of any kind once he'd made sure she wasn't hurt and they'd discussed the implications of Aunt Ada's secret room.

No, they'd been lost in each other's arms. . . .

And that was as much her fault as his.

While the moments ticked away, she waited for him to explain what his new freedom meant to him . . . to her . . . but he didn't.

His face looked strained, as if he were struggling with himself . . . didn't know what to say next.

As if he were trying to figure out how to get from what he'd just said to the true reason he'd asked her for this talk.

Damask's absurd fantasies dissolved. Coldness settled around her heart.

His breakup with Verona had nothing to do with her. If it did, he'd have told her so at once. He wouldn't be sitting there in silence.

The iciness in her breast merged with humiliation. How could she have been foolish enough to think that was possible? He wanted her physically, but that was all. His heart, unlike hers, wasn't involved.

Just like Warren's hadn't been.

She'd be a fool no longer. She'd get this misery over with. Damask raised her chin and looked Braden straight in the eye. "No matter what you say, I'm still going to reopen the inn."

The mixture of emotions on his face faded. He stared at her, frowning. "I know. I told you I wouldn't try to stop you."

"You didn't think you'd have to. You believed I'd fail. Now that you know Aunt Ada made a profit, and I could, too, you've changed your mind."

He still stared, then shook his head. "I don't know where all this came from, but you're wrong. I haven't changed my mind."

Relief—and sudden irrational hope—sprang to life inside her. Maybe she'd been wrong once again. . . .

"Isn't that what you wanted to talk to me about?"

"Of course not!"

His face looked so incredulous, his tones were so vehement, she had to believe him. "Then, what—"

He was up from his chair and pulling her out of the rocker and into his arms before she had time to even finish her sentence, let alone react—or resist.

"You . . . *us*," he said huskily.

As always, the touch of his hands was working its magic, overriding everything else, all her common sense. Damask tried to marshal her thoughts, to tell him to stop, but the hunger inside her was too strong. She slid her arms around his waist, raised her head.

Damask's beautiful eyes gazed into his with a dreamy, dazed look. Her yielding body pressed against him, inflaming his own. Braden felt himself hardening.

Slow down! Only a kiss now. Anything else must wait until later. Until she's your wife . . . or at least agreed to marry you.

His hand on the back of her neck tangled in the thick coil of auburn hair, tugged at it until it spilled loose around her shoulders, down her back, releasing the flower scent that always clung to her, intoxicating him with it. Her hair was so silky tumbling over his hands. He wanted to bury his face in it.

His body reacted instinctively to the enticements bombarding it, paying no attention to his mind's directives.

Damask's lips parted with an invitation he couldn't resist.

Just a kiss, that's all, he repeated to himself desperately. Well, maybe two or three . . . just to get her in the right mood . . . to say yes . . .

Her lips were impossibly sweet beneath his own. Sweeter than the sweetest honey—his tongue probed gently for her to open to him—when she did his tongue slid inside, curling around her tongue, curving into the soft sides of her mouth, then thrusting deep inside.

He heard her gasp, then her tongue tentatively touched his. Fire shot through Braden, his answering gasp blended with hers.

Slow down! he told himself, trying to control his body's urgent demands. This is far enough for now . . . you need to stop.

No, he needed to kiss her deeper, press her willing, soft body even closer to his own. He needed to lay her down on the sofa and get rid of the clothes that hindered his access to her lovely body.

His lips still covering hers, he scooped her up in his arms, walked the few feet to the sofa, and sliding himself onto it, brought her down with him to lie nestled against him.

For a few moments, that was enough, just to feel her pressed tightly against him, feel her soft breasts with their hardened points, the beating of her heart.

A small sound came from the doorway.

Braden stiffened. Oh, God, no, it couldn't be one of the children. Why hadn't he closed the door? Locked it?

Releasing Damask's lips, he raised his head enough to see the door.

Bluebell stood on the threshold, meowing softly. Braden silently cursed himself for leaving a kitchen window open enough for her to enter. But better her than Emmy or Cory.

Braden took Damask's lips again in a deep kiss that promised more, then he raised his head.

She smiled up at him, her mouth soft, her eyes wide and dazed.

"Don't move. I'll be right back," he whispered, then hurried to the door.

"Sorry," he told the cat in low tones, lifting her back over the doorsill. He closed the door, thankful its key was inside in the lock. The click of the lock sounded loud to his ears, and Braden winced.

Turning, he half expected to see Damask up, smoothing her dress, ready to dash out the door.

He breathed a sigh of relief. She lay in the same position. In a moment, he was back beside her again, gathering her close.

You've kissed her more than once. Now is the time to stop while you still can! Ask her to marry you.

His body was stronger than the carping inner voice urgently giving him a different message. Telling him he must have this woman lying beside him—*now.* Everything else could wait. . . .

Braden's hand strayed to the bodice of Damask's gown, searching for the row of tiny buttons. He drew in his breath as his fingers encountered the bare flesh of Damask's throat.

She'd anticipated him and unbuttoned it herself.

His hands trembling, he untied the drawstring of her chemise, pulled it from her shoulders, leaving them and her breasts bare to his touch, his sight.

Her full breasts, with their hardened pink nipples, shimmered in the lamplight, beckoning him to touch them . . . kiss them. . . .

"You are so beautiful," Braden whispered, lowering his head.

Still marveling at her own brazen behavior, Damask

waited for Braden's lips to touch the aching tips of her breasts to ease that ache.

When his mouth closed over one of them, she gasped at the exquisite sensations that went through her. "Yes," she said. "Oh, yes, do that again."

Braden obliged, pulling on the nipple with a gentle sucking motion that made her gasp again. Just like that morning, her breast seemed to be connected to a part of her that was deep inside. It was the most incredible feeling.

It made her push herself even closer to him, to that hardened male part that was made to ease these aches, make these pleasurable feelings grow even stronger.

"Yes," Braden said, his voice sounding strangled. "Keep on doing that."

Damask obeyed. Braden's male part grew even bigger and harder. Almost alarmingly so. Growing up on a farm, she knew about mating, but how could this be the same?

He seemed too big. Damask reached down, found his engorged member, and ran her hand down it through Braden's trousers. She had been right. It felt very large. But she wanted to touch it under his trousers, she realized.

Braden gave a strangled cry and lifted his head from her breast. "Don't do that!"

Damask was surprised. "I thought it would feel good to you."

He groaned deep in his throat. "It feels *too* good. That's why you must stop."

"Oh." Damask didn't understand his reasoning but drew her hand away as he asked.

Braden moaned and buried his head between her breasts. His face was very hot, almost as if he had a fever. But she knew it wasn't that and thrilled to the reason for his heat.

He lifted his head again. "I can't wait, darling," he said, still in that strangled voice, as if he could hardly talk. "Do you know what I mean?"

She smiled at him. "I can't wait, either," she said, although she wasn't sure she meant that. She knew only that she didn't want him to stop these touches, kisses that were making her feel so good.

He groaned again, then moved her over on the sofa, pulled at her skirts, lifted them above her waist. She felt him fumbling at the drawstring of her drawers, and then he was pulling them down to her feet and off.

Damask felt cool air on that most private part of her that a man had never even looked at before, as Braden was looking, let alone touched.

His expression was almost reverent as he gazed at her.

"You are so beautiful," he said again.

Then he touched her, his fingers sliding through the auburn curls at the apex of her thighs, finding the small, hardened nub hidden within.

Damask's body jerked upward. "Oh!" she said, wonder in her voice.

Braden exulted in her response. She was so innocent yet so unconsciously knowing. He gently rubbed the small nub, feeling its pulsing growth, his male member swelling in response.

Oh, God, he couldn't wait another minute or he'd explode. Braden fumbled with his trouser fastenings, jerked them down, kicked them off the couch.

Finally, his bare, heated flesh pressed against Damask's. She bucked upward, gasping, moving her thighs apart instinctively. Braden eased his hand over her mound again.

She was hot and wet. He pushed a finger inside her and she gasped again. Her hand found his, pushed against it so that his finger eased deeper inside.

"Are you ready for me?" he asked, looking down into her gray eyes. "Ready for me to be inside you?"

Damask swallowed, knowing what he was asking, knowing it might hurt her. But she didn't care. She wanted this as much as he did.

"Yes," she whispered, hearing the tremble in her voice. She moved her thighs apart a little more.

Braden's mouth covered hers while he slowly lowered himself over her. She felt his throbbing hardness at her opening, and tensed, a stab of fear hitting her.

Men and women had been doing this since the beginning of time, she told herself. He couldn't really be too big. She just thought so because she'd never done this before.

His mouth still covering hers, his restless tongue exploring, Braden pushed himself inside her a little, then stopped. Oh, he felt so good! She moved upward a bit to encourage him. "Go on, please don't stop," she urged.

He gave another strangled sound, then his tongue thrust powerfully inside her mouth while that other, hot, throbbing part of him thrust into her below.

A sharp pain went through her. She tensed, jerked her head to the side, and started to draw away from him, but his hand was under her backside, pushing her into him so that she couldn't retreat.

"I'm sorry," he breathed into her mouth. "It will be all right in a minute."

In a few moments the pain eased, as he'd said it would, and she felt a sensation of fullness. Braden was inside her as he'd told her he wanted to be. All the way inside her, as far as he could go.

It felt so strange . . . yet at the same time familiar . . .

as if her body had been designed for this joining . . . as if she'd been waiting for it all her life.

Damask turned her head back, found his mouth, opened her own to him. She felt his shudder and heard his sigh into her mouth. He kissed her, and she met each thrust of his tongue with her own.

His body began moving against her own in a rhythm that excited her so much, she could hardly breathe. In a few moments, she'd learned the rhythm, too, and was moving with him, their breaths coming faster, like their movements.

Wildly, Braden moved inside her. Wildly, Damask answered his movements. She heard herself making small moans of pleasure as the tempo increased.

She felt her body building to something, something that was going to happen, but she didn't know what it was. She knew only that she must keep on moving in time with Braden until it did.

Then she felt herself begin to convulse around him, heard his intake of breath.

"Oh, yes, sweetheart," he said against her throat, "that's right. Wait for me if you can."

He moved faster and so did she, and then she felt as if she were coming apart with the pulsing pleasure that took her. Deep inside, she felt Braden's seed spill and that, too, seemed right. As if meant to be.

Finally, he collapsed on her breasts, his breathing hard, his body, like hers, trembling in the aftermath of the fire that had almost consumed them, yet at the same time had eased the fire blazing within.

Slowly, Damask came back to reality. That was what it felt like . . . as if she'd been away from her everyday self yet at the same time had been more intensely herself than ever before in her life.

So this was what lovemaking was all about. Strange and yet at the same time familiar. Somewhere deep inside her, she'd known how it would be, how to respond.

A thumping sound came from the door. Damask tensed, all the sweet, languorous feelings fading.

Was that one of the children? Emmy wanting her after a bad dream? Was the door locked? Or would it open in a second?

No, Braden had locked it, she remembered.

She gazed down at herself . . . her bare breasts, with Braden still pressed against them, her hiked-up skirts with nothing beneath.

Braden was asleep, breathing deeply, a smile curving his mouth upward. He looked so tired, as if he'd not been getting enough sleep lately.

Tenderness swept through her. Oh, how she loved him!

The thumping sound again came from the door. She couldn't ignore it. If it was Emmy, she might start crying in a moment, wake Flora and Cory.

Oh, Lord! She'd have to unlock the door, open it, and slip outside before Emmy saw Braden.

Carefully and quietly, so as not to wake Braden, she eased herself away from his arms. Her drawers were in a heap on the floor. Cheeks flaming, she scooped them up, slipped them back on, and tied the drawstring firmly around her waist.

Her bodice gaped open to her waist. Quickly, she pulled her chemise drawstring tight. Her fingers fumbled, and it seemed an eternity before she got the row of tiny buttons on the bodice fastened, then pulled her hair back, found enough hairpins on the floor to form a knot.

At last she was decent. But her lips still burned from Braden's kisses, felt swollen. If it was Flora at the door, she would guess what had happened in here a few minutes ago.

No, it wouldn't be Flora. Of course not.

She took a deep breath, tiptoed to the door, and turned the key in the lock, then opened it just enough to slip outside and close it behind her.

Damask let out her breath in relief. It was only Bluebell again.

The cat meowed and rubbed against Damask's skirts.

Except for Bluebell, the hallway was quiet and deserted.

Damask let out her breath in relief. "No, not now," she whispered, bending to caress the animal. "Later, you can come in."

She quietly closed the door on the indignant cat and locked it again. She'd take no chances on Emmy or Cory or Flora coming in and finding Braden half dressed on the sofa.

And the half of his clothes that were missing would indeed be shocking.

Her heated flesh was back to normal. Damask felt all the equally heated emotions leaving.

Braden mumbled, moved his hand around on the couch as if searching for something, then raised his head, pulled himself upright, and looked at her. His shirttail didn't quite cover the part of him that had given her so much pleasure.

Her cheeks flaming, she raised her gaze to his face, swallowed as his look seemed to go right through her clothes and find her bare flesh as he had in truth found it only a little while earlier. He gave her an intimate smile, as if all her secrets were now revealed to him.

And they were.

Her face flamed again. She wanted to flee to her room.

She turned away from him and reached for the

door key. While she was still fumbling with it, Braden's hand closed over hers.

"Wait. You can't leave *now*."

He was standing so close to her, she could feel him pressing against her backside. Obviously, he hadn't yet put on his trousers.

Heat went through her. She fought against it. She wouldn't fall into his arms yet again.

She *wouldn't!*

She hadn't been brought up this way. She'd been taught lovemaking belonged only in the marriage bed. She hadn't intended for this to happen.

But you let it happen. You could have stopped at any time and you didn't.

She kept her back turned. "Please go put your clothes on," she said primly.

Damask felt him tense. His hand stayed over hers, holding the key in the lock.

"Only if you promise not to run away while I do."

She felt heat building between them again. She had to get him away from her. "All right," she said.

Her back still turned, she heard him walk to the couch, his clothes rustling as he dressed.

"You can turn around," he said, his voice sounding as tense as she felt.

She did, keeping her back against the door, her hand behind her still holding the key in the lock.

He was fully dressed again, in the white shirt he wore around the inn and old trousers. But he still looked all too good to her.

He frowned. "Will you please quit standing against that door as if you expect me to attack you and come and sit down? As I said when I came in here, we need to talk."

She swallowed. His voice had lost the tenderness it had held when she'd nestled close in his arms.

Naturally, she told herself. He wanted you, as you wanted him. Now his passion is spent. And he doesn't love you—as you do him. If he did, he'd have told you so. He had plenty of opportunities.

The coldness began creeping back into her.

"We already talked. You told me of your broken engagement—and that you hadn't changed your mind about not objecting to my reopening the inn."

He let out a sigh and raked his hands through his black hair. "Yes, but did you forget I said that wasn't why I asked you to come in here?"

Truth to tell, she had. His first touch had erased all thought, left only feeling. But she didn't want to admit that. It made her too vulnerable.

"Please come over here and sit down again. I promise I'll . . . keep my distance."

He frowned again on those last words as if this weren't going the way he'd like it to, as if he hadn't wanted to say that. He sat down in the armchair he'd occupied before.

"All right." Damask walked over and seated herself in the rocker.

Her thoughts and feelings jumbled, she looked down at her lap, picking at a thread. She didn't want to be here with him. She wanted to be alone in her room. She'd behaved wantonly, and she was ashamed of her lack of self-control. If he loved her, it would be different . . . but he didn't.

Scalding pain went through her.

"Damask, please look at me," Braden said. His voice had softened, but it sounded as troubled as her own had a moment before. "I . . . have something very important to talk to you about."

Damask decided she might as well get this over with. Then she could go to her room and be alone with her thoughts and feelings. Berate herself for being such a fool as to give herself to Braden when he didn't love her at all.

She raised her head and gave him a straight look. "Go ahead."

He cleared his throat, and she saw him swallow. "I don't know how to build up to this gradually. Damask, will you marry me?"

"What?" She stared at him, her mouth falling open. Surely she hadn't heard him correctly.

He gave her a smile. "I want you to be my wife as soon as possible."

Joy flared inside her. Oh, she'd been wrong! He *did* love her. He *did!*

Then caution took hold of her.

He hadn't said that. She wasn't beautiful like Verona. She had two children to raise. And wasn't it odd he was asking her to marry him this soon after breaking up with Verona?

The joy faded away.

"You and Verona ended your engagement only last night. Now you're proposing to me the very next day?"

But hope still clung . . . wouldn't quite let go. If he loved her, now was the time to say so. She'd give him that chance.

Instead, he grimaced. "I know how it sounds. I know I shouldn't ask you this soon, but I have a reason for the hurry."

She felt sick inside. Of course he had a reason. But it wasn't love for her. That could mean only that it was a reason that would benefit him.

And it had to have something to do with the inn. She lifted her head. "What is the reason?"

He hesitated. She saw a muscle twitch in his jaw. "I . . . can't tell you."

All at once she understood. Everything clicked into place and made sense. Yes, it was so simple.

The sickness grew and spread. Her movements jerky, Damask got up from the rocker.

At the creek, he'd told her he wouldn't oppose her plans for reopening the inn. But he'd never said he'd changed *his* plans for building a mansion on this hill.

Because he hadn't.

He was no better than Warren. Braden had jilted Verona, as Warren had jilted *her.*

"Can't or *won't?*" she asked, her voice dead and cold.

He grimaced again, shrugged. "Call it what you will."

"I think I'll call it a clever way to try to get what you want. If we married, my family's half of this property would be yours. You could do as you pleased with it."

His startled look was so credible, she almost believed it. *Almost.* He moved toward her.

"Damask! Please listen!"

She backed up. "Stay away! I won't let you try to soften me up again by . . . making love to me."

Her voice faltered on the last words, and she was terribly afraid she was going to cry.

He stopped, his expression appalled. "My God, how could you think I'd do such a thing?"

Damask could feel her heart breaking, but she wouldn't let him see how much she cared when he didn't care for her at all.

"Because you want your mansion more than anything. More than you wanted Verona. And I'm making it harder and harder for you to get it. This would be the easiest way."

His face closed even more. He took another step toward her. "You're completely wrong!"

She backed up again. "I don't think so. It all makes too much sense."

He stopped, shaking his head, his jaw set. "It makes no sense at all!"

"If that's not the truth, then tell me why you want to marry me."

He opened his mouth, closed it again. "I . . . want to protect you. I like and respect you."

Protect. Like and respect.

His words went through her like a knife. Did he expect her to believe those were his true reasons for wanting to join his life with hers?

That wasn't what she needed from him. She wanted his wholehearted love. A man's love for a woman. The kind of love she felt for him.

She whirled away, walked to the door, unlocked it, and turned the knob.

"Damask, wait!"

She ignored him, opened the door.

Bluebell still sat right outside, her round eyes unblinking. She rubbed against Damask's ankles, purring loudly.

The little cat would be of some comfort during the long, sleepless night Damask saw ahead of her.

"Come on, I'll let you stay in my room," Damask said, not quite able to keep the wobble out of her voice. She closed the door behind her with finality.

Braden barely stopped himself from smashing his fist against the wall. Damn, damn, damn. Things had gone impossibly wrong with his plans.

He'd expected some initial resistance when he'd proposed, but he'd never expected Damask to react as she had. To believe he wanted to marry her to gain control of this property. That thought had never once occurred to him.

Damn it all to hell!

Maybe he *should* have told her the real reason he wanted them to marry as soon as possible.

He at once rejected that. No, she wouldn't have believed that, either, although there was a strong possibility it could happen. Verona had a fiery temper, and when he'd left her she'd been hell-bent on revenge since he'd thwarted her terrible plan . . . then had rejected her.

True, but worry about what Verona may do isn't the real reason you want to marry Damask.

You love her, you fool.

His heart lurched in his chest. No, he didn't. He liked her, respected her, and making love to her was nothing short of heaven.

And what do you think love is made of? Castles in the air? Dreams with no foundation?

His heart lurched again. What, indeed!

Gladness suddenly overwhelmed him, swept all his doubts and worries away.

He loved her. He loved Damask Aldon. With all his heart and soul.

He moved forward, his pulse racing. He'd tell her so right now. *Make* her listen.

Damask wasn't in the hall. She was already in the room she shared with Emmy, and the door was firmly closed.

Braden clenched his teeth. He'd better wait. She was too upset to listen to anything more tonight. Tomorrow evening . . . after everyone else was in bed, he'd fall on his knees and take her hand and propose to her the right way, the way he should have, offering her all the love inside him.

Chapter Twenty-Two

Russell Gifford whistled as he drove his team through the early morning, pulling a wagon load of fresh produce down the road toward the Holmes farm to pick up vegetables.

The sun was just peeking over the horizon, and the day was beautiful after the rainy night, which should bring out plenty of people ready to buy.

Maybe he'd catch a glimpse of Verona while he was at the Holmes place.

He grinned. Since they were children, he'd loved to tease her. She went off like a rocket every time.

His grin faded. But he had to figure out a way to get her out of this engagement with Braden Franklin. She didn't belong with that man. Why couldn't she see that?

She belonged to *him*, Russell Gifford, and always would.

All his life he'd known that and was just waiting for

her to grow up. But then she *had* grown up, suddenly turned from a tomboy into a beautiful woman.

One who wouldn't give him the time of day.

The Holmeses' prosperity had came to them about that same time. Verona and her mother had pushed Wallace into completely redoing the house so it looked like a southern mansion. And Verona and Bernice started dressing up all the time, putting on airs.

Worst of all, only the most eligible, well-to-do single men in town were now good enough for Verona or Bernice to consider as possible husbands for Verona. Strangely enough, none of them suited.

Russell had been ready to decide it was time for him to tell Verona what he figured she already knew somewhere deep inside. That she was meant for him and that's why she couldn't settle on any other man.

But before he got around to it, Braden Franklin had come back to town and she'd set her cap for him.

Russell had been so stunned that before he knew what was happening, he somehow let her get engaged to Braden. But it was plain to him from the start that she didn't love Franklin. And Franklin didn't love her, either. He'd bet on it.

Russell set his mouth and shook the reins.

Somehow he was going to get her away from Franklin.

Because he fully intended to marry her himself.

You'd better hurry up and do something. Before it's too late.

Trouble was, he didn't know what he could do except kidnap her and run away and not let her come back until they were married.

His grin at that improbable series of events was

wry. He didn't think she'd come willingly. Not now, anyway.

The road was muddy after last night's rain. The team and wagon kept splashing through puddles. Tree branches lay on the road, too, broken off by the wind that had picked up a few hours ago.

Up ahead was a whopper, off to the side of the road. Looked almost too big to be a branch. He frowned.

Maybe it was some sort of animal. . . .

When he got close, he drew in his breath. It was a person, huddled in a soaking wet cloak, even the head covered, so he couldn't tell if it was male or female.

My God, was the person dead?

Russell stopped the team, clambered down from his seat, and hurried over, afraid of what he might find.

He knelt down beside the figure and, his hands trembling, gently tugged at it.

A hand came up out of the cloak's folds and pushed at his arm. A woman's hand that looked strangely familiar.

"Go away, leave me alone!"

Russell drew in his breath, his mouth falling open. Instead of obeying the woman's directive, he pulled harder, and she rolled over on her back, her hood falling away from her face.

She had a big scratch on one cheek, her blond hair was soaking wet and straggled over her shoulders. Her dress had traces of what looked like bloodstains on its once-white collar.

She looked up at him with the same stunned shock on her face that must also be on his.

"*Verona?* What are you doing here?"

Verona shut her eyes, trying to close out the sight

of Russell Gifford kneeling before her when she must look like something the cat dragged in.

Of all people to find her like this!

"Go away," she said again, her voice wobbling. "Leave me alone."

"In a pig's eye," Russell answered, his voice very firm.

Before she knew what he planned to do, he'd picked her up in his arms and was carrying her to the wagon a few feet away.

She closed her eyes again, not even trying to fight him. She had no more strength left after all the awful things that had happened last night. This was the final humiliation, and she'd just have to bear it.

Very gently Russell laid her down on the wide wagon seat.

She waited, but nothing else happened. What was he doing? Verona cracked her eyes open just enough to see.

Astonishment, and something else, went over her cold, wet, battered body and soul.

He was gazing down at her with his heart in his eyes.

When she looked worse than she ever had in her entire life.

"Verona, speak to me," Russell said, fear in his voice. "Where did the blood come from? Are you hurt?"

Still bemused by that look, Verona didn't know what he meant. What blood?

Then she remembered falling under the porch and hitting her head. It still hurt a little, she realized, but not much. But her ankle felt swollen and throbbed.

"I fell and hit the back of my head," she mumbled. "But I'm all right."

He snorted. "You'll have a hard time making me believe that. Turn over and let me check."

She closed her eyes again. "No. I'm too tired."

He turned her over gently but firmly. Then he pulled her hood down farther and moved the wet strands of her hair apart. For some reason, his hands felt good poking at her, touching her.

It must be because he was warm and she was cold. *So cold.* She shivered.

His hands stopped and probed at her head. Pain shot through her, making her jump.

"That hurts!" she complained.

He grunted and turned her back over. "It's not a very deep cut and the bleeding's stopped. But you have a big lump."

She didn't say anything, just closed her eyes again. She was so cold . . . if she could just warm up . . . she wanted Russell's warm hands on her again. . . .

No, she didn't! She shivered again, harder.

"My Lord, you're freezing." He reached down to her, lifted her, pulled her against his solid, warm chest, his strong arms wrapped around her.

Oh, that felt so good! Involuntarily, Verona burrowed into him. Somehow, her arms slid around his waist so she could get closer to his wonderful warmth.

Gradually, she stopped shaking from the cold. She was feeling deliciously warm now. She could stay here forever.

"Are you ready to tell me how you came to be alongside the road, soaking wet, with your head cut open?"

His words abruptly shattered the warm cocoon she was in. She realized she was cuddled up close to Russell Gifford, her childhood pal. A man she couldn't *stand* now!

She started to pull away from him, but his hands on her back were like iron.

"Wait just a minute," he said.

"Let me go!" Verona demanded. Then she heard sounds . . . a buggy fast approaching.

Oh, God, someone was coming. She couldn't be found looking like this, held in Russell's arms. She started struggling in earnest, but Russell held tight.

She lifted her head and glared at him. "What is wrong with you? Do you want whoever that is to see you holding me like this?"

A slow smile spread across his face. He nodded. "Yep."

Her mouth fell open. "Why? Don't you realize what they'll think?"

He nodded again, his grip tightening, his smile still in place. "Yep."

She stared at him. "I also look as if I've been the loser in a fight."

His grin faltered a little. "I'll think of some way to explain that . . . unless *you* want to."

Verona sharply drew in her breath. No, she couldn't. She could never tell anyone what she'd almost done last night.

"It's no one's business," she said primly.

Russell's grin returned. He nodded. "That's just what I was thinking."

"I didn't mean about you holding me! Let go right now!"

He shook his head. "Can't do that, Ronie my girl."

Russell had suddenly lost his mind, she decided. That was the only explanation she could come up with.

The buggy was slowing . . . stopping. Naturally. The people in it would think there was trouble with the wagon or team since Russell was stopped along the road.

Until they got a good look at her bedraggled self and saw Russell's arms around her.

Verona closed her eyes again. Stopped struggling. Waited for whatever came next.

She'd brought all this on herself. None of it would be happening if she hadn't gotten that awful, terrible idea and tried to execute it.

She heard the buggy doors opening and closing, and then footsteps on the road.

"Verona Holmes! What in—oh, my, I'm going to faint."

Horror seeped into Verona. That was her mother's voice.

Russell still held her in that viselike grip.

She glared up at him. "*Now* will you let me go?"

"All right." He loosened his grip. His smile had faded, but it still tugged at his mouth, and his hazel eyes sparkled.

He looked for all the world as he used to when they'd played some kind of a joke . . . and gotten away with it.

Verona jerked away from him, sitting with her back turned to her parents.

"Here, here, Bernice," Verona's father said, his voice stern. "Sit down for a minute."

Verona heard a plop and pictured her mother planting her ample backside on the muddy road.

She heard more steps and figured her father was approaching the wagon. What would he do? Would he hit Russell?

For some reason, Verona didn't want him to do that, although she certainly felt like hitting him herself.

"Verona, do you know you scared your mother and

me half to death? We found Lady by the barn a little while ago. We went by Oliver's place and they said they hadn't seen you last night."

Papa's voice sounded peculiar, Verona thought. Worried, but not nearly as angry or indignant as it should, considering he'd seen her wrapped in Russell's arms only seconds before.

Another thought hit her, and she stiffened.

Last night! Oh, good Lord. She'd been gone all night, and now they'd found her in Russell's arms.

A loud sniff came from her mother. Verona heard her approaching the wagon.

Verona swallowed. She had to face them. Listen to all the raving and ranting. Frowning at Russell, who still looked as if he thought this was a big joke, she turned around.

Verona's mother, her face pale, her eyes horrified, stood beside her father, who was supporting her.

Her mother clamped her hand over her mouth as she got a good look at her daughter. "What on earth happened to you? Are you hurt? You're muddy from head to foot and you have blood on your gown."

Verona closed her eyes again, trying to think of a believable story. Nothing came to mind. She *had* to say something. She opened her eyes again, forcing a smile for her mother.

"A few minutes ago . . . I . . . slipped in the mud and fell and cut my head a little. But I'm all right."

"Thank God!" her mother said, apparently accepting Verona's account.

Verona breathed a little easier. Maybe it would be all right. . . .

"Oh, how *could* you do such a thing?" her mother wailed, pressing a lace-edged handkerchief against her forehead. "Get out of that wagon. We must get you home at once, before anyone else passes and sees us and gossip gets back to Braden."

Braden? What did *he* have to do with any of this?

Then she remembered her parents didn't know she and Braden were no longer engaged. That she'd planned for last night's events to straighten out all the trouble between her and Braden.

She felt like laughing wildly but controlled herself.

"It doesn't matter, Mama," Verona said. "Braden and I broke our engagement two nights ago."

Her mother gasped in new shock. "What are you talking about?"

Verona sighed. "I lied to you that night when I said we just had a little spat."

Shock struggled with hope on her mother's face. "Oh, but you can make up," she said. "You can go to him and tell him you're sorry—"

"Bernice, stop it," her father said, his voice commanding. "Can't you see it's too late for that?"

He turned back to Verona. "Are you sure you're all right?" he asked in a gentler tone.

Verona managed a smile. "Yes."

How she lied. Nothing would ever be all right again. She had nothing to look forward to but staying at home the rest of her life, turning into a dried-up old maid.

Mama had stopped sniffling and wailing. She looked from Verona to Russell, and something new came into her face.

"Russell Gifford," she said, her tones indignant, "how *could* you take advantage of my poor, innocent Verona like this?"

Verona stiffened. She could feel her eyes bulging. Surely, Mama couldn't believe she and Russell had spent a passionate night together the way she looked?

Then she remembered she'd explained her appearance.

"Mama!" She moved her glance to her father. "Papa, tell her she's crazy!"

She sucked in her breath at the expression on her father's face. Instead of the incredulous look she'd expected to see, he looked pleased.

"Papa!" she said again.

His pleased look vanished, replaced by a stern one. "When two young people have spent the night together, nothing is left but marriage."

"But we *didn't* spend the night together!"

She turned to Russell. "Tell them, we—"

Her voice died away. Russell's expression was a mixture of sheepishness and manly responsibility.

But deep in his hazel eyes a light danced.

He reached over and placed his hand over hers. "I'm afraid they're right, Verona honey. We should have thought more . . . and not let our feelings carry us away."

As mad as she was at him, his warm hand felt good on hers. Reassuring somehow, as if he would take care of her. Never let anything hurt her.

What was she thinking? He'd just told the most outrageous lie. Verona tried to jerk her hand away, but Russell held it fast.

For one of the few times in her life, Verona was speechless.

It might not be so bad, her mind said. *He's good-looking, and his farm is prosperous enough. And for some reason, he's not fighting your parents' plan to marry you to him. In fact, he seems to be in favor of it.*

Why was he? Verona suddenly remembered that look in Russell's eyes when he'd carried her to the wagon.

He'd looked as if he . . . loved her. Truly loved her.

As no man ever had before. Even Braden hadn't looked at her like that. Not once.

A memory came into her mind. Last night, when she'd glanced through the inn's kitchen window, the expression on Braden's face as he looked at Damask was just like the one Russell had worn.

Strangely, that didn't bother her a bit.

A warm feeling started in her chest, in the region of her heart, and grew.

Maybe she hadn't hated Russell, as she kept telling herself. Maybe that was why the thought of sharing a bed with Braden was so terrifying.

She pictured herself kissing Russell, letting him touch her . . . carry her to their marriage bed.

Amazingly, the thought made her cheeks flame but didn't at all scare her. Or disgust her.

Verona swallowed. She looked at Russell and gave him a tiny smile. Deep in her own eyes she felt a spark to match his own.

Surprise showed on his face for a second, then he smiled back, squeezing her hand, the devilish light in his eyes turning into another kind . . . hot and promising.

She'd never be a real lady . . . and Russell was no gentleman . . . but they suited each other. Why hadn't she seen that a long time ago?

Verona sat up a little straighter, keeping her glance on Russell.

"I suppose you're right," she said, futilely trying to inject a rueful note into her voice. "We have no choice but to marry."

Her mother gasped, then dabbed at her eyes with her handkerchief.

"My baby!" she said, her voice trembling. She hurried toward Verona, her arms outstretched.

Over Mama's head, Verona saw her father glance

at Russell. A satisfied glance, as if everything had worked out perfectly.

Verona was sure Russell wore the same kind of look.

As her mother clasped Verona to her bosom, Russell let go of her hand. She felt bereft without that steady, warm touch.

Probably, she'd have to confess to Russell what had actually happened last night. But she didn't think he'd make her tell her parents.

After what you almost did, you're getting off very easy, her mind said. *You don't deserve this.*

Maybe not, but she could do her best to try to make Russell happy. To be a good wife for him.

And she would.

Chapter Twenty-Three

Damask came out of the sitting room, stood in the hall, and listened. All was quiet. She peeked in on Emmy and Cory to find them soundly asleep. No light shone under the edge of Flora's door, either.

As for Braden . . . Damask tensed. He hadn't eaten supper here tonight. She didn't know where he was and she didn't care, she told herself firmly. Braden was no better than Warren. Completely selfish, thinking only of what he wanted.

Which was the same as it had always been from the first day she'd met him.

He wanted this property. He wanted his beautiful house where the inn now stood.

Nothing, nothing at all had changed as far as he was concerned.

She was the one who'd changed.

She'd foolishly made love with Braden. Even more foolishly fallen in love with him.

He merely desired her. And she'd let him have her.

Oh, what a fool she was!

Braden wanted his dream so badly, he'd do anything to realize it.

He wanted it enough to break his engagement to Verona.

And only two days later propose to Damask because she was the key to his obtaining this property.

Would his haste have mattered if he'd come to you with the right reasons? If he'd said he loved you? That he couldn't live without you?

Where had that thought come from? No, she had to admit, it wouldn't have. If he loved her, it would be different. . . .

But he didn't love her. He'd had plenty of chances to tell her and he hadn't. Even in the midst of their lovemaking he'd spoken no words of love.

Pain struck her again. She pushed it away, determined not to think about any of it.

She had to concentrate on more important things—the decision she must make regarding the inn.

After she'd gone to her room last night, a wind and rainstorm had lashed the area.

This morning, the front yard was once again littered with broken slates, and the attic had new leaks.

Edmond, who'd been in an excellent mood, whistling and singing as he worked at finishing touches on the porch, had shaken his head. The inn needed a whole new roof, he said. He hadn't realized what bad shape it was in. Slate was expensive, and it took a skilled worker to put on a new slate roof.

All things she already knew. Damask couldn't seem to make herself care much. All she could think about was Braden and what had happened last night.

At breakfast Flora gave her a searching look, as if she noticed the difference in her. How could anyone not see she wasn't the same person as yesterday before Braden had awakened her to what it meant to be a woman?

But Flora hadn't pried. She'd chattered on about the secret room and how the discoveries there explained why Ada had let things go. It amazed Flora that she'd never once suspected the existence of the room.

Damask had listened and agreed, her mind distant.

Today, she'd doggedly put wallpaper up in another of the guest rooms, but her heart hadn't been in it.

Now, her spirits very low, Damask came back into the sitting room and stood just inside the door.

If she had any practical sense at all, she'd sell her family's half of the inn to Braden before she got any deeper in debt, and buy a small cottage for Flora and the children and herself.

Obviously, that would be the smart thing to do. The townspeople were on her side now, but that could easily change when they found out about the expensive new roof that was needed, and no doubt other things would keep turning up on the old building.

Even if all that could be worked out, and no matter how well she might do if she got the inn reopened, it wouldn't change Braden's plans for this hill. The lengths he'd gone to the night before had proved that.

He would never want what she did.

A wave of despair swept over her. Yes, she should give up now, while she could still come out ahead.

Remember, I told you everything you needed was right here? But you couldn't find all of it until you were ready?

Damask stiffened as Aunt Ada's words sounded in her ear, then she gasped and stared.

Her aunt was seated in the old rocker, but she wasn't smiling. Her face wore a concerned look.

*You have worked very hard . . . but that isn't all that's
required . . . you must also have understanding . . . and
this you do not yet have. . . .*

The image slowly dissipated, but the rockers on the
old chair kept moving for a few moments longer.

Goose bumps rose on Damask's arms.

But, as before, she didn't feel afraid. Nor did she
doubt the reality of the apparition.

What did her aunt mean? Understanding of what?
Find all of *what?*

She waited for something else to happen.

An urge to go into the secret room came over her.
Had it come from Aunt Ada? Damask stood, unmov-
ing. The compulsion grew stronger.

If she was careful, it wouldn't hurt to look around
in there. The children were asleep, so she wouldn't
have to worry about them discovering the room.

Damask walked to the fireplace, found the brick
with the chipped mortar, and pushed on it.

As before, the wall panel slid silently back, revealing
the small room behind it. A shudder went over her
as she remembered the terror she'd felt when she'd
been locked in there.

That wouldn't happen again. Damask moved the
armchair over, wedged it into the opening, picked
up the lamp from the sitting room table, then looked
inside.

Everything in the tiny room looked the same as
before. The narrow cot, the little table with its pile
of books and candlestick.

The urge to go inside kept prodding. Something
was in there that she must find. . . .

Was she imagining all this? Were her low spirits
putting silly notions in her head?

Possibly, but the strong compulsion stayed. Damask
walked to the cot, poked its mattress, sneezing as the

dust flew out. Carefully avoiding the bedposts, she examined the mattress from all angles, turned it over even stuck her hand inside a torn corner and felt around inside.

Finally, she stood back, positive nothing was hidden in the cot or under it.

There were few other places in the small enclosure where anything could be concealed.

No fireplace or even a stove. No chests of drawers or other furniture.

Only the table and the items on it were left. Damask went to the table and sat down on the chair. Could Aunt Ada have hidden money inside one of the books? No, that didn't make sense. If her aunt had money, she would have used it to repair the inn.

But still . . . Her heart beating faster, Damask picked up the first book and shook it gently. Only a little dust floated out. She'd have to go through its pages one by one and those of the other two books.

Half an hour later, Damask replaced the last book in the neat stack, her mood even lower.

There was nothing in any of the books, not even a scrap of paper.

She tightened her lips. She *had* imagined she'd seen and heard her aunt a few minutes ago. She was a silly idiot and she would go ahead with her decision to sell her family's share of the inn to Braden.

You haven't looked everywhere yet. Open your eyes.

Startled, Damask's glance flew to the rocking chair No ghostly image sat there now, but the rockers moved very slowly.

No, she wasn't imagining all this. She wasn't that fanciful a person, no matter how discouraged she felt.

Damask looked back at the table. The only thing she hadn't examined was the candlestick. She reached over and picked it up, then rotated it in her hands. What could possibly be hidden in a candlestick?

Turning it over, she looked at its bottom. Solid pewter, no holes where something could have been poked inside.

She grasped the ancient candle and tried to twist it. It was wedged solid, with melted candle wax gluing it firmly to the sides. Damask scraped at the melted wax with her fingernails, again tried to twist it. Finally, the candle moved and her next tug brought it out of the holder.

Damask turned it upside down. No holes in it, either. It was just an old candle, needing to be discarded. She lifted the holder and looked inside, finding more candle wax. Scraping at it, she felt a roughness beneath her fingers, almost like a hinge.

Her breath caught. Damask quickly scratched the rest of the wax away.

It *was* a tiny hinge with a notch on the other side. Her hands shaking, Damask pried at the notch.

With a click, a small lid sprang open. Hardly breathing, she looked inside.

What she saw made her mouth fall open.

Her hands still trembling, Damask reached her thumb and forefinger inside the candlestick base.

Braden walked up the stairs in the quiet inn, wondering if he'd waited too long. He'd deliberately stayed at the store and had Jacob bring him some food from Goose Creek's one restaurant. He wanted everyone else in bed before he talked to Damask. He'd gambled that she'd stay up later than the others, as she usually did, reading in the sitting room.

But maybe he'd lost the gamble.

Gaining the top of the stairs, he looked down the hall and his heart sank. The bedroom doors were all closed. The sitting room door stood open, but no light came from the room.

Walking toward the room, Braden cursed himself for a fool. He should have shown up for supper. How did he think he could win Damask's love behaving like this?

Reaching the sitting room door, he glanced inside. His heart jumped.

No wonder he'd thought the room empty. The lamp stood on the small table in the secret room.

Damask sat at the table, her head bent, the lamp light bringing out auburn gleams in her hair. She was looking intently at something cupped in her hands.

What was she holding?

There was only one way to find out. Braden crossed the room, his shoes making no sound on the old rug. Reaching the entrance to the secret room, he cleared his throat.

"Damask . . ."

She jerked her head up. Her big gray eyes stared at him. But he hadn't frightened her, he saw. She looked dazed, as if something had greatly surprised her.

She wasn't frightened and she wasn't angry. He had to take this chance while he had it.

Braden eased himself around the chair in the door's opening and came inside the room.

Damask relaxed the curve of her hands.

"Damask," he said again, "I want to—"

A red flash came up from her hands, made sparkles of light dance in his eyes.

He blinked, moved closer, then looked at Damask.

again. She was smiling but not as if she were happy. It was the strangest smile he'd ever seen, as if it trembled on the edge of tears.

A ring set with a large ruby lay in Damask's hands.

He raised his eyes to hers again. "Where did that come from?"

"I found it in the candlestick."

Damask heard the unsteadiness in her voice. That was nothing compared to the shakiness she felt inside.

Amazement still coursed through her, but now, with Braden standing just across the table, that emotion was overshadowed by others more powerful.

The love she felt for him was still there. She guessed it would be until the day she died. But resentment and anger and sadness were mixed with it. As well as relief.

She didn't care if he saw the other emotions, but she hoped he couldn't see the love, because he didn't want it.

He stared at her, his eyes darkening, for long moments.

"Who put the ring there?" he finally asked, his voice tight.

"Aunt Ada. Oh, I assure you she meant it for me. I found a letter in her Bible soon after I came here, saying she'd left something for me, but I had to find it."

I told you more than that . . . you mustn't forget it.

The whisper, with its note of slightly reproachful warning, faded away. Confusion swept over Damask. What did her aunt mean?

"And you never told me about this letter?"

Doubt was in Braden's voice.

Anger banished Damask's confusion. He didn't believe her. He was going to fight her to the end. He would try to claim part of this ring so he could still have his way.

Damask rose, her head high. "Why should I have? I had no idea what she meant until tonight. I'll get the letter. I'll prove it to you."

Braden shook his head. "That won't be necessary."

"All right, then. I can pay for the inn repairs now, even a new roof," Damask said, glad her voice was stronger.

"I can take a chance on the inn making a profit. The children and I and Flora can hold out as long as necessary. Until you get tired of waiting and decide to go build your mansion somewhere else."

Damask swallowed, shivering at the look on Braden's face. She sat back down because her knees suddenly felt weak.

His eyes had darkened, his face tightened. "Do you know why I came in here tonight? Why I was looking for you?"

She forced herself to steadiness. Not for anything would she let him see how much she loved him, when he cared nothing for her.

"Probably for another try at convincing me to marry you to give you control of this property," she said coolly. "Now you're angry because you know I can hold out against you as long as necessary."

His eyes grew darker, his face cold. "You're right— at least in the first part of what you said. I *was* planning to ask you to marry me. But—"

"I had experience with a completely selfish man like you," she cut him off, her voice bitter.

Nothing had changed from last night. He was still pursuing his plans. "He jilted me when my parents died because he didn't want the responsibility of raising Emmy and Cory."

His fist came down on the table so hard, the lamp wobbled.

"Dammit! I've never seen such a stubborn woman!"

Damask heard a small scuffling sound from somewhere outside the room. Oh, Lord, was Emmy up? Had she heard them quarreling?

Damask pushed by Braden into the sitting room. The room was empty. She hurried to the door and looked out into the hall. It, too, was empty, all the bedroom doors closed.

Relief surged through her. She was wrong, thank goodness. She couldn't have stood for Emmy to have heard their bitter words.

She felt Braden behind her and turned, lifting her chin. "Now, are you going to sell me your half of the inn? Or are you still going to continue with this stalemate?"

His face became stony. "You can have the whole thing. Tomorrow, I'll go to the lawyer and get the inn deeded over to you. I'll also move out."

Damask drew in her breath. She stepped back and he went by her and out into the hall, walked to his room and closed the door behind him.

Slowly, Damask's anger drained away, leaving only pain.

Her troubles were over. She had achieved her objective.

Her family, including Flora, could stay here. Even if the inn never made a profit, with the proceeds from the sale of the ruby, they would have enough to live on.

She should feel wonderful. And, of course, she did feel a deep relief.

But she felt no triumph or satisfaction from Braden's capitulation.

Only sorrow. And love, of course.

The love that Braden would never know she felt for him.

Because he'd never return it.

Chapter
Twenty-Four

What was that banging sound? Was someone knocking at the inn door? She must get up to see who it was. . . in just a minute. . . .

The banging came again, louder this time.

"All right, I'm coming!"

Damask struggled up through layers of sleep to realize she was lying on the sitting room sofa, still fully dressed.

Day was just breaking, feeble light coming through the windows. She pushed herself upright. What was she doing here?

From the table beside her a red flash came.

In a rush, last night's events returned to her mind.

The discovery of the ruby ring . . . Braden's arrival . . . their quarrel . . . his capitulation.

Misery washed over her. She buried her face in her hands. Oh, why had she ever come here? Why hadn't she stayed in Tennessee? If she'd never met Braden, she wouldn't have to live with this pain the rest of her life.

The banging came again, even louder, and Damask realized it was wind tearing at a loose shutter. A storm was brewing. A bad one, from the sound of that wind.

She was exhausted, as if she hadn't slept a wink. She'd go to the room she shared with Emmy and try to sleep a little longer if the storm would let her.

The hall was dark and quiet. Damask opened her bedroom door and went in. She stopped short just inside the doorway, her heart skipping a beat.

The covers were thrown back on the bed she and Emmy shared, and Emmy was gone.

She couldn't be far, Damask tried to tell herself. She must have just gotten up early.

Before daylight? When had Emmy ever done that?

Maybe she'd awakened, scared because Damask wasn't beside her, and gone to find Flora. Yes, that must be what happened.

Her worry lessening, Damask eased open Flora's door. Flora lay in the middle of the bed, covers mounded. She was alone.

Fear hit Damask. She quietly closed Flora's door and stood in the hall.

Then another fear hit her. *Cory.*

She hurried to his door, opened it, then gasped. His bed, too, had thrown-back covers and was empty.

Damask hastened from the room and went downstairs.

Neither child was anywhere to be found, either inside the house or at the barn.

Back inside, her alarm increasing, Damask went upstairs again, where she checked all the guest rooms. She even opened the secret room, but of course it was empty.

A gust of wind hit the house, and the sturdy old structure seemed to shudder under the onslaught.

Urgency filled her. Emmy and Cory were out somewhere and a bad storm was brewing. She had to find them.

Braden's door opened. He stood in the opening, looking at her in surprise. He, too, was fully dressed. Had he slept in his clothes as she had?

"What's wrong?" he asked.

"The children are gone," she said in a rush.

"What do you mean?"

"Gone! I've looked everywhere, even in the barn. They're nowhere. And a storm's coming."

Damask's hair was mussed, and she looked like she'd slept in her clothes. She had dark circles under her eyes. She'd had about the same kind of night he had, he realized.

A wave of tenderness went over Braden. His anger at Damask had died. He wanted to hold her, comfort her. Love her.

Even after what she put you through last night?

Yes. Love didn't seem to end because the loved person didn't reciprocate.

And besides, he'd put *her* through a lot these last few weeks.

"Come on," he said, forcing confidence into his voice. "We'll find them."

Damask's face relaxed a little. "Do you have any idea where they could be? Or why they left—"

Her voice broke off and she put a hand to her mouth. "Oh, do you think they *did* hear us quarreling last night? I thought I heard a noise, but I checked and didn't see anyone."

He remembered when she'd gone to the door. His mind went back to what they'd been saying. "That was right after you said your fiancé had jilted you because he didn't want the responsibility of the children."

Damask looked stricken. "Yes. Do you think they could have heard?"

"It's possible."

More than possible. He and Damask had raised their voices. They'd been very angry with each other.

Shame went through him. He'd slammed his fist down on the table.

Violent-acting adults scared children. He knew that better than most people.

Emmy and Cory could have heard, then fled as he used to flee, scared to death, when his drunken father raged around their shack.

Another gust of wind battered the inn.

He'd had somewhere to flee to.

And Emmy and Cory did, too.

"Come on," Braden said. "I know a place they may be."

"Where?" she asked.

"A cabin in the woods. I used to . . . stay there sometimes."

She nodded. "All right. Let's go."

The rain hadn't started yet, but the roiling black clouds promised it soon would. As he and Damask hurried through the woods, wind lashing them, he prayed the storm would hold off until they reached the cabin.

And he prayed he was right and Emmy and Cory were safely inside.

Safe? In that old shack? With its door hanging by one hinge? God, why hadn't he repaired that door long before now?

Damask bumped against him. He reached over and took her hand. She tensed but didn't draw away. Her hand felt small and cold in his grip but infinitely dear. He wanted to tell her she'd be safe with him always.

As soon as the children were found and everyone was safely back at the inn, he was going to make her listen to him if he had to gag her first.

And this time he'd do it right.

Last night's doubts rose up.

What if she didn't love him? She'd never said that, even when she was taking such pleasure from his lovemaking. Was he willing to make a complete fool of himself?

Yes. He was willing to do anything to win her love, to marry her.

He squeezed her hand, and after a moment, she squeezed back. Was that a sign she was softening toward him, or only gratitude for a little human comfort because she was so scared for the children?

He didn't know, but he wasn't going to let go of her hand.

The sky got darker, almost dark as night. It wouldn't be long now before the storm hit in all its fury. God, he hoped the children were at the cabin. At least it offered some shelter.

What if they weren't? Then where could they search?

He pushed down the fear that thought brought. He had no time or energy to waste on fear.

"It's so dark," Damask said. "How can you tell we're on the right path?"

She was trying to keep her voice from trembling but not succeeding.

"I know these woods like the back of my hand," he assured her, making his voice confident.

Or at least he used to—back when he was a boy.

He clenched his jaw, refusing to let doubt enter. He still did.

"Good," Damask said, her voice relieved. "Because I don't have any idea where we are."

Was he sure he did?

Braden also forced down those doubts. Yes. He had to be on the right trail.

But it seemed to be taking a long time . . . longer than it should. . . .

The sky steadily darkened . . . lightning flashed and thunder rumbled . . . closer now . . . much closer.

Braden's tension grew. He hurried his steps. Damask struggled to keep up with him, stumbling once or twice.

It was too dark to see any landmarks at all. Braden was relying now on pure instinct—and beginning to fear that wasn't enough.

Suddenly, the cabin's bulk loomed ahead. His heart jumped and he sighed in relief. "There it is."

Damask squeezed his hand again, hard. "If they're not here, I . . ."

He returned the squeeze. "Let's see right now."

The door still hung by one hinge. Braden pushed it open, holding his breath.

It was dim inside, but he made out two small figures huddling together on the old cot.

"Emmy! Cory!"

Damask ran to them and hugged them both at once. Braden followed.

"Are you all right?" Damask asked, her voice sharp with worry and relief.

"Yes, Damask," Cory said in low tones. Emmy nodded.

"Didn't you know I'd be scared to death?" Damask asked.

They both nodded, mute.

A hard gust slammed against the side of the old cabin, and it shuddered. Then the rain came, pounding in its fury. The door slammed back against the wall, and the one remaining hinge gave way. The door crashed to the floor.

A jagged flash of lightning came, followed by a loud clap of thunder. Windswept rain drove through the now open doorway into the small interior.

Emmy grabbed Damask around her neck and clung, hiding her face in Damask's chest. "I'm scared!" she whimpered.

Damask sat down beside her on the cot. "It's all right," she said. Cory edged closer to his sisters, holding his mouth tight, obviously determined not to show any fear.

Braden hurried to the door. He struggled to right it and close it against the storm.

Cory jumped up and brought one of the wooden chairs, and the two of them managed to prop the door in place, then wedge the chair under the knob.

"There, maybe that will hold. Thanks for helping," Braden told Cory.

"I wanted to," Cory said manfully, but his face was pale. He went back to the cot.

Damask glanced over at Braden. He was looking at her in such a peculiar way . . . his mouth firm, his gaze intent.

Then, as if he'd made up his mind about something, he strode across the room and stopped in front of her.

She looked at him in surprise.

Braden placed his hand over her mouth. "Don't say anything, please. Let me talk. I've wanted to tell you something for two days now and haven't made it. This isn't the ideal time or place, but I'd better go ahead while I have the chance."

His big, warm hand felt good on her mouth. It made

her remember how wonderful it had felt touching her at other times . . . in other places.

But it couldn't mean anything. Braden didn't love her as she loved him. Pain went through her at this familiar thought. He cared for the children, and he was strong and brave. He was nothing like Warren.

But he didn't love her.

He loosened his hand and gave her a questioning look.

"All right," she agreed, holding her voice steady. "Go ahead and talk."

His hand left her mouth, found her free hand, and clasped it in his own.

Then he knelt before her.

Damask gave him an astonished look. "What—"

He smiled at her. "Shhh. Remember, you promised to let me talk."

Suppressed feelings surged up in her. She swallowed, then nodded silently.

"That's better," Braden said approvingly. He took a deep breath, then let it out. He looked so deep into her eyes, she felt dizzy . . . but held the glance.

"Damask Aldon, I love you with all my heart. I want to marry you for no other reason. Can you believe that? Will you do me the great honor of agreeing to be my wife?"

Damask stared at him, stunned into speechlessness. Braden had said the words she'd longed to hear, despaired of ever hearing.

A tug came at her sleeve. "Say yes, Damask," Cory urged.

"Oh, do, Damask!" Emmy echoed.

Braden's sea green glance was mesmerizing her. She felt as if he could see all the way through her . . . into her heart and soul.

And she could see inside him, too. See that he was

kneeling before her with only truth and love in his heart and soul.

The problems between them seemed to dissolve like the storm raging outside would dissolve an ant-hill.

No, that couldn't happen. Their lives were set on different paths. Braden still wanted his grand mansion. She still wanted the inn.

More than she wanted Braden's love?

No, of course not. She wanted Braden more than anything . . . *loved* him more than anything. . . .

More than the inn?

Yes . . . of course! She didn't care where they lived . . . as long as they were together.

Damask felt her lips curving in a wide smile. She turned her hand over and squeezed his hand once, hard.

"Yes, I will marry you, Braden Franklin. I love you, too. With everything inside me."

"Oh, good, Damask!" Cory and Emmy said in unison.

Braden smiled, too. A relieved, satisfied smile. "I don't believe in long engagements."

Something in his smile made her redden, bringing back those moments they'd spent in each other's arms, promising her there would be many, many more of them.

"Neither do I," she answered.

Another flash of lightning came, followed at once by a reverberating crash of thunder.

Emmy screamed. Cory jumped.

Braden encircled all three of them with his strong arms.

"It's fine. I'm here. I will always take care of all of you," he said, his voice as firm and strong as his grasp.

"Do you mean that?" Emmy asked in a small voice.

Braden drew back a little and looked at her in surprise. "Of course I mean it. Why would you think I didn't?"

Emmy bit her lip and hung her head.

Cory spoke up. "Last night Emmy came and told me that"—he glanced up at Braden—"that you didn't want to take care of us. Just like Warren didn't. So we thought . . ."

"We were going back to Tennessee," Emmy said. "So we wouldn't be in your way anymore."

Damask's horrified glance met Braden's.

"Look at me," Braden told the children. "You will never, ever be in my way. I love you both and couldn't do without you."

"Neither could I," Damask said.

Emmy's face broke into a smile. So did Cory's.

"I guess Emmy just misunderstood what she heard," Cory said in a manly voice.

Emmy bobbed her head in agreement.

"Yes," Braden said. "That's what happened." He gave Damask a look full of meaning for their future.

There had been a lot of misunderstandings between them, she thought. But God willing, that was all in the past.

Another flash of lightning came, followed at once by a thunderclap that made even Damask jump and clutch Emmy tighter.

In a moment, Emmy eased away, glanced at Braden. "Mr. Braden, didn't you get scared when you stayed here all by yourself? Did it ever storm?"

A faraway look came to his eyes, as if he remembered those days all too well. "Yes, I was scared."

Of course he had been, Damask thought. His childhood had been a nightmare. No wonder he now felt he had to prove himself to Goose Creek.

Why that need had taken him to extremes.

Why he needed that house on the hill . . . that she would share with him.

"I think it's starting to ease up," Braden said, getting to his feet, smiling down at all of them.

"Yes," Damask agreed, smiling back.

She could let him have his dream. She loved the inn, but she loved Braden more.

Half an hour later, they came out of the woods into the clearing behind the inn. Thank God they were home, safe and sound.

Home . . . a small, bittersweet feeling went through her.

How she wished Braden felt the same for this old inn as she did. Then, everything in their lives would be perfect.

Her glance went to the inn. She stopped, gasping in shock.

A big walnut tree had fallen onto the side of the building. Part of the roof was smashed in—slates and broken glass were everywhere. Several branches stuck through windowpanes.

Tears sprang to her eyes. She couldn't stand to look at the destruction.

Braden put his arm around her shoulder. The back door burst open and Flora came hurrying out, her face beaming with relief.

"Oh, thank God all of you are safe! I was so worried!"

She hurried over and embraced them, one at a time, then stood back, worry returning to her weathered face.

"See what the tree has done to the inn?" She wrung her hands. "It is bad, so bad."

Damask turned to Braden, swallowing a lump in her throat. "I guess you were right all along. The inn *is* too old. It's outlived its usefulness."

He frowned at her. "Did I say that?"

She gave him a surprised look. "Of course you did. More than once."

He shook his head. "I don't know what was the matter with me."

Braden waved his hand at the fallen tree. "We can get that sawed up and out of there in no time."

She stared at him, an incredulous hope dawning. "What do you mean?"

"The stone is hardly damaged. Like you and Flora said, this old building will outlive us all."

Flora beamed at Braden. "Yah, that it will."

Her eyes went from one to other, took in Braden's arm clasped possessively around Damask's shoulder, the way Damask leaned into him.

"And also the children and grandchildren you and Damask will someday have."

Damask felt her mouth falling open.

Grandchildren?

Braden's arm tightened around her.

"There's no doubt in my mind about that," he said, his voice ringing with confidence and happiness.

"Nor in mine," Damask said in a moment.

You see, everything has worked out just as it should. I told you it would. . . .

Damask could almost see Aunt Ada's satisfied expression, hear her laugh.

You were right, Damask silently told her. We were two stubborn people.

Stubborn people are also strong people. You will be happy here. . . .

Damask looked up at Braden, her love overflowing. "I know we'll be happy," she said softly. "I know that very well."

Braden lifted one brow, then gave her a slow smile and nodded.

Epilogue

"I wish I could make tiny stitches! Mine are big and clumsy——like me."

Laughing, Verona threw down the tiny outing flannel gown she was working on and rubbed her rounded belly.

Damask smiled back at her. "Compared to me, you're still small.

"And so are you," Damask said, turning to Geneva, who held her own baby garment and sewed with frowning concentration.

Geneva glanced up, her frown lines smoothing out.

"That's only because you started sooner," she said pertly. "I think all of us must have gotten pregnant on our wedding nights."

"You're no doubt right," Verona agreed, picking up the gown again with a sigh. "With husbands like ours, we'll probably stay that way most of the time."

"Verona!" Damask said. The three women shared a conspiratorial laugh.

Braden was as ardent a lover as any woman could want. He was a wonderful husband in every way. And Emmy and Cory adored him.

His energy left her breathless. Besides running his department store, his plans for opening a new store next year in a town farther north were nearing completion.

As were the inn repairs. Once Braden realized how much he, too, loved the old structure, he'd thrown himself with unlimited enthusiasm into the task. And as he'd always wanted, Braden now had the town's liking and respect.

Restoring the inn had become a town project, with most of the able-bodied men pitching in and many of the women helping her and Flora cook for the workers. The residents were proudly delighted that next month Goose Creek Inn would be reopened. Ads had been placed in Philadelphia newspapers as well as those in Baltimore and elsewhere. The interest shown in the historic inn had been remarkable.

Flora was beside herself with happiness. Especially since she and Harold had married the previous month. Harold had moved into the inn, keeping himself busy with the countless small repairs always needed.

And Braden had found his sister, living in a town not too far away. She was married, with two children, and the families often visited back and forth. Like Braden, she'd finally made her peace with Goose Creek.

Damask drew her needle in and out of the soft fabric, and a beam of late winter sunlight hit the ring on her right hand, making a deep red flash.

"That is the most beautiful ring I ever saw in my life," Verona said, a trace of envy in her voice.

But only a trace. It was amazing how she'd changed since her marriage to Russell.

"Yes, it is," Geneva agreed. "And I don't give a fig for jewelry." Geneva had lost none of her independence since she and Edmond married.

Damask glanced at the ruby in its simple gold setting.

"Aunt Ada . . . left the ring for me. It was very special to her. I'll hand it down to our first daughter."

A second note, also found in Aunt Ada's Bible, had explained . . . most things. Her lost love, who'd been killed during the war, had given her the ring. She couldn't bear to part with it, even for her beloved inn. But she'd left it for Damask to sell if she must.

Damask heard footsteps in the hall, and in a moment Braden came into the sitting room. He wore an old shirt and trousers and had a smudge of dirt on one cheek. His black hair was somewhat mussed.

He looked so good, Damask wished the two women were gone and she and her husband were alone together.

"There you are." Braden came across to the old rocker where Damask sat, and he kissed her cheek. Again, she wished they were alone so he could give her a real kiss . . . maybe more.

But it wouldn't be long until night. She blushed at her thoughts.

"The workers have gone for the day, and I'm going to take Cory and Emmy fishing at the creek," he said, his smile and glance telling her his thoughts were much like hers.

"All right," Damask agreed, smiling back at him.

"We were just talking about Damask's beautiful ring," Verona said.

No one would ever know she was once engaged to Braden, Damask thought. Thank God, neither of

Elizabeth Graham

them seemed to feel awkward in the other's presence. In a small town like Goose Creek, that would make life very difficult.

"It means a lot to us, doesn't it, dear?" Damask asked.

If she hadn't found the ring . . . if Emmy hadn't heard their bitter argument and she and Cory run off to the cabin . . . if she and Braden hadn't forgotten their quarrel in order to search for the children . . .

So many ifs. But somehow it had all worked out.

"Oh, indeed, it does," Braden agreed.

The rockers of Damask's chair moved just a tiny bit, not enough for anyone else to notice. A soft whisper floated in the air around her.

You were so stubborn. I thought you'd never understand that the real treasure I'd left you wasn't the ring at all.

Damask smiled.

I always knew you and Braden were perfect for each other.

Braden leaned over and kissed Damask's temple. "I'll see you in a little while."

"Don't stay too late," she said.

"I won't." He gave her one last, lingering smile that warmed her to her toes and was rich with promises for the night to come . . . and for all their years together.